A
SKIMPTON
COMPENDIUM

JOHN C. BIGGINS

🏆 TROPHY PRESS

Life was hierarchical and whatever happened was right. There were the strong, who deserved to win and always did win, and there were the weak, who deserved to lose and always did lose, everlastingly.

– George Orwell, *Such, Such Were the Joys*

John C. Biggins was born in Leeds in 1958.
He works as an actor, writer and graphic
designer, and lives in London.
A Skimpton Compendium is his first work of fiction.

CONTENTS

ONE

THE BOMBAY
BOMBSHELL

'Look Piggot, just finish the tidying up and get out would you!' barked Skimpton at the rather plain-looking third-former whose job it was to keep the older boy's belongings in order.

'But Skimpton,' pleaded the youngster through his unflatteringly protruding teeth, 'I have hardly started on the bookshelves!'

'You can finish those to-morrow,' retorted the senior angrily, 'now just leave me in peace.'

Piggot was out of the door quick as lightning and down the stairs in seconds, quite unaware that Skimpton had punctuated his departure by hurling a silver boxing trophy at the door after him.

At last, Skimpton was alone in his study. The day seemed to have been an endless succession of infuriating interruptions; by masters seeking his attendance in the classroom and boys badgering him for advice on any number of trifling matters.

Setting his lips tightly, the reliable House Captain resolved to allow nothing further to come between himself and the matter in hand – a problem of some delicacy which demanded immediate and careful attention.

He was an attractive, amiable young man, widely held to be the most popular boy in the school. Having made his mark at Faysgarth initially as a sportsman of quite startling ability, Skimpton was now revered by his schoolfellows both as a good-natured Deputy Head Boy and an even-handed captain of Second House. Today, however, he was far from his easy-going self, as Piggot had discovered to his cost.

As skipper of Faysgarth's First Eleven at soccer, it was Skimpton's job to pick the team for Saturday's final against arch rivals Rainingham, current holders of the Monktonshire Minor Public Schools' Challenge Cup. Faysgarth had been turning in some pretty impressive performances in recent weeks, and Skimpton rather fancied his team's chances against its fiercest adversaries.

Pausing over the team sheet, the captain troubled over the number nine position, and with some irritation reached into his blazer pocket and produced a crumpled sheet of paper – the cause of his present dark mood. He then read, for the hundredth time that day, the words written thereon:

> *My Dear Skimpton,*
> *Forgive me for imposing on you at this late stage before the*
> *Rainingham match, but I am requesting that you pick me as*
> *centre-forward. I am certain that I will not let the team down.*
> *Regards,*
> *Mohan Khan*

Khan, or 'Pearly' as he had been dubbed by his schoolfellows, was the son of a wealthy doctor from Bombay, and had arrived at Faysgarth the previous term. Normally his request for inclusion in the First Eleven would have posed no problem, for, as the

Indian was a hopeless footballer and would have been hard-pressed to secure a place even in the junior side, there would have been no question of the entreaty being granted. But this occasion was different. Some days earlier Khan had covered for Skimpton at some considerable risk to himself over an unsavoury incident involving a third-former, a hockey stick and a bag of fruit bonbons. And although Skimpton still felt indebted to the Indian for helping him on that occasion, selecting him for the Rainingham match by way of reward seemed to be stretching gratitude way beyond its acceptable limit.

And what of Marcus Dent, the undisputed School Scoundrel, whose custom it was to take the centre-forward's position in this fixture? How would he react to being dropped in favour of a well-known duffer? Dent, although undoubtedly a vicious and despicable fellow, exerted not inconsiderable influence at Faysgarth, amongst both boys and staff. In addition, his combative presence in the attack would be invaluable in the tussle against Rainingham's powerful defenders. Not normally known for his interest in sports, Dent always made sure to turn out in any soccer final, attracted by the sizeable contingent of female onlookers which generally arrived by bus from Faverstock, and in front of whom he could display his undoubted skill with the leather.

Crumpling the offending note into a ball and firing it vengefully in the direction of the waste bin, Skimpton felt himself close to making a decision on the matter. Everyone knew that Khan could not kick a football to save his life, let alone wallop it into the Rainingham net from twenty yards. Indeed, if his pitiful displays during PT were anything to go by, the young colonial would have his work cut out to tie his boot laces with any degree of conviction. Dent, on the other hand, had turned in a stylish performance last season, netting two excellent strikes, even though Faysgarth had been beaten by the odd goal in five. No: the matter was resolved – Khan's request must be rejected.

As he was setting himself to pen a reply to the audacious Indian, a liquorice toffee popped into his mouth to aid concentration, there was a smart knock at the door. 'Who is it now?' rasped Skimpton impatiently. The door creaked open, and in the gloomy corridor, Skimpton could just make out the shadowy presence of Mohan Khan.

'Ah, Pearly,' said Skimpton crisply, 'just the man. Come in.'

'I see you have received my note,' said the other. 'I hope I am not presuming too much if I intrude upon your time with a view to pressing for a response?'

'Not in the least. Sit down.' Skimpton turned to face his visitor and, leaning backwards in his chair, took a couple of moments to study Khan closely. He was a presentable enough fellow, of quite stocky build, and with a gaze of such piercing intensity that it gave the impression that he was permanently in search of approval. Skimpton had always found him to be a reliable fellow and his impeccable manners more than reassured the House Captain of his breeding. 'Pearly,' he said presently, 'I am well aware of the considerable debt I owe you over the Dodsworth incident, and I do not think I have yet had the opportunity to thank you fully for the part you played in resolving the issue in my favour. If, in the future, I can be of any help to you – in whatever way – I will of course be only too happy to oblige. However, I am far from sure that I can comply with your wishes with respect to the Rainingham match.'

At this, Khan became agitated, his breathing visibly quickened and he began drumming his fingers nervously on the arm of the chair.

'I regret to have to force the issue,' he said, 'but once you know the full facts, I am certain you will reconsider. You see, my father is an old Faysgarthian, and his fervent wish is to see his son score against Rainingham. There exists a long-standing wager between himself and his brother in Bombay, set down when my uncle's son and I were infants. My cousin is now at St Hugh's College, and suffering the same torment from his father as I am from mine.'

'And has he also made no impression on his First Eleven at St. Hugh's?'

'On the contrary; Sanjit is an excellent footballer, but his captain refuses to play him anywhere other than at right full-back. From that position I gather he stands only marginally more chance of scoring a goal than myself.'

'True. And your father is determined to break the stalemate, you say, to see your name on the scoresheet against Rainingham, and win the bet?'

'That is correct. I don't know if you are aware, but my father is an influential figure behind the scenes at Faysgarth, and a considerable benefactor of the school. His patience is already running out, and I fear that if he is not soon satisfied, he will remove me to another institution and curtail the generous financial support he affords the school.'

'This bet sounds mightily important. How much is it for?'

'Ten rupees.'

'Ten rupees! Is that all?'

'It is not the money that is important, Skimpton. The issue has become a matter of pride between my father and uncle, and the two families have been in a state of prolonged conflict over it for several months. My father and his brother appear to have taken the animosity they felt towards Rainingham as schoolboys, and turned it against one another!'

Skimpton whistled to himself. Seldom had he been confronted with so tricky a dilemma. With the school's finances at risk, not to mention his own reputation if his team lost the game, what should he do? And then there would be the undoubted outcry from Marcus Dent once he had discovered that he hadn't been picked! In the end, he tossed a coin, took no notice of the outcome, and fixed a determined gaze on Mohan Khan.

'Have you ever played top-flight schools' soccer before, Pearly?' he asked.

'I am afraid not, Skimpton. As you know I am entirely useless at sports.'

Skimpton smiled wanly, stroked his chin, and thought for a second. 'Meet me at lunchtime to-morrow on the football pitch in full kit,' he said. 'We'll thrash the leather around for half an hour.'

'Thank you, Skimpton,' said Pearly, a broad grin spreading over his face. 'I promise you I will do my best not to let you down.'

'I am sure you will, Pearly,' said Skimpton. And as the Indian turned to leave, he pencilled his name onto the team sheet. 'Oh, and Pearly...' he added.

'Yes Skimpton?'

'See if you can manage the odd sit-up or two before then, will you?'

*   *   *   *

'My giddy aunt!' shrieked Binns the next day. 'Skimpton's gone stark raving mad! He's picked Pearly to play against Rainingham!' A group of Main House boys had gathered around the noticeboard in the Senior Common Room, where Skimpton had posted the team sheet for Saturday's game. A sizeable majority of them were openly aghast at the captain's astounding team selection.

'And at centre-forward as well!' piped up a voice from the back. 'Old Dent will have an opinion on that!'

Instantly, Marcus Dent appeared, smoking a small Cuban cigar. Smiling, he strode to the noticeboard, boys hastily removing themselves from his path. As his eyes scanned the team sheet he began chuckling malevolently. 'So,' he murmured to himself, 'it's true. Skimpton's dropped me to left-half and picked that weasel Khan as centre-forward.'

'That's right Marcus,' shouted Binns, 'what do you have to say about that?'

Dent paused for what seemed like an eternity, drew deeply on his cigar, scanned his audience through heavily lidded eyes, and only when the last vestiges of smoke had been expelled from his mouth, said, 'I didn't know they played footer in the colonies.'

'They don't,' said Skimpton from the doorway, having observed the brouhaha with mounting unease. 'I've picked Pearly because I was impressed by his determination to succeed. Besides, we could do with a little muscle in the final third.'

'But Skimpton!' yelled Binns, 'Dent's our best forward, everyone knows that. Why on earth would you want to play him at left-half?'

'Because that is where I feel he will be of most use on Saturday.'

'We'll see about that,' muttered Dent.

'Besides,' continued Skimpton, 'bearing in mind the number of cigars he smokes these days, I doubt very much whether Dent would be able to keep pace with the rest of the attack!' A stunned silence greeted this comment, and Skimpton, sensing that he had perhaps been too provocative – bearing in mind the frailty of his case – turned briskly and walked away.

Dent, furious, stubbed out his cigar on the floor, marched to the noticeboard and crossed his name off the team sheet. Then, in capital letters, he scrawled 'NOT AVAILABLE' next to it, breaking the pencil in half in the process, before striding purposefully over to the door. 'Binns! Spate!' he fumed. 'My study NOW!'

*   *   *   *

Once outside, Skimpton, sensing the possibility of danger, Dent and his adjuncts only a few seconds behind, prudently increased his pace, making off in the direction of the soccer pitch. After changing, he ran out with a ball and met Pearly Khan, shivering in the goalmouth.

'I wish to thank you Skimpton,' offered the Indian boy through chattering teeth. 'I have seen the team sheet.' In addition to his footer kit, Khan also wore gloves, three scarves, a balaclava, a bobble hat and a pair of swimming goggles. Round his neck, hanging from a piece of string, was a circular pendant. It looked like bone, stained red, and on it was a rather child-like depiction of an elephant.

'That's an unusual piece, Pearly,' said Skimpton, 'what's it made of?'

'Ivory,' explained Khan, sniffing all the while. 'I was given it by an old soothsayer in Bombay. It is reputed to bring good luck.' The Indian boy then sneezed mightily, almost falling over in the process.

'Are you suffering from a cold, Pearly?' enquired Skimpton, testily.

'Perhaps I am not yet accustomed to your English winter,' came the snivelling reply. 'In Bombay we have sunshine all year round, except in the rainy season.'

'Well, you'd better get used to it pretty quick, for there are only five days to go before you're due to turn out for the First Eleven.'

'Worry not, Skimpton. My lucky charm will ensure that I do not let you down.'

'Hmmm. Well, let's start with some physical jerks, shall we?' Skimpton dropped to the grass and commenced a burst of press-ups whilst Pearly looked on. 'Think you can do a few of these?' he asked, looking up at the weaker boy.

'I'll try,' replied the Indian, at which he began tentatively lowering his limbs to the ground, groaning as he did so.

'Come on, man,' encouraged the sportsman, 'surely you can manage a dozen press-ups!' Pearly lay face down, placed his palms on the ground beside him and pushed for all he was worth. Try as he might though, he could no more complete one press-up than he could fly to the moon, and after a seemingly interminable performance of huffing and puffing, the Indian gave up, utterly exhausted.

'I'm sorry Skimpton,' he gasped, 'I appear to have no strength whatsoever in my arms. Perhaps we could try something else?'

A number of boys had gathered on the touchline, alerted to Pearly's feeble endeavours by Binns and Spate, on their way to lunch. Some began jeering the young Indian mercilessly. 'I don't know about Pearly Khan,' quipped one of them, 'looks more to me like Pearly can't!'

'Take no notice,' said Skimpton, helping the other boy up, 'let's try some running on the spot, shall we?' Thankfully, though, the session was interrupted before Pearly could test his stamina further, when Piggot arrived bearing a letter for Skimpton. 'Go and get changed, Pearly,' said the fitter of the two resolutely, 'we'll have another bash to-morrow.' A desolate-looking Khan then trudged off in the direction of the changing rooms, hoots of derision ringing in his ears.

'What's this then Piggot?' questioned Skimpton, taking delivery of the missive from his trusty fag.

'Looks to me like a letter from your father Skimpton,' replied the ever-perceptive Piggot, 'if the handwriting on the envelope is anything to go by.'

'Very good. Now run along and supervise Khan in the shower for me. And make sure the water's freezing for him, would you?'

A letter from his father was such a rare event that Skimpton felt compelled to mark the occasion by purchasing some fruit bonbons from the tuck shop and retiring immediately to his study to give it his full attention. Aware that such a plan meant him probably skipping double geography, he instructed Jack Varley to make his excuses for him, plying his housemate with sweeties for his pains and pleading an headache by way of explication of his absence.

The news that his father intended to visit Faysgarth the following Saturday would ordinarily have been a cause of considerable celebration for Skimpton, since these days he so rarely managed to meet with the old fellow. On this occasion, though, his pater's overture provoked mixed feelings in the young man.

Skimpton's father was a high-ranking government accountant whose work frequently took him away from home. This meant, even during the holidays, Skimpton's only contact with his sole surviving parent was the odd postcard, often sent from some far-flung outpost of the Empire. That weekend, though, he was due to attend a conference on the subject of penal budgets in nearby Crownbridge, and would be well-placed to put in an appearance at Faysgarth after wrapping up his business on Saturday afternoon.

Skimpton's father had, however, promised to visit his son at school on numerous other occasions but had never appeared, and Skimpton half hoped that this time would be no exception. For, although he enjoyed seeing him enormously, he was anxious that his father should not witness any ignominious defeat suffered by his team at the hands of the Rainingham boys.

Although in his heart of hearts he knew that the cause was in all probability already lost, the determined all-rounder settled into his armchair, took pen and paper and began formulating a rigorous training schedule for Pearly Khan. Fully aware that Marcus Dent had by now almost certainly removed himself from contention, he decided that if all else failed he would play centre-forward himself, moving the Indian into defence and allowing him first shot at any penalty which came his team's way. And although he knew that there was very little chance of it reaching its destination before the weekend, he also penned a short note to his father, care of the Home Office in London, in an attempt to subtly dissuade the latter from visiting Faysgarth the following Saturday.

*   *   *   *

Meanwhile, over in Main House, Marcus Dent was holding an impromptu meeting with his chums on the subject of the day's humiliating events. Pacing the room restlessly, the bounder was becoming increasingly irritated by the whole business. How, puzzled the blackguard, could he turn the embarrassing situation to his advantage? His face crimson with rage, he scoured his rancid imagination for a retributory ruse of sufficient maliciousness that – through it – his reputation as School Scoundrel would be considerably enhanced.

'What on earth's Skimpton thinking of, picking the Indian!' screamed Binns. 'Why, he'll give the match away!'

'Precisely,' agreed Dent. 'Apart from that, his stupidity could well set a dangerous precedent. Before long, these colonials will be beating us at our own games, and we can't have that. For, after all, what's the point of inventing a sport if you can't then be assured of beating every other bugger at it!' Unsure whether or not their leader's rhetoric demanded a verbal response, those present followed Spate's lead and broke into polite applause. 'Stop all that,' snapped Dent acidly, 'I need to think!'

The three minutes' silence, which he had previously demanded should follow any utterance tinged with more than a whiff of rancour, enabled Dent to pour himself a stiff drink, settle on his chaise longue and formulate a plan of action. 'Binns,' he commanded presently, 'organize some transport, a charabanc will do. And Spate, get on the blower to the landlord of The White Swan in Faverstock. Inform him that we shall require use of his upstairs room on Friday night from about eight.'

'Certainly Marcus.'

*　　*　　*　　*

Towards the end of the fifth afternoon's training session, Skimpton and an exhausted Pearly Khan found themselves enjoying each other's company in the long-jump pit. Having all but abandoned any notion of building up the other's fitness and strength, Skimpton had decided to spend the hours available to them trying to improve the Indian's limited skills with the ball – a time-consuming exercise which involved the sports supremo crying off afternoon lessons all week. They had been working on Pearly's penalty kicking that last afternoon, and – aware that his protégé had put everything he had into the previous few days' work – Skimpton felt that a few words of encouragement might be appropriate.

However, after much soul-searching, he found himself unable to summon up the required positivity for such a task, and decided instead to be brutally honest. 'Pearly,' he said grimly, 'you've worked jolly hard this week, and I'll say this for you: you're a plucky fellow. I've been impressed also by your politeness and affability, and on those counts you deserve a chance to fulfil your father's ambition for you. However, I feel I must tell you that, despite my tuition, you are no better a footballer now than you were when you first came to me with this hair-brained scheme. If anything, your level of skill is slightly worse than it was at the beginning of the week. In fact, my fag Piggot is far better than you and he's only a junior.'

'What are you implying, Skimpton?'

'Very well, I shall endeavour to be more forthright. Your chances of scoring against Rainingham to-morrow are approximately nil, my friend. I therefore recommend that if you wish to avoid heaping disgrace upon both yourself and your school, you cry off with an injured leg. I shall of course provide corroboration for any such public statement.' Pearly turned away, unsure how to respond.

'Well?' prompted Skimpton. 'What do you say to that?'

'My father has sent word from Bombay that he will be dispatching a representative to oversee the match on Saturday. I cannot answer for the consequences if he finds out I did not make the team.'

'But you must understand, Pearly,' insisted Skimpton, 'that on present form there is no possibility of you scoring. Can you not convince your father and his brother that they should forget their childish wager?'

'I suspect not. I do have another suggestion, though.'

'And what is that, pray?'

'I gather there is a new rule in operation this season with respect to the use of substitutes, is that right?'

'Correct. The footballing authorities have decided to try it out in schools' soccer initially, with a view to extending the regulation to the professional game, in the fullness of time.'

'Then perhaps you could be persuaded to let me start the match, on the understanding that if things go badly, I will feign injury and allow you to replace me with another player.'

'Not a bad idea. We haven't had recourse to use one this season, but I'll see if I can encourage young Terry Dunstan to don the substitute's jersey. Failing that I suggest you retire to your study and pray for a heavy downfall of snow.'

*   *   *   *

In the event, the sun shone brightly the following morning. Skimpton, watchful for any early sign of his father, had trotted out just after breakfast to put Pearly through his paces in the penalty area. Unwilling to entertain the thought of his father arriving at Faysgarth only to witness his son's team beaten roundly by Rainingham, Skimpton left strict instructions for Piggot to place a fine bottle of brandy in the staff-room, and introduce the old fellow to it early on. If precedent was anything to go by, such an enticement would doubtless retain his attention, out of sight of the soccer pitch, until the final whistle.

As was usual, a crowd had gathered on the touchline, eager to glimpse more of Pearly's bunglings with the ball. Numbered amongst them was Marcus Dent, looking slightly the worse for wear after having reputedly spent the previous evening making merry with his chums at The White Swan in Faverstock.

'Come on Pearly,' mocked the school villain, 'let's see what you're made of! Summon us up some Oriental magic with the old leather!'

Apart from this final coaching session with Pearly, Skimpton had another reason to vacate Second House earlier than usual that day. Colonel Coombes, the irredeemably short-sighted chemistry master, had become suspicious of the sportsman's excuses for missing lessons all week, and was said to be on the warpath. Everyone knew that the volatile master's viciously haphazard use of the cane, coupled with his fearsome temper, had on many occasions left boys in need of lengthy hospital treatment. Indeed, Skimpton himself had suffered at the hands of the demonic chemistry man some years before, and had no intention of repeating the experience today. The brutal encounter had happened when the irate Colonel had smashed a tennis racket over Skimpton's head after having accused him of smirking without permission on school premises. The unlucky third-former had merely paid a routine visit to the dentist that afternoon and returned with his mouth slightly contorted as a consequence of the anaesthetic. He spent the rest of the day in the casualty department of Barnchester Royal Infirmary having seven stitches inserted into his head.

That afternoon, though, it was Skimpton's hope that the Colonel might have his hands full running the line at the football game, rather than devote his attention to pursuing Skimpton for his alleged absences. Aware that his eyesight problem had lately been the cause of considerable controversy as a result of several fiercely disputed offside decisions, Colonel Coombes had recently adopted the bizarre tactic of attaching himself by a length of rope to a first-former named Kydd, who would accompany him at the touchline and advise the master about tricky decisions. Indeed, so dependent had the Colonel become on his young accomplice that during the hours of darkness he could often be seen being led around the school by him like a perplexed dog on a lead.

With the crowd swelling in number and kick-off time rapidly approaching, Skimpton placed the ball on the penalty spot and invited Pearly to have one last crack at bursting the net. 'Just keep your head down and belt it as hard as you can!' he instructed, taking up a position in goal. But Pearly's poor level of expertise, even after five days' intensive instruction, allowed for no such accomplishment. After a brief, uncertain run-up, the Indian swung his right leg awkwardly, missed the ball entirely, near-somersaulted, and ended up flat on his back in the mud.

'I say Pearly!' hooted Marcus Dent from the touchline. 'How about taking up gymnastics? I'm sure you'd make a grand fist of the parallel bars!' At which all present fairly whooped with laughter, including, it has to be said, some of the masters.

With only a few minutes to go, and Colonel Coombes ready and tethered to his assistant on the half way line, Skimpton felt a pang of trepidation shudder through his limbs, for the strapping fellows from Rainingham were now taking to the field. They were a fairly homely bunch, widely held to be from a slightly lower social class than the fellows at Faysgarth. Many members of the team, it was rumoured, were scholarship boys, and their untutored accents as they called to one another brought to mind popular characters from radio comedy programmes. However dubious their origins though, the Rainingham lads had already enjoyed a spectacularly successful season, and had only that week secured top place in the Monktonshire Minor Public Schools' League Championship (upper division). This game represented Skimpton's last chance of the season to wrestle some glory from their grasp.

'Skimpton!' bellowed Colonel Coombes from the touchline. 'I'd be very grateful if you would see me after the game today, as I must speak with you urgently on the topic of your classroom attendance this week!'

'Of course, Colonel.' replied Skimpton blandly. That was the last thing he needed. How in Heaven's name would he be able to concentrate on the game with the promise of an hideous punishment from the Colonel hanging over his head? And where on earth were his team? Surely they must have clambered into their togs by now!

Eventually, the Faysgarthians emerged. But they resembled nothing like the side he had picked. In fact, the outfit which took the field was primarily made up of players from the Junior Eleven, supplemented by various oddities from elsewhere! Riley, the lanky fourth-form 'cellist appeared to be playing in goal, and taking up a position rather reluctantly on the wing was the infamous surrealist Rodney Carstairs, whose father was reputed to run an African-style dance troupe in Finland.

'What in God's name is going on?' demanded Skimpton of his diminutive fag Piggot, as the latter joined him in the centre circle.

'It was Dent, Skimpton,' returned the junior bleakly. 'He took the First Eleven out revelling last night in Faverstock, and they are all so ill as a consequence that we youngsters have been forced to take their places!' With a toss of his head, Piggot indicated a group of grey-looking fellows huddled behind the visitors' goal. Dent had joined them and was surreptitiously distributing Cuban cigars.

'What a bunch of asses!' exploded Skimpton. 'Getting themselves into that state the night before an important match. And as for that rotter Dent, why, I've a good mind to...'

'It's useless, Skimpton,' interrupted Piggot. 'Kick off's in one minute and the referee's waiting to start!' Skimpton, unable to contain his fury, kicked the air in frustration, a large lump of mud from his boot flying off and hitting Pearly Khan full in the face

'What's the matter Skimpton,' bellowed Dent from the touchline, 'lost your marbles as well as your team? I'd stick to chemistry in future if I were you, that way you might stay out of trouble!'

'Take no notice Skimpton,' urged Piggot, ushering his rattled fag-master towards the centre spot. 'We'll win this game if we have to run ourselves ragged!'

Just then, a flurry of activity near the school end corner flag heralded the arrival of three individuals so heavily insulated against the cold that they were almost impossible to identify as human. Pearly Khan shuffled over to Skimpton, and, with an air of resignation, intoned, 'It is my father. He has travelled from Bombay with his brother to watch the game.'

'Poor show,' sympathized Skimpton, scanning the crowd, 'and there's no crying off injured either, Pearly, for there goes my substitute.' The skipper directed Khan's attention to the other end of the field, where an unsteady and pale-looking Terry Dunstan was being led away by Binns after collapsing on the touchline as a result of extreme dehydration.

'By the bye,' asked Skimpton, 'who's that other fellow with your father and uncle?'

'That is my cousin Sanjit. He has come to look round the school. My uncle is considering transferring him to Faysgarth next term with a view to him playing in an advantageous position in the First Eleven.'

'We'll see about that,' frowned Skimpton cheerlessly, taking his position to face the first onslaught from the Rainingham forwards. 'Come on chaps!' he cried, summoning up every last vestige of inspiration. 'Let's give these fellows what's for!' At which the crowd cheered, the referee blew his whistle, and battle commenced.

*   *   *   *

By half-time, Faysgarth, playing with a strong wind behind them, considered themselves lucky to be only four goals down. Pearly Khan, apart from woefully mis-kicking an early chance some six yards out, had hardly touched the ball, and although putting all their might into the fray, the junior Faysgarthians were no match for Rainingham's muscular team. Skimpton's cause had not been helped when Carstairs had put through his own goal in a misguided attempt to assist his chum Riley after a corner. Bizarrely, the young surrealist punched the ball into his own net, assuming the mantle of goalkeeper after spotting his musician friend unconscious on the ground. The latter, entirely unchallenged, had disastrously collided with a goalpost minutes before and had lain comatose for some time.

Khan's father, on the touchline, could hardly conceal his disgust at his son's performance. After the young Indian had scuffed a clearance into the crowd, a furious Dr. Khan had angrily hurled a muffler at his son. When, much to the dismay of the crowd, it missed, an inattentive Khan instantly obliged by tripping over the item and falling face-down in a puddle.

'That's the ticket Pearly,' whooped Marcus Dent, 'save yourself the bother of a bath afterwards!'

Skimpton was aware, as the game progressed, that the touchline quips at the young colonial's expense were affecting Khan deeply, and was on the point of suggesting he retire when the whistle blew for half-time.

'Come on Pearly,' the worthy young captain urged, 'I have a notion these Rainingham chaps will tire in the second half – their defence looks groggy already. Chin up! We'll get you that goal if it's the last thing we do!'

In the event, the second half was only seven minutes old when the opportunity he had been waiting for presented itself to Skimpton. Rainingham, now six-up and beginning to lark about, gave the ball away on the left wing. Piggot, speeding down the line, dribbled past the full back with an emphatic feint and sent over a ripping centre. Lunging backwards, hopelessly out of position, the Rainingham 'keeper fisted the ball across the mouth of his goal. Skimpton, thundering in at the far post, expertly trapped the leather at the feet of Pearly Khan only two feet from the goal line. Stepping backwards out of his way, the captain had presented the Indian with an unmissable chance, the empty net gaping in front of him.

'Whack it in Pearly!' cried the Faysgarthians.

'Come on Mohan,' yelled his father, 'put the ball in the net!' And with the defence stranded, Pearly withdrew his leg, faltered, and blasted the ball blindly wide, his miserably sliced effort eventually coming to rest only a yard from the corner flag.

'Right in front of the bally net!' groaned Skimpton. 'It was an absolute sitter!' Pearly, utterly deflated, trudged away, his head bowed in shame. Dr. Khan, quite beside himself with frustration, sunk to his knees in despair, as his brother chuckled to himself, content that there was no way on earth, given his nephew's astounding ineptitude, that the wager would ever be settled in anyone's favour other than his own.

By twelve minutes from the end, Rainingham were holding onto a nine-goal lead, and it seemed that only a miracle could save Faysgarth from one of the most humiliating sporting defeats in its history. As the ball rocketed past Riley in the Faysgarth goal for Rainingham's tenth of the afternoon, Skimpton's plucky troupe of youngsters dragged themselves into position to face yet another irrepressible bombardment by the Rainingham lads. As he placed the ball onto the centre spot, Skimpton looked around at his bedraggled team-mates and prepared to will them on for one last effort. Then he noticed the absence of Pearly Khan. 'Why, the blighter's sloped off without permission,' he exclaimed, 'leaving us with only ten men!' So incensed was he by the Indian's insubordination that he took the ball from the kick off, raced goalwards, slid through the Rainingham defence and belted the leather resolutely into the opposing net from fifteen yards out! Ten - one!

Skimpton's feat, however, could raise little more than an half-hearted, ironic cheer from the crowd, who were beginning to drift away disconsolately. That was until the dramatic reappearance of Pearly Khan. Amidst unspeakable insults from the Dent contingent, the Indian pelted onto the pitch during a brief interruption. Seemingly revitalised, he quickly dispossessed a Rainingham forward, waltzed into the penalty box and delivered a defence-splitting pass to a team-mate, who duly prodded the ball home! Goal! The crowd, sensing the remote possibility that Faysgarth may yet squeeze a scrap of dignity from the match, duly went wild, and their cheers seemed to propel the boy from Bombay into even greater feats of footballing magic.

Ten-two down with only seven minutes to go, and Pearly took a few seconds' breather to confide in his captain.

'It was my lucky charm,' he whispered. 'I lost it a few days ago in the dressing room. Without it I am lost!' Skimpton recognized the colourful talisman which Khan now wore around his neck as the one he'd seen him sporting at the first training session earlier in the week.

'If that's all it takes to get the best out of a fellow,' laughed Skimpton, 'then put me down for a dozen! Come on, Pearly, let's get you that goal and have no more done about it!'

Certainly, it was a new Pearly Khan who had taken the field in those final minutes. His speed and intricate footwork brought two more goals – one from a lively Piggot who had pounced on a thirty-yard screamer from the Indian which rebounded at his feet from a post, another a spectacular diving header dispatched by Skimpton from a pinpoint cross by the Bombay Bombshell. But try as he might, the Indian could not score himself. It seemed incredible that, with goals now going in at the Rainingham end every few seconds, Pearly could not find the target. Even Riley, the lanky goalkeeper had wandered up and nodded one in from a free kick! And Carstairs, his unconventional sidekick, had sent one rocketing into the top corner via his pelvis!

With the score standing at ten-nine and only two minutes left, a determined Pearly collected the ball on the halfway line, strode manfully up field, with it seemingly tied to his boot, wriggled through a platoon of defenders, and placed a precise shot towards the bottom corner of the goal. The Rainingham 'keeper flung himself across his six-yard box, but to no avail, for the leather was already way beyond his reach and heading for the net. Then, from nowhere, a burly full-back launched himself at the line in an attempt at a spectacular last-ditch clearance. The crowd gasped in amazement as he made contact with the ball, but his tenacious kick only sent it rocketing into the roof of his own net for a spectacular own goal! Ten-all and Pearly had still not managed to score!

What a game, thought Skimpton, and for the first time he scanned the faces in the crowd, desperate that his father's should be amongst them.

Then, with only seconds left on the watch, a clear chance for victory presented itself. Pearly had wriggled into a dangerous position in the left of the Rainingham penalty box, and slotted the ball through to Skimpton, a few yards to his right, in acres of space and with only one defender left to beat. Selling the Rainingham full-back a perfect dummy, the Faysgarth skipper deftly pushed the ball through his challenger's legs and bore down on goal, preparing to round the 'keeper and slam the ball home. The visitors' last line of defence, though, had other ideas. Skimpton feigned to shoot then flicked the ball to the left some six yards out, and the Rainingham 'keeper flung himself at the Faysgarthian's feet bringing him crashing to the ground with a blatant rugby tackle! Foul!

Skimpton knew, even as he heard the whistle blow for a penalty, that he would play no further part in the game, for he had fallen so heavily that his right foot had become twisted under him, and his ankle injured in the process. As he lay prostrate in the penalty area, somewhat dazed from the assault, Skimpton was vaguely aware that Marcus Dent appeared to be running onto the pitch. Before the skipper had quite recovered his bearings, he felt his shirt being pulled roughly over his head. 'What on earth are you doing, Dent?' he demanded.

'In the absence of any other suitable candidate,' explained the bounder, 'I am taking your place in the team.'

'Over my dead body!'

'I am afraid, Skimpton,' said Dent, donning the latter's jersey, 'that you have no choice in the matter. When a player's injury prevents him from taking any further part in the game, a substitute can be used – that, as I am sure you are aware, is the new rule. I am stepping into the breach.'

Skimpton, struggling to his feet, his ankle throbbing agonisingly, was in no position to argue, and with the aid of his trusty fag Piggot, he hobbled bravely to a position just beside the visitors' goal, cursing Dent under his breath.

The crowd was in uproar subsequent to the foul being committed. Fierce arguments broke out the moment the seriousness of Skimpton's injury was confirmed, for the thorny question then arose as to who should take the penalty. Dr. Khan insisted his son should be given the job, though many around him, his brother included, thought otherwise. Pearly's cousin Sanjit, obviously wishing to distance himself from the dispute, kept his own council. Binns and Spate, though, were in little doubt as to who should be entrusted with the final kick of the game. 'Why everyone knows it must be Dent!' screamed the louder of the two. 'With all due respect, Doctor Khan, your son has played a blinder for the last ten minutes but seems singularly incapable of putting the ball in the net!'

At one point a contingent of prefects sought to bring Colonel Coombes into the fracas, but the chemistry man was busy trying to disengage himself from his young assistant Kydd. The master had ended up practically strangling the youngster after the rope used to connect the two of them had become tangled around a goalpost.

In the end, it was down to Skimpton, as captain, to decide.

'Bearing in mind his sensational contribution to the game this afternoon,' he pronounced, 'and since my injury precludes me from doing so, I should like to offer my friend Pearly Khan the opportunity to win the game for Faysgarth!'

Behind the goal, Dr. Khan looked to the heavens, gave out a cry of thanks, and rubbed his hands in anticipation of his son's impending triumph from the penalty spot. Pearly though, appeared troubled, and after a brief word with Skimpton, marched over to the referee, took the ball and handed it solemnly to Marcus Dent. There sounded a series of gasps from the crowd, followed by an eerie silence, punctuated only by a further strangulated wail of anguish from Pearly's father.

'Thanks, Pearly,' said Dent slyly, taking the ball from the

Indian boy. 'No hard feelings eh?'

'Not in the least,' replied Khan casually. 'I understand that none of your comments this afternoon have been directed at me personally.'

'Good show. Always best to put school before self, eh?'

'Well played Pearly!' called out Binns from the touchline.

At this point the Rainingham keeper piped up. 'Do you think,' he sighed, a trifle impatiently, 'that we could get on with it? I'd like to get back in time for tea.'

Dent, after a brief perusal of the crowd to make sure his female friends were present to admire his sensational last-minute contribution, stepped up to the penalty spot with the ball. After placing it carefully on the ground, he took three steps back, wiped his cheek with the arm of Skimpton's soccer jersey, and looked the 'keeper straight in the eye. He then glanced first left, then right of the hefty Rainingham goalie, as he made up his mind which corner to aim for.

A hushed silence descended the field as all waited in unbearable anticipation. Finally, Dent ran forward, placed his left foot onto the ground beside the ball and swung his right boot into the leather, propelling it powerfully goalwards. The 'keeper though, had only to thrust upward a fist to keep it out, for Dent had cannoned the ball straight at him! As the leather flew skywards, the Faysgarth forwards stood motionless in stunned amazement, in contrast to the Rainingham boys, who fairly flopped to their knees in relief. Only one figure in the twenty-two retained his wits in those crucial final seconds, and that boy was Pearly Khan. Sensing that the ball was hurtling earthwards only two or three yards in front of him, he raced forward and thumped a perfectly timed volley straight into the back of the net! The whistle blew and that was that! Faysgarth had won, eleven goals to ten – all thanks to the battling boy from Bombay!

'Hurrah!' came the cry from behind the ropes. 'Pearly's done it! Faysgarth's won the cup!'

Within seconds, ecstatic members of the crowd had hoisted both Skimpton and Pearly Khan onto their shoulders, propelling them joyously towards the cricket pavilion, where lemonade and sandwiches awaited, by way of an accompaniment to the presentation of the trophy by an esteemed member of the local Rotarian society.

Meanwhile, on the field, Marcus Dent was being consoled by his usual coterie of sycophants.

'Never mind, Marcus,' squawked Binns. 'At least you didn't miss the target! Good job Pearly was following up though, otherwise my guess is you'd've been extremely unpopular!'

'For mercy's sake button it, Binns,' snapped Dent wrathfully, 'and get me my blazer.' Before he could don his school jacket and slouch off unnoticed though, Dent was intercepted by an uncommonly agitated Colonel Coombes. Recently released from his entanglement with young Kydd, and, as a result, desperately lacking the visual assistance afforded by the youngster, the master stopped Dent as he was leaving the sports field. He accomplished this by simply walking straight into him.

'Ah, Skimpton!' he exclaimed. 'Just the young man I've been looking for. Do not think that because you have triumphed in the sporting arena today that I have forgotten your scholarly transgressions earlier this week!'

'Colonel Coombes,' said Dent calmly, 'there seems to have been some mistake. You see, I am not the individual whom you wish to upbraid, but an entirely...'

'Do not attempt, young man, to pull the wool over my eyes. Are you not wearing a jersey with the number seven emblazoned across its back?'

'Yes sir, but if you would let me explain...'

The Colonel's face was beginning to redden and his left leg had started to make its characteristic jerking movements – a sure sign that the temperature of his anger had reached such a dangerous level that only extreme violence would extinguish it. 'According to my team sheet,' he continued, 'that position was filled today by a boy named Skimpton,' he rattled, 'whom I am rather keen to interview in connection with his absence from afternoon lessons this week.'

'But Colonel Coombes...'

'Enough! I will tolerate no further interruption! Take yourself off to the gymnasium at once! Your impudence demands no less than a thorough beating, even before the more serious matter of your truancy is addressed. Now go!'

Having dispatched Dent to prepare himself for the inevitable thrashing and consequent sojourn in hospital, Colonel Coombes strode off purposefully to his study with a view to carefully choosing a weapon whose size and maleficence might do justice to his fury.

*   *   *   *

A little later, the Monktonshire Minor Public Schools' Challenge Cup having taken pride of place in Faysgarth's trophy cabinet, Skimpton, his ankle securely strapped, was limping towards the senior changing rooms. Outside the door, arguing the finer points of football, he encountered Pearly Khan's father and uncle. They were a curious looking pair, clothed in a peculiar combination of Oriental formal dress and English woollies. 'But you must understand,' insisted the latter in mellifluous, exotic tones, 'that after the penalty has been missed a member of the defending team must touch the ball before it can be kicked by an opposing player!'

'That is only if the goalkeeper has not touched it first! On this occasion, the ball clearly struck the Rainingham 'keeper on the hand before my son blasted his shot into the net!'

'Excuse me gentlemen,' interposed Skimpton. 'I don't suppose either of you has seen Pearly, I mean Mohan, Khan have you?'

The doctor, evidently rather annoyed by the interruption, turned to face Skimpton. After positioning very deliberately a pair of wire-rimmed spectacles further up his nose, he peered quizzically through them at the soccer captain.

At length, he replied disinterestedly, 'My son is inside the changing area with his cousin.' He then removed his spectacles, returned to his brother, and resumed hostilities. 'Now hand over the ten rupees Vasu,' he insisted angrily, 'or I shall be compelled to write to my wife's uncle who is a barrister in Calcutta!'

Inside the steamy changing rooms, Skimpton could just make out what he took to be the figure of Mohan Khan showering alone. The rest of his team, being juniors, he assumed were busy changing in their own facility elsewhere. 'Pearly!' he declared, 'I'm glad to have caught you. That was a wizard game, what?'

'It certainly was by jingo,' replied a third, fully clothed young man stepping forward from the gloom. 'Skimpton,' said he, as his countryman emerged from the shower, 'I would like you to meet my cousin Sanjit, one of my country's finest footballers.'

'You mean...'

'Yes, Skimpton. It was Sanjit who came on, not me, in the final ten minutes of the game.'

'But Pearly...'

'The improvement in performance had nothing to do with my lucky charm, it was Sanjit who scored the winning goal.'

Pearly's cousin stepped forward and proffered Skimpton his hand. 'I am pleased and honoured to make your acquaintance,' he said.

'My cousin and I felt that he possessed far more chance of scoring a goal and putting an end to our family feud than I did,' continued Pearly. 'We quickly changed clothes when no-one was looking. He did a fine job don't you think?'

'Why yes, but...'

'We knew that in all probability no-one would notice the difference – after all, in the eyes of a white man, one coloured fellow looks very much like another. Besides, Sanjit and I are used to exchanging identities, our families see so little of us these days that they are unsure which of us is which. And today my father and uncle were far too concerned with their petty rivalry to notice anything was amiss. I hope you will not think too harshly of us.'

Skimpton, somewhat staggered by Pearly Khan's extraordinary revelations, took a few seconds to survey the two young men who stood before him; one clad in overcoat, scarf, gloves and woollen hat, the other stark naked and dripping water onto the floor. In that the colour of their skin was identical, the two did indeed appear somewhat similar. Their facial features though, were obviously entirely different, the cousin even sporting a putative beard, apparently tolerated at St Hugh's after the relaxing of rules with regard to facial hair. In summary, Skimpton felt rather a chump, having allowed himself to be tricked into believing the two colonials to be the same person.

'Do not feel foolish, Skimpton,' said Pearly, 'you were far too involved in the game to realise that Sanjit had taken my place. You are first and foremost a sportsman, and one of quite astounding talent and commitment, and it is in this field of endeavour where your perceptivity lies – not in the more aesthetic arts.'

'But Pearly,' Skimpton protested, 'judging by today's performance everyone at Faysgarth will expect you to turn out for the First Eleven on a regular basis! I couldn't possibly sanction Sanjit stepping in for you again!'

'Of course not. My cousin is also needed over at St Hugh's to add mettle to their first team's defence. But if you will agree to keep today's deception a secret, Skimpton, I will, before the start of next season, announce my retirement from the game on health grounds.'

Seating himself wearily on a nearby bench, Skimpton shook his head in a baffled gesture of resignation. 'I'll say this, Pearly,' sighed the skipper, with a wry smile, 'your way of doing things is rather queer. But I'll say no more about it if you don't.'

'I had made a promise not to let you down, Skimpton,' said Pearly, 'and knew that whatever happened I must keep my word.'

Which, in a way, he had. Skimpton now turned his attention to Khan's cousin, Sanjit. Handing the shivering youngster a towel, he said, 'As for you, young fellow, though not exactly condoning your behaviour, I'd like to pay tribute both to your fine display this afternoon, but more importantly, to your selfless decision in refusing the opportunity to take the final penalty.'

'I did not feel confident of scoring, that is why.'

'I thought you had lost your nerve, Sanjit!' said Pearly, teasingly.

'It was more important that the team win than it was for your father to feel satisfied, Mohan,' replied his cousin.

'Nevertheless,' said Skimpton, 'such magnanimity and loyalty to team-mates I am sure makes you a great asset to the First Eleven at St. Hugh's. My hope is, for the sake of the opposition at least, they keep you at full back, where you can inflict least damage!'

Pearly placed a hand on Skimpton's shoulder in a brotherly fashion, and smiled broadly at his somewhat restive conspirator. 'Thank you, Skimpton,' he said, 'for all the help you have given me in the last few days. As far as football is concerned, I think I would make a fine club doctor. Wouldn't you agree?'

'Possibly. You'd have to promise not to send your cousin to treat the injured players though, when you didn't feel like it!'

'Nonsense!' put in Sanjit, 'I intend to train as a veterinary surgeon. The two disciplines are pretty much identical, are they not?'

'Sanjit!' warned Pearly. 'Do not be mischievous! Skimpton has had a very confusing time of it already today.'

'But Mohan, I still stand by the point, the common-or-garden General Practitioner is no better qualified than the average Veterinary Surgeon!'

'That is patently absurd...'

And as the two cousins continued to squabble over the relative merits of their intended careers, Skimpton quietly removed his togs and, unnoticed, stepped into the shower.

*   *   *   *

On his way to Second House, half an hour later, Skimpton noticed a dwarfish figure in full footer kit standing guard at the school gates. Closer investigation revealed it to be his diminutive fag, Piggot.

'Ho ho, young shaver!' hailed the Senior. 'What concerns you here at this late hour? Shouldn't you be at supper?'

A shivering Piggot flashed his unruly teeth in a deferential grin in the direction of his hero, and replied, 'I am on the lookout, as you requested Skimpton, for your father, who I believe is due at Faysgarth some time today!'

Skimpton looked at his watch, lamented the trouble caused by the two other parents that day, and for a moment believed that he might be better served staying well clear of all family entanglements for the foreseeable future. 'I very much doubt,' he said, 'whether my father will turn up today. He has probably been detained in Crownbridge on government business and intends to take the last train back to London.' An accurate conjecture, as it turned out, for at that moment, his pater was in fact seated in The Railway Tavern in Faverstock, accompanied by a copy of *The Illustrated London News* and a copious brandy, awaiting the eight forty-seven to Paddington.

'I say what a pity!' said a crestfallen Piggot. 'I was so looking forward to meeting him. Has he sent you no word of his intended movements?'

'Good Lord no! That is not his style.'

'It's a shame he couldn't have been here to see the match. What a scorcher it was too, eh? That would certainly have been a satisfaction for you had he been present! Tell me, what's he like?'

Skimpton paused for a moment. In truth it had been so long since he'd seen his father that he had about as little idea of him as had Doctor Khan and his fractious brother of their interchangeable sons Mohan and Sanjit.

Laying his blazer over Piggot's shoulders, and strolling in amiable silence with him down the drive, Skimpton pondered the question further, and struggled to formulate an adequate reply. As they rounded the corner of Main House, the youngster preparing to peel off in the direction of the junior changing rooms, Skimpton gazed over towards the farthest end of the quad where the warm lights of the refectory beckoned in the late winter gloom. 'My father...' he mused, somewhat ruefully. 'Well, Piggot, he's got grey hair and a rather unruly moustache. And I gather he works for the government. Further to that, I suppose you'd have to ask his friends in the Home Office.' And on that note, the two Faysgarthians parted.

TWO

SKIMPTON CONFUSED

Although not normally given to public displays of anger, nothing roused Skimpton's ire more than the spectacle of an older fellow bullying. He had been engaged in a rather perfunctory inspection of his chum Jack Varley's cricket bat near the entrance to Second House when his attention was attracted to a rather unsightly scramble at the chapel end of the quad.

With the new cricket season now well under way, Varley, an accomplished performer at the crease, never wasted an opportunity in detaining Skimpton to enthuse on the subject of his batting average. The present exchange aroused no more than the usual thinly disguised indifference in the non-cricketer. Indeed, so engrossed had Varley become in his verbose and detailed admiration of the bruised willow that he failed to notice that his chum had departed his presence and was proceeding with some urgency in the direction of the nearby scrum.

Closer inspection revealed the screams of pain to be emanating from a rather rancid-smelling third-former, the new boy Blane, about whom Skimpton knew very little, apart from the fact that the youngster had – of late – been making rather a name for himself in the Junior Eleven as a fast bowler. The perpetrator of the violence, on this, as on so many other occasions at Faysgarth, was the undisputed School Scoundrel, the contemptible Marcus Dent.

Skimpton had been vaguely aware of a preliminary cuffing having been administered to the youngster by Dent, and had taken this as no more than a minor abuse of the Senior's position. But when the ruffian, encouraged by his scruffy companions, had proceeded to twist the youngster's arm so viciously that it appeared to be in danger of breaking off, Skimpton judged the moment right to intervene.

'I say, Dent,' interposed the Deputy Head Boy, 'I'd be very much obliged if you would release that young man's arm immediately, as it is required to help secure victory over the Village Ladies' Eleven to-morrow afternoon.'

Dent, somewhat startled by Skimpton's intervention, discharged the youngster to the ground with the nonchalance of a hardened smoker discarding a spent match.

'Well, look who it is,' sneered the blackguard, 'my old friend Skimpton, guardian of Faysgarth's sporting heritage. Well I tell you this, my friend, the outcome of the cricket match to-morrow bothers me not one jot. What does concern me, though, is when some malodorous young brute rummages through my belongings. Then I adjudge it my duty to afford the fellow immediate punishment.'

At this juncture, noticing that Blane had staggered to his feet, Dent launched a hearty kick at the youngster's stomach, sending the latter careering backwards and into the arms of Faysgarth's hopelessly short-sighted chemistry master, Colonel Archibald Coombes.

'What on earth do you boys think you are doing?' screeched the bespectacled boffin, and turning to confront the stinky third-former, now doubled-up in pain, he demanded, 'And who – or more precisely what – are you?'

Blane, though, felt even less inclined than did Marcus Dent to engage in conversation with the pitiless Colonel, as they all knew that the chemistry man would already be concocting some heinous punishment in his twisted mind. So, rather than respond to his question, the youngster simply turned on his heel and ran, closely followed by the screeching bully Dent and his cowardly chums.

'Well?' persisted the master, vaguely aware that some adjustment in personnel had taken place, but unsure of who, precisely, remained present. In the end, a cautious Skimpton stepped forward to explain the pandemonium.

'Perhaps I can be of some assistance, Colonel?' offered the sports champion. 'Some of the boys have been engaged in a little good-natured scragging over a loose tennis ball, nothing more. You became embroiled on your way to the staff room, which is, by the way, in that direction.'

'I am perfectly aware of the exact location of the staff quarters, thank you very much!' barked the myopic menace of the science laboratory. 'Perhaps you could enlighten me as to why pupils are wasting their free time with tennis balls when they would certainly be better engaged at the nets in preparation for to-morrow's match against the Village Ladies Eleven?'

'I regret to say that I have no idea, Colonel Coombes,' replied Skimpton, apologetically.

'Then kindly keep your own council, and remind me of the whereabouts of Main House.'

Skimpton, having gallantly manoeuvred the Colonel towards his destination, was instantly rewarded with five hundred lines for his pains. Piggot, the former's faithful fag, who happened to be passing, was ordered to the gym for a severe beating after the Colonel inadvertently knocked him onto the grass with his stick. 'Who let that dog into the school grounds?' demanded the master, as the second battered and bewildered third-former of the afternoon staggered to his feet.

'Do not concern yourself unduly, Colonel Coombes,' said Skimpton, 'I shall have the animal destroyed immediately.'

The annual fixture between Faysgarth's Junior Eleven and the Village Ladies' outfit was a curious event dating back over some thirty years, and was organised by the local church. Although Skimpton had no great love for the sport, especially this particularly bizarre contest, he realised that the youngsters from Faysgarth might be hard-pressed to make an impression without the considerable skills of young Blane. And it was to this puzzling individual that Skimpton's mind kept returning as he later copied out his wretched lines, confined to the recesses of the library for two hours.

Why had Blane been rooting through Dent's belongings? Was the youngster a thief? And if so, should there be any place for such as him in a Faysgarth sports team? These questions were still troubling the likeable young sporting stalwart as he returned to his study, fully expecting to discover Piggot busy preparing a cool glass of lemonade. Instead, he found his quarters empty, a note on his desk informing him that his young servant had been rushed to hospital in Faverstock as a result of the wounds inflicted upon him in the gym by a more than usually irate Colonel Coombes.

Settling back into his favourite armchair and biting into a crisp Granny Smith, Skimpton pondered for a moment on the relative barbarism of life at Faysgarth. Was it really necessary to inflict such injuries by way of punishment? Would it not be wiser to cajole good behaviour through reward, rather than merely terrify individuals into conformity? Aware that such thoughts might be considered subversive if allowed to flourish, and suspecting that – in any case – he may be entering unchartered, dangerous territory should he continue to pursue such a line of speculation, the pragmatic Skimpton settled his attention on a subject closer to his heart: fruit bonbons.

It was as he was rummaging in a drawer looking for a bag of his favourite sweeties that Skimpton noticed a queer smell in the room. His curiosity aroused, he sniffed about the place and discovered the odour to be exuding from behind a curtain which moved slightly as he approached it. Convinced of the presence of an intruder, the young boxing champion brought up his guard. 'Come out at once or I might very well knock you to the floor!' he challenged firmly. There was no response. 'Alright then, you've jolly well asked for it!' At which point he launched himself at the curtain.

Some time later, extricating himself from the tangle of drawstrings, wires and embroidered fabric which constituted the drapery, a breathless Skimpton stationed himself squarely in the middle of the room, preparing to do further battle with the soft furnishings.

'Good afternoon, Skimpton,' came a calm voice from behind him.

'Good God!' exclaimed the House Captain, turning abruptly and sending several trophies crashing from the mantelpiece. 'It's young Blane! What on earth are you doing here?'

*   *   *   *

Meanwhile, over in Main House, Marcus Dent and his infantile band of cronies were holding an impromptu meeting to discuss events of the day.

'I say!' screamed the ever-voluble Binns. 'Did you see the look on old Skimpton's face when Archie Coombes gave him that roasting? I'll wager he won't be too pleased with those five hundred lines!'

'And I'll wager you won't be too pleased with my foot eighteen inches up your arse,' snarled Dent menacingly, 'but you can be certain that uncomfortable fate awaits you if you don't pipe down.'

After the customary three minutes' silence which usually followed one of Dent's more savage outbursts, the school bully's companions breathed a collective sigh of relief as their mentor settled into his chaise longue with a small Cuban cigar and a vodka and tonic. Dent, they had concluded, was behaving even more unpredictably than usual that afternoon, and on these occasions everyone present was wont to fear for his life. 'The question is,' pondered Dent, jiggling the ice cubes in his tumbler, 'where is that weasel Blane and what was he doing going through my things?'

'Probably after some tuck,' assured his predatory cohort Spate, tentatively. 'But don't worry Marcus, we'll catch up with him at supper and give him a thorough scragging.'

'You don't understand, Spate,' retorted the bounder, 'I suspect that stinking little sniveller has appropriated something of mine.'

'I say! What exactly?'

'An item of considerable sentimental value.' The timbre of Dent's voice afforded such undeniable gravity to this pronouncement, such ponderous portent, that none present doubted the seriousness of his loss. After a lengthy pause, during which Binns felt himself close to evacuating his bowels through nervousness, Dent rounded on his band of mercenaries. 'There's something fishy going on,' he pronounced, 'AND I WANT TO KNOW WHAT IT IS!!!' At which, he pounced on the hapless Binns and sent him crashing to the floor with an incisive jab to the kidneys.

Exactly three minutes later, Spate ventured forth with an hypothesis. 'I saw the little rodent earlier looking for something in the quad and chased him into Second House. Perhaps he's still holed up there?'

'Possibly,' conceded Dent. 'He's probably keeping out of harm's way until this wretched cricket game to-morrow.'

'Perhaps we could organise a kidnap,' croaked Binns from the floor.

'Not a bad idea,' mused Dent, perusing his drink thoughtfully. Binns smiled in a brief moment of self-congratulation; an expression Dent instantly removed by mirthlessly flinging what remained of his vodka and tonic into his friend's face.

*　　*　　*　　*

'What an extraordinary tale!' exclaimed Skimpton, wafting air from the open window into the room in an attempt to neutralise the curious smell oozing from the youngster Blane. 'You must give me a moment to take it all in!'

The latter's explanation of his presence in Skimpton's study did indeed invite close scrutiny; a task Skimpton began to fear might severely strain his credulity, for the boy's story seemed almost too preposterous to be believed. 'Let me get this straight, Blane,' said Skimpton. 'During a family holiday some years ago on the Loire, your sister struck up a friendship with an older boy who was vacationing with his parents nearby. And as a parting gift she presented him, in error, with an antique brooch, a family heirloom. More recently, though, your family has fallen onto hard times after your father died a bankrupt, and an attempt to recover the brooch, which has subsequently been revealed to be worth a small fortune, was instigated. Is that correct?'

'Yes.'

'Your sister, not wishing to reveal to her family that she had given away the item, wrote many times to the young man pleading for its return, but to no avail. The individual steadfastly refused all requests to discuss the matter. Is that right?'

'That's about the size of it, yes.'

'What an utter bounder!' declared Skimpton, his keen sense of injustice propelling a closed fist down hard onto the surface of the desk. 'Who is this fellow?'

Blane looked down at the floor, a tear moistening his smooth, girlish cheek. 'The boy's name,' he said, 'is Marcus Dent.'

'I might have guessed,' said Skimpton, casting a rueful eye across the quad in the direction of Main House, within whose walls his fiendish nemesis resided. He then turned an admonishing gaze on his young companion. 'You are aware, though,' he said sternly, 'that it is strictly against school rules to go rummaging around in a fellow's study, to say nothing of gaining entry into my room here and secreting yourself in the drapery?'

'I fully appreciate how unconventional, not to say underhand, my actions might appear, Skimpton. Though I am sure that you will exercise a tolerant understanding once you are conversant with all the facts.'

'And what's it like, this brooch?'

'Circular, about the size of a small pocket watch. Ceylon sapphire, fifteen-carat. Worth rather a lot of money.'

His family's financial position, he explained, had reached such a calamitous state that he and his sister had devised a plan to enrol him at Faysgarth, deferring the payment of fees until the end of term, thus giving him ample opportunity to retrieve the gaud from the clutches of her erstwhile beau before parting with any cash its sale might generate.

That afternoon, apparently, as Dent was out hunting badgers with his pals, a chance had presented itself. Blane had sneaked into Dent's quarters and, after a lengthy search, had located the brooch – only to be interrupted in his escape by Dent and his chums returning early. A fierce chase had ensued, concluding in the violent scuffle in the quad. During the struggle, Blane explained, the brooch had slipped from his grasp, and he now had no idea of its whereabouts.

'Is the item perhaps now in the possession of Marcus Dent?' enquired the tennis champion.

'Possibly' came the youngster's reply. 'Though my guess is it's still knocking around the quad, if it hasn't been picked up by someone else, that is. I daren't venture out to look for it myself in case either Dent or his comrades are lying in wait for me.'

'I see,' said Skimpton.

'I am very sorry to impose on your generosity, Skimpton, but as you can understand, I must avoid further injury if I am to take part in to-morrow's cricket match.'

'Oh, bother the cricket match for a minute! Let me work out what is best to do.'

Almost despite himself, Skimpton found his irritation with the youngster growing. Cricket was his least favourite sport, and he had no real desire to embroil himself in Marcus Dent's sordid business. He also, suddenly, felt his quarters somewhat invaded and was frustrated at his own seeming inability to devise a scheme by which to rid himself of the rancorous youngster's company.

'Of course, should you choose to help me,' said Blane, 'I am sure my mother would be more than willing to accommodate you with some sort of reward.'

This reference to the boy's mother produced a level of uneasiness in Skimpton which might cloud a less determined young man's vision. On top of everything else, and in addition to the previous references to his sister, Blane was shamelessly flouting a cardinal – though unwritten – rule of Second House prohibiting the mention of women. Though he detested such flagrant abuse of tradition, Skimpton decided to say nothing, take deep breaths and plough on.

'I won't pretend, Blane,' he said, 'that I have a great deal of sympathy with your methods. However, it would be churlish of me to ignore your family's plight. I therefore intend to organise a discreet search party so that this wretched bauble, upon which you have placed so much reliance, can be retrieved, and your family allowed once more to take its rightful place in society. Your sister's judgement, I am afraid to say, leaves much to be desired, and she has – to a large extent – only herself to blame for her family's predicament, through having become involved with Dent in the first place.'

'I shall forward your opinion to her at the earliest opportunity, Skimpton.'

'Good. In the mean time I suggest that you avail yourself of my washing facilities and endeavour to banish that appalling smell from your person. In addition, I recommend you peruse this slim volume by the estimable Lord Baden-Powell. I draw particular attention to the chapter entitled "How To Avoid Getting Into Trouble".'

*   *   *   *

Across the corridor, Skimpton's chum Jack Varley was enjoying the company of young Dick Parr, a fine cricketer and captain of the Junior Eleven. His tutorial was interrupted by the sound of Skimpton's voice and a knocking at the door. 'I say, Jack!' shouted Skimpton, 'might I intrude?'

A silence ensued, and some minutes later, Varley appeared. 'Come in, Skimpton,' he said. 'You know young Parr? He and I were just trying to work out where I'd mislaid my cricket bat. You haven't seen it have you?'

'Afraid not old man.'

'No matter, I'm sure it'll turn up. We've also been discussing team selection for to-morrow's match against the Village Ladies Eleven, haven't we Dick?'

'I was wondering,' put in the youngster, 'if young Blane will be fit to open the bowling after his skirmish with Marcus Dent?'

'That is precisely the subject about which I have come to talk with Jack,' asserted the polo captain. 'Now get out would you, Parr, and leave us in peace.'

After the young colt had scampered off, Varley filled the kettle, offered his chum a Garibaldi biscuit, and invited Skimpton to compose himself on the bed. A brief silence followed, during which Varley poured milk into two china cups. 'Needed you to be quite so abrupt with the little fellow?' enquired he presently, after seating himself with his favourite cushion on the window sill.

'Don't talk to me about third-formers, Jack, I've had it up to here with them.'

'What's the matter old bean, something eating you?'

'Two things: cricket and young Blane. Furthermore, if I hear another mention of a woman I shall more than likely take a knife to my throat.'

'I say, calm down, won't you!' interrupted Varley, jumping down to remove the whistling kettle from its fiery perch.

Varley was an handsome, even-tempered fellow who had assisted Skimpton on many occasions in the past, when the sports champion's passions had threatened to overwhelm him. Although he shared many of his chum's suspicions of the opposite sex, Varley's burgeoning misogyny was far less vehement. He had vowed to keep out of the way of women until such time as it was deemed prudent to marry for the sake of appearances. When that hour came, he resolved to select a plain-looking specimen whose gratitude and subservience would be such that she could also function as a parlour maid, cook and general domestic servant, thus reducing household costs should money ever become tight.

Skimpton, on the other hand, found it nigh on impossible to contemplate even the idea of a woman. Being an only child, reared by his father before prep., he had reached his seventeenth year never once having so much as spoken to a member of the opposite sex. During his time at Faysgarth he had assiduously avoided the Matron, stayed in his study during the cricket match against the village ladies, and had all meals brought to him by his fag Piggot, thus eliminating the need for any contact with the serving girls in the refectory. On the few fateful occasions when Skimpton *had* found himself imprisoned by the company of ladies, he would usually lapse into an embarrassing bout of paralysis – a condition of such catatonic severity that he would normally have to be carried away and placed in his bed, where he might sometimes lay completely rigid for hours.

Varley poured the steaming water into the teapot, and offered Skimpton the packet of biscuits. Pretty soon, the House Captain's black mood had subsided, and he turned to Varley, his face bearing an earnest expression.

'Let me ask you something, Jack,' he said.

'Fire away old man.'

'Exactly how hard up is Faysgarth, at the moment?'

'The place is practically bankrupt, Skimpton, everyone knows that. Always has been.'

'I see.'

Skimpton jumped to his feet and gazed out of the window, surveying the quad, thoughtfully. Stroking his chin in the manner of an Hollywood sleuth, he turned to his friend. 'Look, Jack,' he said, 'I've a little job that requires doing and I need your help.'

* * * *

Some time later, over in Main House, Marcus Dent and his companions were priming themselves for a raid on Skimpton's quarters with the intention of abducting young Blane. Their preparations took the form of an extended drinking session during which many present became rather shaky on their feet. Dent had recently taken custody of a stolen consignment of Russian vodka, procured from a nearby public house by a shady cellar man called Ronnie. As it was their first experience of the potent Bolshevik fire water, several boys fairly threw the stuff back as though it were lemonade, and as a result many had taken to singing and lolling about the furniture. Binns in particular looked much the worse for wear, after downing a full pint of the stuff for a bet, and was crashing around the room like a boisterous rhino unsure of its bearings.

Eventually, their leader gathered his wits and, somewhat unsteadily, mounted the sideboard, from where he delivered his call to arms. 'Quiet everyone!' he snarled, consulting his wristwatch. 'The hour has arrived. Take up your weapons and prepare for battle!'

Needing no further prompting, Binns jumped to his feet, saluted triumphantly, and emptied the contents of his stomach over a boy named Pinkerton, who had merely wandered in from the corridor brandishing a cricket bat. 'I say you chaps,' asked the unfortunate intruder, as all present peered in his direction, acquainting themselves with the precise composition of Binns's culinary preferences over the previous twenty-four hours, 'does anyone know who this belongs to?'

'I couldn't be certain,' drawled Dent,' but I'd hazard that most of it belongs to the landlord of The White Swan in Faverstock!'

At which, all present whooped with hilarity, including Binns, who tasted the stuff and confirmed the veracity of his chum's witty conjecture.

*   *   *   *

It was at around ten o'clock in the evening when Dent's army of inebriated brigands encountered Skimpton's search party in the quad. The sports captain had assembled a squadron of reliable youngsters, including Piggot and Dick Parr, to assist himself and Varley in the search for Blane's missing brooch. Just outside Main House, Marcus Dent's shadowy form lurched onto the gravel to block their path, his steaming warriors bringing up the rear. 'Looking for something, Skimpton?' demanded the young liar.

'Nothing in which you might be remotely interested, Dent,' came the firm reply.

'It wouldn't be an antique brooch, would it? Worth rather a lot of money?'

'As a matter of fact,' put in Jack Varley, 'we were hoping to find my cricket bat which was lost earlier during the bullying ballyhoo.'

'Oh yes?' slurred Dent. 'And what bullying ballyhoolying… ballying bull…bully…hooler…ing might that be?'

'You know very well which bally bullying ballyhoo,' said Skimpton. 'For you were the main perpetrator.'

'Is this the missing bat?' roared Binns, raising the item in question above his head as though it were nothing more than a cheap football rattle.

'Hand that to me, Binns,' insisted Varley angrily, 'and I shall put it to good use by delivering you with a comprehensive beating about the ears!'

'Come now, Varlish…Varleyman,' garbled Dent. 'I'm sure Binns only intended to borrow your equipment, and would doubtless have returned it in due course. We have had need of it of late, have we not, Binns?'

'What?'

'My friend has been putting up shelves for me and needed something to bosh…bash…drive in the nails. Isn't that right, Binns?'

'Indeed Marcus!'

'Why, you…'

Skimpton gasped in amazement as his chum rounded on Dent and his allies, for never before had he seen Varley in such a fume. 'Hand over that bat immediately, Dent,' he demanded, 'or I shall punch your face for you!'

'We'll see about that!' retorted the most arrogant boy present, and baring his knuckles at Varley, hollered, 'At 'em fellows!'

The resulting mêlée, the culmination of many months' feuding between the rival factions, was contested with such ferocity that night that many boys came close to losing their lives. Skimpton himself suffered a slight knife wound to the abdomen, sufficient to rule him out of the high jump championships the following week. Bearing in mind the amount of noise produced by the combatants, it was a miracle that none of the masters were woken, or else most certainly a call would have been made to the local constabulary. During the hostilities, Jack Varley was roundly beaten with his own bat, Binns had part of his ear sliced off by one of his own side wielding an antique sabre, Dick Parr was severely bitten by a German boy named Wolf, and Piggot was very nearly beheaded when attacked with an axe by Dent's savage sidekick Spate. Indeed, the wound in the youngster's neck was so deep that Skimpton was later to remark archly that he would no longer have any trouble finding a place to park his Grecian Flyer bicycle.

Marcus Dent, by contrast, kept himself well clear of the fray, conducting his troops from the roof of the refectory whilst guzzling more of the stolen vodka. He did not, however, escape injury that night; whilst clambering down a drainpipe he lost his footing, crashed to the ground and fractured his leg in three places.

It was only the sobering appearance of the local vicar, the Reverend Kenneth Hargreaves, making one of his night-time visits to the younger boys' dorms, that invoked an uneasy truce. The churchman had been offering spiritual guidance to some of the less experienced cricketers, nervous about to-morrow's game, when one of his charges had drawn his attention to the battle raging in the quad. He would, he said, say nothing about the matter if everyone involved retired to bed immediately.

The Reverend Hargreaves was a stringy, uninspiring figure, whose lengthy sermons had been known to dispirit boys of a more nervous disposition, almost to the point of suicide. And the prospect of a spontaneous lecture on the subject of Loving Thy Neighbour was, on that evening, sufficient to clear the quad in seconds.

As the last footsteps disappeared and the Reverend's motorbike roared off into the Monktonshire night, Colonel Coombes, waking from his slumber, appeared at his study window in daintily striped pyjamas, and confirmed that all was well with the world. To him, at least, the quadrangle was a silent lake of green, bathed in moonlight, as was its custom at this hour. He consulted his newly acquired pocket watch and ascertained the time to be somewhere between eleven-thirty and a quarter past five.

*　　*　　*　　*

Early the next morning, Skimpton awoke with a start on the floor of his study. He recalled having been placed there the previous night by his chums. A sharp pain shot through his lower abdomen as he attempted to move, and his head throbbed as if it had been hit with a large bag of ball bearings, which in fact it had – the previous night. His limbs felt like lead as he tried to haul them into some sort of recognizable arrangement on the floor, and one of his upper molars appeared to have strayed from its mooring in his mouth.

Young Blane was at that moment boiling a kettle on the old primus, after having taken up residence in Skimpton's bed the night before. 'Three sugars for me, if you don't mind,' gasped the Senior, collapsing into his favourite armchair.

'Skimpton! You're awake!' said the uninjured boy. 'I gather last night was something of a bloodbath. I do apologise.'

'You and your wretched sister's brooch have caused mayhem in Faysgarth over the last twenty-four hours. My man Piggot very nearly found himself decapitated on your behalf last night.'

'Is there anything I can do?' offered the youngster, weakly.

'All I require from you at the moment, Blane, apart from a strong cup of tea, is that you make yourself as inconspicuous as possible in my quarters. Have you bathed?'

'I availed myself of your washbasin last night whilst you were out, Skimpton.'

'Well I'm afraid that's not good enough. You still appear to be exuding an odour the rancidity of which I have never before encountered. I therefore insist that you take yourself off to the showers at once!'

'But Skimpton, such a course would reveal my whereabouts to the other boys, and within minutes Marcus Dent and his recalcitrant pals will doubtless apprehend me.'

'I care not, Blane, to be quite frank. I wash my hands of you.'

'But Skimpton,' pleaded the junior, 'what about the brooch?'

Skimpton breathed a painful sigh, gazed momentarily up at the ceiling and clasped his hands together in a gesture of exasperated communion with his maker. 'Before we were set upon last night by Dent and his cronies,' he explained, 'my companions and I managed to conduct a thorough exploration of the quadrangle and its immediate environs. I am afraid to no avail. The jewellery in question appears to have disappeared.'

'It must be somewhere,' insisted the third-former, 'and if I don't locate it soon I shall be forced to leave Faysgarth, for without the brooch my family is penniless!'

'Young man,' said the more hygiene-conscious of the two, 'I can only remind you of the words to the school hymn.' Skimpton then straightened himself in the chair and began a strenuous rendition of the first verse of the famous anthem, plundering simultaneously the keys of both F sharp minor and B flat major:

> *He who would valiant be*
> *'Gainst all disaster*
> *Let him in constancy*
> *Follow the master.*

As a result, Skimpton assumed, of this stirring musical performance, the youngster was now close to tears. 'But what am I to do?' pleaded the junior, his voice fraught with despair.

'Return to your quarters immediately,' came the firm reply, 'and pack your belongings in preparation for departure. This afternoon, go out onto the cricket field and play the game of your life. That way you are assured of a rousing send-off from your fellow Faysgarthians. Further to that, you have a number of options.'

'And what are they?' pleaded the lachrymose third-former.

Skimpton could now see that his young charge was weeping openly, and reached into his pocket for a handkerchief. 'You can either attempt to join Her Majesty's Navy, possibly as a cabin boy or suchlike,' he suggested, 'or seek immediate employment with one of the more radical political organisations which I gather are springing up in the larger towns and cities. The socialists in particular are always on the lookout for penniless stragglers with emotional defects. Why not write to them?'

Blane's response was to throw himself blubbering at Skimpton's feet, his pitiful wails prompting the introduction of a consolatory arm around the youngster's shoulder. 'Come now,' said Skimpton, proffering a hanky, 'dry your eyes.'

For all his dispassionate advice, Skimpton could not help but be moved by young Blane's plight, and aside from his tears and foul odour, the laddie had begun to appear almost personable, attractive even, in his vulnerability. Skimpton was wrestling with conflicting responsibilities for which his education at Faysgarth had hardly prepared him. And as he gazed into the young boy's tear-strewn face, uncertain of what to say or do, his mind turned to a similar occasion from his early days at Faysgarth.

As a third-former himself, a confused and unsettled Skimpton had occasion to visit the quarters of an older boy named Giles Curbishley. Aware that an unsavoury skirmish on the rugger field had left Skimpton humiliated and in need of solace, Curbishley took time to counsel the young man. But when even kind words failed to stem the flow of tears, the older boy resorted to more venal methods, an approach Skimpton now resolved to try himself. 'Would you like a fruit bonbon?' he asked Blane, kindly.

'Yes, thank you,' came the predictable response.

'You know, Blane,' continued Skimpton, 'there are many things in this world far worse than poverty.'

The young third-former finished chewing, blew his nose on the handkerchief, and looked up at Skimpton. 'Like what?' he asked, blankly.

Skimpton hesitated. He opened his mouth to speak, but knew that in truth, nothing in his experience had equipped him to tackle so fiendishly difficult a question. As a result, he offered no reply, only the hand of friendship.

'There is one person I must confront with this problem before I go,' said Blane, resolutely, 'and that is Marcus Dent. I shall seek audience with him at once.'

'That's the ticket, Blane,' encouraged Skimpton, grinning. 'Like a true Faysgarthian – battling through the eye of the storm and onward into the lion's den!'

And at that, Blane turned on his heel and left.

Within seconds, Piggot appeared, his neck heavily bandaged – a clumsy attempt by first aiders the night before to prevent his uppermost extremity from detaching itself from the rest of his body. 'Where's that stinky toe rag off to?' complained the fag, opening another window. 'They say he never takes a bath or changes his clothes. Should I set about fumigating the room?'

'Look here, Piggot,' retorted Skimpton, tersely. 'Young Blane's personal habits may leave much to be desired, but I tell you now that he has more blind courage in his little finger than the average Faysgarthian possesses in his entire body. And that includes you!'

'But Skimpton...'

'I will hear no ill of him, Piggot, especially from your particular corner. Your pitiful display in the fracas last night combined with a deeply unpleasant and overweening arrogance leads me to conclude that, at the moment at least, you represent no more than a very large pain in the neck! Do I make myself clear?'

'Perfectly, sir.'

'This afternoon, however, you have an opportunity to redeem yourself at the crease. I am aware that my knowledge of the game of cricket is somewhat rudimentary, but I expect no less than a swift and efficient dispatch to the boundary of any suitable ball delivered at you by the village ladies. That is, of course, if you rein in your cockiness, concentrate properly, and do not lose your head.'

'I'll do my best, Skimpton.'

*   *   *   *

Meanwhile, over in Main House, Marcus Dent, his leg encased in plaster, was reclining on his chaise longue and listening with mounting frustration to his chums' recollections of the previous night's revelry. 'Did you see how I extracted young Parr's thumb-nails!' wailed Binns, never one to conceal his achievements from his pals. 'That's one junior batsman who won't be clocking up a century this afternoon!'

'Be quiet Binns!' growled Dent. 'Or I'll slice your other ear off.' There was something about Binns's voice, its volume and particular timbre which was always certain to rile Dent. Indeed, he had begun to suspect that, in a curiously perverse way, he actually enjoyed losing his temper with this most irritating of cohorts, for his violent outbursts in Binns's direction served not only to relieve his own frustrations, but also established his bullish superiority in the eyes of the others.

After the customary three minutes, the icy silence was broken when Dent spoke again, this time in calm, menacing tones. 'The fact remains,' he stated, 'that I have yet to recover what is rightfully mine, namely, the brooch. And to do that we must locate that putrid slime-pit Blane, and pronto.'

At that precise moment, there was a sharp knock at the door. Binns opened it, and there, in the corridor, much to the amazement of all, stood the fetid youngster in question. 'I have come,' stated Blane, entering the room and addressing the worst of them, 'to reclaim my sister's brooch which was given to you in error some two and a half years ago.'

'Ah,' breathed Dent, wagging his finger, in recognition, 'then you *are* related to Charlotte Blane. I suspected as much. The plot coagulates.' Dent paused to allow all present to murmur their appreciation of his characteristically picturesque terminology. 'Kindly inform your sister,' he resumed, 'that the trinket to which you refer was afforded me as a gift and as such is – and shall continue to remain – my property. You may also inform her, however, that the aforementioned bauble, alas, no longer resides in my possession. I had assumed, young Blane, that you had taken custody of it yourself, but your presence here would imply the contrary. I must therefore conclude with some regret that it is lost and suggest that, should you in the future by any chance retrieve it, you return it forthwith to me. That is, if you value your life.'

Dent settled himself comfortably on his chaise longue, clasped his hands together loosely, and closed his eyes. Satisfied that his verbal dexterity had breathed energetic life into his cause, he now waited to receive the inevitable gesture of admiration from his peers.

It was left to Spate to initiate the round of applause, which quickly gathered pace down corridor and dormitory, and within a minute had spread across the quad and into the classrooms. Pretty soon, the entire school, every Junior, Senior and member of staff was applauding enthusiastically, though very few knew precisely why. Even Wilf, the Groundsman, raking the long-jump pit at the far end of the sports field, laid down his tools and joined the tribute, tears welling in his eyes. At its height, though, the acclaim was interrupted by an audacious interjection from young Blane. 'If it is indeed the case that the brooch is mislaid,' he said crisply, 'then I can do no more. But should I, in the future, hear that you have regained its possession, I warn you now that I shall mobilise all legal steps open to me to return the said item to its rightful home.'

Dent turned his gaze on the youngster, and in an almost placatory tone, said, 'Comes to something when a fellow's asked to return a gift which he had accepted in good faith, wouldn't you say, Blane?'

'Comes to something when a fellow knows he holds the future of a recently bereaved family in his hands yet chooses to do nothing about it,' came the terse reply.

'Would you like me to maim him in some way, Marcus?' enquired Spate, helpfully.

'No, leave him be,' replied Dent, 'I like him. He has a fine tongue in his head which belies his youth.' Dent stood up, hobbled over to the fireplace, stoked the embers briefly and then turned to face his visitor. 'Young man,' he said, 'you have shown considerable, some would say almost reckless, courage in coming here today. Being the abstruse type of person that I am, I can only find such abject stupidity admirable. I should very much like it if you would consider joining my staff.'

The assembled cronies gasped in amazement at this unexpected turn of events, and Binns was encouraged by Spate to pick his jaw up from the floor, before all present returned their attention to the junior to await his response.

'Dent,' said the young fast bowler, smiling, 'nothing could persuade me, no amount of money, nor any grievously applied torture could impel me to join you in your disgusting den of moral decrepitude. I would rather die penniless in a sewer than be seen associating with your shabby gang of mercenaries. The company of a poisoned snake would be preferable to me than...'

'Alright, alright,' interrupted Dent, 'I think we get the picture. If that is your final decision then so be it. You must therefore excuse me if I don't see you to the door.'

Blane turned to leave, passing Binns on his way out. 'You smelly little cunt,' murmured the ruffian, under his breath.

*   *   *   *

It is one of those curious idiosyncrasies of life at Faysgarth that the quadrangle, centre of so much noteworthy activity at the school, is, in fact, a total misnomer, the area in question being enclosed on only three sides. To the north is Main House, opposite is Second House, and in between, the master's quarters and refectory. The open side, to the east, is bordered by the gravel drive, beyond that are the playing fields, which in turn give way to the rolling Monktonshire Downs.

Just like the question of whether it was wise to place the dangerously myopic Colonel Coombes in charge of the chemistry laboratory, or indeed allow him to mete out such barbaric punishments without supervision, the issue of the quad not actually satisfying the basic requirements of a compound so named, never really arose. But then, no-one ever chose to question the motives of Wilf, the Groundsman, whose preoccupation with the long-jump pit, especially during junior games, might in other circumstances have aroused comment. Or indeed many of the other puzzlingly pointless, and on occasion hazardous, traditions which had become a feature of life at Faysgarth. The misnaming of the quadrangle, then, was a minor eccentricity, for when one attended a school as idiosyncratic as

Faysgarth – where unalloyed barbarism and academic anarchy often held sway – what need was there to concern oneself in architectural pedantry?

It was, therefore, no surprise to Skimpton, on the afternoon of the annual cricket match, to witness the charabanc carrying the Village Ladies' Eleven, pass his window five times. The driver, he presumed, had been given precise instructions, as always, to deliver his passengers at a location where a small welcoming party would await them in an enclosed courtyard which didn't actually exist.

Eventually, though, the rickety old vehicle drew up with a rancid belch from its exhaust pipe, its exasperated driver scratching his head in bewilderment, as the ladies were disgorged onto the lawn. The quadrangle sparkled in the sunshine as Skimpton, from the safety of his study, observed the odd assortment of souls as they bustled and clattered their way to their changing quarters. As was usually the case, the school kitchens had been made available to them for this purpose, and it was Skimpton's schoolfellow Jack Varley who had been entrusted with the unenviable task of overseeing the team's billeting.

A wry smile crept over Skimpton's face as he watched his hapless housemate herding the gossiping ladies towards the refectory, and the amiable Deputy Head Boy surprised himself with the degree to which his interest in proceedings had grown. This was partially, he presumed, as a result of his entanglement with Blane – but also because nothing much else of consequence seemed to be happening that afternoon.

The ladies made up a curious band of individuals, all of different shapes and sizes. For Skimpton it was almost like encountering beings from another planet, and he took up his small telescope to facilitate more detailed study.

Not only did their apparel mark them out as totally different from his chums, but they seemed to *move* in an entirely bizarre fashion; either shuffling along like hedgehogs or giving the impression of floating above the ground like butterflies.

Shaking his head in utter bafflement, and conscious that he was breaking his tradition, Skimpton took up his blazer, picked an apple for later and left his study with the intention of seeking a good seat from which to observe the afternoon's sport.

Passing behind the pavilion, he encountered Reverend Hargreaves parking his motorcycle. 'I say Reverend,' quipped the schoolboy playfully, 'how do you fancy your ladies' chances this afternoon?'

'Never dismiss the meek, for they will inherit the earth. John, chapter four, verse five,' came the less-than-accurate reply. 'I suspect, Skimpton, that you may be surprised by the depth of skill and commitment in this year's team. We have some useful newcomers from the Faverstock Townswomen's Guild who could well trouble your youngsters!'

It had been the vicar's custom to umpire this fixture in previous years, though even with the aid of his blatantly prejudiced decisions, the ladies had never once succeeded in securing a victory. Perhaps, mused Skimpton, this time would be different. Tarrying to observe the wiry cleric as he unfastened his bicycle clips, Skimpton prolonged the banter with further reference to the forthcoming contest. 'I hear Colonel Coombes will be overseeing proceedings this time, Reverend,' he joked, 'I sincerely hope his eyesight is up to the task of umpiring!'

'Indeed,' nodded the clergyman, 'we must hope so, for I shall be unable to fulfil my customary duties this year as I have parish business in Barnchester which will require my absence for at least two to three hours.'

'Poor show! Can't you put it off?'

'God's work, I fear, cannot be set aside so easily, even for the sake of a cricket match! I shall only tarry here long enough to see the first over bowled.'

'In that case, we Faysgarthians might have to take it upon ourselves to give the ladies some encouragement!'

'I doubt whether that will be necessary,' smiled Hargreaves, a puzzling note of irritation creeping into his voice. 'Now if you will excuse me, I have a pep talk to deliver.' And with that, the Reverend scampered off in the direction of his chattering charges.

*　　*　　*　　*

By the middle of the afternoon, with the summer sun casting its benevolent gaze over Faysgarth, all seemed to be progressing according to precedent; the ladies, who had elected to bat, had lost their seventh wicket for a total of only fourteen runs. The main damage had been inflicted by young Blane, whose demonic bowling had so devastated the opposition's attack that he had required very little assistance from his team mates, an indifferent bunch who seemed unable to muster much enthusiasm for the event.

Apart from some predictably eccentric umpiring from Colonel Coombes, the afternoon's endeavours seemed to be passing without much noteworthy incident. That was until the arrival at the crease of Miss Emily Fortune-Bingham. A gangly young woman with flowing red hair, she reminded Skimpton of a painting he had often scrutinised in his father's study depicting a vacant-looking nymph reclining in a rowing boat. However ungainly her appearance, Miss Fortune-Bingham's stroke play proved to be exemplary, and before long an elegant sweep over cover brought the ladies' total to a respectable forty-seven for eight.

Just as it seemed that no amount of effort by young Blane at the pavilion end could unseat her, an astonishing decision by Colonel Coombes gave the young batswoman out leg before – an arcane judgment since the ball appeared to go nowhere near her pads! In fact, she had clipped the delivery skilfully from well outside leg stump, past first slip for a rather neat four! No amount of protestation from Miss Fortune-Bingham could convince the squinting chemist that his decision was in error, and, spurred on by the cynical jeering of Marcus Dent's chums, gathered around their leader's wheelchair behind deep mid-wicket, the erratic Colonel promptly issued the hapless redhead with five thousand lines, to be completed by Monday morning at the latest.

The remaining batswomen added no more runs before the last tail-ender was clean bowled by young Blane, and the innings reached its conclusion at fifty-five all out.

As the ladies prepared to take to the field, Skimpton reflected on the tedium of the game. Cricket was a sport which never failed to disappoint him, both as a player and spectator. When, on the rare occasions that he had ventured forth with the bat, his impatient technique invariably resulted in him being out first ball. His attempts at bowling were only marginally more successful, as he soon became bored with the seemingly interminable standing around. He even suggested on one occasion that two balls should be used, with overs being bowled simultaneously from both ends to speed things up, but the consequent outcry was so violent and so severely was he abused by his schoolmates that he resolved never to venture anywhere near the game again.

He was on the point of retiring to the gymnasium to do sixty press-ups when Piggot appeared with a cooling glass of lemonade. 'Is this an attempt to make up for your previous deplorable behaviour, Piggot?' enquired the Senior.

'Yes, Skimpton,' came the sheepish reply. 'I am afraid the procurement of this refreshment amounts to a thinly disguised attempt to curry favour with the Faysgarthian I admire most.'

A puzzled Skimpton paused for thought, his attention momentarily fixed on Piggot's awesomely protruding teeth. 'And who might that be?' he asked, mischievously.

'Why you sir, of course!'

'Very good. Now shouldn't you be padding yourself up in preparation for battle?'

'Yes, sir. I'll get on with it right away, sir.'

'Good luck, Piggot.'

'Thank you, sir.'

Satisfied that, although on this occasion he was not at the epicentre of the school's sporting endeavours, his exalted place in the esteem of the other boys appeared secure, Skimpton surveyed the cricket pitch from his vantage point close to the pavilion with a sense of both pride and fatherly devotion. His warmth even extended towards the players of the opposition – that bizarre collection of womenfolk who had temporarily invaded his domain. There was the elderly Lady Farkham-Trillyon, sipping tea at deep mid-wicket, and chatting with the equally geriatric Mrs. Fforde-Wellesley, reputed to be distantly related to the Duke of Wellington. Also numbered amongst them was the young Miss Fay Manners-Henderson, about whose looks some of the more gregarious older boys had been volubly enthusing all afternoon. And then there was the unsettling Emily Fortune-Bingham with her flowing red locks and undoubted skill at the crease. Where had she accumulated such strength and technique?

What disturbed him most, though, as he watched the ladies casually discussing tactics, was that there seemed to be no sense of competition between them; very little evidence of the petty rivalry and gratuitous bullying which he had come to accept as the prerequisites of civilized life. Perhaps they had agreed to set aside their differences in pursuit of victory over the common enemy? Or possibly they just didn't care two hoots who won? Either way, it amounted to a pretty baffling state of affairs, and it was with more than a degree of satisfaction that he noticed a tetchy Miss Fortune-Bingham, at the scoreboard end, barking orders at one of her more dilatory colleagues. At least one of them, he mused, was concerned about the outcome of the match.

Beginning to tire of his inertia, Skimpton concluded that his reflections that afternoon had served at least one purpose: to confirm his intention to stick to the company of his own sex wherever possible. And as he watched the attractive figure of young Blane practising his strokes, silhouetted against the sun, low in the blue English sky, it occurred to Skimpton that it might very well be a jolly good thing if school were to go on forever.

The Junior Eleven's innings opened disastrously, with wickets toppling at an alarming rate. Only young Parr, his thumbs heavily bandaged after the skirmish the night before with Binns, managed to remain at the crease with any degree of authority. Again, it was the unorthodox figure of Emily Fortune-Bingham who inflicted the most grievous damage, although, as the crowd were only too aware, the resistance proffered by the Faysgarth batsmen was little more than negligible. The onlookers were in uproar as normally respectable middle order men were dismissed offering only indifferent opposition. A courageous stand by the bandaged Piggot, batting at number six, was brought to an abrupt halt by a particularly malicious delivery which reared up from the turf and almost dispatched the youngster's head to the boundary over fine leg.

Miss Fortune-Bingham's devastating bowling style could only be described as vigorous and comprehensive; in turn she delivered googlies, yorkers, and an array of full tosses which would have troubled many an accomplished amateur. She bowled over and around the wicket, at medium and fast pace, and occasionally threw in the odd spun ball which totally confused her wicket keeper, Baroness Griselda Edwardes-Hawke. The resulting byes accounted in total for the measly nine runs which had accrued for the home side when young Blane arrived at the crease.

A humiliated, totally mystified hum circled the pitch as the assembled Faysgarthians prepared themselves for the unthinkable: defeat at the hands of the Village Ladies' Eleven. Dick Parr, the opener not known for his fast scoring rate, hung his head in shame for he had been at the crease for well over an hour without scoring a single run.

Even Colonel Coombes saw fit to intervene, optimistically promising a valuable prize for the first Faysgarthian to notch up a six. However, through a combination of ineptitude, indifference and ill-luck on behalf of the home side, there appeared to be little chance of anyone taking up his offer.

So, as young Blane set himself to face the first ball from the fiery Pre-Raphaelite, he knew that, as the weakest batsman in the team, he was staring failure full in the face, and that his dreams of leaving Faysgarth a hero stood in tatters.

Had it not been for an amazing twist of fate, this disappointing scenario would indeed have been the most likely conclusion to the match. But the events which followed were of such catastrophic import, such enormous seriousness, and would produce such a profound effect on the proceedings that afternoon, that none present – even in his wildest dreams – could have imagined them happening. The details which follow are etched into the memories of all concerned, and were destined to be passed down through the generations, to equally disbelieving listeners, as one of the most astonishing narratives ever to emanate from Faysgarth School – an institution which, over the decades, had endured its fair share of controversy.

Although an easy catch had been dropped at square leg off the fourth ball, young Blane had managed to survive his first over. It seemed only a matter of time, though, before the inevitable capitulation. Skimpton, unable to stomach the distressing spectacle of his school's humiliation at the hands of a bunch of women, and unwilling to witness the demise of his young chum Blane dispatched into ignominious anonymity by an eccentric flame-haired debutante, folded his deck chair and headed back in the direction of his quarters.

As he disappeared behind the pavilion, his hands thrust sombrely into his pockets, sarcastic cheers from Dent and his chums stinging his ears, Skimpton noticed the Reverend Hargreaves's motorbike leaning against the games hut. Closer inspection revealed a neat pile of clothing on the ground nearby, together with a small box bearing the imprint of James & Jardine, theatrical costumiers of Market Street, Faverstock.

In a thrice, the young sprinter put two and two together and strode purposefully onto the field. A hushed silence greeted his arrival, the players themselves stood in complete puzzlement as Skimpton stepped forward to confront Emily Fortune-Bingham in full flight. As she belted towards him, preparing to let rip with another fearsome delivery, Skimpton withdrew his arm, thrust it forward, and punched the young woman squarely in the jaw! An astonished gasp rose from the crowd, followed by what can only be described as a stunned silence, broken only by the shrieks of pain as Skimpton proceeded to wrestle manfully with the woman on the ground. This spectacle proved too much for many of the ladies; the first, second and third slips all fainted simultaneously, followed a few seconds later by gully, cover point and silly mid-off, alias Mrs. Forde-Wellesley, who sadly never regained consciousness.

Finally, the Colonel, who was unaware that anything untoward had taken place until Jack Varley rushed onto the field and suggested he intervene, called proceedings to a halt and summoned the two miscreants to the popping crease to explain themselves. It was then that Skimpton was able to reveal that the ladies' superior all-rounder was not quite what she appeared; that the ungainly Miss Emily Fortune-Bingham was in fact none other than the Reverend Kenneth Hargreaves, Vicar of the Parish of Faverstock, disguised in a floral summer outfit and ridiculous ginger wig! The House Captain then proceeded to demonstrate this be removing the rascally cleric's headgear and over-garments, leaving him squealing with indignation wearing only a singlet, long johns and lurid, tartan socks! This resulted in an almighty cheer from behind the ropes, which in turn provoked Baroness Griselda Edwardes-Hawke into an epileptic fit of gargantuan proportions behind the pavilion-end wicket.

When confronted by Colonel Coombes, the wretched clergyman offered no tangible explanation for his extraordinary prank, except to plead that he had done it all for his ladies in the hope that a victory might maintain their flagging enthusiasm and ensure the fixture's survival for future generations. (Later investigations, however, proved that the errant minister had placed a large sum of money, pocketed from his Sunday collections, on the outcome of the match, and that he had planned a visit to various continental hotspots with his winnings.)

'I take note' pronounced Colonel Coombes, imperiously, 'of your feeble attempt to cite a concern for tradition by way of excuse for your distasteful behaviour here today. However, given that you stand before me in your undergarments, having just been revealed as nothing other than a cowardly churchman with a liking for ladies' clothing, I must take with something of a pinch of salt your protestations of concern for the customs of these parts. I therefore insist that you depart Faysgarth forthwith, and never set foot in its grounds again. Do I make myself clear?'

'Perfectly Colonel Coombes.'

'And furthermore, I also intend to issue you with a hefty punishment of lines. You shall write out, in capital letters, 43,000 times, "I must not take part in cricket matches dressed as a woman". Do you understand?'

'Fully, Colonel Coombes.'

After Hargreaves had been marched away by a battalion of burly sixth-formers, a brief conference involving Lady Farkham-Trillyon, Colonel Coombes and Skimpton, as representative of the boys, decided that the match should continue. For although the light was fading fast, there appeared to be no reason why the extraordinary events should curtail proceedings prematurely.

The Faysgarth score stood at only nine runs with only Blane and Parr left to bat. After the ladies had been revived with smelling salts, and the unfortunate Baroness Edwardes-Hawke taken away in an ambulance and replaced with a third-former whose name no-one could ever remember, young Blane steadied himself to face the first ball from the ladies' new bowler. Her genteel delivery was promptly dispatched over deep extra cover for a magnificent four. The crowd roared its approval, and Skimpton fairly willed his penniless protégé into greater feats of cricketing magic.

With the aid of the dogged Parr, Blane was able to keep the strike and had soon pushed the score to forty-five, just ten runs short of victory, with the gathering gloom allowing only one more over to be played. An air of anticipation gripped the large crowd, Faysgarth's biggest for years, their numbers swelled by local people hoping to hear more of the vicar's misdemeanours.

A quiet chat with both batsmen reaffirmed Colonel Coombes's intention to award a special prize for the first six scored, and with Blane facing the bowling, the young tail-ender smiled across at Skimpton confident that he could deliver what his school expected of him.

The first ball of the over brought Blane two runs, enabling him to keep strike. The following delivery he nudged to third man – two more runs. From the next three, however, he amazingly failed to score, only managing to block each of the finely judged leg breaks. So! A six needed to win, and the young urchin prepared to face the final ball of the match.

At that moment, however, all eyes turned to the driveway as a booming, authoritative voice bellowed out, 'STOP THAT GAME IMMEDIATELY!' It was an elderly lady of considerable bulk, waving a parasol in a threatening manner and shuffling uneasily across the gravel.

'And who, young sir, might you be?' questioned Colonel Coombes, after the woman had hauled herself breathlessly to within his field of view.

'I,' proclaimed the formidable newcomer, 'am Miss Emily Fortune-Bingham of the Faverstock Women's Over Sixties' Bowling Club, and I demand that I take my place in the team!'

'But madam,' protested the Colonel weakly, 'the game we are here engaged in playing is cricket!'

'I am well aware of that my man. Unlike yours, my eyesight functions perfectly.' At which the plucky septuagenarian transported her sizeable self to within a foot of Colonel Coombes, and with parasol firmly tucked under her arm, and fists clenched determinedly by her sides, gave full vent to her fury. 'That miserable oaf Hargreaves promised me a game against your boys this afternoon, and I have been looking forward to it for weeks. When, however, the promised transportation failed to appear at twelve-thirty sharp as arranged, I was forced to make my way here on foot. I do not intend to leave without taking some part in the game!'

'On foot, eh?' quipped Dent from his wheelchair. 'That's one and a half miles in just under five hours. Perhaps we'd better enlist the old fool in the cross-country team as well!' Everyone laughed heartily before breaking into another enthusiastic round of applause.

'But madam,' pleaded the Colonel, 'the light is rapidly fading and there is only one ball left to bowl.'

'In that case,' resolved Miss Fortune-Bingham, adjusting the waistband of her dress to allow for the freer movement of her legs, 'that ball shall be delivered...BY MYSELF!'

A huge cheer resounded from behind the ropes, and a resigned Colonel Coombes, after consultation with Lady Farkham-Trillyon, finally gave permission for the village veteran to bowl the last ball of the day.

Evidently relishing the prospect of doing battle, and having ascertained that she might yet save the day for her team, the ageing aristocrat speared the ground with her parasol, took the ball from a colleague and covered it in a thick wad of spittle. After glaring at her opponent with a spiteful stare which lasted a full minute and a half, and might easily have sent WG Grace into the pavilion feigning injury, the Faverstock over sixties' bowls champion turned smartly on her heel and strode off with the ball. Parting the crowd, she continued in the direction of the running track, all the while rubbing the red leather vigorously against her thigh. When she had reached a position on the rugger pitch some three hundred yards away, Miss Fortune-Bingham turned, let out a piercing yell reminiscent of an hyena in childbirth, and began her tumultuous run-up.

All dived for cover as the spunky spinster thundered towards the wicket, and Colonel Coombes found himself literally flying through the air as her indomitable momentum brushed him aside. Young Blane, at the crease, felt a bead of sweat spring from his brow as the monstrous dowager bounded up and released a ferocious under-arm delivery which skidded towards him across the turf. Raising his bat and preparing to deal as best he could with the grotesquely swerving ball as it bobbled first this way then that, the youngster could hardly believe his eyes when it hit a stone some three yards from the crease, and flew upwards into the air! An eerie silence descended as everyone followed the arc of the ball as it descended directly in front of the batsman.

'Hit it, Blane!' shouted Skimpton, a lone voice in the void. And his young chum did just that. Quickly adjusting his feet, Blane swung his weapon and hit a sweet drive high into the air towards deep mid-wicket. Everyone knew from the moment it left the bat that it was a certain six, for the sound of leather on willow was so sweet that nothing less was conceivable.

None present though, least of all Marcus Dent and his chums, could have predicted what would happen next. As the ball plummeted from the heavens in their direction, Binns, Spate and the rest of the cowardly clan leaped for cover, leaving Dent alone to try and manoeuvre himself and his wheelchair out of the way. Looking up at the very last moment and seeing the ball hurtling towards him, the school braggart let out an almighty yell, a scream instantly cut short as the ball landed squarely between his teeth, its momentum sending the young wretch careering backwards into a ditch!

'Hurrah!' cried the jubilant young Faysgarthians as they flooded onto the pitch. 'Well played Blane! Good show!'

Later, it was a proud youngster who received his congratulations, first from Skimpton and then from Colonel Coombes, who ushered him onto the steps of the pavilion to receive his prize for scoring the first – and only – six of the innings. 'Blane,' pronounced the Colonel proudly, as the entire school gathered around, 'you have performed jolly well this afternoon, not only as a batsman but as a bowler as well, and I have no hesitation in paying tribute to you as a credit both to your family and to the school. And, in recognition of your fine achievement, I have great pleasure in presenting you with this attractive pocket watch.'

'Hurrah!'

The myopic chemist then reached into his pocket and, much to everyone's intense amusement, produced a small brooch and handed it to Blane. The youngster was speechless in the midst of the hilarity, for he instantly recognized the bauble as the one he had lost in the quad the previous day.

'This fine timepiece,' continued the Colonel, encouraging its recipient to hold aloft the brooch for all to see, 'came into my possession only yesterday when I discovered it in the quad. Since nobody has reported it missing, I must presume that it had been resting in the bushes for some time. Therefore, I think it only fair that it should go to a good home.'

The resulting sniggers from some of the older boys drew the attention of Binns, who was nearby, wheeling Marcus Dent in the direction of Main House. 'But Colonel Coombes!' cried the young knave, 'that brooch belongs to Marcus Dent!'

'Brooch? What brooch?' demanded the confused master, taking the medallion from Blane. 'What we have here is a precisely functioning pocket watch. Is that not correct, Blane?'

'Certainly, sir.'

'I know that because I have been using it to tell the time for the past day and a half!'

'Well whatever it is, sir,' persisted Binns, 'it belongs to Marcus Dent. He had it stolen yesterday.'

A worried Blane shot a desperate look towards Skimpton, who had been monitoring events from close by. An intervention was obviously required to ensure that justice was done, and the House Captain met the challenge unflinchingly. 'Can I suggest, Colonel,' he said, 'that we ask Dent himself about the item?'

The flustered master then turned his defective gaze on the nearby School Scoundrel, slouched in his wheelchair, a cricket ball lodged in his mouth. 'Well Dent,' demanded the Colonel, 'is this true? Are you the rightful owner of this pocket watch?'

Dent looked up and grunted, saliva dripping from his face. By way of further response, he could only manage an uncomprehending roll of his eyes and a series of grotesque facial twitches. He then passed wind and jerked his head in a stupefied gesture of indifference.

'Well if that's the best you can do,' concluded the Colonel, 'you don't deserve any consideration in the matter.'

All present laughed heartily, as Binns's pathetic explanations were rewarded with three and a half thousand lines and a promise of a severe caning by the Colonel for wasting everyone's time.

Skimpton turned to congratulate his young friend, only to discover that Blane had disappeared. Probably, thought Skimpton, to inform his family by telephone of their newly re-acquired wealth, and to secure from them a commitment to keep him at Faysgarth for the foreseeable future!

*   *   *   *

When, a few minutes later, the sports supremo approached his quarters, his euphoria was such that he failed to notice that the door was slightly ajar. Casually pushing it open, intending to take a few minutes to refresh himself before supper, he was confronted with a sight which was destined to etch a permanent picture into his memory. Nothing of the preceding events, astounding as they had been, could have prepared him for the vision which now presented itself before his eyes.

The spectre of a naked woman positioned uninvited and entirely unannounced in his study was one which would certainly alarm any schoolfellow. But for Skimpton, such an event produced so profound a paralysis that any onlooker could easily have assumed that his entire body had turned to granite.

The female who was busy washing herself at his sink did not notice Skimpton at first, and the silence which accompanied his immobility had the effect of forcing him to study her closely. The curve of her back, the roundness of her buttocks, her delicate neck and slender waist all pointed to one thing. Skimpton cleared his throat and ascertained that he still possessed the power of speech. 'Blane,' he said flatly, 'I do believe that you are in fact a woman.'

The startled young lady reached immediately for a towel to cover herself, and an uneasy silence enveloped the room. Fixing Skimpton's gaze, the female half-smiled and took a step towards him, the previous foul smell having been banished from her person and replaced with an altogether more acceptable bouquet which Skimpton assumed to be perfume.

'I must apologise,' she said, 'for imposing upon your hospitality once again, and, indeed, for deceiving you. I hope that you will understand why I was forced to first invent, and then *become* my younger brother in the last few months.'

Skimpton remained silent.

'Desperation, nothing else, impelled me to resort to unconventional methods in order to regain from Marcus Dent what was rightfully mine, though you were right to point out the folly of ever getting involved with such a villainous individual in the first place. Perhaps had it been you I met on holiday things would have concluded differently. I have to admit, Skimpton, that over the last few days I have grown rather fond of you, in a funny sort of way, and hope that you will not think too unkindly of me as a result of my actions. My name is Charlotte Blane.'

She then took another step towards her host and proffered a hand. Skimpton was befuddled, his understanding of her still lay somewhere between the present and the immediate past; the barely-concealed female form now before him, and the lively young boy practising at the nets in the sunshine earlier in the afternoon. A lump appeared in his throat, and he found himself trembling slightly. With considerable difficulty, he managed to offer his hand to the other. 'I am happy to meet you Miss Blane,' he uttered falteringly.

'Would you mind,' said she, 'facing the door whilst I change?'

'Of course.'

As he perused the grain of the wood, Skimpton became acutely aware of the luxuriant sound Charlotte Blane's clothes made as they brushed against her limbs, and felt an immediate tensing in his extremities. It was a sound the likes of which he had never before encountered; of silken, feminine fabrics settling themselves comfortably over smooth, delicate skin – an experience which Skimpton would remember for a long time, reminiscent of waves gently lapping at the shore, and one which he did not find altogether unpleasant.

'You see now, Skimpton,' she said, 'why I had gained something of a reputation as a slacker for personal hygiene. I couldn't risk bathing in front of the other boys for I would immediately have revealed myself as...well, different from them! And six months without bathing produces bodily odours practically unrecognisable outside of the lower orders.'

'And what of the cricket?'

'I was taught the game as a youngster by my father in the colonies, and knew that I could hold my own in Faysgarth's junior ranks. It was for this reason that the school's governing body relaxed the rules regarding the payment of fees. I hoped by playing well today that my debt might be written off, though as soon as I saw that religious fellow pretending to be a woman, I knew I would be hard pressed to make an impression.'

'But if you knew he was pulling such a stunt why did you say nothing?'

'I did! I approached him quietly and accused him of being a man masquerading as a woman, at which, he promptly denounced me as a woman masquerading as a boy!'

'Then why did he not reveal your skulduggery when I confronted him with his?'

'That I cannot tell you. The Lord works in mysterious ways. You may turn now.'

She now stood before him wearing an elegant pale green dress in printed shot silk with matching shoes. Her face now bore the traces of a subtle lipstick, her cheeks glowing an appealing shade of peach.

'Mind you,' she continued, 'he was a clever fellow. My guess is he filled those little boys' minds with religious mumbo-jumbo during his visit to their dorms last night. No wonder they were so preoccupied and ineffectual during the game.'

She then checked her makeup in the mirror, delicately removing a stray eyelash from her cheek, picked up her handbag and smiled warmly at Skimpton. 'Time I was getting along,' she sighed, and, perched momentarily on her tiptoes, kissed him lightly on the forehead. As she was leaving, she turned in the doorway and spoke. 'As promised,' she said, 'my family will forward a sizeable monetary reward as recompense for your inconvenience, though I do not doubt that, being the type of fellow that you are, you will donate the entire sum to the school you love. That is why I have left a small token for you in the top drawer of your desk.'

Skimpton, though, was too disorientated to comprehend.

* * * *

About an hour later, after he had fully recovered from the rictus which was the inevitable consequence of Charlotte Blane's parting embrace, Skimpton settled wearily into his armchair and reflected upon his experiences of the previous two days.

'What an extraordinary sequence of events,' he mused, and was forced to conclude that, had the story been depicted in a work of fiction, the average reader would doubtless have dismissed it as implausible. Indeed, had it not been for the lingering fragrance of scent in the room, Skimpton himself might well have judged that he had dreamed the entire episode. And then he remembered the gift which awaited his attention in the top drawer.

A quick investigation revealed that Charlotte Blane had left him a small package. Its simple wrapping of brown paper was easily discarded to reveal a small illustrated book: *Cricketing for Beginners* by Major Ronald Blane CBE. Inside the front page, a brief inscription had been written. It read:

> *For my chum Skimpton, a jolly good sport.*
> *Fondest regards,*
> *Charlotte Blane*

Later, having read the work from cover to cover, Skimpton was forced to concede that he was no less baffled by the game than he had been before. But then, given recent events, his capacity for bewilderment seemed to know no bounds.

THREE

ET TU, SKIMPTON?

'Watch where you're goin' on that bike you young rascald!' thundered Constable Stubbs as Skimpton skidded past him on the driveway to Faysgarth School.

'I'm frightfully sorry Constable,' gasped the rugger captain, 'but I'm on my way to the gym, you see. I'm late for training!'

'There's no excuse for ridin' without lights,' retorted the portly PC, angrily, 'particularly when it's dark!' Constable Stubbs was a sizeable fellow, widely held to possess somewhat limited intellectual prowess, a disability thought to have resulted from too much rumbustious rugby in his youth.

Aware that he must quickly placate the policeman over his minor dereliction, Skimpton's knowledge of the former's erstwhile endeavours with the oval ball led to him choosing a sporting platform from which to fashion his defence. 'I'm down to give a rousing team talk in five minutes to the First Fifteen,' he said, 'for to-morrow sees our final match of the term!'

The constable manoeuvred his weighty frame into a position from which he could more effectively scrutinise the schoolboy. 'It's Master Skimpton isn't it?' he enquired.

'That's right sir!'

At which, the policeman's demeanour visibly softened. 'I saw you score a fine try last week against a rival team. Manly stuff!'

'Thank you, Constable!' said the talented fly-half. 'I'm very sorry about my lights, sir, but my bally dynamo's been playing up.' Skimpton leant his bike against a nearby wall, removed his cycle clips, and re-joined the bobby on the drive.

'In that case,' beamed the corpulent constable, 'don't worry yourself. When a vital school sportin' fixture's at stake the law must take second place.'

'That's a jolly decent attitude Constable,' said Skimpton, quietly pleased at having won the policeman round.

Constable Stubbs had achieved his position as chief custodian of the law at the nearby small town of Faverstock not through any astute understanding of, or desire to implement, the principles of justice, but through a bureaucratic blunder which promoted him from air raid warden to police constable at the end of the last war. Rather than seek to overturn this grotesque procedural error, the local people seemed content to tolerate the constable's stolidity, since his shortcomings made easier their manipulation of him into disregarding any nugatory transgressions which they might commit. And as long as he concentrated most of his attention on his very personal and sometimes bruising crusade against the local villainy, most residents were happy to maintain their unstinting support, supplemented by large quantities of Battenberg cake, a confection to which the portly policeman was particularly partial.

'What brings you to Faysgarth, Constable, might I ask?' enquired Skimpton presently.

'A spate of burglaries, sir, in the surroundin' villages. I've just been 'avin' a word with your Colonel Coombes in the 'ope that 'e might hencourage a campaign of vigilance so that the culprits can be caught.'

'My word!' said Skimpton. 'What clues do you have so far?'

'We believe that a local backslider by the name of Jimmy Swarthy might be involved, but as yet we 'ave no hevidence with which to put 'im behind bars.'

'Any sign of the loot?'

'Hunfortunately not.'

'Well, I'll certainly keep a lookout, and encourage my schoolfellows in Second House to do the same!'

'Take great care though, Master Skimpton, for we 'ave good reason to believe 'e may be dangerous, as drugs may be involved.'

'I will, Constable. Now if you'll excuse me, I'd better get on.'

'That's the ticket, Master Skimpton. Keep up the good work!'

As the constable proceeded down the drive towards the school gates, Skimpton returned to his bicycle with a view to wheeling it into the sheds behind Main House. Some minutes later, whilst kneeling to check a tyre, he became aware of urgent footsteps approaching from behind, and mindful of the policeman's advice, prepared himself for the worst. Spinning round, poised to defend his person from attack, the tennis champion found himself confronted by his young manservant, breathing heavily and evidently somewhat flustered. 'Piggot!' said the Senior. 'What on earth's the matter?'

'Do you think I might have a word with you, Skimpton?' rasped the perspiring fag.

'When?'

'Right away?'

Skimpton sighed and looked at his watch. 'Can't it wait?' he said. 'I'm late for rugger training.'

'I'm afraid it is rather urgent.'

'Very well. We'd better go to my study for I have to collect my kit. And for mercy's sake, stop panting like a gun dog!'

*　　*　　*　　*

Meanwhile, over in Main House, Marcus Dent was presiding over a meeting of the Speculative Finance Committee, a shady organization which amounted to little more than a convenient front for illicit games of dice, blackjack and roulette. These gatherings usually took place in the school rotter's sumptuous quarters, with the curtains drawn and the door securely locked. Dent and his chum Spate took a generous commission from these occasional ventures, as many of the wealthier boys gambled huge sums on ludicrous bets. At the last symposium, a first-former, the son of a rich lingerie manufacturer, had wagered some fifteen hundred pounds on the contents of a sandwich which rested on a plate some distance away. Dent (having placed the catering order himself) maintained it was roast beef, and the youngster thought chicken. A cursory inspection proved it to be filled with boiled ham, but Dent confiscated the youngster's money anyway.

On this occasion, the 'committee' had organized a guest speaker to host a seminar on 'Merchant Banking'. This turned out to consist of the local one-handed card-sharp Jimmy Swarthy doing tricks and taking bets on the Monktonshire St. Leger.

Swarthy was a colourful character whose unctuous personality seemed to consist of an exaggerated impersonation of himself. He was of stocky build with jet-black hair and a thin moustache which lined his upper lip. Rumour held that his right hand had been confiscated by irate East End gangsters, furious that Swarthy had apparently swindled them over some stolen jewels. The reality, though, was somewhat more mundane; it had been severed in a mincing machine when Swarthy was apprenticed in a Faverstock butcher's shop as a youth. The resulting stump seemed to present him with little difficulty in his profession as a card-sharp. Indeed, Swarthy's salty attitude to his handicap was aptly encapsulated in the tattoo he'd had inscribed just above the wrist: 'hands off' it read, followed by an entirely unnecessary exclamation mark.

'How's tricks, Jimmy?' enquired Dent, smoothing his way into the petty crook's presence, after the latter had wound up the evening's activities.

'Mustn't complain Your Honour!' came the affected cockney reply. 'Another glass of this lovely port wouldn't go amiss, though!'

'Get another bottle, Spate.'

Swarthy settled himself into an armchair and accepted with flamboyant gratitude one of Dent's small Cuban cigars. 'Where, might I enquire,' he intoned, 'is my good friend Master Binns tonight? Not still smarting over that five hundred I took off him last time, I hope?'

'Not in the least.'

'Good. After all, he knew what he was taking on.'

'Indeed. For a one-handed man, Jimmy, you play a mean game of billiards. No, Binns is busy rehearsing for the school play. He's taken the lead in Shakespeare's *Othello* which opens next week.'

'Blimey! Highly high-brow.'

Dent's relationship with Swarthy was an unsettling one to behold. Each seemed overly intent on impressing the other, whilst at the same time desperate not to appear to be doing so. This made for puzzling exchanges in which they seemed to compete with one another for the prize of most ironical conversationalist.

'Can I interest you in a tip for the St. Leger, Master Dent?' asked Swarthy, presently.

'No thank you James. I don't bet on horses; too many variables. I prefer to fix my own odds.'

'In that case what about a small wager on the outcome of the rugger game to-morrow.'

'Foregone conclusion; Faysgarth's bound to win. Skimpton's on top form as usual.'

Swarthy nodded in smarmy acknowledgement. 'Plus ça change,' he agreed.

Just then their attention turned to an unsightly commotion in the doorway as Binns fought his way towards them through the departing crowd. Toppling backgammon boards and scattering chairs, the unruly Senior made a bee-line for the lemonade in the drinks cabinet, leaving a trail of destruction in his wake.

'Do excuse me, James,' said Marcus Dent dryly. 'It appears I have business to attend to.' The school bounder then cleared his room of visitors, methodically cleaned up the detritus left by Binns's extravagantly untidy entrance, and adopted a composed posture on his chaise longue. 'So, Binns,' he said resignedly, 'tell me what precisely is troubling you.'

*   *   *   *

'You mean Prof. Beedon has dropped Binns from the play and wants me to take over with only a week to go?' exclaimed Skimpton, in a rather clumsy ejaculation reminiscent of third-rate drama. He had been collecting together his notes for the pep talk he intended giving the First Fifteen after training when Piggot had blurted out his news.

'That's about the size of it,' replied the junior, sheepishly.

'But I've never acted before in my life!'

'He knows that, but he's desperate, and feels certain that he can rely upon you to learn the lines accurately.'

'Me? Surely there are other fellows far more qualified!'

'I would have thought so, Skimpton, but the Prof. seems intent on having you play the part. He seems to think that, as you're the most popular boy in the school, you might bring an added dimension to the role and provoke sympathy for the character in the audience.'

'I see.' When Skimpton had been accosted by Piggot on the school drive a few moments earlier, he assumed it to be about some petty squabble in the junior ranks. Nothing had prepared him for this extraordinary turn. 'How big a part is this *Othello* fellow?' he demanded.

'It's the title role Skimpton. The play pretty much revolves around him.'

Skimpton put down his kit bag, folded his papers and took a few moments to consider. 'And do you think,' said he, 'from your experience of the play in preparation, that I would be suitable to undertake the role?'

'Let's put it this way, Skimpton, you couldn't possibly do any worse than Binns.'

'Really?'

'I am afraid the rest of the cast threatened to withdraw unless he was sacked.'

'I see. And what part do you portray in this theatrical extravaganza, Piggot?'

'Should you choose to take on the lead role, Skimpton, you will find yourself playing opposite me, as I am fulfilling the part of your wife, *Desdemona*.'

'Oh dear.'

'A woman you suffocate to death in the final act.'

Skimpton's approach to the whole business brightened considerably at the thought of publicly 'murdering' his own fag. What a hoot it would be, he thought, and what an achievement if he could complete the dastardly act without laughing!

'The Professor is aware of my sporting obligations, I assume?' he said, grandly. 'Naturally I could not contemplate taking any part in proceedings until after the rugger final to-morrow.'

'Of course. The Professor acknowledges your immediate priority must be in the sporting arena, Skimpton. Though he did indicate that I should inform you that, in all probability, talent scouts from the professional theatre will be present at the performance, and the possibility of lucrative West End contracts cannot be ruled out.'

'Really?' said Skimpton, intrigued. 'And who might these 'talent scouts' be? Anyone famous?'

'Friends of the Professor's from London, I assume. He mentioned no names.'

Skimpton, gazing out at the quad thoughtfully, popped a fruit bonbon in his mouth, adopted the pose of a noble tragedian in pensive mood, and turned smartly from the window. 'Very well,' said he, 'tell the Professor I accept his offer, and will be available to practice to-morrow evening after rugger.'

'Good show!' triumphed Piggot, beaming. 'I should tell you, however, that in the theatre we refer to it as "rehearsing", Skimpton.'

'What does it matter what it's called, fathead! So long as we all have a giddy time!' And throwing his kit bag joyfully over his shoulder, added, 'Now hie thee hence, firrah, for I have waiting team-matef to infpire!'

*   *   *   *

'I say!' burst forth Binns, at an ear drum-shattering volume. 'These fig biscuits are jolly scrumptious!' He had been placed on Dent's leather armchair immediately after Jimmy Swarthy, on his departure, had vacated it, and plied with copious amounts of tuck in an attempt to abate his fury. Having achieved this goal at the cost of three bags of biscuits, four Swiss Rolls and a couple of bottles of fizzy pop, Dent luxuriated on his chaise longue, eyes closed, and listened as his voluble cohort bemoaned his humiliating predicament. 'I'll never be a professional actor now,' groaned Binns. 'My dad will be furious. He had me earmarked for a small part in his next West End show.'

His father, Barney Binns, was a producer of some notoriety, mostly of inferior, rather tasteless musical entertainments, and had promised to attend the performance of the school play with a view to deciding upon his son's suitability for a career in show business. Binns, his anger rising once more, reached for a box of marshmallows and let out another hail of rancorous invective. 'I'll kill that filthy communist Beedon!' he screamed, 'How dare he sack me! I say Marcus, pass me over the cherryade would you?'

Dent, his patience receding, walked over to the drinks cabinet and procured yet another placatory bottle for his chum. 'Binns,' he said calmly, 'tell me...why is it that whenever you have anything to say you invariably bellow it at the top of your voice?'

'Do I?' bellowed Binns at the top of his voice. 'I didn't realize.'

'Indeed you do.'

'In that case, I apologize, Marcus.'

'It's just that,' sighed Dent, 'perhaps if you had exercised a little more vocal restraint during rehearsals, you might yet be delivering of your *Othello*. Instead of which, it appears that prissy little schoolgirl Skimpton is on the point of grabbing all the glory once again.'

'I know,' sneered Binns, 'he's such a sissy I hate him. Can't we devise a plan to wipe him from the face of the earth?'

Dent's eyes rolled briefly in their sockets, eventually coming to rest in the direction of the heavens. A brief knock at the door then heralded the reappearance of Spate, waving an impressive wad of notes. 'I've just finished the accounting with Jimmy,' he said, making for the Turkish Delight. 'Here's our commission from the St Leger.'

'Excellent.' Dent took the money and placed it in the safe, set into the wall behind one of the small Gainsborough portraits he'd accepted the previous month from a third-former as payment of a debt.

'He said he'd see us next week.'

'Who did?'

'Jimmy. He said he was looking forward to another convergence of the committee next week.'

'The fool! I told him the meeting was cancelled due to this blasted school play!'

'Would you like me to go after him, Marcus, and inform him as such?'

'No, leave it to me. The thing is there'll be no-one about next week, they'll all be glued to Skimpton strutting about *The Rialto*.'

'I'd do anything to see him come a cropper,' put in Binns, moodily stuffing profiteroles into his face.

'And I'd dearly like to thwart that snivelling little socialist Beedon as well,' added Spate. 'He gave me five hundred lines yesterday for refusing to sing *The Internationale* in his English lesson.'

'Slimy Bolshevik,' snorted Dent. 'Where on earth does this place find such low lifes? You are right: we must concoct some scenario to put paid to this theatrical event. Binns...'

'Yes Marcus?' shouted he, standing to attention.

'Come to my study after dinner to-morrow and we shall discuss the matter. In the mean time I shall put my thinking cap on. Oh, and Spate...'

'Sir?'

'Organize some ear plugs for me before then, would you?'

*   *   *   *

Early the following evening, Skimpton, having played a blinder in the final rugger game of the term, stood squarely in his study and prepared to set about tackling his next assignment. In one hand a copy of William Shakespeare's drama of power corrupted by passion and jealousy; in the other, a slim volume by one Rose Tennent, entitled *Acting Made Easy*.

Being somewhat short on rehearsal time, the young all-rounder felt he should combine his learning of the words with some useful tips on technique. To this end, Rose Tennent's handy pamphlet was proving invaluable. Approaching the mirror above his hand basin, he proceeded to follow the author's simple instructions. Pursing his mouth and grasping his lower lip with his left hand, he thrust out his lower jaw and let out a portentous 'aaah' sound, a noise so deep and seemingly profound that the aspiring thespian perceived it as emanating from the very core of his being. 'Aaaay,' he breathed. 'Orrrr...'

'I say Skimpton! What on earth are you up to?' It was his pal Jack Varley, peering quizzically through the half-open door.

'Preparatory work, Jack,' explained Skimpton airily, 'for this wretched play.'

'I don't know about any play,' joked his chum, 'looks to me like you are trying to perform a tonsillectomy!'

'Don't be a silly chump,' said Skimpton, contorting his features further and dripping saliva onto the porcelain, 'these exercises are imperative if I'm to avoid damage to my vocal cords on the night of the performance.'

'Poppycock!'

'It's true. The part I have undertaken to play is one of the most demanding in the whole theatrical canon, so I am led to believe, and not one which should be approached casually. After all, I wouldn't attempt an assault on the County Tennis Championships without rigorous preliminary work on my ground strokes, so why should this be any different?'

'I see,' said Varley, '*Othello* played then, did he?'

'Don't be fatuous, Jack, for it doesn't become you. Now here,' said the House Captain, chucking his chum the script, 'test me on my lines.'

Varley settled into the armchair and fished out his reading glasses as Skimpton took up a declamatory pose opposite him. 'Let him do his spite my services,' he proclaimed with exaggerated gravity, 'which I have done the signory shall out!'

'I say, steady on old man!' laughed Varley. 'Don't you think you are going about this rather heavy-handedly?'

'What do you mean?'

'I don't know much about it but I'd hazard that if you hammer away at your vocal cords like that you'll more than likely do some permanent damage!'

Skimpton looked deflated, and in the style of a petulant debutante in a poor drawing room farce, threw down his script. 'You're right Jack,' he sighed, collapsing onto the bed. 'I'm just not cut out for the artistic side of things.' Varley's response took the form of a diligently crafted silence, punctuated only by the sound of him crossing his legs. 'The thing is,' continued Skimpton, 'Prof. Beedon seems to think I'm perfect for the part, and I really don't feel inclined to let him down!'

'He's a rum fellow that Beedon,' quipped Varley. 'I can't say I'll be sad to see the back of him at the end of term. Are you sure this isn't one of his tom-fool pranks?'

'Piggot appears to think he's pretty serious.'

'If that's the case, why's he always laughing himself into a stupor at the slightest provocation?'

'I don't know! Besides, I owe it to the school to do my best; all sorts of local dignitaries have been invited. Oh, Jack, what are we going to do?'

'We?' protested Varley. 'I, my friend, have far better things to do than to get caught up in a load of potty theatricals.'

Skimpton laughed mockingly. Varley was always pleading that he was too busy whenever his pal needed serious assistance. 'What better things?' he demanded.

'Chess, for instance. I've a game lined up this very evening with your man Piggot.'

'What's he doing playing board games? I was led to understand that he'd taken the part of *Desdemona*. Why isn't he learning his lines?'

'My dear Skimpton, unlike yourself, Piggot has enjoyed the luxury of some three months' rehearsal, and as a consequence knows his part inside out. And yours, probably.'

'Hmmm. Well, make sure he doesn't miss practice tonight, for I shall require the little blighter to serve me my cues.'

'Then *Desdemona* too played tennis? With such a lot in common it is astonishing the marriage didn't last!'

Skimpton flung a towel at Varley, and as the latter scooted from the room, took up his pose once more. Stretching out his arm in the manner of a mighty warrior, and thrusting forward his chin, the renowned javelin champion pronounced:

'To know which when I knew that boasting is an honour,
I shall promulgate...promulgate...promulgate...'

*   *   *   *

Later the same night, in Main House, a somewhat lubricated Marcus Dent and his brainless crony Binns were plotting Skimpton's downfall. 'I know,' hooted the doltish sidekick, 'why don't we just burn the hall down on opening night?'

'Wonderful idea, 'said Dent sarcastically, 'then we would have nowhere to hold next term's Fescennine Music Hall, and

I've already booked the snake act. No, whatever skulduggery we contrive must take place during the actual performance, so that when it is cancelled we can move in and cream off the youngsters for an impromptu meeting of the Speculative Finance Committee.'

'In that case, why don't I just don a toga, walk on stage at the appropriate moment and stab Skimpton to death with a real dagger?'

'That's *Antony and Cleopatra* you blithering idiot! For an aspiring actor, Binns, you display a remarkable ignorance of dramatic literature. What on earth do you do during English lessons?'

'Masturbate, mostly.'

Dent considered soaking Binns with what remained of his eggnog, but instead cut him dead with a weary stare. 'This *Othello* chap,' he said presently, 'would I be right in assuming he's something of an army man?'

'Prof. Beedon reckons he's a tragic figure against whom the locals conspire because of the colour of his skin.'

'Which is?'

'Black as the ace of spades.'

'Hmmm.'

'I tried to get something of that persecuted quality across in my rendition.'

'I'm sure your fellow cast members were very helpful in that respect.'

'They were indeed most accommodating!'

'But tell me, what precisely happens to this fellow in the end?'

'When everything gets on top of him, he throws an almighty wobbler, murders his wife and then does away with himself.'

'I see. Am I to assume that this militaristic victim of ancient prejudice wields some sort of weapon about the stage?'

'A whacking great sword, yes.'

'Splendid.' Dent knocked back the remainder of his drink then lit a small Cuban cigar, from which he drew smoke deeply into his lungs. 'Tell me, Binns,' he said, exhaling resolutely, 'do we still have a key to the chemistry laboratory?'

'I, erm...yes. I think Spate keeps all his duplicates in the cellars with the dead boys.'

'Excellent. Now: you see that book on the top shelf, with the purple binding?'

'The one next to the collection of Beardsley engravings, yes. *Fun With Compounds?*'

'That's the one. Get it down, would you?' Binns clambered up the shelves, somewhat unsteadily, and eventually produced the dusty volume for Dent's perusal. 'Look up "adhesives" would you?' requested the bounder. 'Chemical composition thereof...'

*   *   *   *

Professor Denys Beedon, PhD, had arrived at Faysgarth the previous term, and during the last few months his youthful, unorthodox presence had generated some controversy in the English Department. His means of transport was immediately the subject of some considerable comment, for he had arrived at the school in a curious French motor van which, had it not been for the manufacturer's name on the back, one could easily have believed he had constructed himself using iron railings and rusty old cheese graters.

Like most of his colleagues on the staff, Beedon sported a beard. But unlike the other masters, his facial hair, rather than resembling an unruly forestation wandering aimlessly over his face, was cropped closely about his chin in the manner of a Russian revolutionary. In common with his fellow masters, Beedon also wore a corduroy blazer and smoked a pipe, though his jacket was of such an unconventional cut that it reached to well below his knees, and his smoking apparatus invariably contained a foul-smelling substance, the inhaling of which usually resulted in him collapsing into paroxysms of laughter. Indeed, the young master's capacity for mirth had begun to cause some concern at Faysgarth, and he had been warned on many occasions against continuing his practice of enticing boys into his quarters and sending them out half an hour later, falling over in the corridors in fits of uncontrolled merriment. Once, during full school assembly, the Professor had greeted the grave news of a fourth-former's untimely death in a boating accident with such raucous guffaws that, during the minute's respectful silence, he had to be forcefully led from the hall, slapped about the face, gagged and locked in his room.

It was during one of these unseemly bouts of risibility, prompted by an article Beedon had just read in *The Barnchester Chronicle*, that Skimpton first approached the Professor at the start of his initial rehearsal for *Othello*. 'Ah! My replacement Moor!' greeted the master, stifling the last of his chortles. 'Welcome to *The Rialto*. You've learned your lines I hope?'

'Young Piggot has been good enough to recite them to me in my sleep, sir,' came the reply. 'I believe that to be an efficient method of cramming, according, that is, to this splendid book by Rose Tennent...'

'Yes, yes, yes,' interrupted Beedon. 'Now: I have chosen you for this part, Skimpton, because I believe you to be naturally a man of action, and not so much a brain worker, very like the character himself, in fact. Would you concur with that assessment?'

Skimpton was unsure whether an agreement with the Professor's hypothesis would mean an implicit acknowledgement of the latter's blatant slight on his intellect, and instead of responding, he retired behind a semi-hostile silence.

'Like many soldiers,' continued the Prof.,'*Othello* lacks intellectual acumen, psychological insight and, at times, plain common sense. Qualities which I am sure you will be able to highlight without much difficulty.'

'Now look here, Professor Beedon...'

'Good. Let's get on with the first scene then, shall we?'

The Professor's provocative manner had by now aroused Skimpton's anger, and he was on the verge of challenging him over his remarks when Piggot intervened. 'Don't worry, Skimpton,' reassured the youngster, *sotto voce*, 'he's always like this. You just have to get used to it – he means no harm.'

'Very well,' said Skimpton. 'I shall endeavour to disregard his rudeness for the sake of art.' As he strode purposefully to the stage, Skimpton noticed Colonel Coombes, who was playing *Othello*'s malevolent sidekick *Iago*, with his face buried deep in his script. Obviously not yet secure with his lines, the chemistry man seemed to be hiding behind a piece of scenery some way towards the back. By contrast, it was an assured-looking Skimpton who immediately took up a position at the very centre of the stage. There was a hushed silence in the hall as the rest of the cast waited to see how their new leading man shaped up.

> *Let him do his spite my, services which I have done*
> *the signory...*

'No, no, no, no, no, no, no!' bellowed the Professor. 'We can't have that!'

There was a pause as Skimpton approached the edge of the stage and peered through the lights into the auditorium. 'Is there a problem, Professor Beedon?' he enquired tersely.

'Yes,' came the reply. 'It's that bit of scenery there. What on earth are we doing with an ornamental tree on stage? This is supposed to be seventeenth-century Italy!'

'The Venetian buildings are still being painted,' explained Colonel Coombes. 'This section of Oriental garden is all that remains of the set for last year's highly acclaimed production of *The Mikado*, which I myself produced. Today, though, it is standing in for the Doge's Palace.'

'I see. Very well, carry on.'

'Don't be put off,' whispered the Colonel. 'He gets like this. It's the creative juices at work.'

The cross-country champion took up his position to begin again, but this time his concentration had deserted him and his mind went blank.

'Please continue,' urged the Professor. There then followed an unbearably embarrassing silence as Skimpton scoured his memory for the words. 'Feel free to use a book if you need,' added Beedon. 'I'd rather not be hindered by retentionist technicalities at this stage.'

Skimpton sighed, looked to the floor and began to wonder why he had ever consented to get involved in such a project. Varley was right, he concluded with a ponderous sigh, this was no place for him; he should stick to the sports field, where his talents were more gratefully and indeed more intelligibly received.

'Think about the character's attempt to disguise a profound lack of confidence in an alien environment,' offered the Professor helpfully. And for the first time that day, Skimpton felt he fully understood what the man was talking about.

*   *   *   *

Colonel Coombes's absence from the chemistry laboratory, meanwhile, had left the way clear for Marcus Dent and his friends to have *Fun With Compounds*, as they adapted some of the more spectacular experiments in Dent's handbook of the same name.

Aside the bubbling concoctions which kept Binns's feeble mind occupied, Dent and his cohort Spate, at the blackboard, were working on a formula which they hoped might produce an adhesive so powerful that they would be able to put it on the market and retire on the proceeds. Binns, though, had more immediate rewards to share with them. 'I say chaps!' he hooted. 'Watch this!' He then proceeded to pour a flask of liquid chlorine into an already unstable mixture containing benzoyl peroxide and cyanide.

The resulting explosion, which dispatched the stuff eight feet into the air, produced a cloud of gas so noxious that it sent all three of them clambering in the direction of an open window to recover. Dent, having taken the precaution of placing a handkerchief over his mouth, was the first to return to the remains of Binns's experiment. After the poisonous gas had cleared, a swift inspection of the debris revealed that both the conical flask and the Bunsen burner over which it had been placed had become firmly glued to the bench!

'Well blow me down with a feather!' he exclaimed. 'This stuff's just what we're looking for! Well played, Binns!'

But the scientist responsible for the breakthrough was unavailable to receive the congratulations offered him, for he was on his hands and knees, fingers thrust firmly down his throat in a desperate attempt to expel the poisonous vapours from his person.

Astounded that, no matter how hard he tried, he could not prise what remained of the apparatus from the bench, Dent called again to his pals. 'I say! Come and look at this!' he cried. The effects of the explosion, though, also precluded Spate from sharing his chum's excitement. As a result of an attempt to place his hands in front of his face for protection from the blast, he was now fully engaged in trying to remove them from the window frame to which they had subsequently become resolutely attached.

*   *   *   *

'How's the acting going Skimpton? All set for opening night?' Jack Varley had been on his way to the post box some days later when he had encountered his friend reciting his lines from a seated position atop the cycle sheds.

'Don't bother me now, Jack,' said Skimpton, his gaze fixed on a distant spot, 'for I must concentrate on my breath control.'

'I do apologise. Wouldn't want to come between you and the estimable Rose Tennent!'

'Don't be sore Jack, I'll only be a few seconds.'

Varley hung around for a couple of minutes, waiting for his rather embarrassing friend to complete his respiratory routine. Finally, though, he gave up and marched off.

'Where are you going, Jack?' shouted Skimpton, after him.

'I have to post my football coupon,' came the tetchy reply.

Skimpton exhaled vigorously, jumped down from his perch and joined his chum as he headed towards the drive. 'As a matter of fact,' he said, 'I've discarded my acting manual on the advice of Prof. Beedon, who reckons I should rely more on my instincts.'

'Is that a fact?'

'Says that too much theorising can get in the way of natural talent such as mine.'

'Does this mean no more late-night bouts of stage fighting in your study?'

'The Prof. prefers them to develop "organically" in rehearsal.'

'Well I'm glad to hear it. My windows were rattling until three the other morning. And I shall be surprised if all that low-slung chanting nonsense hasn't damaged the foundations.'

'Sorry about that old man. I'm afraid young Piggot and I have been getting rather carried away of late. Wine gum?'

'No thanks.'

'Actually, the Prof.'s turning out to be quite a decent fellow. He says that, if the show's a success, he sees no hindrance to me eventually becoming an Hollywood star!'

'Does he really? I can think of one major obstacle for a start.'

'What's that?'

'You can't act.'

'Apparently that's of no importance these days. Looks are what count, and I certainly have those in abundance, according to the Professor.'

'I suppose he pointed out that your natural modesty would further endear you to the public, did he?'

'He didn't touch on that, but now you mention it...'

'Yes, yes. Now if you'll excuse me, Skimpton, I should like to avoid missing the last post.'

Just then Skimpton spied his fag Piggot slouching near the entrance to Second House, and bade farewell to Varley with the intention of reproaching the youngster for his sloppy demeanour. 'What's the matter with you, Piggot?' he growled. 'Stand up straight, your posture is an insult to everyone in Second House!'

'I am sorry Skimpton,' came the weary reply, 'but I fear that too many nights spent repeating Shakespeare in your ear instead of sleeping in my bed may well be having a detrimental effect on my general well-being.'

'Nonsense! You are a youngster and as such should require only negligible sleep. Why, when I was your age, training for the Junior Decathlon, I went a whole term without so much as resting my eyes for five minutes!'

'Did you really Skimpton?'

'Pretty much, and what's more I won comfortably. Now run along and don't let me see you dawdling on school premises again!'

*   *   *   *

The remainder of the weeks' rehearsals progressed satisfactorily, as far as Skimpton was concerned, and although Colonel Coombes's insistence on hiding his face behind his script throughout caused some general consternation, it was with an air of cautious optimism that all involved retired to refresh themselves the night before the show.

'Piggot,' said Skimpton, having settled himself in his bed with a mug of hot cocoa, 'tell me, how do you rate my performance so far?'

His bleary-eyed manservant was swaying nearby, trying desperately to focus his attention on yet another night's Shakespearean recitation of his hero's lines, in an attempt to secure them in the latter's memory via his unconscious. 'Well Skimpton,' said the exhausted youngster, flatly, 'if I were the producer, I might venture to suggest that you pay a little more attention to the actual sense of what you are saying on stage, rather than merely opting to impress with the musicality of your rendition. That way you might be able to put some of the stresses in the right place.'

'I see,' retorted the Senior tartly. 'And if I were in charge, I would advise you to try and bring a little more enthusiasm and energy to your performance as the tragic *Desdemona!*'

'But Skimpton,' protested the fag, 'you don't seem to realise – I have had no sleep for a week!'

'That is beside the point. Now, on the subject of this fellow Beedon and his delirious giggling: what do you reckon he puts in his pipe?'

'I cannot be sure, Skimpton, but I've seen him handing over money to that suspicious-looking fellow from Faverstock in exchange for small packages wrapped in newspaper.'

'Hmmm...whatever it is it certainly doesn't seem to do much for his powers of concentration. Tonight he set off on one of his ludicrous theories about *Othello*'s 'neuroses' only to lose his thread half way through. He'd not only forgotten what he was talking about, but also precisely where – and who – he was! And as for getting me to black up with makeup for rehearsal – I had no idea my character was a coloured fellow! I thought the Moor of Venice was a stretch of uncultivated land somewhere in Northern Italy, possibly used for grouse shooting!'

Skimpton finished the remainder of his cocoa, placed the cup beside the bed on the floor, adjusted his two pillows and closed his eyes. 'Let's start with act three, scene two, shall we?' he breathed.

Good Michael, look you to the guard tonight...

But as he waited for Piggot to recite the words in his ear, he found himself setting out for the Kingdom of Slumber quite unaware that his nocturnal companion had, some minutes before, already made a similar journey, curled up in the hearth. Transported in his dreams to an extravagant Venetian landscape many moons away, the youngster was mouthing silently the poetry pertaining thereto, the delicious fruits of an Englishman's luxuriously fertile imagination:

That poor soul sat sighing by a sycamore tree
Sing all a green willow
Her hand on her bosom, her head on her knee
Sing willow...willow...willow...

*   *   *   *

'Yoo hoo! I say, Barney Binns isn't it?' yodelled Lady Edgerton as the chauffeur drew the Rolls to an imperious halt outside Faysgarth's Main Hall the following evening.

'I say Celia, do pipe down would you?' hissed her husband Lord Rupert, through gritted teeth. 'You are attracting unwanted attention.'

'Oh, do belt up,' came the swift reply. 'If you'd wanted us to arrive incognito we should've come on bicycles. Look, it's my old friend Barney Binns. I haven't seen him for aeons.'

'Celia daarling!' boomed Binns Senior, sidling up to the rear passenger door. 'I mustn't have clapped eyes on you since, what was it, *Bringing Up The Rear* four, five years ago! How the devil are you?'

'Hideously unhappy darling. Trapped in a disastrous marriage with this awful little man here.'

Barney Binns then angled his head to peer past her, manufacturing a sympathetic expression for the benefit of Lady Edgerton's husband. 'My deepest condolences, Lord Edgerton,' he said. 'Celia was an absolute nightmare to work with in the theatre, she must be impossible to tolerate as a wife. Your life must be purgatory.'

'It is,' spat the Lord, as he turned stiffly and stared out of the other window.

'So, Barney,' wailed the chemically enhanced blonde as she stepped from the motor-car, 'what brings you to these parts?'

The greasy theatrical offered Lady Edgerton his arm and sighed with exaggerated resignation. 'My son is taking the lead in tonight's production,' he said, 'and I promised to lend my celebrity to the occasion.'

'Which celebrity might that be, pray, one of your illustrious associates?'

'Why myself of course, you cheeky vixen!'

As the two erstwhile colleagues chatted animatedly, crossing the gravel drive, Lord Edgerton was left alone in his car, staring into the middle distance and ruing the day he had ever set eyes on the appalling young woman he now felt obliged to call his wife.

'Of course, Rupert insists we turn out every year as he's on the Board of Governors,' trilled Lady Celia. 'Last year's effort was quite ghastly – *The Mikado*, I think it was – though it could just as easily have been set in the wild west as Titipu, for all the shouting and screaming!'

The distinguished erstwhile dandy Lord Rupert Edgerton had lived in the area for some time, and as a colourful patron of the arts and distinguished connoisseur of painting, his annual presence at the school play always added a certain lustre to the occasion. Lady Celia, a former actress, was considerably younger than her husband, and had married him as a dare a few years previously, during a lull in her career. These days she was widely held to be something of a sensation in fashionable circles, with her vibrant tongue and forthright manner. Her frequent, often bitterly fought, battles with her husband were legendary. These days, it was thought by many who had known him for some time that this turbulent relationship was beginning to get the better of Rupert Edgerton. As something of a snappy dresser and gregarious socialite in his day, he was now seen as having lost some of his lustre – a state of affairs which frequently reduced him to bouts of rancorous melancholia, especially when his garrulous wife was at her most demanding.

'Rupert!' she commanded from the entrance to the hall. 'Go and conjure up some liquid refreshment whilst I denounce you to my chum!' At which, the sour-faced peer descended his motor -car and instigated a weary search for alcohol.

Meanwhile, backstage, Professor Beedon was delivering a lengthy pep-talk before curtain up. In measured tones he presented the assembled cast with a wide-ranging lecture on the meaning of Shakespeare's play, with numerous references to what Beedon described as its 'political context'. 'The day will come,' he concluded gravely, 'when the shackled masses will discard their chains and take up weapons against their oppressors. In all corners of the earth, enslaved peoples will embrace once more the cultural heritage so long denied them, in a mighty process of global redemption. Meanwhile, their imperialist tyrants will be left grovelling in the quagmire of their moral decrepitude. And in our own land men, women and children will emerge from the mines and factories...'

'Excuse me sir,' interrupted Piggot, 'but I seem to have mislaid my handkerchief!'

'Well use someone else's for pity's sake!'

'But it's a vital prop sir!' insisted the goofy third-former. 'And its colour matches my costume.' Piggot was wearing an elegant bottle green robe in crushed velvet, with lace accoutrements. Together with a flowing blonde wig he looked almost fetching. Until, that is, he opened his mouth.

During the ensuing frantic search about the wings and dressing rooms for Desdemona's hanky, Skimpton, having finally given up trying to glean any meaning from Professor Beedon's address, sought refuge in the sage words of Rose Tennent.

> *Q 237: Is there any way of preventing stage fright taking hold before a performance?*
> *A. No, not entirely. Weather permitting, step outside and take a few deep breaths.*

*   *   *   *

Over in Main House, Marcus Dent was briefing Binns on the subject of the evening's mischief. 'Now,' he said, 'you know what to do with the adhesive compound?'

'I do indeed Marcus.'

'Good. Did you remember to add that other stuff to Skimpton's makeup as I instructed?'

'Of course I did! Do I look like a fool?'

'Yes, as a matter of fact you do.'

'I mixed it in when everyone was having tea.'

'Excellent. Now get along and report back to me once the fireworks have started.'

'Will you not be present to see the results of our handiwork Marcus?'

'Unfortunately not, I shall have to rely on you to provide a detailed summation of events. Spate and I must remain here and entertain Jimmy Swarthy when he arrives, and prepare for what could yet be the most lucrative meeting of the Speculative Finance Committee!'

Binns made to leave, a determined expression carved into his face, and a securely corked test tube resting in his sticky hand.

'Before you go,' uttered Dent, 'I think it might be wise if you adopted some sort of disguise before going backstage, so that no-one suspects anything untoward.'

'Righto!'

* * * *

At precisely seven thirty-four pm, the house lights in Faysgarth's Main Hall dimmed, the audience curtailed its chatter, and the curtain rose on Professor Denys Beedon's controversial production of William Shakespeare's famous tragedy *Othello*. With the palpably agitated director hovering at the rear of the stalls, the young Faysgarthian entrusted with initiating proceedings shuffled into place amidst the luscious fabrics and ingeniously marbled pillars, and the performance began.

> *Rodrigo: Never tell me; I take it as much unkindly*
> *That thou hast, Iago, who hast had thy purse*
> *As if the strings were thine, shoulds't know of this -*
> *Iago: 'Sblood, but you'll not hear me.*
> *If ever I did dream of such a matter*
> *Abhor me.'*

As he spoke, for the first time without his face hidden behind a script, it became clear that Colonel Coombes, whilst concealing his visage from view in rehearsals, had been perfecting a catalogue of bizarre grimaces and lascivious sneers the likes of which had never been witnessed on a stage. Indeed, his facial contortions involved such a monstrous twisting of his muscles that his words were all but unintelligible. Instead of the customary scheming and subtle malevolence which were generally presented as the impetus behind the character's complex persona, the Colonel's *Iago*, from the outset, became a figure of intense pity, resembling the less-than-fortunate victim of an unpleasant nervous disorder.

As the minutes ticked by, his grotesque facial distortions became even more exaggerated, and soon the audience's sympathy began to evaporate. Many even began tittering at the twitching Colonel. Professor Beedon meanwhile, seated himself disconsolately near the exit, his head firmly placed in his hands.

Backstage, Binns, having thrown on a costume from a previous production of *She Stoops To Conquer*, was hovering suspiciously around the table upon which the props were placed.

'What do you think you are doing, Binns?' hissed Skimpton, emerging from the lavatory for the third time that night. 'And why are you dressed like that?'

'I'm...I'm...' Binns was obviously up to no good, but Skimpton was in no position to deliver an adequate reprimand, for he was due on stage in a matter of seconds. 'I'm playing *Tony Lumpkin!*' blathered the startled Senior.

'Who on earth's he?'

'A character from a Restoration comedy by Oliver Goldsmith I believe,' came the cocky reply. 'Prof Beedon thought my surprise appearance tonight might have a profoundly alienating effect on the audience.'

'Any appearance by you is guaranteed to provoke a profoundly alienating effect, Binns, no matter the audience. Now stop talking utter balderdash and hand me my sword.'

*　　*　　*　　*

'Gin and tonic alright for you James?'

'That would be most welcome,' replied Jimmy Swarthy, seating himself on the leather armchair in Marcus Dent's sumptuous study.

'I am afraid,' continued the school cheat, 'that we were unable to contact you with regard to this week's meeting.'

'Oh yes?'

'It's been cancelled due to the school play. However, we do hope to have something arranged for the end of the evening. In the meantime, what about a game of backgammon?'

'No thanks.'

'How about poker then? I have some very rude playing cards which I feel certain you would enjoy viewing.'

Swarthy seemed somewhat preoccupied as he glanced furtively about the room. Dent and Spate, who were trying their best to entertain him, put this down to a slight irritation that the evening's gambling, which he was expecting to oversee, appeared to have been overlooked. 'Don't worry Jimmy,' said Spate frankly, 'we'll drag some poor punter in before the night's out – there's no danger of you going home empty-handed. Meanwhile, what about letting us sample some more of that merchandise we smoked last week?'

'As a matter of fact, I received a new consignment only this morning.'

'Wizard!'

Swarthy gulped down his drink, handed the glass to Dent for prompt refilling, and took out a long clay pipe. 'Gosh!' cried Dent, 'that looks like one of those things you see in old farming photographs!'

'Quite possibly,' came the jocular reply. 'Agricultural workers used to smoke these things in the last century.'

'Well,' put in Dent, 'if it's good enough for those old skivvies, it's good enough for us, eh, Spate?'

'Abso-bloody-lutely!'

Swarthy filled the pipe and handed it to Spate to light. 'I expect Mr Binns is in the middle of his turn by now, eh?' enquired the conman, shifting position so as to avoid Spate's ostentatious exhalation.

'Afraid not,' replied Dent, throwing back his fifth vodka and tonic. 'He was sacked last week. However, we've come up with a rattling good plan to scupper his replacement, haven't we Spate?'

Dent's comrade, though, offered no reply, for at that moment he was sprawled face down on the Persian rug, completely insensible to the world. 'Crikey, James!' laughed Dent uneasily. 'This stuff's jolly potent isn't it?'

'He'll be alright in a minute,' said Swarthy, offering Dent the pipe. 'Here, try some yourself.'

*   *   *   *

'Do stop cackling, Celia, you are making things worse!' snapped Lord Edgerton, his mouth concealed behind his hand. He had only recently returned to his seat after his lengthy search for alcohol, with a bottle of vodka in a paper bag, procured from Mr Kellington, the dipsomaniacal Head of Latin, who he'd found dozing in the staff room. Edgerton's wife was now taking sizeable and frequent gulps, between frenzied bouts of laughter.

Lady Celia's piercing howls of hilarity had commenced soon after Skimpton had arrived on stage, and her rollicking response to his presence was soon threatening to infect the rest of the audience.

After a confident start, the young sportsman had made the mistake of reaching for his sword to illustrate a dramatic point during scene three. Having completed an heroic gesture with what he considered to be more than a touch of style, he replaced the sabre in its scabbard, only to discover that it was quite impossible for him to detach the weapon from his grasp!

> *Yet by your gracious patience I will*
> *A round unvarnished tale deliver*

...intoned he, whilst striking the cutlass violently against the boards. To no avail, however, for the wooden sword seemed to be glued to his hand!

A scene and a half later, amid much laughter, Skimpton had managed to prise the prop painfully from his possession, only to find himself, seconds later, bestride an untethered gondola, with his right hand firmly adhered to a pillar. In an attempt to assist, Colonel Coombes had inadvertently attached himself to Skimpton's other hand, and his furiously grimacing *Iago* was forced to devise his evil campaign with the proposed victim only inches from his face.

The audience was in uproar as the Colonel, his features maniacally contorted into what the performer considered to be the very personification of evil, pulled himself free and careered off backwards down the Grand Canal, demolishing the Doge's Palace *en route*.

The interval curtain fell with a furious Skimpton sliding about the stage, trying literally to shake off a screaming eunuch. Amid scenes of some confusion backstage, a giggling Professor Beedon attempted to restore calm by embarking on an impromptu lecture on the importance of the Paris Commune, a subject in which, for obvious reasons, few members of cast appeared remotely interested. Skimpton managed to extricate himself from the mêlée by dodging out of the back door.

> *Q. 249: Is there anything that can be done when everything goes wrong?*
> *A. No, not really. As before, and weather permitting, step outside and take a few deep breaths.*

Agonizingly, he was attempting to peel the hardened chemicals from his hands under a nearby tap, when he spied Binns trotting joyfully over the quadrangle lawn, having just exited Main House. In a thrice the hundred-yarder had bounded over and collared the delinquent as he was about to sneak through the refectory on his way back to the Main School Hall. 'What do you mean coating my sword with glue, you dirty rotter?' demanded the incensed House Captain, pushing the knave towards the driveway and thrusting his head into the nearest privet hedge. 'That filthy stuff's got all over the set, putting the second half of the show in jeopardy!'

'Disfigure me by all means, Skimpton,' screamed the wretched villain, 'but please, please promise you won't slay me!'

The possibility of murder hadn't actually occurred to Skimpton, though given the circumstances, he was certain that such a course should undoubtedly earn him the respect of many a Faysgarthian for generations to come. In the event, he chose to release his quarry as, at that moment, his attention was drawn elsewhere.

'I'll do anything for you, Skimpton,' wept Binns from the thicket, 'but please spare me my life!'

'Shut up, why don't you!' snapped Skimpton, and Binns immediately ceased wailing. As the numbskull tentatively withdrew himself from the bush, Skimpton pulled him across the drive to a position behind a tree, immediately overlooking the masters' car parking area. 'Now who's that?' whispered the diligent Deputy Head Boy, referring to a dark figure with a canvas bag who was loitering suspiciously around the vehicles.

'What?'

'Keep your voice down! Who's that over there near the cars?'

There was little doubt in Binns's mind as to the identity of the sinister character, but in response to Skimpton's question he made every attempt to keep his quivering lip tightly buttoned. 'If you know,' said Skimpton, fixing the miserable toady with a determined glare, 'you must tell me. Otherwise...' Here, he paused deliberately before continuing, and looked about him to indicate the seriousness of his intent. 'Otherwise, Binns, I shall have no other recourse but to kill you.'

'It's Jimmy Swarthy, Skimpton,' came the instant reply. 'I can't be sure but I think it's Jimmy Swarthy !'

'The local one-handed card-sharp and all-round good-for-nothing?'

'The same.'

'He's just come from the master's quarters with that bag. I'll wager anything it's full of stolen goods.'

'Crikey!' shrieked Binns.

Much to Skimpton's intense consternation, the volume of Binns's outburst was such that Swarthy looked round, appeared to panic, jumped in the nearest car and started up the engine.

'Come back here at once!' shouted Skimpton. But it was too late, the vehicle had spluttered into life, reared up and skidded off down the drive. 'Why,' cried Skimpton, 'that's Prof. Beedon's van Swarthy's just stolen!'

'The filthy renegade!' snorted Binns, in rather unconvincing indignation.

'Give me your clothes at once,' demanded Skimpton. 'I intend to give chase.'

Fearful of another scragging, Binns duly began disrobing himself of his Restoration costume, and handed it over to Skimpton. 'Now listen carefully,' said the latter. 'Go immediately and get word to Jack Varley as to what has happened. I shall follow this fellow on my bicycle whilst Jack telephones the Police. You understand, Binns, what will happen to you if you do not carry out my orders?'

'Yes, Skimpton, you will end my life for me, prematurely and permanently.'

'Correct. Now, after that, your task is to take my part in the play.'

'What?'

'I assume you still know the lines?'

'Well...yes, but...what about the makeup?'

'I've used it all up, you'll have to go on as you are. Now get a move on, there are only a few more minutes before curtain up on part two!'

And so, as Skimpton pulled on the boots, breeches, shirt and waistcoat which had comprised Binns's earlier disguise, and the other drew about him the majestic robes of a renaissance statesman, theatrical history was made. For that night, Faysgarth School witnessed not only the world's first black *Tony Lumpkin* but also its only Caucasian *Moor of Venice...*

*   *   *   *

'Well, Barney,' sniggered a squiffy Lady Edgerton as the interval drew to its close, 'bit of a disaster all round for your young brat in the title role, eh?'

Barney Binns scoffed dismissively and cast a weary sidelong glance in the direction of his would-be tormentor. 'I'm afraid you're mistaken there, Celia,' he said. 'That young fellow was no relation of mine.'

'Oh, really?'

The greasy entrepreneur's smug grin took rapid flight though, when the lights dimmed and the curtain rose for the second half. For there, a few moments later, quaking in terror on the centre of the stage, he saw an entirely different *Othello*, one whose skin colour was remarkably similar to everyone else's, and whose facial features bore an even more noticeable resemblance to his own. 'No, that wasn't my son,' he stuttered, eyes fixed forward in disbelief. 'But that is!'

'Will you think so?' recited Colonel Coombes, turning casually to present his fellow actor with another of his unhandsome scowls. Binns, taken somewhat aback, stood frozen with fear for at least twenty seconds before responding:

Think so, Iago?

Colonel Coombes, also entirely unprepared for what stood before him, swayed with incredulity before staggering backwards to the prompt desk for his spectacles. 'What, to kiss in private?' he continued from the wings, his face now utterly drained of expression in the darkness.

Lady Edgerton turned to a baffled Barney Binns and smiled. 'There's a turn-up for the books,' she mused. 'That puts a whole different complexion on things. Wonder what Old Will would've thought!'

* * * *

'STOP!' bellowed Constable Stubbs, his hefty policeman's arm held aloft as he stepped into the road, just outside Faysgarth village. 'Where do you think you're goin' on that bike without any lights, you young pimp?'

'I can explain, Constable,' pleaded Skimpton as he swung his Grecian Flyer to a skidded halt.

'Be silent, for I am going to 'ave to locate my notebook and take your name, with a view to reporting you to a local magistrate!'

'But sir, my chum Varley was meant to have...'

'Quiet, you young savage! And don't try any of your monkey business or I'll likely take my belt to you 'ere and now. Name?'

'Skimpton, sir.'

'Don't be funny with me, son, for I can very easily 'ave you locked up and arrange for the key to be thrown away.'

'But Constable, you don't understand, this is theatrical makeup! I've tried but I can't seem to get it off. Now if you'll just...'

'I don't know 'ow they do things in your Godforsaken country, laddie, but over 'ere we 'ave laws to uphold – and that sometimes means lockin' villains up first and askin' 'em questions some considerable time later. So, I'll put it to you again: name?'

Realising that he was getting nowhere with the appallingly impercipient custodian, Skimpton decided that matters were too urgent for further frustrating debate. Grasping the initiative, he affected an instant removal of Constable Stubbs from the case by merely charging at the fellow and pushing him into a nearby ditch. Clambering onto his bike, he then rode off at considerable speed.

'Get back 'ere you filthy little swine,' roared Stubbs, reaching for his whistle and rolling over in the mud in an unsuccessful attempt to right himself. 'I'll 'ave you disembowelled for this!'

By this time, though, Skimpton, having reached Faysgarth village, was proceeding with some caution down one of the side roads on which were situated many large and luxurious houses. Secreted just off the driveway of one of them, he noticed Prof. Beedon's van, pulled onto a grass verge and parked under a tree. Discarding his bicycle, Skimpton made his way up the drive and headed for the enormous mansion which loomed in the moonlit distance.

A few moments later, climbing through a conveniently open downstairs window, he moved stealthily into what he assumed was the drawing room. Even in the gloom he could see that the place was literally teeming with expensive antique furniture and priceless works of art; a veritable treasure-house of auspicious-looking paintings and expressive sculptures. Suddenly, there was a noise behind him and he waited a second or two before turning abruptly. Silence. Then he felt a sharp pain on the back of his head and, as he fell, his vision blurred crazily and he rapidly lost consciousness.

Regaining his senses some time later, his head thumping painfully, Skimpton staggered into the hallway. Once there, he rested for a moment, leaning against the bannister. Hearing a noise and looking up, he was greeted by none other than Constable Stubbs charging towards him from the open door like an incensed rhino, and brandishing a truncheon.

Presently, he awoke with a second throbbing injury, this time on his forehead. As his vision cleared, he could clearly make out the gargantuan presence of Constable Stubbs stationed, with his back to him, some yards away in the drawing room, his notebook at the ready. He also ascertained that the policeman had taken the precaution of tying his wrists to the bannister with a length of stout rope. Glancing around, he searched in vain for something sharp with which to affect his release, but to no avail. Until, with a gorgeous stroke of luck, he spied a small knife nearby, just beneath the hall table – one that he assumed would normally be used to open the mail – and set about retrieving it with his feet with a view to cutting himself free.

Seated on the piano stool immediately opposite Constable Stubbs was a slight, bespectacled man in a dressing gown, wringing his hands and smoking nervously. Somewhat painfully, he appeared to be scouring his brain for the particular details demanded by the bobby. 'That's right,' sighed the man, as the constable copied down the words in block capitals, 'that's Cézanne with a big "C".'

Silently, Skimpton worked away with the knife, until eventually he was free. Crawling past the staircase, down the length of the hall, he stole silently through the conservatory, and a few seconds later, disappeared into the rainy night.

'Now just to recapitulate,' said the meticulous constable, 'these missin' items are the property of your employers. Is that correct?'

'That is indeed so, yes.'

'Lord and Lady...would that be Hedgertond with an "h"?'

The man, reaching the end of his patience with his interrogator, pursed his lips and closed his eyes momentarily, before responding. 'I shall leave that to your creative discretion, Constable,' he said.

*   *   *   *

'And furthermore,' pronounced Colonel Coombes weightily, 'everyone concerned, myself included, would like, I am sure, to offer their thanks to Professor Beedon – not only for his tireless and indeed inspiring work on the production side, but also for the informative and entertaining address we have just enjoyed. Who amongst us would have thought that an account of the October Revolution would have made so fascinating, and indeed rousing, a talk!'

The Colonel had taken to the stage as the rather sluggish applause afforded the performance had died down, and was now in danger of sending the audience to sleep with his tedious meanderings, so exhausted were they already, after ninety minutes of Binns's ear-shattering declamation.

'Now,' continued the chemistry Colonel, 'I should like, if I may, to call upon our esteemed, and some would say tireless, benefactor Lord Rupert Edgerton, who is here tonight with his lovely daughter, to propose a final vote of thanks.'

Amid a further lacklustre offering by way of applause, the bitter and flamboyantly twisted peer took to the stage, accompanied by his rather unsteady and obviously disinterested spouse. 'Firstly, I should like to thank the cast on a most arresting performance,' he muttered, making no attempt to conceal the undercurrent of tired sarcasm in his voice, 'and in particular the leading player for presenting us with such an impressive and unconventional *tour de force.*'

'Hear hear!' slurred his wife.

The speaker was right to call attention to Binns's performance, for it was remarkable by any standards. His momentous rendition of the title role had sustained such a relentless level of volume that a sizeable proportion of the audience had sat through the entire second half with their fingers thrust deep into their ears. Indeed, so severe was the assault on their senses that many, Binns's father included, had inserted improvised ear plugs, by way of refuge from the abominable racket. Some, who had drifted off to sleep, were startled somewhat, when Binns decided, independently of any direction, to illustrate *Othello*'s epileptic fit by hurling himself writhing and twisting into the auditorium. Several boys were carried out injured as a result of him barging into them, and a member of the Faysgarth Women's League seated in the third row, was taken to hospital after Binns – gripped by the character's *truance* – stamped on her foot repeatedly and broke three of her toes.

Even without the aid of cotton wool, Skimpton's flagging fag Piggot, as *Desdemona*, had lapsed into so profound a slumber at the end, that he had to be woken from his death bed for the curtain call. Now, as Lord Edgerton praised his performance in particular, he stood in a daze on the edge of the stage, in danger of toppling over through sheer exhaustion.

As the esteemed Peer proceeded with his half-hearted peroration, Jack Varley puzzled as to why Skimpton had not put in an appearance in the second half, and concluded that his chum had probably cried off in disgrace, after the humiliating chaos of the first half. He would, he thought, in all probability have retired to bed, quite wisely intending to put the whole sorry episode behind him.

Just then, there was a commotion at the rear of the hall. The exit doors were flung open and a gust of wind billowed up the aisle, announcing the arrival of none other than Constable Stubbs. The portly policefellow placed himself with some ceremony in the doorway, rain dripping from his uniform, self-importance radiating from his enormous face.

'I 'ave come,' he stated solemnly, 'with grave news. A robbery 'as taken place this evenin' at the residence of Lord and Lady Hedgertond!' The constable's habit of scattering consonants where none were required momentarily confused the gathering, and it was a few seconds before the more etymologically astute amongst them fully appreciated the immediate gravity of his report.

'Did you hear that Rupert?' screeched Lady Celia. 'How exciting!'

'I am very distressed to 'ave to inform you, Your Lordship,' continued Constable Stubbs, 'that a number of quite valuable works of hart 'ave been stolen!'

*   *   *   *

The resulting gasps of horror could be heard quite clearly over in Main House, where Marcus Dent was recovering from his drug-induced stupor. From a position slouched over the chaise longue, his forehead buried in the ashtray, Dent let out a groan which nudged his cohort Spate from his coma. 'Are you alright, Spate?' he asked, rubbing ash from his eyes.

'I think so Marcus,' replied a groggy Spate, gathering himself up with some difficulty from the carpet.

'How long have we been out?'

'I have no idea. I can't see the clock for the room is still spinning.'

'My mouth is terribly dry.'

'So is mine.'

'I think I should like to sleep forever.'

'Me too.'

*   *   *   *

'And what about the Constable, Constable?' asked Lord Edgerton urgently.

'Peg pardon sir?' came the baffled reply.

'What did Fellowes say about the oil painting by Constable?', asked Lord Edgerton, more deliberately.

'Ah, I see.' Stubbs consulted his notebook at length, as many present shuffled impatiently in their seats. 'Would that be the *Boat Building Near Flatford Mill, 1814*, sir?'

'That's right, yes!'

'By one, John Constable of 'Ampstead?'

'Yes! Yes!'

'Oil on canvas?'

'Yes!'

'Gawn sir!'

'Good God.'

'Isn't this an absolute hoot?' whooped a revitalized Lady Celia, from her position next to Professor Beedon on the stage. 'I haven't had this much fun in years! Think of the insurance!'

'As, I am afraid,' continued Constable Stubbs, 'is the sculpture entitled *Torso Of A Young Girl With Serpent* by one August Rodin.' The assembled cognoscenti winced audibly at the policeman's shamelessly boorish pronunciation, and Lord Edgerton, mopping his brow with a silk handkerchief, made a mental note to instigate moves to have the policeman transferred elsewhere at the earliest opportunity. Professor Beedon, meanwhile, smiled serenely, lit his pipe and handed it on for Lady Celia to sample its pungent contents.

'What of the Gauguin?' enquired Lord Edgerton nervously.

'Would that be a Monsieur Paul Gauguin of Tahiti?'

'Yes, yes!'

'His woodcut of 1893 depictin' *Les Femmes A La Riviere?*'

'That's right!'

'Gawn, sir!'

Lord Edgerton, utterly deflated and with tears in his eyes, sank into his seat, placed both elbows on his knees and thrust his head into his hands. It appeared that most of his prized art treasures had been stolen, and if the present representative were anything to go by, the chances of the local constabulary retrieving them were negligible.

'What about my favourite, Rupert?' put in a giggling Lady Celia. 'that nice one with the pretty horses by...oh, whatsisname?'

'Stubbs.'

'Yes sir?'

'What about the Stubbs Constable Stubbs?'

'Beg pardon, sir?'

'The painting by George Stubbs!'

'George? George who sir?'

'George Stubbs, Constable! His name is also Stubbs!'

'Ah yes. According to your fellow...'

'Fellowes.'

'I only hinterviewed one member of your staff, Lord Hedgertond.'

'Constable Stubbs,' sighed the broken peer, 'the butler's name is Fellowes.'

'Indeed it is, sir.'

'Now, about the Stubbs, Constable?'

'Gawn sir.'

All present retained a stunned silence as they observed the grieving Lord writhing on stage, in a state of some considerable dismay. Indeed, the performance was so compelling that no-one noticed the arrival of Dent, Spate and Jimmy Swarthy as they insinuated themselves into the hall through a side door, eventually taking up a position at the rear of the auditorium.

'However,' exclaimed the constable, emerging confidently from his notebook, 'I do 'ave a suspect!'

'And who, pray, might that be?'

'A young kaffir whom I apprehended at the scene of the crime, so to speak.'

Urgent whisperings followed, in hot pursuit of this latest revelation, and a gaggle of boys had collected behind the policeman, craning their necks in an effort to glimpse the pages of his all-important notebook.

'And where is this fellow now?' asked Lord Edgerton.

'He was about to attack me, your Lordship, until I hincapacitated 'im with my truncheon.'

'Well done, Constable. And what has become of him?'

'Whilst hinterviewin' your fellow...Fellowes, I took the precaution of tying the sooty-faced blackguard to your bannister.'

'Good thinking. And is he still so restrained?'

'Not exactly, sir.'

'Not exactly?'

The constable shifted his weight guiltily and began fidgeting with his notebook. 'I used a double knot, Your Lordship' he pleaded, 'and sturdy twine...'

'Where is he, Constable Stubbs?'

'Gawn, sir.'

All present groaned loudly in a gesture of disappointed solidarity with the desperate Lord Edgerton.

'However,' resumed the policeman positively, 'I 'ave circulated 'is descriptiond by telephone and am confident that either 'e, or one of 'is tribesmen will be captured very soon, when they will be locked away in a police cell and tortured until they confess.' At this, the constable smiled resolutely, delighted with his evening's work.

'I don't think such drastic action will be necessary, Constable,' said a voice from the back of the hall.

'That's the maniac!' cried Stubbs, launching himself down the aisle towards Skimpton. Luckily though, a battalion of burly sixth-formers were seated nearby and managed to restrain the demented policeman from reaching his prey. As they propelled him back down the aisle, pinning him against the stage, Skimpton took a few steps forward. Studiously, he cleared his throat in preparation for the lengthy and detailed explanations which were to follow.

*　　*　　*　　*

'But why,' quizzed Lord Edgerton, some fifteen minutes later, 'are you attired in eighteenth-century apparel?'

'This was a disguise, Your Lordship,' explained Skimpton, 'adopted by another boy, by the name of Binns, I believe, to afford him access to the props table during the performance. I later caught him outside and was about to deliver him with a ticking off when I noticed Swarthy lurking in the staff motor-car parking area. We swapped costumes, I gave chase on my bicycle and he took my place in the play!'

His astonished inquisitor now turned his attention to Jimmy Swarthy, casually smoking at the rear of the auditorium. 'James Swarthy?' he quizzed.

'That's right, Your Honour.'

'Is this boy's testimony correct? Were you in the vicinity of the master's car parking area at the time stated?'

'Certainly not, Your Worship. I was with these gentlemen all night.'

'That is correct,' interposed Dent, 'Spate and I have been entertaining Mr. Swarthy in Main House all evening.'

'That's not true!' came a booming voice from behind the curtain. After he had fought a lengthy battle with the red velvet and barged onto the downstage area, Binns, for it was he, adopted one of his declamatory poses, intended to magnify the momentousness of his contribution. 'Swarthy's lying,' he declared, 'for I visited Dent's study during the interval!'

'What do you mean, Binns?' barked Dent.

'You told me to report back to you, don't you remember Marcus? That's what I'd been doing when Skimpton collared me in the quad.'

'And what did you find during this alleged visit to your schoolfellow's study?' demanded Lord Edgerton.

'Well, sir...' faltered Binns.

'Come on man, spit it out!'

'Dent and Spate dead to the world!'

'And Swarthy?'

'No sign of him sir!'

A further gasp was emitted by the audience as all eyes turned to Jimmy Swarthy. 'You're forgetting one thing,' he said, 'I couldn't possibly have nicked a car, like this boy says.'

'And why not?'

'I can't drive!' Swarthy then held up the grisly stump where his right hand had once been. 'How would I grasp hold of the gear stick with this?'

'That is precisely why,' pronounced Skimpton portentously, 'you required an accomplice!'

Amazed murmurs quickly circled the room, and Jimmy Swarthy began to look decidedly uneasy. Marcus Dent, sensing that it might be prudent to do so, moved a little distance away from his one-handed business partner, an expression of innocent bafflement having been quickly applied to his face.

'And do you have any idea of the identity of this confederate, young man?' asked Lord Edgerton, of Skimpton.

'My guess is,' replied he, 'that your butler Fellowes might well be worth investigating. For, listening to the constable's testimony earlier, it strikes me that, for someone of his station, Fellowes's knowledge of the Fine Arts appears rather too thorough. I would also go so far as to hazard that he is outside at this very moment, preparing to drive Mr. Swarthy and the booty away, confiscating Prof. Beedon's motor-van for the purpose!'

'The slimy little queer!' squealed Lady Edgerton, leaping from the stage with remarkable athleticism. 'Quick! Let's get him!'

'Not so fast Lady Celia!' chuckled Prof. Beedon from behind a cloud of rancid-smelling smoke. Some seconds later, when it had cleared, he was revealed to be flourishing both an uncharacteristically earnest expression, and a frighteningly convincing revolver, both of which were directed at Constable Stubbs. 'Nobody make a move,' he instructed, 'or Sherlock Holmes here gets it.'

It would be dishonest to report that no-one present considered tackling the Professor, regardless of – or indeed inspired by – the threatened consequences to the policeman. Indeed, Lord Edgerton quietly encouraged his wife to make an attempt, in the vain hope of killing three birds with one stone. But in the end, a combination of cowardice, indifference and a hint of old-fashioned humanitarianism took precedence; the stunned congregation sat in total silence as the Professor leaped from the stage and manhandled his quivering hostage to the door.

'Denys! Wait for me!' cried Jimmy Swarthy. 'I'm coming with you!'

So – that was the story, thought Skimpton: Swarthy and the communist Prof. in cahoots!

'I'm afraid not, Jimmy,' said Beedon, 'Where I am going there is no place for such as you.'

'But I thought we were partners!'

'In my line of business, one makes little distinction between the ruling and criminal classes.'

'But what about my paintings?' cried Lord Edgerton, his querulous voice saturated in anguish.

'You can rest assured,' said Beedon, breaking into another of his pathetic giggles, 'that your prized possessions will be ransomed and the proceeds forwarded to a radical socialist cause. Do not grieve for their loss, Lord Edgerton, for they will soon be recognized as the worthless baubles they have always been; the banal playthings of a bourgeois culture teetering on the edge of extinction. In fact, not dissimilar in kind to yourself and your lovely wife!'

'How dare you!' snarled Lady Celia. 'I have never been a worthless bauble. Rupert! Defend me from this scurrilous attack.'

'Shut up, Celia,' hissed Lord Edgerton, as all present gasped at the violence with which he delivered his rebuke.

'I see. You're going to allow this filthy little communist here to besmirch my name, are you?' Lady Celia's eyes were beginning to glaze over as the combination of alcohol and whatever Prof. Beedon had put in his pipe began to take their toll.

'Yes I am,' replied her husband flatly, 'for at the moment you are the least of my worries.'

'Of course, I had forgotten your precious paintings,' retorted Lady Celia. 'Well, I'll tell you, Rupert Edgerton, this is what I think of your precious paintings!' Then, before all present, she took off both her shoes and hurled them at her husband, hitting him squarely on the nose with both of them. She then launched herself at Beedon, who promptly stepped out of the way and allowed her to career head first into Piggot, who at that moment finally toppled, utterly exhausted, from the stage. (Although Piggot was eventually helped to his feet, Lady Celia was knocked unconscious in the fore-stage collision, where she lay until the following morning, when her husband finally got around to sending someone to pick her up.)

Pausing only to borrow a box of matches from an admiring sixth-former to light his infernal pipe, Prof. Beedon then made for the door. Dragging the quaking constable behind him, he disappeared into the darkness, roaring, 'Up The Revolution!' as he went.

'Quick! After them!' implored the Lord, blood dripping from his nose.

'Don't worry,' assured Skimpton, 'they won't get very far. I took the liberty of piercing a small hole in Prof. Beedon's petrol tank with my penknife. It should be almost empty by now.'

There then occurred an explosion of such magnitude that the Faysgarth School Hall fairly shook to its foundations, as, outside, a spark from Prof. Beedon's match ignited the petrol and ripped the motor van apart. When the building had stopped shaking, Lord Edgerton jumped to his feet, his face grey with trepidation, and gasped, 'My God! The paintings!'

The ensuing commotion was interrupted by the sensational re-appearance of a dishevelled Constable Stubbs, making his second dramatic entrance of the evening at the rear of the auditorium. His uniform in tatters, his face blackened by the explosion, he staggered the length of the hall and came to an heroic halt at the foot of the stage.

LORD EDGERTON: (*hopefully*) My paintings, Constable..?
STUBBS: (*dolefully*) I'm sorry, sir.
LORD EDGERTON: (*fearfully*) Not...
STUBBS: (*regretfully*) I'm afraid so, sir.
LORD EDGERTON: (*agonisingly*) You mean...
STUBBS: (*finally*) Gawn sir, yes.
SKIMPTON: (*inquisitively*) And Beedon?
STUBBS: (*triumphantly*) Blown to pieces sir!

The hall emptied in seconds as the assembled Faysgarthians made straight for the debris outside, where they fought viciously over grisly mementos of the scattered socialist. Skimpton, meanwhile, approached the sorry pile of rags which now constituted the local bobby. 'I suppose,' he said, 'I should scald you, Constable, for your stubborn obstructiveness earlier.' And then, making grim reference to their blackened features, added, 'But instead I shall proffer the hand of friendship and welcome you to the ranks of the Colonial Constabulary.'

*   *   *   *

The next morning found Skimpton in his darkened study propped up in bed, a mirror in his hand, ruefully examining both his bandaged crown and his murky complexion. The two head injuries he had sustained the previous night – one as a result of what he assumed to be an attack by Jimmy Swarthy, the other precipitated by what he knew was an assault at the hands of Constable Stubbs – had consolidated their presence in his skull overnight. Consequently, his head now throbbed with a dull persistence, and he had become acutely sensitive to any noise. It was with some urgency, then, that he dived for cover, placing a pillow around his ears, when a jaunty, voluble Jack Varley breezed into the room carrying with him a small package. 'Good morrow, noble sir!' declared he, expansively.

'Do you have to be so raucous, Jack?' pleaded Skimpton, venturing forth his face tentatively from beneath the blankets.

'Haven't managed to shift the makeup yet I see!'

'Colonel Coombes reckons the dye Binns added to it means I shall be stuck like this for at least a month!'

'What fun! What are you going to do in the hols, go out onto the streets and see if you are treated any differently as the result of your transformation?'

'If my reception by Constable Stubbs is anything to go by, I think I'll be better off staying in my room here at Faysgarth. They've given me permission since my father is away on business. Anyway, what news on *The Rialto*, Jack?'

Varley filled the kettle, placed it on the old primus and opened the curtains, the resulting shards of sunlight consigning Skimpton once more to his refuge under the blankets. 'Well, apparently,' enthused Varley, 'Prof. Beedon was no professor at all, neither was he a PhD!'

'Really?'

'According to Jimmy Swarthy, via Constable Stubbs, he wasn't even English but a Frenchman called Denis Laval! He'd been travelling around the country for some time securing employment in minor public schools such as Faysgarth, situated in wealthy areas, mounting ridiculous productions of classic plays, and then plundering the local houses of artworks, with the aid of the local villains, whilst the owners attended the shows! The proceeds of his crimes have supposedly helped finance social unrest in dozens of countries including Spain, Germany and his native France!'

'I say!'

Varley handed Skimpton a cup of sweet tea and fidgeted excitedly with the parcel he had brought with him. Sensing that Varley was desperate that he do so, Skimpton resisted the temptation to request that he reveal its contents. 'You haven't seen Piggot have you, Jack?' he asked instead, 'For I need him to run some errands for me.'

'Don't expect that little fellow to be around for a while, Skimpton,' came the reply.

'Why not?'

'He seems to have struck it lucky with Barney Binns, who's offered him a part in his next musical, *What's Up Jack?* or something like that. Sounds highly questionable.'

'Good Lord.'

'As for Binns Junior, he was foolish enough to confide in his father over his part in Dent's dirty tricks campaign. As a result, it looks as though he'll be keeping you company at Faysgarth over the forthcoming hols.'

'What? Why?'

'Binns's father reported him to Colonel Coombes, who's issued him with three quarters of a million lines for fooling about in the chemistry lab – to be completed before next term!'

'Good show!'

Varley settled into Skimpton's armchair and mused for a few moments over the remarkable events of the previous day. 'I must say, though, Skimpton,' he owned, 'it was uncommonly bright of you to catch Swarthy out like that. However, it puzzles me to know what made you so sure he had an accomplice?'

'I wasn't certain at first, but when he held up his right arm by way of proof that he could not manoeuvre a gear stick I knew I had him cornered.'

'How exactly?'

'You see, only in the case of a left-hand drive vehicle would Swarthy's disability have mattered – with reference to a gear stick, anyway. I hadn't at that point mentioned Prof. Beedon's French motor-van as being the one used in the robbery, so Swarthy's brandishing of his right stump, rather than proving his innocence, implicated him in the crime beyond all reasonable doubt! Besides, I then realized that I'd seen him getting into the vehicle via the right-hand passenger door – indicating that someone else was probably in there already and took responsibility for the driving!'

'Pity you pointed the finger at the wrong man, though, Skimpton.'

'You can't have everything, Jack, and that Fellowes fellow did seem a trifle rum. Remember though, I had placed my trust in Prof. Beedon, for as director of the play he had been responsible for getting me up on stage and delivering a rattling performance!'

'He was, however, also culpable of sneaking out during the interval, driving off to do the burglary with Swarthy, and returning to the school hall just in time to give his thank-you speech!'

'Exactly. It was a most ingenious plan. The audience imagined he was backstage trying to get the performance back on the rails, whilst the cast assumed he was in the auditorium schmoozing with his pals! Meanwhile, Swarthy knocks the ruffians out with drugs and drink, and nips off to do the robbery. After which, he then returns to Main House just as the chaps are regaining consciousness, with a watertight alibi. What they didn't bargain on, though, was Binns returning to Dent's study during the interval, and finding Jimmy Swarthy absent.'

'Precisely. But why, Skimpton, did you not send word with Binns that you were giving chase? That way all that nonsense with Constable Stubbs might have been avoided?'

'I gave him strict instructions to inform you of my intentions, Jack, but the silly chump must have been so preoccupied with getting into character that he forgot! Just shows what happens when you rely on one of Marcus Dent's cronies, especially one as stage-struck as the pea-brained Binns.'

'Speaking of whom, that bounder Dent will be mightily dismayed at having lost all his winnings from the gambling club.'

'You know, Jack, I feel it was almost worth seeing those works of art go up in smoke just to catch sight of Dent's face when he realized that Swarthy had robbed him, and that all his filthy money had been destroyed in the explosion.'

'You are such a philistine, Skimpton.'

'But not a bad detective though, eh Jack?'

'Indeed. I take my hat off to you in that respect.'

Varley poured more tea, and remembered the packet of Garibaldi biscuits in his pocket. He took out a couple and ate them greedily before presenting Skimpton with the package he had brought with him.

'What's this?' said Skimpton.

'It is a present for you,' came the jocular reply.

'Great pip! What on earth is it?'

'Open it. I won thirty shillings on the football pools this week, Skimpton, so I have bought you a chess set.'

The sports champion manufactured a grim smile. 'Wonderful!' he said wanly, removing the wrapping.

'I thought it might keep you out of trouble! What about a game? I'll teach you the rules. Clear the desk!'

'What...right away?'

'Why not?' Varley opened the board eagerly and emptied out the pieces. 'Now,' he said, 'who's black and who's white...'

FOUR

ON THE ROPES!

'Ah, Skimpton,' said Marcus Dent, his voice betraying a hint of nervousness as he showed his schoolfellow into his study, 'I thought you might drop by. Some refreshment? I am afraid I have only water at the moment, can I get you a glass?'

It was early evening at a troubled Faysgarth, the darkness beginning to descend like a conspiracy of silence, concealing a multitude of sins.

'No thanks,' came the reply.

Dent seated himself on a simple wooden box in his study, from where he indicated that Skimpton should make use of an upturned milk crate near the window.

The School Scoundrel's room was eerily sparse in appearance, a far cry from the brash opulence that was said to comprise, until recently, Dent's living quarters. Skimpton had heard many times of the groaning bookshelves, heavy with popular magazines and racy detective novels, to say nothing of the famous drinks cabinet teeming with exotic concoctions. He had seen the effects of Dent's collection of disturbing hand-coloured etchings depicting scenes in a lunatic asylum, the mere sight of which had been enough to disturb the equilibrium of a number of younger Faysgarthians unfortunate enough to find themselves in their presence. Skimpton had heard, too, of Dent's jaguar skin rug, his sumptuous four-poster bed, and ostentatious chandelier, supposedly looted from the Amber Palace in Jaipur. And, of course, there was the bounder's exquisite chaise longue, from which the filthy rotter had masterminded so many of his troublesome campaigns.

Today, though, all were conspicuous by their absence, and as Skimpton surveyed the room, bereft of its adornments, and illuminated by a single candle – placed in a saucer in the middle of the floor – he almost felt the walls heaving and moaning about him, pleading for help.

Dent, seeking temporary respite from the unease he felt at Skimpton's presence in such threadbare surroundings, rolled a cigarette. Placing it nervously between his lips, the tobacco tumbling clumsily from its tip, he lit a match and began smoking in the presence of the Deputy Head Boy. Skimpton, though, chose to disregard this blatant breach of school regulations, for, almost despite himself – and for the first time in his life – he had begun to feel sympathy for the wretched figure who was once his most powerful and fervent adversary.

Over in Second House, Skimpton's young fag Piggot gazed pensively over the gloom-laden quad, the chapel bell echoing into the chilly evening. Like a ghoul emerging from behind a tombstone, the moon appeared and illuminated the youngster's face at the window of Skimpton's study. A single tear now tracing its way down his cheek, Piggot – his ears still ringing from the severe beating he had just received – slowly lowered himself to the floor and began sobbing quietly. He wept not only for himself but for the school he loved, now transformed into an unrecognizably infernal domain, devoid of humanity. For Piggot, there was no escaping the fact that Faysgarth had become a place of misery and brutal oppression for himself and so many of his schoolfellows.

A few miles to the east, across the rolling Monktonshire Downs, lies the small market town of Faverstock. With its streets of Georgian houses, dotted with half-timbered Tudor residences, it is considered by many to be the most idyllic in the county. Its police station, situated near the old Wool Exchange, rarely finds itself embroiled in any investigation more serious than the odd minor motor accident or the loss of an household pet. Fortunately so, for the local constable – PC Albert Stubbs – was not thought by many to be a man of enormous investigative capacity. This meant that when a crime of any significance did occur, cerebral reinforcements were invariably called from headquarters in nearby Barnchester.

In the case of the recent murder enquiry at Faysgarth School, a diminutive Detective Inspector by the name of Haddock had been assigned the case, somewhat reluctantly uprooting himself from his desk to lead the hunt for the killer.

The chief suspect, a senior boy from the school by the name of Spate, had been questioned at length by the insouciant detective, but since the victim's body had disappeared soon after the alleged crime, and before it had been properly examined for clues, he had returned to Barnchester with a feeling that little more could be done. This left the impercipient Constable Stubbs in charge of the case, and he was in no mood to let a suspected murderer loose on the community without being certain that it was safe to do so.

To this end, PC Stubbs had manufactured a charge involving the theft of a number of bicycles, and persuaded a local Magistrate, the aging Justice Pimbleton-Daze, to remand the boy pending further enquiries. After all, reckoned the portly custodian, how could he possibly consider releasing an individual who had been seen committing a brutal murder by a reliable witness? For, although the corpse had yet to be retrieved, it would only be a matter of time before the guilty youth would be brought to justice, and invited to acquaint himself with the hangman's noose. The suspect had turned eighteen a week before the crime was committed, a fact the policeman had established with some delight very soon after the arrest had been made.

For his part, Spate had begun to view himself as something of a permanent resident in the tiny cell which had been his home for the last three months. Seated on a plain, wooden bench opposite his equally spartan bed, Spate now occupied his time filling out the many complicated forms which comprised his corpulent captive's official paperwork.

Laying down his pen for a moment, he drifted towards the tiny barred window, his eyes roaming listlessly in the direction of a distant steeple, its dissonant bells singing out across the pastures. With a feeling of longing, the young man could just make out the buildings immediately behind the chapel as belonging to his school, Faysgarth, and he sighed, quite unaware of the precise reasons why he should at present be detained in such dreary surroundings. For, even more seriously than the others, Spate found himself yet another victim of the appalling turn of events which had in recent months swirled around Faysgarth like a particularly malevolent virus. A catastrophic regime of persecution which had left the school's pupils and staff – in Piggot's case literally – on their knees.

To explain this unfortunate state of affairs, it is necessary to recount in some detail the events of the previous quarter, starting with the school's boxing championships in March. For it was then that the sorry sequence of events began; the malicious and ill-conceived plotting which would leave Skimpton and so many of his schoolfellows well and truly 'on the ropes'!

*   *   *   *

'And now, Ladies and Gentlemen,' announced Colonel Coombes, into the microphone which had been lowered from the ceiling of Faysgarth village hall, 'it is indeed my pleasure to introduce – or present – to you, now, the final bout – or contest – of the evening. As many of you present will know from previous years, at this point in the proceedings we select a member of the audience to do battle with one of our finest contenders.'

The usual derisory applause greeted the short-sighted Colonel's characteristically long-winded address, for – as was his custom when nerves took hold during public pronouncements – the hopeless chemistry dolt was tiresomely dispensing synonyms like unwarranted detentions. 'As is customary,' he continued, 'I shall now ask – or request – that the hall lights be lowered so that I might pick out – or select – the volunteer with my flashlight!'

Skimpton, who had already seen off his opponent in the middleweight division inside the first two minutes, had showered and changed briskly, and was seated in the audience between his chum Jack Varley and a rather lumpy fifth-former by the name of Tubby Malkin. With a trophy already under his belt, Skimpton was content to be excluded from the concluding contest, which usually provided an amusing finale to the evening's activities. The young sports supremo was consulting his programme gleefully, trying to ascertain which of the evening's successful pugilists was down to tackle the unlucky volunteer, when the lights flickered off.

'Just one moment, everyone!' cried the dim-sighted professor as he searched for his flashlight. 'I'll be just a moment!'

Ninety pitch-black seconds later, amid good humoured cat-calls, the hopelessly myopic chemistry man located the switch on his torch and directed its beam across the excited crowd. After dithering briefly on various boys, all of whom unvaliantly pleaded ineligibility through ill-health, the light finally settled on an uncomfortable Tubby Malkin, squirming in his seat beside Skimpton. 'But sir!' pleaded the podgy youngster, 'I can't possibly fight, I'm far too fat!'

'Nonsense,' retorted the Colonel amid howls of delight, 'dispatch yourself to the changing rooms immediately and climb into your togs!'

'But sir, I haven't got any!'

'Then borrow some, you fool! Now get on with it before I'm tempted to issue you with lines for unmanliness!'

Tubby Malkin was an unpopular boy, mainly because of his disgusting personal habits and pusillanimous nature. Indeed, some even thought him quite the most repulsive young man ever to pass through the gates of Faysgarth, and as a result, he had been bullied mercilessly since his arrival at the school. Quickly set apart as something of a loner, he made friends in his third year with a German boy who was later withdrawn by his parents to join a group in his homeland known as *The Edelweiss Pirates*, a particularly gruesome division of the Hitler Youth which specialised in interrogation methods for the under-nines.

Since that brief, yet intense, liaison, Malkin had succeeded in antagonising his schoolfellows with his irritating attempts to ingratiate himself into their company, to such an extent that many had taken to ignoring him completely. Indeed, on one occasion when the youngster was trapped up a tree in Dead Man's Wood, his pleas for assistance fell on deaf ears for a day and a half. Wilf, the groundsman, finally took pity on Malkin and accommodated the youngster in his growlery for a week of strenuous convalescence.

It was as a result of one of Malkin's pitiful displays of grovelling that the fleshy fifth-former had contrived, at the night of the Boxing Championships, to place himself in the seat next to Skimpton. His hope was that, as the most well-liked boy in the school, some of Skimpton's popularity might rub off on himself. To no avail though, for as the sports champion propelled a reluctant Tubby in the direction of the changing rooms, it was amid as raucous a chorus of disapproval as the unpleasant youngster had ever experienced.

'Look,' said Skimpton, manhandling his writhing charge through the doorway, 'just protect yourself as best you can and wait for an opening. Your opponent is a particularly beastly individual named Spate, one of Marcus Dent's pals. Now, he's likely to try various underhand tricks, but he is a flyweight, so you should have no trouble using your not inconsiderable bulk to repel his attack.'

'But Skimpton,' pleaded the flabby yellow belly, 'I'm not used to violence, I've only ever utilised it against animals, and then only very small ones!'

'Rubbish,' came the stern reply, 'put these on.' Using safety pins, Skimpton had constructed an enormous pair of trunks from an old Union Jack which was lying about, and was now looking around for something with which to fashion a singlet.

'But Skimpton,' protested Malkin weakly, 'can't I wear your kit?'

'Not a chance. It would never fit you. Besides, I don't relish having to clean the resulting mess from my togs once Spate has burst those abominable facial lesions of yours. Now here, put this on.' Skimpton held out a section of carpet from which he'd chopped a hole for the boy's head. Tubby gave out a rancid-smelling sigh and pulled on the appallingly improvised vestment.

'I thank you for your assistance, Skimpton,' said the fatty, passing wind nervously, 'but I am really not sure if I can go through with all this.'

'Nonsense. Look, if you back out now the Colonel will be livid, and there's no telling what he might do to you in that kind of mood. How about if I pledge you a topping feed if you win, what do you say to that?'

'I think I should rather starve.'

'Don't be a silly chump. Now put this round your waist.' Skimpton helped Tubby loop a length of string around the dilapidated remnant, securing it tightly about the youngster with a double reef knot.

'But Skimpton,' gasped Tubby, 'I can hardly breathe.'

'Don't be a sissy. This way, you see, your carpet won't get frayed during clinches.'

Spate was already waiting in the ring, dancing about and punching the air daintily, when Tubby Malkin appeared. The crowd whooped with hilarity as the combined strength of five burly sixth-formers struggled to hoist the bloated contender onto the canvas. Sullenly, Malkin made straight for his corner and placed his enormous behind resentfully onto the stool, breaking it in half.

'Now look,' said Skimpton, arriving at his side, 'there may be quite a bit of barracking from the crowd, but try to take no notice. Just do as I have said and you will be alright.'

'But Skimpton,' argued the monstrous coward, 'Spate hates me – you can see it in his eyes!' Skimpton found it difficult to disagree, for there, only three feet away, was his malevolent opponent, perfectly still, glaring menacingly at Malkin. Although slight of frame, Spate made a convincing boxer with a compact frame, muscular arms and a powerful neck, some three inches wider than his head. He was a sinister fellow at the best of times, who carried about him a seething violence which surfaced spectacularly once he had removed his school uniform and donned the togs of a pugilist.

Presently, Colonel Coombes brought together the two schoolfellows in the middle of the ring and embarked on a lengthy summation of the rules. With this characteristically protracted lecture threatening to prolong the evening's activities beyond their allotted time, an impatient young Faysgarthian on the front row decided to take matters into his own hands and rang the bell for the first round. 'Good Lord!' laughed Jack Varley, as the Colonel hastily exited the ring, and the two fellows commenced the contest, 'what on earth is Malkin wearing?'

'I think that it might be described as a badly worn carpet!' quipped Skimpton.

'Indeed,' chuckled Varley, somewhat surprised at the ingeniousness of his chum's wit.

The flabby fifth-former had anchored himself squarely in the centre of the ring in a pool of perspiration, with his gloves around his head for protection, and it was in this position that he remained throughout the first round. By contrast, the sprightly Spate was hopping about like a kangaroo, jabbing and teasing his opponent, much to the joyous amusement of the crowd.

Wobbly handfuls of Tubby's grey flesh had begun to poke through holes in the carpet as Spate dealt his adversary several vicious body blows in the final seconds. As the bell sounded, Tubby presented a sorry sight to the assembled Faysgarthians; his Union Jack trunks had all but disintegrated around him and large sections of the carpet had been wrenched from his person by spectators, and strewn about the ring. Bruised, battered, semi-naked and humiliated, the friendless fifth-former threw himself to the floor in his corner.

'Good show, Tubby!' encouraged Skimpton, unconvincingly. 'You are putting up a simply super fight. If I'm any judge you are ahead on points!'

'Skimpton,' gasped the exhausted youngster, far from convinced, 'I think I should much rather die than go out for the second round.'

'Oh, for Mercy's sake man,' returned Skimpton impatiently, 'you've soaked up more punishment in one round than many chaps take in a year – and you're still on your feet! Look: wait until Spate starts larking about for the crowd, which knowing him he surely will, then simply bash him on the snout!'

But, prostrate in his corner, Tubby Malkin was showing distinct signs of imminent collapse, and it was only with the aid of strong smelling salts that his eager trainer was able to revive the heavyweight contender for the second round. 'Careful with your feet, Tubby,' cried a third-former, 'and don't trip over the carpet!'

The second round progressed very much as had the first, with Tubby firmly rooted to the middle of the ring, and his opponent dancing energetically around him. With a few moments left to the bell, Spate, having choreographed an impressively balletic manoeuvre across the canvas and landing a fearful blow to Tubby's spine, began pleasing the crowd further with an extraordinary display of acrobatics. A series of spectacular somersaults interspersed with dainty left jabs at his adversary's head, followed by a magnificent back flip, left a grinning Spate straining on tiptoes, awaiting his applause. It was then that Tubby Malkin decided to offer his only punch of the bout. Withdrawing his left arm out of sight of his prancing opponent, the fatty brought it round and smashed it with astonishing power into the back of Spate's head, sending the flashy flyweight literally soaring through the air and out of the ring. All eyes looked on in silent amazement as they followed Spate's broken body as it flew over the crowd and crashed to earth face-down in the region of row five!

'Bless my soul!' mouthed a stunned Jack Varley. 'That was some sock on the bean!' Moments later, Skimpton led a victorious if slightly confused Tubby Malkin in complete silence from the ring. Down the aisle they walked, startled Faysgarthians lining the route, their mouths agape, past the shattered remains of his opponent and into the dressing rooms.

'Now then, champ,' said Skimpton once they were inside, 'I vote we retire to my study for a jolly good feed, what?'

*   *   *   *

'I say! Are all those travel books yours, Skimpton?' enquired Tubby, nosing about the older boy's bookshelves some time later.

'They are indeed,' came the laconic reply, 'I intend becoming an explorer when I grow up.'

'How frightfully ambitious of you! I'm marked down for a career in the Civil Service, I'm afraid. Not much excitement there.'

Skimpton was reclining on his bed pretending to read a novel. Satisfied that he had fulfilled his culinary obligations with regard to the voracious fifth-former, he now awaited – with receding patience – Tubby's departure. For his part, the visitor had polished off all Skimpton's provisions in seconds, and now prowled the study searching for any excuse to remain.

'You have so many trophies and medals, Skimpton,' whinged

the less popular of the two, 'I do so wish I were successful like you, but I am afraid I lack confidence.' As he spoke, Malkin seemed forever to be scratching his face and toying with his pimples, a habit Skimpton found frankly disgusting. 'You see, Skimpton,' he continued, now poking at his nose and discarding the resulting detritus onto the floor, 'people don't seem to like me, and I can't for the life of me fathom why.'

At this point, his host resolved to ignore the boy and his repugnant mannerisms, in the hope that he would realize that his presence was no longer welcome, and take himself off. No such luck, though, for the beast seemed intent on punishing Skimpton further with his company. 'Can I get you anything?' he fawned, 'a cup of tea, perhaps?'

'No thanks. As a matter of fact, Tubby, I shall be retiring to bed pretty soon.'

'Don't mind me, I'll just potter about. Is that *Around The World In Eighty Days* you are reading?' persisted the wretched sycophant. 'I've read that thirteen times, you know. Would you like me to tell you what happens in the end?'

'No thank you, Tubby,' interrupted Skimpton crisply, 'I think I should prefer to enjoy the conclusion of the book myself.'

'I do so love reading. I'm racing through a rather weighty tome at the moment by an Austrian fellow called...'

'I don't think I've heard of him.'

'I adore movies, too. Have you by any chance seen a German film entitled *Triumph Of The Will?*'

'Look,' said Skimpton, closing his book, 'if you don't mind, I'd like to go to bed now.'

'Of course. I shall come back to-morrow and we can discuss politics. Have you heard of Oswald Mosley?'

'No.'

'What about the National Socialists in Germany?'

'Please, Tubby, just leave me in peace.'

'I hear there are some very interesting developments in Italy at the moment.'

'GET OUT!'

'Have you read Nietzsche by any chance?'

Skimpton then forced the door closed on Tubby Malkin, bolted it and rolled onto his bed. Outside in the corridor, the fanatic continued to spout for some five minutes before he was ejected from the building by a group of irate housemates. As silence descended at last, Skimpton gave out a momentous sigh of relief and closed his eyes, only to be startled a few seconds later by the sound of Tubby's voice echoing around the quad. 'Skimpton's my chum!' was his triumphant cry. 'Listen to me everybody! God Save The King! Skimpton's my chum!'

*   *   *   *

Early the next morning, Skimpton was woken by an unwelcome knock at the door. It was seven-thirty and barely light when he staggered to his feet to greet Tubby Malkin carrying a tray and dripping water onto the floor. 'I have brought you breakfast, Skimpton,' he beamed, 'and have taken a freezing shower in an attempt to rid my skin of its unsightly pallor.'

Skimpton squinted at his tormentor through flickering eyelids, weary with sleep. In the grey, early morning light Tubby's explosive complexion looked if anything worse than usual. 'This is very kind of you, Tubby,' yawned the House Captain, 'but I do have a fag who takes care of these things for me.'

'But I have just cycled down to the village to procure fresh rolls from the bakery!'

'Very well. Come in.'

Tubby stayed until eight-thirty, chattering incessantly about nothing of any importance, then followed Skimpton to Full School Assembly where he placed himself beside the sportsman on the front row of Second House. He appeared again at lunch and then at dinner, promising to pop over to Skimpton's study later that evening for a chat about Richard Wagner and the German romantic poets Ludwig Uhland and Joseph von

Eichendorff. Skimpton sought refuge in Jack Varley's room.

'The thing is, Jack,' he lamented, 'the monster's latched onto me, convinced I'm his friend. He keeps trying to entice me to political meetings in Faverstock and I just can't shake him off!'

'Calm down old boy,' reassured Varley, 'things can't be that bad. Here, enjoy a fruit bonbon and relax.'

Skimpton settled himself on his friend's bed, unwrapped the sweetie and popped it smartly into his mouth, luxuriating in the tangy flavour as the liquid interior escaped its crunchy coating. 'You don't know what he's like, Jack. He keeps going on about these black-shirted fellows all the time, and I'm afraid I haven't the faintest idea what he's talking about.'

'And I'm sure neither does he, half the time. Don't worry yourself, Skimpton. In my experience if you ignore these chaps for long enough, they eventually drift away.'

'If only I could be sure that were the case with Tubby.'

'Look, Skimpton, let's try and forget about Tubby for the time being, shall we? I am sure there are more interesting topics of conversation. Lemon tart?'

'Rather.'

Varley was reaching into his tuck box for a napkin when there was an abrupt knock at the door. Skimpton jumped to his feet instantly. 'Don't answer it Jack,' he hissed, 'for I know it to be Tubby!'

'Leave this to me.'

'I know you are in there, Skimpton,' hollered the unwanted intruder through the keyhole. Smartly, Varley approached the door and opened it a couple of inches, discovering Tubby Malkin on his knees in the corridor.

'Just what exactly do you think you are doing?' he enquired loftily.

'Ah, Varley,' intoned the pest, struggling to his feet and feigning condescension, 'I was looking for my skum Chimpton... I mean my chum Skimpton. He isn't in there by any chance, is he?'

'I am afraid not,' came the stern reply. 'Skimpton is elsewhere cramming for his Latin and wished me to request that you seek company elsewhere for the next few months.'

'He hates me, doesn't he?' said Tubby, sulkily.

'Not in the least. He merely requires a period of isolation so as to concentrate on his school work.'

'He's just like the others,' blurted the bloated fifth-former, 'pretends to be a decent fellow and then turns into a stinking Judas!'

'I say, steady on there!' returned a rattled Jack Varley. 'I won't have language like that in Second House. If you want to speak of a fellow Faysgarthian in that way I suggest you take up residence in the sewers, where I am sure the vermin will keep you company.'

'And you are no better,' snarled the young brute, undaunted. 'I know what you get up to in your free periods, with young Parr down at the long-jump pit. But I'll show you! I'll show you all!'

By this time, the corridor had filled with boys, eager to offer their housemate encouragement in his feud with the most hated individual at Faysgarth. Buoyed by their presence, Varley ventured forth a forceful response to Tubby's accusations. 'Now watch what you are saying, Malkin,' he stated, 'or I might very well punch your spotty face for you!'

'Oh yes?' sneered the fatty. 'Well, you'd better be careful or you'll end up in hospital like the last fellow who tried!' He then turned his attention to the other boys present. 'And you chaps had better watch out, too,' he said, 'for I know all about what goes on after lights out in Second House too!'

Varley then stepped out into the corridor, his face fairly steaming with fury. 'Look, just get out, you footling little nitwit,' he demanded wrathfully 'before I kick your backside for you!'

'I'm going,' jeered Malkin, 'but I warn you, all of you, you are all going to come a cropper one of these days, you...you...you beastly load of buggers!'

Varley waited until he heard the outside door slammed shut

before returning, somewhat shaken, to his room.

'Well,' commented a thoughtful Skimpton, 'that turned out to be rather a shindy. Plum?'

'No thanks.' Varley, evidently still unsettled by the encounter, perched on the end of the bed, his back to Skimpton, and waited a few seconds until he had regained some of his composure. 'Something must be done about that boy,' he said presently, 'and soon.'

'I agree,' said Skimpton. 'But what?'

* * * *

In the event, it was left to Marcus Dent's vicious confederate Spate to deal with the luckless Tubby. Furious at the beating he had taken in the boxing ring earlier in the week, Spate returned from Barnchester Royal Infirmary fully recovered and determined to teach his erstwhile opponent a lesson. To this end, he thrashed Malkin so comprehensively with a rounders bat that the ill-fated fifth-former died of his injuries.

Varley, who witnessed the assault on his way to cricket practice in the gym, alerted Colonel Coombes, who promptly pronounced the victim deceased after a fruitless search for the boy's pulse. The police were immediately telephoned, and soon after the arrival of Constable Stubbs from Faverstock, the body was moved to the staff room, awaiting the arrival of a doctor.

A statement was taken from Jack Varley, whose cogent and precise account of events greatly impressed the constable, and shortly afterwards Spate was placed under arrest and taken off to Faverstock Police Station for further questioning.

It would be inaccurate to report that either Skimpton or the majority of his schoolfellows took any delight in the demise of Tubby Malkin, nor indeed the removal of his young murderer, Spate, from the school. Yet to imply that anyone expended a great deal of concern on either of them would be dishonest. In any case, there was little opportunity to dwell on the issue, since events took an even stranger turn the following morning.

It was Piggot who brought Skimpton up-to-date on the way to Full School Assembly. 'I say, Skimpton!' hooted the youngster, his protruding teeth thrust forward gleefully, 'have you heard the latest?'

A certain relief at being spared further contact with the awful Tubby Malkin, thanks to Spate's violent intervention, meant that Skimpton had slept soundly the previous night and – having risen late – was crossing the quad without having spoken to anyone that morning. 'If you mean Spate's killing of Tubby Malkin,' he snorted, 'then yes, I have.'

'You don't know the half of it,' returned Piggot. 'Malkin's body has disappeared from the staff room!'

'Didn't the ambulance arrive to take it away?'

'It suffered a flat tyre outside Barnchester and didn't get here until midnight. By that time the corpse had simply gone.'

'Then it is obvious what has happened: Dent has stolen it in an attempt to get his chum off the murder charge.'

'He denies it flatly, having already denounced his friend as a monstrous killer who should be locked up forever. Besides, Constable Stubbs has already conducted a thorough search of the bounder's quarters, with no result. Colonel Coombes has cancelled games and intends organizing a vigorous exploration of the school grounds this afternoon.'

Skimpton stopped abruptly, for never in his years at Faysgarth had he heard of so preposterous a narrative. He'd been party to, and even suffered the consequences of, many of the Colonel's potty gimmicks in the past, but this project quite took the biscuit – and all because of a measly missing cadaver! 'CANCELLED GAMES?' he exclaimed. 'WHATEVER NEXT?'

'Apparently, the constable's keeping Spate under lock and key pending further enquiries.'

'Good for him. Let's hope for all our sakes that his investigations are of the long and drawn out variety, for – as far as I am concerned – the middle of the next millennium would be too early to consider Spate for release. That brute needs to be taught a lesson. You can't go around battering people to death with sports equipment just because they happen to be miserable little toadies, Piggot! You'd wipe out three quarters of the Foreign Office if that were the case!'

'Perhaps that might not be such a bad thing, Skimpton.'

'Possibly, but not here at Faysgarth. Think of the scandal that has been brought upon the school.'

'There have already been newspaper reporters from Barnchester asking questions.'

'Well, there you are.'

'But Colonel Coombes sent them packing. Told them they should get proper jobs and stop wasting everyone's time.'

'Quite right. Look, Piggot,' said Skimpton rather painfully, 'you wouldn't mind getting me some aspirin, would you? I'm afraid this business is beginning to get on top of me somewhat.'

*   *   *   *

Throughout the remainder of the day, school conducted its affairs in a suitably restrained manner, all mention of the previous day's grisly events having been strictly forbidden. As a result, meals were taken in strained silence and school work tackled without much enthusiasm, as boys struggled to suppress their longing to discuss the week's dramatic incidents.

Colonel Coombes's search party failed to locate Tubby Malkin's corpse, as everyone predicted, even after a three-hour exploration of the school grounds. Constable Stubbs, accompanied by a decidedly unimpressive police officer of limited stature named Haddock, carried out further interviews with Jack Varley, to very little consequence. In the absence of any body to speak of, the miniature detective returned with negligible reluctance to the comfort of his office in Barchester, leaving rather vague instructions for Constable Stubbs to keep him informed of any developments.

That night, it was a somewhat subdued Skimpton who

turned in early. Finding Mr. Jules Verne's narrative somewhat lacking in excitement compared to recent events at Faysgarth, he discarded his book and drifted off to sleep.

Later that night, as the brave young explorer was dreaming of hacking his way through the dense undergrowth, deep in the Tibetan jungle, Skimpton was disturbed by a tap-tap-tapping sound which appeared to be emanating from a nearby tree. Halting abruptly, he turned about and eyed with some suspicion the column of strapping Masai warriors, specially requisitioned for the expedition from reliable suppliers, and after waiting a few seconds, proceeded with caution.

Tap-tap-tap.

Once again, he stopped, the sinister sounds of the jungle bearing down on him from all sides.

Tap-tap-tap.

A young black boy appeared at his side, seemingly arriving from nowhere, and handed him an envelope. 'Sahib,' he gasped, 'this is for you.' Skimpton took the letter, opened it swiftly with his knife and unfolded the crisp white paper. It was a short, handwritten note on official stationery, and read:

> *My Dear Skimpton,*
> *I fear your life may be in danger, please send word of your*
> *position immediately.*
> *Regards,*
> *Clement Jamamal, Governor.*

Tap-tap-tap. Tap-tap-tap.

Skimpton woke with a start, the insistent rhythm forcing its way into his consciousness. Slipping silently from between the sheets, he made his way cautiously across the floor in the direction of the noise. Pulling open the curtain, he was confronted with a sight so hideous, so terrifying that for a moment he was convinced that he must still be dreaming. For there, outside in the darkness, its distorted features thrust against the glass, was an horrific slimy presence, its ghoulish face glistening in the moonlight, its hair matted in scabrous streaks across its pate, its manic eyes glaring inwards from the gloom. Skimpton gave out a petrified shriek and retreated into the room, for he could now see that the appalling creature was making a desperate and determined attempt to gain entrance. At that moment, having pushed open the window, it spoke in tones which were immediately recognizable. 'Can I come in, Skimpton?' asked the beast.

'Tubby Malkin!' exclaimed Skimpton. 'What on earth are you doing here? We thought you were murdered!'

'Not really,' laughed the reincarnated fifth-former, climbing in with his briefcase, 'I feigned my own death, you see! Isn't it a simply topping jape?'

'You are a perfect menace, Malkin,' rasped a furious Skimpton. 'Go and report your existence to the authorities immediately.'

'Do you think I might have something to eat?' asked the brute, dripping filthy slime onto the carpet. 'For I have been mostly hiding in the sewers since last night and there's not much down there apart from excrement, and I didn't fancy partaking of any of that, even in the present circumstances.' Tubby made straight for Skimpton's recently replenished tuck box and began scoffing the contents like he hadn't eaten for weeks. 'I did find the body of an old boy down there, though,' he added, casually.

'What!!?'

'I thought I might have been able to feed on him until closer inspection revealed that the rats had already picked his bones dry.'

'Who was he, for Heaven's sake?'

'I can't be sure, but do you remember a boy named Miles Brody?'

'About your age, disappeared last year?'

'That's the fellow, I suspect it was him. He's pretty well rotted away now, but I think I recognized his spectacles.' Tubby then produced a rather rusty old pair of wire-rimmed glasses from his pocket and thrust them at Skimpton, who withdrew immediately. 'My guess is he fell down a manhole and never made it back.'

'What a perfectly ghastly story,' said Skimpton squeamishly. 'Now, as soon as you've finished that pork pie you can tidy yourself up and report to Colonel Coombes.'

'Oh, I shan't be doing that,' said the other resolutely.

'And why not?'

'Because I must continue with my Master Plan, of course!'

'And what might that be, might I ask?'

'I will tell you later. In the meantime, look at this.' Tubby flicked open his briefcase, emptied out a half pint of grimy sewage and pulled from it a large wad of soiled banknotes.

'Crikey!' ejaculated Skimpton. 'There must be hundreds of pounds there!'

'Fifteen thousand in all, as a matter of fact. I drew it from my bank account in Faverstock yesterday. This money was left to me by my adopted parents before they disappeared. It is meant to pay for the remainder of my education and secure me a comfortable position in the Ministry of Agriculture and Fisheries.'

'What has all this to do with me?'

'Because, Skimpton, if you help me with my Master Plan, then five hundred of it will be yours!'

'I want nothing of your money, Malkin, nor your so-called Master Plan.'

Tubby looked momentarily crestfallen, though Skimpton was unsure quite whether he was the cause of this disappointment or it was as a result of his uninvited guest having just finished off the last of his food. Presently, Malkin turned to Skimpton, and, with an earnest look on his face, explained, 'I am an orphan, Skimpton, with neither friends nor family to look after me. This is my very last chance to make something of myself before disappearing into the obscurity of the Civil Service. As a budding explorer I am sure you understand my desire to achieve something and gain a little respect from my peers. I ask only for the opportunity to explain my intentions to you, and then you may make up your own mind whether or not you are prepared to assist me.'

Skimpton viewed, with considerable suspicion, the pitiful excuse for a Faysgarthian standing before him. Tubby Malkin looked frankly unspeakable as he dripped foul-smelling substances onto the floor, his battered face covered in dried blood from the beating he had received the previous day, his grubby fingers toying nervously with the banknotes. 'Start talking,' said the Deputy Head Boy, 'and make it quick.'

*   *   *   *

Some time later, after Tubby had outlined his scheme, Skimpton was even more adamant in his refusal to help. 'It will never work, Tubby,' he said. 'Besides, what happens to Spate in the meantime, languishing in gaol?'

'They can't keep him on a murder charge without a body,' replied Tubby optimistically, 'even Constable Stubbs couldn't get away with that. No, Skimpton, don't you see? It's a truly inspired stratagem. Tubby Malkin will simply disappear, vanish from the face of the earth, just another one of Faysgarth's mysterious missing boys, like Miles Brody and numerous others!'

Skimpton gave Malkin's scheme a further moment's consideration before restating his position. 'I am sorry, Tubby,' he said, 'but I cannot possibly allow myself to get involved with your ridiculous Master Plan. Perhaps one of the other boys...'

'I am afraid it has to be you, Skimpton, as you are the only one in possession of the expertise required to see the thing through.'

'Tubby, I am House Captain, and as such must set an example! If any of this should come out...'

Tubby hurled the banknotes petulantly onto the bed and strode towards the window. 'So,' he scoffed, 'you are intent on letting me down.'

'I am afraid so.'

'Very well, then I must to resort to more unpleasant methods of persuasion.'

He turned to face Skimpton, a fiendish smile contaminating his filthy face. 'Your friend Varley,' he said, sneeringly, 'you like him very much, don't you?'

'You leave Jack out of this, you dirty little dog,' warned Skimpton, rounding on the greasy blackmailer.

'You might be interested to know,' resumed Tubby blandly, 'that I have some pretty sordid information regarding your pal Varley and a member of staff from the Science Department.'

Skimpton grasped him by the throat and thrust him angrily against the wall. 'Carry on,' he hissed menacingly.

'Information which,' gasped Malkin, 'if made public might very well cause considerable embarrassment to the school.'

'Why, you barmy little snake,' growled Skimpton, his thumbs pushing forcefully into the younger boy's windpipe. 'I've a good mind to finish Spate's work for him here and now!'

'Think about it,' croaked the young bastard, 'is it too much for me to request your co-operation in this small matter, if, as seems to be the case, you are to deny me your friendship?'

Presently, Skimpton released Tubby from his stranglehold, tossed the miserable toady onto the armchair and stood motionless by the open window. 'Get out,' he said.

As the vermin withdrew to his sewer for the night, Skimpton began to try and work out what best to do, and resolved to keep an eye on his chum Jack Varley, especially when in the company of Colonel Coombes.

*   *   *   *

Eight weeks later, at the County Boxing Championships in the Empire Hall, Barnchester, the sizeable contingent of Faysgarthians in the audience were buzzing with talk of their school's newest contender for the heavyweight title – a wealthy American boy recently arrived from Texas by the name of Guy Rangers.

The megalithic Yank had seen off an opponent from St.

Chad's College within thirty seconds, in an unruly qualifying heat, and was now bouncing confidently into the ring to await his next conquest. 'I say Skimpton,' beamed Jack Varley, 'this Rangers fellow is quite something isn't he?'

'Yes, I suppose so,' replied an apparently unimpressed Skimpton.

'That was an almighty left hook he produced to dispatch that fellow in the last heat!'

'Hmmm.'

'Well come on, old man, try and summon up a bit of interest. I know you've already bagged your trophy tonight, but this is the big one we're talking about – The Monktonshire Minor Public Schools' Undisputed Heavyweight Crown! Faysgarth hasn't produced a champion at this weight for over a decade.'

'Yes, I know,' offered Skimpton listlessly.

'Skimpton,' queried Varley, 'is there something amiss? You have been acting jolly strangely these past few weeks. Have I given you any reason to be distant with me?'

'What? No, sorry Jack. I can't seem to summon up much enthusiasm for boxing at the moment. Perhaps my mind is occupied with next month's athletics championships instead.'

An enthusiastic cheer was raised as the assembled Faysgarthians were treated once more to the sight of Guy Rangers's impressively muscular physique. A truly magnificent specimen of boyhood, the Texan displayed an emphatic pair of shoulders, a sturdy neck, and an amazing chest of awesome proportions. His stomach muscles reminded one of powerfully clenched fists and his legs were akin to those of a thoroughbred racehorse (except, of course, that he possessed only two of them). His vivacious, sculpted chin and steely gaze gave the impression of a ruthless, indestructible fighting machine that would stop at nothing to get its way.

It was with some obvious trepidation that his adversary from St. Chad's College climbed into the ring, fear written all over his face, and looking very much like a small boy about to do battle with a fully-grown beast.

As the bell sounded for the opening round, Rangers, having discarded his amateur vest to allow the steam to rise impressively from his back, charged at his opponent in a thundering and violent pugilistic display which owed more to Attila The Hun than it did to Gentleman Jim Corbett.

By the end of the first round, the crowd was on its feet, many infected by Rangers's combative display, and fighting amongst themselves. As the round progressed, it was clear that the other boy possessed considerably more skill than did Rangers, though this did not prevent the pugnacious Faysgarthian from flooring his adversary with a low punch which elicited an instant public warning from the referee.

The opening of round two saw Rangers stalking his prey relentlessly about the ring, as the St. Chad's man attempted to weave his way out of trouble. The fight was turning into a classic struggle between technique and robust, unbridled passion, when a series of scrappy clinches offered Rangers the opportunity to weaken his opponent with a devastating series of stout body blows.

After the referee parted them, a momentary lapse in concentration left the contender from St. Chad's with his head unguarded. Spurred on by the hysterical crowd, Rangers ploughed in with a stunning sequence of jabs, followed by a right, a left, an even more powerful right, and an unstoppable left hook which sent the plucky college boy crashing to the canvas, his face all over the place.

The towel came in within seconds of the count and the victorious Faysgarthians went wild, for once more their school could boast an heavyweight champion! The triumphant Guy Rangers was hoisted high into the air by several burly sixth-formers, and shouldered from the ring. 'Hurrah!' they cried. 'Good old Guy!'

Rangers had insisted that, should he win, the American National Anthem be played, and as the strains of *The Star-Spangled Banner* crackled through the public address system, he saluted manfully from his position high above the crowd, and encouraged all present to join him in singing along.

> *Oh, say can you see by the dawn's early light*
> *What so proudly we hailed at the twilight's last gleaming?*

'I say,' mused a pensive Jack Varley, 'I'm not sure I approve of that.'

'Approve of what, Jack?' asked an equally thoughtful Skimpton.

'Any of it,' came the troubled reply.

*   *   *   *

In the weeks which followed his remarkable victory, Guy Rangers enjoyed unparalleled popularity at Faysgarth, and soon boasted a devout following amongst the junior ranks. This outbreak of unbridled hero-worship also influenced some of the more impressionable members of staff, many of whom even began attempting imitations of the Texan's southern drawl during their classes.

Vulgar American colloquialisms began to be bandied around the quad as Faysgarthians started to refer to one another as 'Jack' and 'buddy' – much to the annoyance of Jack Varley, who began investigating the possibility of changing his name through the official channels.

A musical appreciation society was formed with the express intention of promoting American composers' work, and everywhere boys could be heard attempting the slow movement from *The New World Symphony* on mouth organs. Many were caught wearing ten-gallon hats in the privacy of their quarters, and an impromptu rodeo brought serious complaints from a local farmer whose cattle had been cynically abused.

Guy Rangers, capitalising upon his growing reputation, transformed his ad-hoc band of acolytes into a platoon of confederate-style soldiers who marched and saluted to the sound of a bugle and the raising of the *Stars and Stripes* each morning.

Meanwhile, it did not go unnoticed that the singing of the National Anthem during Full School Assembly was being undertaken by many with more than a degree of indifference. Indeed, some of the boys began mouthing red-neck rebel songs under their breaths, producing an appalling cacophony not heard since Riley – the fourth-form 'cellist – performed his latest Stravinsky-inspired sonata, accompanied by another boy on tuba, the previous term.

Rangers's intense love of his country appeared to be boundless, and his disdainful attitude to school tradition was matched only by his dismissive and sometimes excessively harsh treatment of foreign boys. Initially, he took it upon himself to forbid any of them from participating in any extra-curricular activities, then arranged for them to be actively hounded from their quarters, so that many – forced to sleep on the sports field – pleaded with their parents to be transferred to other schools.

Aided by the establishment of a well-drilled and ruthlessly efficient militia, drawn from the ranks of the third and fourth-forms, and issued with strict orders to clamp down heavily on any lapses in discipline, the monstrous Texan's influence could be felt in every corner of school life. His rigid stranglehold, founded on a combination of brute strength, seemingly unlimited funds and a heady, North American jingoism, made Marcus Dent's previous skulduggery seem like an outing of the Faverstock Ladies' Croquet Team.

A notable low point was reached when an unfortunate Trinidadian boy, the son of a respected diplomat, objected to being called a filthy name by Rangers during an history lesson. His reward for challenging the despotic Texan was to be lassoed to the chapel pulpit whilst further abuse was hurled at him by the more febrile members of the American's ecumenical contingent. The victim was, soon after, withdrawn from Faysgarth by his irate father.

Marcus Dent, to whom the West Indian owed a large sum of money, approached Rangers in his headquarters to plead for greater tolerance, since many of his debtors were now being driven from the school by the American. The erstwhile undisputed School Scoundrel was the instant recipient of a comprehensive whipping for his pains, and every last vestige of his belongings were confiscated until further notice.

Indeed, Rangers's brand of 'doodle dandy'-style terror was so universal during this time, that Jack Varley was moved to joke grimly that the only safe Faysgarthian was probably Master Spate, still detained at His Majesty's Pleasure by Constable Stubbs, in connection with the murder of Tubby Malkin. The sole individual afforded any degree of courtesy by the tyrannical cowboy was Skimpton himself – it was assumed because of the latter's quick grasp of baseball, a game Rangers had recently instigated at Faysgarth in preference to cricket. This seemingly cordial relationship between the Deputy Head Boy and the American soon began to cause considerable friction between Skimpton and many of his schoolfellows, including his old ally Jack Varley, who had suffered the loss of his favourite cricket bat to one of Rangers's young satellites. He later witnessed the treasured item being thrown onto a bonfire during the Fourth of July celebrations.

*   *   *   *

And so, it was against this tempestuous background of turmoil and terror, perpetrated by the totalitarian Texan, that Skimpton found himself paying his first-ever visit to his impecunious former nemesis Marcus Dent, in his now barren and squalid boudoir.

Turning from the window, Dent fixed Skimpton with a disbelieving stare after the latter had been speaking for some considerable time. 'Do you seriously expect me to believe,' said the broken bounder, incredulously, 'that this Rangers fellow is actually Tubby Malkin?'

'I am afraid so,' said Skimpton, 'for that is the awful truth. After faking his own death, the sniveller blackmailed me into participating in his Master Plan. Hiding in the sewers for eight weeks, the monstrous skunk embarked on a vigorous training schedule which he insisted I formulate for him. Having furnished me with sufficient funds, he had me supply him with special provisions daily, which constituted a strict diet.

'With the boxing championships approaching, he re-emerged, enrolling himself at the school under his new identity using money left to him by his adopted parents. By this time, he had grown a good six inches and shed every ounce of excess fat.

'It never occurred to me that his reappearance might fool anyone, but there you are, such was the magnitude of the fellow's transformation. He'd perfected the accent some years ago on summer camp just outside Houston.'

'I see.'

'Believe me,' implored Skimpton, 'had his threats been of a less serious nature I would have had nothing whatsoever to do with him.'

'I understand,' said Dent thoughtfully. 'I shall not enquire as to the precise details of the scurrilous young lizard's menaces, but must conclude that we are in urgent need of a finely wrought counter-strategy to repulse them. In other words, a plan which will discredit our American cousin so severely that, should he choose to reveal his unpleasant intelligence, it will be dismissed out of hand.'

Skimpton was impressed by Dent's immediate grasp of the situation, as well as with the latter's ability to communicate his interpretation of the dilemma using taut, economical phraseology. After scouring his intellect in an effort to compete with the young stylist's grandiloquence, the sportsman opted for a simple, uncluttered response. 'I agree,' he said presently.

'Meanwhile,' resumed Dent, 'my chum Spate remains in custody on a piffling, trumped-up theft charge.' For some minutes he stroked his heavily whiskered chin, before finally standing up. 'Thank you for your assistance, Skimpton,' he said.

'I only wish I could have come earlier,' explained the other, 'but the filthy rotter kept intimidating me. Were it myself under threat from his libellous assertions, then the story might well have been different, but as his allegations concern others, close to me, I could not risk disclosure.'

'Perhaps we could meet to-morrow evening after we have had time to consider a suitable course of action?'

'Good idea,' said Skimpton, unsure as to whether he was capable of devising such a scheme. Then, for the first and only time in their lives, the two shook hands, before Skimpton departed.

*   *   *   *

The following afternoon saw Guy Rangers, alias Tubby Malkin, wreaking havoc on the sports field. A plucky fourth-former from the Belgian Congo had reached the final of the school's discus competition, ousting one of the American's personal guard from the contest. Enraged, the cynical pseudo-Texan had ordered both the youngster's arms broken by one of his cronies.

Skimpton, who had been relying on the black boy's participation in the forthcoming Athletics Championships, was beside himself with fury. After confronting Rangers near the running track, he was delivered with an immediate and scornfully dispatched left hook to the temple, which sent the sports captain reeling into the cricket nets in front of the entire school.

Skimpton's young manservant Piggot attempted to intervene on his fagmaster's behalf, and was awarded with a severe beating by Rangers and his vicious cohorts. This casual brutality, even more venomous than that which had just been unleashed at himself, convinced Skimpton that he must try his utmost to provide Marcus Dent with any assistance, in whatever scheme was agreed, to rid his battered school of Rangers's abominable presence.

*   *   *   *

Later that night, Skimpton found himself in the company of Marcus Dent and his chum Binns, drinking hot milk and plotting in the former's study. 'What we need,' announced Dent, 'is a body. Binns, go look in the cellars.'

'No use, Marcus,' said Binns, 'Spate removed all the remains of his victims some time ago.'

'What?' cried Skimpton, quite unable to believe what he was hearing.

'Why don't we use the skellington from the biology laboratory, Marcus?' offered Binns.

'Don't be ridiculous,' said Dent, 'it's held together with metal pins.'

Setting aside his reservations about the veracity of the previous exchange, Skimpton ventured forth with a suggestion. 'If it is a decomposed body you require,' he said, 'I may be able to help you. In the sewers under Second House lay the remains of a boy named Miles Brody, who disappeared some time ago.'

'I remember him,' said Dent, 'a fourth-former with glasses. Spate killed him last year.'

'I beg your pardon?'

'Quite accidentally, you understand, in an argument over examination papers.'

'Spate *murdered* him?' blurted Skimpton.

'Technically I suppose he did, yes.'

'Does it all the time,' laughed Binns, 'usually at the request of parents.'

'Makes a tidy income from it actually,' put in Dent, airily. 'I've tried to dissuade him, but to no avail.'

'I see,' muttered Skimpton, uneasily.

'How did you hear about Brody's body?' enquired Dent.

'Tubby came across it in the sewers, where he was hiding after faking his own death,' explained Skimpton.

'Really?' said Dent. 'Binns, go and fish out this cadaver immediately.'

'Why me?' protested the nitwit.

'Because I have no intention of going into the sewers, and I am sure our friend Skimpton hasn't either.'

'But Marcus, it will be simply beastly down there!'

'Then take an overcoat and some smelling salts! Now get out before I tell Rangers about your subversive nocturnal activities!' Binns had been secretly defacing Rangers's recruitment posters for his Counter Intelligence League, and was so terrified of exposure that he was out of the door even before Dent had finished threatening him.

'So, Marcus,' said Skimpton eagerly, 'what's the plan?'

'Well,' replied Dent, pausing conspiratorially, 'I intend to put paid to Guy Rangers by having him convicted of a murder.'

'But of whom?'

Dent stroked his cheek coolly before confidently smiling at Skimpton. 'Tubby Malkin,' he said.

'Good Lord! But they are the same person!'

'Exactly.'

'So how will you do it?'

Dent paused and cleared his throat before proceeding with the outline of his plan.

'First, we need a school uniform to drape around this corpse of yours,' he explained, 'because if my guess is correct, young Brody's will have disintegrated by now.'

'No problem. I have Tubby's – he left it with me when he took on his new identity.'

'Excellent. We also require your chum Varley to retract his evidence implicating Spate in the murder of Tubby.'

'Why, exactly?'

'Because I intend to prove that he was actually killed at a later date.'

'Look,' said Skimpton, enthusiastically, 'we might be able to let Jack's evidence stand, and disprove it in court, for I know for certain that, the day after his supposed slaying, Tubby nipped out from his hiding place in the sewers to pay a visit to his bank in Faverstock. They are sure to have a record of the withdrawal he made.'

'Magnificent! Next, we need some personal items belonging to Guy Rangers, preferably including a weapon of some kind.'

'I shall borrow them from him under some pretext.'

'Good. Then, we shall hide the body where it can easily be found, with the incriminating evidence close by.'

'But what about a motive?'

'I assume Rangers, I mean Malkin, still has his money stashed away somewhere?'

'I expect so.'

'Then there, my dear friend, is the American's rationale for murder. An open and shut case!'

'Dent,' beamed Skimpton, 'you are a spanking genius!'

'I know,' agreed the rejuvenated school bully, 'how about a game of draughts?'

'You're on!'

*　　*　　*　　*

A short time later, with Dent leading four games to one, Binns arrived, out of breath and dragging behind him what appeared to be a filthy sack. 'I hope I'm going to get paid for this,' groaned the silly billy.

'At last!' greeted Dent. 'Now let's have a look at the fellow!' Binns emptied the contents of his sack onto the floor, and amongst the evil-smelling detritus that came out with it, was the grimy skeleton of Miles Brody, a few pitiful threads of school uniform clinging to it like seaweed on a weathered old shipwreck.

'He's a handsome beggar!' joked Binns.

'Do you think he will pass as Tubby?' asked Skimpton uncomfortably.

'He's about the right height,' said Dent, 'and once we've put some clothes on him, we'll shove a few sweetie wrappers in his pocket just to make sure. Now get rid of him, Binns.'

'Why can't he stay here?'

'Because he gives me the creeps, that's why. Now push off and hide him in your room.'

'If you ask me,' said Binns, caressing one of Brody's eye sockets suggestively, 'he livens the place up a bit.'

'Don't be disgusting,' said Dent, genuinely sickened.

'Well, it is rather grim in here at the moment, Marcus, if you don't mind me saying so.'

'Well I do mind you saying so. Now take yourself off with your haunted friend and await Skimpton's arrival with Tubby's clothes and a few personal items. Then dump him on the playing fields near a ditch, that way we can account for the rapid deterioration in his condition.'

'We can suggest that he has been eaten by rats,' added Skimpton helpfully.

'He *has* been eaten by rats,' said Dent, 'quite comprehensively by the looks of him.'

'What a wheeze!' screeched Binns. 'Setting up Tubby for his own murder!'

'Breathe a word of this to anyone, Binns,' warned Dent soberly, 'and I shall personally see to it that you enjoy a similar fate to that of young Brody here, only worse. Do you understand?'

'Yes Marcus.'

There was a brief pause as the three conspirators stood in silence, contemplating the enormity of their undertaking. Presently, Dent turned to Skimpton. 'We'll leave it at four-one for tonight, shall we?' he said dryly.

* * * *

'Do you think I might borrow your Bowie knife, Tubby?' requested Skimpton later that night, whilst entertaining the individual formerly known as Tubby Malkin in his study.

'Hey! Don't call me Tubby!' snapped Tubby in his American accent. 'Whaddya want it f'r anyways?'

'I'd like to scare a few boys from the Modern Music Society.

That wretched Eastern European plinky-plonk stuff they play drifts across the quad and keeps me awake.'

'Why certainly Skimpton,' drawled Tubby, removing his weapon from his belt and hurling it nonchalantly at the dart board. 'Why doncha just go ahead and mark one of 'em with it?'

'I don't think that will be necessary, they're mostly sissies anyway. A quick flash of the blade should do the trick.'

Tubby wrenched off his cowboy boots, stretched himself on Skimpton's favourite armchair and lit a cheroot.

'Make yourself at home...er...Guy,' said Skimpton, summoning up as much sincerity as he could muster. 'Listen, I'm awfully sorry about that unpleasantness earlier...on the sports field.'

'Hey! Get outta here!'

Skimpton made to leave but was instantly called back. 'Where ya goin'?' demanded Tubby.

'I'm leaving, as you instructed, Tubby!'

'I meant f'rget about it, schmuck! Siddown!'

'No,' insisted Skimpton, 'you were quite right to punish me. I deserved worse.'

'You want f'r me to break y'r legs?'

'I... erm...not just at the moment, for they are required next month at the County Athletics Championships. Can I get you anything, Guy? I'm afraid I appear to be right out of baked beans, but I could rustle us up some coffee...?'

'Great idea.'

'Why not loosen up your holster, let me take your jacket?'

Tubby removed his prize Wild West jerkin extremely gingerly and handed it to Skimpton. 'Be very careful with that,' he said. 'You got any cookies?'

'Cookies?'

'Better still, hold the cookies. You gat any vodka? Gimme a Piledriver.'

'Right away sir.'

*   *   *   *

Later, as the small hours ticked away into larger ones, a lone owl hooted in Dead Man's Wood. In their respective beds, Skimpton and Marcus Dent lay awake thinking about Guy Rangers, who in turn was elsewhere dreaming of punching cattle and world domination.

Some distance away, prostrate in the tiny cell located in the bowels of Faverstock's miniature police station, lay young Spate, now beginning to tire of his incarceration, and vowing never again to involve himself in homicidal activities, unless, that was, he deemed them either to be absolutely necessary or financially advantageous.

Meanwhile, on the farthest edge of the playing fields, out past the boundary of the cricket pitch, some distance to the east even of the long-jump pit, Binns was assembling, in as pleasing an arrangement as he could muster, the earthly remains of Miles Brody. Now decked out in Tubby Malkin's grubby school uniform, the former fourth-former looked almost pleased to be out in the open air again. The owl hooted for a second time, and Binns bade a last farewell to his transfigured friend and trudged off in the direction of Main House and his waiting bed.

*   *   *   *

The following lunchtime, a meeting was taking place in Main School Hall of the Faysgarth Senior Poetry Society, during which Riley, the lanky fourth-form 'cellist, was attempting to curry favour with Guy Rangers, who was seated in the audience. To this end, the stringy aesthete had selected works by American writers, and had embarked on a reading which comprised excerpts from the poems of Walt Whitman.

Rangers, though, was unimpressed, and only a few seconds into the recitation, jumped to his feet and let loose a vituperative torrent of abuse, railing against 'art for art's sake' and other such theories which he apparently found distasteful.

He was cut short in his invective by the arrival of Detective Inspector Haddock from Barnchester CID, who was accompanied by the redoubtable Constable Stubbs.

The Inspector, hands thrust deep into his raincoat pocket and pipe securely clamped between his teeth, ambled up the aisle and placed his diminutive frame next to the ranting Rangers. The Policeman's close proximity sufficiently distracted the Texan, and within seconds, he had coolly elicited what appeared to be a premature curtailment of Rangers's profanity. Removing his pipe very deliberately, the detective began slowly shaking his head, taking his time and choosing his moment very carefully before speaking, so as to imbue his imminent utterance with maximum significance.

In the event, Constable Stubbs, zealous as ever to steal the limelight, got there before him. 'Guy Rangers?' he demanded.

'Constable!' snapped the detective rancorously, 'I, as the senior officer present, shall ask the questions!'

'Very good sir.'

'Are you Guy Rangers, young man?' said Haddock.

'Yeah,' came the sloppy reply.

'As a result of information received, I have come here today to arrest you for the murder of one Tubby Malkin.' At this, several members of the Senior Poetry Society sank to their knees in a dramatic gesture of thanks, some even breaking down in tears, so joyous to them was the news imparted by Detective Inspector Haddock. Rangers merely looked to the heavens and began laughing uproariously.

'I must warn you,' interjected Stubbs, 'that anything you might wish to say could well be recorded in my notebook, and at a later date used in hevidence, some of which is 'ighly likely to be disadvantaginous to your case. Do you 'ave anythin' to say?'

Rangers turned his face to the constable, spat out a

large mouthful of chewing tobacco onto the floor and smiled contemptuously to himself. 'Stick it up y'r ass, copper!' he said.

'Thank you, Constable,' said Haddock. 'You may now make use of your handcuffs.'

'Very good sir.'

* * * *

On the fifteenth of July that year, the following report appeared in the Barnchester Chronicle:

DRAMATIC TURN IN FAYSGARTH MURDER TRIAL
– defendant makes astonishing claim on final day
by Aubrey Prince

American student Guy Rangers (18) of Houston, Texas, accused of murdering his schoolfellow Thomas 'Tubby' Malkin at Faysgarth last April, today amazed the court at the Monktonshire Assizes in Barnchester by claiming to <u>be</u> his fifteen-year-old alleged victim.

At the commencement of his week-long trial, Rangers had astounded the court by dispensing with his counsel, choosing instead to conduct his own defence.

Throughout proceedings, Rangers stood in the dock wearing a large 'cowboy' style hat, neckerchief, suede rustling jerkin with frayed trimming, sheriff's badge, trews and knee-length boots.

After previously denying that he had been present at the school at the time of the murder, the muscular Texan later insisted that, in the person of Thomas Malkin, he had faked his own death in order to take on a new identity.

Prosecuting, Mr. Gerald Brody (49), whose son also disappeared from the school last year, described Rangers's story as preposterous – 'the desperate ramblings of a guilty man'. Mr Brody, wearing a charcoal grey pinstriped suit with black Italian snake-skin shoes and a flame-red tie with a lizard motif, had previously called as a witness a pupil from the school, Marcus Dent, who gave his age as eighteen. He claimed to have seen the accused loitering about the school grounds the day after Malkin's supposed slaying by another boy.

Dent, sporting the school's distinctive bottle green blazer with yellow and black striped tie, proffered the theory that Malkin, who has no living relatives, was unhappy at being bullied at school and had indeed staged his own death in an attempt to garner sympathy.

Julian Spate (18), also of Faysgarth, had been arrested on suspicion of killing Malkin with a rounders bat on that occasion, but when the alleged victim's body disappeared soon afterwards, Spate remained in custody on a theft charge.

The erudite Dent then went on to speculate that the victim had fallen into Rangers's clutches the day following his supposed murder, and was persuaded by the American to make a substantial withdrawal from his bank in Faverstock.

A bank clerk, Miss Muriel Downes (36) of Rainingham, wearing a navy-blue pinafore-style suit with matching shoes, appeared to corroborate Dent's conjecture when she recalled serving a young man of Malkin's description in the Faverstock branch of the Frugal Savings Bank in Market Street, the day after the latter's alleged slaying by Spate. The register of withdrawals indicated that the boy had left the bank with some £15,000 2s 6d in cash.

Detective Inspector Norman Haddock (48) of Barnchester CID, in an elegant Harris tweed sports jacket, ochre woollen tie, beige trousers and mottled brogues, said that, acting upon information anonymously received, his men had located what they believed to be Malkin's badly decomposed body in the grounds of the school some three months later. Nearby was a knife and a pair of spurs belonging to the accused. A search of Rangers's study revealed a stash of money amounting to some £13,000 19s 4d, hidden in the dead boy's briefcase, under the bed. The numbered notes were traced to Malkin's account in Faverstock.

A master at the school, Colonel Archibald Coombes (52), wearing a brown corduroy jacket, grey 'v' necked pullover, paisley patterned bowtie, azure cotton slacks and sturdy shoes, admitted when questioned by Mr. Brody that he may have been mistaken when, at the scene of the fake murder, he pronounced Malkin deceased. And when pressed further, could not actually remember having taken the boy's pulse.

In an impassioned defence, during which Rangers appeared gradually to misplace his American accent, the Texan maintained that he had loaned his knife to another boy the night before his arrest. Mr. Brody countered that fingerprinting tests carried out by forensic scientists at the Home Office had shown no other hand on the weapon other than that of the accused. As for the spurs, Rangers had no idea how they came to be found near the body.

Still maintaining that his true identity was that of Thomas Malkin, the American concluded his defence by demanding he be released, and insisting that the £13,000 19s 4d be returned to him forthwith, as the money was rightfully his.

A verdict is expected later today.

*　　*　　*　　*

The last day of term saw the finals of the Monktonshire Minor Public Schools' Athletics Championships, held that year at Faysgarth. Skimpton, tenacious as ever, won the hundred-yard dash, 440 yards' hurdles, long jump, high jump, hop-skip and jump, javelin, shot putt, hammer and pole vault, playing a vital part in his team's narrow victory over its nearest rivals from St Chad's College.

When helping to clear away the bunting afterwards, Skimpton came across his chum Jack Varley, enjoying the company of young Dick Parr, captain of the Junior Cricket Eleven, in the long-jump pit. 'Jack,' he hailed, 'am I interrupting anything?'

'Not at all,' came the hearty reply. 'Run along now, Parr, and remember what I have said, always keep a straight bat and watch out for the googlies!'

'Toodle pip!'

Skimpton's friendship with Varley had been clothed in

somewhat formal weeds of late, partly because of the sportsman's perceived former cameraderie with the convicted murderer Guy Rangers, but also because of Skimpton's uncertainty with respect to his friend's dealings with Colonel Coombes. In an attempt to clear once and for all the nasty taste left by Tubby Malkin's insinuations, Skimpton braced himself to confront Varley with his suspicions. 'Jack,' he said tentatively, 'I've something rather delicate to discuss with you.'

'Oh yes?'

'A matter that has been of considerable concern to me for quite some time.'

'Go on.'

'This might be a trifle embarrassing, I'm afraid.'

'Well come on, spit it out old stick!'

Just then, they were interrupted by a first-former who joined them brandishing a note. 'Varley,' panted the junior, 'I have an urgent message here, addressed to Colonel Coombes.'

'What of it?'

'He instructed me to give it to you when it arrived since he said you would know where to find him.'

'Not again,' groaned Varley. 'He'll be in the White Swan at Faverstock. Last time he kept me there talking for hours about recent attempts at splitting the atom!'

'Oh yes?

Varley took the note and dismissed the youngster, tossing him a ha'penny for his trouble. 'When I finally got away,' he said, 'if I remember rightly, I discovered Tubby Malkin had been spying on us!'

'When was this?'

'Three, four months ago. Not long before he died.'

'Tubby Malkin?'

'Yes. When I confronted him, he threatened to broadcast it all over the school!'

'Broadcast what, Jack?'

'Why, that I'd been drinking in the public house with Colonel

Coombes, of course! He'd only bought me a half of bitter, for Goodness sake, but strictly speaking, I'm still under-age!'

'So, what did you do?'

'About what?'

'Why, Malkin, of course!'

'I booted his backside for him, and continued to do so on many other occasions when he had the audacity to bring the subject up!'

It took Skimpton some seconds to fully comprehend the enormity of what he had just been told. He had made assumptions, foolish ones, the consequences of which had indirectly led to a boy being incarcerated for his own murder for a very long time. In something of a quandary, he found himself unsure whether or not to confide his secret to Varley. 'Jack,' he said presently, 'I've been an awfully silly chump these last few months.'

'Well, what's new? Now what did you want to discuss with me?'

Skimpton looked up from contemplating the palm of his hand, sighed and said, 'Jack, I am considering giving the boxing a miss next year. I feel that I might have taken a few too many punches.'

'Good idea. Look, Skimpton, I'd better get this note to Colonel Coombes. How about if I pop round later and demonstrate my new crystal set to you? Or perhaps we could enjoy a rattling game of tiddlywinks together?'

'That would be dandy.'

After watching his housemate depart, Skimpton lowered his weary frame into the long-jump pit and reflected further upon recent events. Sifting the sand through his fingers, he felt a creeping sense of unease at the way things had been resolved.

Some feet away, he noticed a stray discus half buried in the sand like a forgotten clue in a crime mystery, the murder weapon finally discovered that would nail the culprit. Picking it up and weighing it in his hand, he brushed the grains of sand from its pock-marked surface and studied closely the scratches accrued through decades of use by generations of Faysgarthians, each one the testimony of a determined young athlete's endeavour.

Taking the wood firmly in his right hand and striding out onto the shale, he began rotating his body, slowly at first, somehow testing his resolve, before pushing himself more purposefully. As the school buildings, playing fields and hills beyond began blurring in his peripheral vision, his head seemed to float, as if he had been somehow transported into the eye of a storm. For a brief moment, he felt utterly detached from the world and its wretchedness, for nothing else seemed to matter but the whirlwind he had created with his swirling body.

Now spinning wildly, on the very edge of control, Skimpton knew he should let go the disc, but held on, spinning faster and faster until he could hardly breathe. Within an ace of oblivion, he released his grip and watched as the flying discus hurtled skywards. Higher and higher it flew, gleaming in the evening sunshine, soaring up through the clouds and floating off into the heavens, never to be seen again.

*   *   *   *

Returning to his quarters some time later, he was hailed by Marcus Dent, who was lazing on a bench in the quad, in an attitude of utter contentment.

'Congratulations on a fine display this afternoon, Skimpton,' grinned the reinstated rotter. 'I hear you practically won the athletics cup single handed.'

'Did I?' came the dreamy reply. 'How's your chum Spate?'

'Keeping out of trouble, I am happy to say,' replied the rogue, unconvincingly. 'I think that spell in clink set him worrying about his ways.' Dent leaned back on the bench, luxuriating in the last rays of sunshine, hands in his pockets, eyes closed and legs outstretched. 'You know, Skimpton,' he conjectured, 'if you're beginning to harbour any misgivings about the methods we adopted in disposing of Tubby Malkin, then don't. My guess is, he'll be far happier with his lasso, rounding up the inmates in the asylum to which he has been dispatched. Guy Rangers will afford him much more respect than he ever elicited from Faysgarth, or indeed anywhere else, in his previous unpleasant guise. For, unfortunates such as he invariably find themselves persecuted by society, whatever their age or circumstances. It is in their nature, almost, to provoke such a reaction.'

Skimpton seated himself beside Dent on the bench. 'Perhaps you are right,' he said. 'Do you mind if I ask you something?'

'Go ahead.'

'Do you ever reach a point where you feel like a complete fool?'

'Often.'

'And what do you do at such a time?'

'I try and forget about it by consuming large quantities of strong drink.'

'And you find that does the trick?'

'Usually.'

'I see.' And without offering any further comment, and dispensing with any valedictory salutation, the House Captain set off at a brisk pace in the same direction as had his chum Jack Varley, intending to join his pal and the verbose Colonel Coombes in a flagon or two at The White Swan Inn at Faverstock.

FIVE

VARLEY'S AUNT

September found Faysgarth in its autumn garb. The fading blooms of summer mingled cordially with the scattered fruits of the orchard bough. Nearby, its seasonal bounty long since gathered in, the vegetable patch clung to a solitary lettuce for company. In the off-duty corridors, the silent walls stood at ease, awaiting the imminent return of their charges, and prepared to echo once again with the saltpetre of young boys' summer exploits.

As well as being a time for renewing old friendships, September was also the month for playing old tricks on new boys. Some seasoned hands would even now be devising dastardly schemes for newcomers, as recompense for previous knaveries they themselves had suffered. At this time of year, even the ancient quad took on a rebellious air, as its austere windows and portals smiled conspiratorially in the direction of the chapel steeple, which, temporarily relieved of its spiritual duties, now appeared to sway frivolously in the autumn breeze. And the cricket pavilion close by, home of so much clandestine activity in term time, now floated in mischievous collusion with its neighbouring sheds and equipment stores, like a pirated Indiaman bobbing alongside an assortment of skiffs in a sea of green.

It was two days before the commencement of a new school term when, unbeknownst to the architectural plotters, an intruder had arrived under cover of darkness and beneath their very noses. At crack of dawn, donning running togs and shoes, the interloper had snaked off while the school was still asleep. Down the leafy byways he ran, tracing an arduous route which he hoped would eventually lead to a winner's medal in the County Cross Country Championships some six weeks hence.

A little time later, as the morning sun coaxed richer hues from the walls of Faysgarth School, they began to reverberate, faintly at first, with the steady patter of a runner's feet. And as he neared the quad, their capricious thoughts of rebellion set aside for another year, the ageing walls quickly donned the more respectable mantle of responsibility, and saluted once more the individual whose achievements and general first-class behaviour demanded admiration from all quarters. A boy whose extraordinary disciplinary record and exemplary sense of fair play was an inspiration not only to his contemporaries and those who instructed them, but also for the very fabric of the institution to which he belonged.

Nearing the breathless completion of his morning's exercise, and now traversing the quad at breakneck speed, was a conscientious young fellow named Skimpton. Not for him the tortuous planning of the inevitably anti-climactic first day jape; he would leave that to others with little better to do. For this young man had far more challenging goals in sight: a whole year of sporting records to break, an army of opponents to see off and trophies to hoist, his immediate concern being the Cross-Country Championships later that term.

The previous year, according to his fag Piggot's possibly suspect timekeeping, Skimpton had completed the fifteen-mile course in just under fifty-eight minutes, making an average speed of over sixteen miles an hour – a remarkable pace even by Skimpton's standards. Nonetheless, tradition dictated that he must at least equal his achievement this time round.

Choosing to banish any lurking suspicion regarding Piggot's arithmetic, the determined and attractive champion had resolved, over the holidays, not only to match his previous record but to substantially better it in the forthcoming race. And though it would be fiendishly difficult to achieve, to shrink from the challenge – in Skimpton's eyes at least – meant nothing less than to brandish himself a coward.

As he showered briskly, the young rouser reflected on how successful his training schedule, begun some weeks earlier at home, was progressing, for he now felt fitter and more determined than ever. Then he turned his attention to the cheery prospect of greeting his particular chum Jack Varley, who was due to arrive the next day. Although by no means an accomplished sportsman, except, of course, at the popping crease, Varley was quite the most level-headed fellow Skimpton had encountered at Faysgarth, and the young inside-forward had been more than happy to be guided by his pal's excellent advice on many an occasion. An indubitable ally, Skimpton had frequently found himself grateful to Varley, relying on the latter as a buffer between himself and his more outlandish follies.

Friction occurred most frequently between them when Varley's words of undoubted wisdom on the subject of Skimpton's indifferent academic performance were rejected by the sportsman. In these instances, Varley would retire to his study in frustration, and the Deputy Head Boy would contemplate his position in the gym. The life of a sportsman, he invariably concluded, is rarely reliant on meticulous intellectual analysis, but demands, rather, the single-minded fortitude of the often-foolhardy explorer. And since his sporting successes, in the fullness of time, would undoubtedly constitute a prestigious platform from which to launch himself at the British Empire, should they not take precedence over school work? After all, what need would he have, say, in the jungles of Nyasaland, for the niceties of the Gregorian Chant or the intricacies of the Binominal Theorem? Where, in the treacherous rapids of Indo-China would he find use for the works of Lucretius or the origins of the Wilton Diptych? Besides, was he not the most popular boy in the school, amongst both boys and staff? And after all, he had never actually *failed* an examination. Indeed, as long as he continued to heap sporting success on the school only rarely did anyone, Varley and the appalling Colonel Coombes aside, appear remotely interested in anything other than his sporting progress. The other exception was, of course, the school magazine, *Fractured Lives* – and even that mainly restricted itself to ridiculing his notoriously eccentric renditions of the school song in Full School Assembly.

All this mattered little though, to the boy who was now climbing silently into his clothes in the gloom of the Senior Changing Room, for he had already decided that the new school year would be approached with the same combination of vigour and fortitude which had delivered him with so many triumphs in the past. His inspiration, as always, would be the words of his great sporting hero, the celebrated distance runner and sage, Sir Frederick W. Ludlum:

> *Even if the tactics be flawed and the game all but lost,*
> *The shots at goal will always be worth a cheer.*

*   *   *   *

At dinner, Skimpton, forced to take his food in the refectory in the absence of his dutiful fag Piggot – who would normally deliver his meals to him in his study – was surprised to find himself in the company of his nemesis Marcus Dent, who had also arrived early for the new school year. 'Good evening, Dent,' offered

Skimpton, in the spirit of cautious amicability. 'I trust you have enjoyed your summer hols?'

'Pretty much,' came the reprobate's semi-coherent reply. 'What's for dinner?'

'Steak and kidney pud. Tastes like one of matron's poultices.'

'I am sure it is delicious.'

Dent, obviously the worse for drink, was toying moodily with a rather grim-looking spotted dick. Finally giving up, he tossed aside his spoon. 'I saw you out running earlier Skimpton!' he slurred.

'You want to get a bit of exercise yourself, Marcus,' admonished Skimpton, moving away, 'might do you good!'

'I get all the PT I want, thank you very much, in the company of the more curvaceous athletes from St Bridgit's College. Some of those girls could give you a run for your money, I can tell you.'

'I am not in the least bit interested in your smutty conjecture, Dent,' dismissed Skimpton, seating himself at the farthest end of the table. 'Furthermore, I would be most grateful if you would remain silent whilst I await my food and study my training plan.'

'And so you should, for I suspect you might have a rival for the cross country crown this year.'

'If you mean Algernon Grimshaw...'

'Forget that slack-jawed commoner, look closer to home, Skimpton. My chum Peacock was expelled from St Hugh's last term for eccentric behaviour, and has transferred here.'

'Would that be Horace Peacock, the runner?'

'Indeed. He's a wizard over the last mile.'

'So I hear. But isn't he also something of a sissy?'

'Mildly eccentric perhaps, with a modicum of affected effeminacy thrown in for good measure. But you know this place, they'd enrol old Caligula if he coughed up the fees.'

Skimpton did not reply, for in his eagerness to partake of dinner, he had forgotten that he might have to converse with the serving girl, Nancy, after the recent demise of the aged retainer Dingle. Her presence brought on the customary bout of temporary paralysis, which abated only marginally after she had left for the kitchens, having delivered a bowl of decidedly bleak-looking soup. Thankfully Dent was too far away to notice his discomfort.

'If I were you, Skimpton,' teased the bounder, on his way out, 'I'd be a tiny bit wary of Cocky Peacock. Who knows, he may even usurp your position as Faysgarth's favourite sportsman. Aren't you a little afraid he might prove a bit of a handful on the home stretch?'

'N...n...not in the least.'

'I see. Well, enjoy your cabbage soup.' And with that, the frisky Main Houseman bounded off into the kitchens in search of Nancy, where, buoyed with the over-confidence that accompanies too much alcohol, he demanded that she visit a local picture house with him the following night.

*   *   *   *

Later, in Main House, the School Braggart, slightly unsteady on his feet and belching with consummate regularity, unpacked from his suitcases the bottles of liquor he had plundered from his parents' supplies. Settling himself dizzily on his chaise longue with a large vodka and tonic, Faysgarth's most battle-scarred blackguard considered his position at the onset of possibly his final term at the school.

Not for him the wholesome challenge of ball-in-face and chafing jockstrap, nor the inevitable implications of unmanliness which accompanied academic success. This young knave sought an entirely different brand of recognition; one which he hoped would continue to sustain him as it always had, by dint of unbridled saturnalia and downright beastliness, maintained by a corrupt and ruthless autocracy with himself at its head.

First things first, though, thought the rascally Main Houseman; he must concoct an autumn jape of such wizard proportions that his infamous name would stand atop the league table of filthy rotten blighters for generations to come. For, at the age of twenty-three and now contemplating the inevitable curtailment of his time at Faysgarth, Dent was determined that, at his departure, he should take with him a reputation which would render his future colleagues at varsity quaking in their boots at the thought of his impending arrival.

Having previously contrived to fail the previous five leaving examinations in an attempt to prolong indefinitely his attendance at the school, Dent now found himself faced with an ultimatum from his family. Until recently, he had encountered little difficulty in persuading his indifferent parents to part with the sizeable fees required to maintain his unruly presence in Main House. That was until he wrecked his father's Daimler on a riotous night out in London the previous summer. So incensed was Dent Senior by his son's recklessness, which also dispatched to hospital a junior member of the government who happened to be passing, that an ultimatum had been drawn up: either his son passes the Oxbridge entrance exam at Christmas, or forego his allowance until he was married. And as he had no intention of harnessing himself to such a tedious and outmoded institution for at least a decade, the undisputed School Scoundrel finally resigned himself to a life – for a few years at least – lived amongst the dreaming spires.

Dent's advancing years had forced him to acclimatise himself to being something of an anachronism at Faysgarth, being older even than some of the masters. Indeed, the youthful Mr. Frobisher, a German tutor, had been compelled to resign his post at Faysgarth, his preparatory work the previous term having suffered as a result of him being issued with too many detentions by Dent.

In addition, the subject of Dent's age meant that there was another reason for him to surpass, this year, his previous autumnal devilry; he was in danger of being treated as a source of amusement amongst the lower orders. Some had recently taken to referring to him as The Old Man of Main House behind his back, and a scurrilous article in the school magazine had mischievously suggested that encroaching senility was threatening his position at the school.

Knowing full well that mud, however witlessly strewn, has a tendency to stick, Dent calculated that his strategy for the autumn jape could – if successful – rake away the offending muck quickly. If it failed, however, the resulting insubordination might leave a stain on the rest of the term and possibly even befoul his legacy forever.

The question remained, against whom should his seditious contrivances be perpetrated this year? Previous victims included Colonel Coombes, the clueless chemistry clot, tricked into believing that he had participated in grotesque satanic rituals. A notorious night's bedevilment left the squinting scientist stricken with such profound terror that even an extended sojourn in a sanatorium could not erase the guilt he felt at apparently having ordered the slaughter of a dozen new-born lambs by fourth-formers in his study. The truth, of course, was that he had been drugged by Dent, forced to witness the faked event when semi-conscious, and then sent photographs of himself apparently conducting the gruesome proceedings from his bed.

Another year, Dent had issued the entire first-form with fake exam papers on the first day of term, with a list of severe punishments for any boy answering incorrectly. Questions included:

> *How erotic was the Indian Mutiny?*
> *Keep answers brief. To save time, it is advised that you write on both sides of the answer paper simultaneously.*

And then there was the sorry tale of young Donald McRae, an impressionable new boy who had arrived at Faysgarth from his father's estate in a remote region of Scotland. Dent persuaded the whole of Main House, where McRae had been billeted, to adopt a conspiracy of silence in his presence. This situation persisted for most of the autumn term until Dent put it about that the boy's unpopularity was due to the shape of his ears. McRae's father withdrew his son from the school after the youngster sliced off portions of the offending appendages in the biology laboratory, and pinned them to the Senior Common Room notice board, in a futile attempt to gain acceptance.

And so today, as Dent slid into a deep and troubled sleep, fully clothed and replete with vodka, it was a measure of the seriousness with which he approached his immediate task that, even in this pitiful state, he had managed to set an alarm clock for an unholy hour, and placed it next to the chaise longue on which he now lay sprawled, with the intention of making an early start on the matter in hand.

*   *   *   *

The following day saw much to-ing and fro-ing about the place, as Faysgarth's young protégés drifted back from their vacations. Cars drew up on the drive and boys were hurled from them along with their luggage, before the vehicles reversed at speed out of the school gates, the departing parents eager to return to their lives at home, troubled no more by their tiresome offspring.

Fresh from a challenging session on the parallel bars, Skimpton noticed gleefully that the door to Varley's study was ajar. 'Jack!' he greeted. 'You are back early! I wasn't expecting you until this evening!'

Varley was unpacking his things in a somewhat distracted manner, and barely looked up at his chum. 'Weren't you?' he said.

'What's the matter old man?' queried Skimpton, immediately sensing that something was up. 'Surely you are not unhappy to see me?'

'What?' said Varley, thrusting the empty suitcase under his bed and then brightening up considerably. 'No, of course not old boy. How are you?'

'Very well thank you,' replied Skimpton, proffering the other his hand, 'and yourself?'

'Fair to middling I am afraid. And once I tell you the reason for my premature return you will understand my discomfort.'

'What is it old bean?'

'You'd better sit down, Skimpton, I don't want you lapsing into one of your catatonic states.'

Skimpton placed himself with some ceremony on his pal's bed and awaited Varley's explanation. 'Well?' he said, at length.

'I am to receive a visit from my aunt Lucinda later today.'

'Great Scott!'

'Now before you go all queer on me, I should point out that it is not my aunt that is the cause of my consternation, it is her wretched dog. A ferocious little brute if ever I saw one.' Here, Varley moved to the sink, filled the kettle and prepared the teapot for the first brew of the new term. 'I shall be most surprised,' he continued, 'if the little monster doesn't devour one of the new boys unless we are extremely vigilant. I say, Skimpton, you don't happen to have any milk, do you? Skimpton? Where the devil are you?'

Skimpton, however, was no longer in attendance, having taken himself off – at the first mention of Varley's relative – in the direction of the gym, with the intention of punishing himself with 500 press-ups, his usual method of regaining full use of his limbs.

*   *   *   *

Meanwhile, over in Main House, Marcus Dent was listening to gypsy music playing on his gramophone, when he was disturbed by a commotion in the corridor. The school rotter had been recovering from the previous night's over-indulgence by relaxing on his chaise longue and nonchalantly hurling darts at a photograph of one of the crowned heads of Europe, when he recognized the booming voice whose owner he assumed was responsible for the fracas outside. 'Make way!' it demanded. 'VIP arriving!' So violent were the speaker's footsteps that the resulting vibration sent the needle dancing crazily about the gramophone record, before the entire cabinet hurled itself from its perch and crashed to the floor.

Just then the door was flung open and several hefty trunks came flying in, landing on the Persian carpet and rattling the chandelier. 'Careful with those,' scowled Dent attempting to reassemble his gramophone player, 'you'll have that Lalique vase over and it's worth a fortune.'

'Sorry Marcus.' It was Binns, thrusting his blubbery frame through the door and flashing his master a lop-sided grin.

'Is Spate with you?'

Just then the fellow in question appeared behind Binns in the corridor. 'I am indeed, Marcus,' he intoned, 'greetings.'

'Guess how many boys he hurled from the train this year?' demanded Binns loudly.

'Shame they didn't include you, you fathead,' returned Dent. 'Well, Spate?'

'Only three I am afraid, Marcus.'

'You are slacking. I shall expect you to make up for it by being doubly psychotic this term.'

'You may count on it Marcus.'

'We met an old chum of yours on the train, Marcus,' put in Binns.

'Binns...'

'Yes, Marcus?'

'You do realize that you are stationed little more than two feet away from me, don't you?'

'I'd say eighteen inches at most. So what?'

'So why are you bellowing at me like a blasted foghorn, you dirty great clod?'

'Sorry Marcus.'

'If anything, you are even louder than usual. What has happened?'

'I might be able to shed some light on that subject, Marcus,' explained Spate. 'You see, I accidentally set off a firework in

Binns's ear when he was asleep on the train. I suspect he might have gone a trifle deaf.'

At that moment, Horace 'Cocky' Peacock breezed into the room, arms outstretched in the manner of an ostentatious theatrical, and hugged Dent warmly. 'My dear Marcus,' he beamed, 'how simply saucy to see you!' He was wearing a rather fetching georgette blouson in royal blue with moleskin trimming, and his affectionate greeting left Dent with a vibrant lipstick mark on his cheek.

'Cocky Peacock!' laughed he. 'You've met my chums, Binns and Spate?'

'Cocky was good enough to pay our excess fares, Marcus,' boomed Binns, 'we were in First Class without permission.'

'How uncommonly generous of you Cocky.'

'Yes, it was wasn't it?' Peacock had by now made for the mirror and was busy adjusting his makeup and hair.

'Spate had been letting off fireworks you see,' added Binns, 'and we were escaping the guard.'

'Fascinating,' said Dent, indifferently. 'Now, Cocky, I dare say you'll want something stiff inside you after your arduous journey.'

'Very presumptuous of you, Marcus, but on this occasion a simple glass of tonic water should suffice.'

'Binns...'

'Not for me thanks, Marcus. Bit early in the day.'

'Never mind "bit early in the day"! Get Cocky a blasted drink you fool!'

Binns sulked off in the direction of the drinks cabinet whilst Cocky seated himself next to Dent on the chaise longue. Spate, meanwhile, hovered around menacingly, munching a brandy ball.

'So, Cocky,' said Dent expansively, 'how is your mischievous brother?'

'Dickie is resting in his flat in Hammersmith after some disastrous jape at college involving the Dean and a bag of flour.'

'How very dull.'

'I agree. I trust that you have a few more inventive rags up your sleeve for this term, Marcus?'

'I'm working on it.'

'Well I hope you will be quick, otherwise I might very well die of boredom in this ghastly place. How on earth do you stand it?'

'Actually,' roared Binns, hurling his voice across the room ferociously, 'I think Faysgarth's rather jolly!'

'I am sure you do,' snapped Cocky, 'but I do not recall your views being sought on the matter.'

'I...I only meant...'

'I care little for what you meant, you loud-mouthed oaf. It was the volume at which you distributed your opinion that concerns me. Now bring me my drink or I shall devise some heinous punishment for you.'

A gentle thud was heard as Binns's jaw detached itself and dropped feebly to the floor. In a state of severe shock, he gazed at it for some seconds, then picked it up and re-attached it to his face, before delivering Cocky Peacock with his glass of Indian tonic water.

'Take no notice of him, Binns,' said Dent, 'his bark is worse than his bite.'

'Nonsense,' dismissed Cocky, 'I bit an impudent boy on the nose last week at the Faverstock Summer Fete, and was paid handsomely for it by a Girl Guide.'

Cocky Peacock had been something of an outrageous character almost since birth. He wrote an obscene novel at the age of nine, was briefly imprisoned in a juvenile correction facility for lewd behaviour in a billiard hall, and spent three months in an utopian enclave run by a bearded sculptor and religious fanatic. Nowadays though, he cut something of a solitary figure, his sharp tongue and risqué conjecture having accounted for many an attachment. His intense friendship with a Polynesian boy at St. Hugh's the previous year almost destroyed him. When the individual departed the school, a minor disagreement between the two having been left unresolved, a furious Peacock was left railing at the world, and suffering from an obsessive tendency to preen himself in public.

To the lower orders he was seen as a fearsome though somewhat distant individual whose scathing put-downs could leave a boy staggering in their wake.

Apart from his unrivalled eloquence, Cocky was also a surprisingly good runner, and would use sporting occasions as much to show off a new haircut or taffeta singlet as he would to display his undoubted speed over the final mile. Indeed, it was one such occasion, during his last term at St. Hugh's, which saw the final act of vanity result in his expulsion. A quarter of a mile ahead of his nearest rival, and with only 500 yards to the tape, Cocky had taken out a comb and was so embroiled in sculpting his golden locks, in preparation for the photographers who awaited his victory at the finishing line, that he very nearly gave the race away, having to come from behind and pip another boy at the post. He was instantly summoned to the headmaster's office and told to seek an alternative school the following term. Having been turned down by several, on account of his reputation, he now found himself at Faysgarth, an institution so desperate for funds that people joked that a baboon would probably be offered a place if its owners coughed up the requisite fees.

Some years earlier he and Dent had formed a happy, breezily subversive union at prep, even though the latter was somewhat older than Peacock. Together they produced a juvenile literary magazine of such profound depravity that a copy found its way to the Lord Chamberlain, who pronounced it quite the most degenerate publication he had ever encountered. Unable to instigate proceedings against the authors, as they were both under-age, the guardian of public morals ordered every copy in existence destroyed.

Cocky, though, had managed to retain one issue, and – having now delighted Dent by producing it – was busy entertaining the small gathering with a dramatic rendition of a mildly suggestive sonnet, recited from its pages.

A girl I knew with auburn hair
Would lay her assets all but bare
And with her husband also there
The two would f---- without a care.

Before he could continue, though, there was a knock at the door. Cocky, who happened to be nearest, opened it.

'I am looking for my nephew, Mr. Jack Varley,' the stranger stated. It was a young woman of about thirty, with short, brown hair and pretty enough features. She appeared to be struggling to control a small dog which wriggled about in her arms.

'I am afraid, madam,' replied Cocky, with measured politeness, 'that I am new to Faysgarth and am therefore, as yet, unacquainted with the young man to whom you refer.'

'This is Second House, is it not?' she asked assuredly.

'There I *can* assist you. This building is Main House.'

Here, Dent intervened. 'Second House,' said he, 'is on the opposite side of the quad, madam. There, in all probability, you will discover your nephew, most likely engaged in a titanic tussle over the chessboard with one of his many creditworthy chums.'

'I am certain of it. Thank you, both of you.'

The young woman then turned smartly and took both herself and her dog off down the corridor, leaving Dent and Peacock smiling archly at one another.

'I say!' said Binns, butting in between the two of them and squinting off after the young woman. 'That's a healthy bit of skirt if ever I saw one!'

'And what would you know about it?' retorted Cocky. 'Are you an expert?'

'Well, no.'

'Do you have any notion of what an *unhealthy* bit of skirt looks like?'

'Not in the least.'

'Then kindly spare us your vulgar remarks.'

'There's no need to take that tone.'

'I shall take whatever tone I wish with you, young fellow, until you repay the 3/6 you owe me for the train. Now toss off with your sidekick and summon up some tea and crumpets for Marcus and myself.'

A quick nod from their leader, and within seconds both Binns and Spate were absent, leaving Dent to refill his pal's glass. 'I am glad to see,' he intoned dryly, 'that you have wasted no time in establishing affectionate sway over my minions.'

'Such irksome little toadies, and uncommonly plain, both of them. Where did you find them?'

'Binns, I suppose, is part of the furniture, and Spate, I think, came free with a bottle of rat poison.'

'What about this fellow Skimpton,' said Varley, 'is he to compete in this year's County Cross Country race? I hear he's rather an accomplished athlete.'

'You shouldn't find him much trouble, Cocky. The fellow's stark raving bonkers. Seizes up, apparently, in the presence of women.'

'How bizarre. Let's hope there are plenty in the crowd on the day of the race!'

'It can be arranged.'

*   *   *   *

'Get down Barclay!' implored Varley's aunt as her dog wrestled her nephew onto the floor of his study. 'I'm awfully sorry, Jack,' she sighed, 'it's something about strangers he doesn't like.'

'It's quite understandable,' said Varley, gripping the writhing creature by the throat, and holding it at arm's length, 'I am sure I deserve it.' Handing over the yelping pup, Varley eyed ruefully the holes in his blazer and brushed himself down as his aunt used a length of rope to bind the dog securely to a chair leg.

'Any chance of a cup of tea?' she enquired.

'Lucinda,' returned Jack with a hint of impatience, 'I shall consider providing you with refreshment when you have informed me of the reason for your visit.'

His aunt was now inspecting the cricket bat situated nearby, and which still bore the marks of the previous season's bowling. 'What's your current average, Jack?' she asked.

'I shall tell you that when you answer *my* question. To what do I owe the pleasure of your company, Lucinda?'

'Do you have a bowl of water?'

'Whatever for?'

'Why, I intend to dive into it and perform the backstroke of course! It's for the dog, you chump!'

Varley's aunt Lucinda was seen as something of a mysterious character in the family, though her rumbustious, good-natured manner always provoked immediate acceptance at gatherings. Unmarried, she was reputed to hold down a relatively powerful position as a research scientist at one of the government's laboratories nearby, but had always been very reluctant to discuss the precise nature of her work.

Judging by the origins of the many postcards she sent to him from all over the globe, Varley wondered if she may even be a spy, but when on the one occasion he confronted her with his suspicion, her response was to laugh uproariously in the manner of a raucous schoolgirl.

Varley had always got on well with his aunt, and their easy banter had provided a cheerful accompaniment to many family holidays, when she had often taken charge of her nephew during boating expeditions. Once, when staying in the family cottage in France, so happy had been their time together, that Varley briefly thought that he might be in love with her – a notion quickly banished once he returned to Faysgarth and re-acquainted himself with the pleasures of the long-jump pit.

Family tittle-tattle maintained that she was involved in a long-standing liaison with a gentleman some years older than herself, and alongside whom she worked at the MOD. But Varley's enquiries in that respect had gleaned even less information than had those relating to the nature of her work – and provoked from her a similarly robust and mirth-filled response.

Having stated that Varley's relationship with his aunt was generally an amicable one, it would be misleading to imply that the pair saw eye-to-eye on everything, particularly with respect to her dog Barclay. Quite why his aunt should procure the company of so aggressive a brute was beyond Varley, and his open hostility to the wretched creature frequently left him shaken, grazed and punctured, and his friendship with Lucinda decidedly strained.

'Leave the dog here?' he exclaimed presently. 'At Faysgarth?'

'Why not?' Lucinda had finally got around to revealing the reason for her visit, having proposed that her nephew take custody of the atrocious canine whilst she attended to business abroad.

'Apart from anything else the rules forbid the keeping of animals anywhere on school premises!'

'But Jack,' pleaded his aunt, 'couldn't you keep him hidden here in your room?'

'Lucinda,' Varley replied firmly, 'he would tear me to pieces in my bed!' At that, the tenacious Barclay dragged himself, and the chair to which he was tied, into the doorway, spun around several times, freeing himself to squeeze through the door and scuttle off down the corridor. Varley had flung himself onto the floor in a vain attempt to restrain the beast but had suffered the indignity of having his face trampled over by Barclay on his way out.

'Leave him, Jack,' said aunt Lucinda, 'he won't get very far.' Varley's aunt then proceeded to light the stove and fill the kettle, whilst attempting to change the subject with idle chit-chat. 'So,' she remarked, 'this is Faysgarth?'

'Indeed it is. And I will not have its tranquillity disturbed by your beastly bow-wow!'

'And what of your chum Skimpton, Jack, am I to meet him?'

'Assuming he has not been savaged by the hound, I suspect those may be his footsteps even now.'

A few seconds later, Skimpton appeared in the doorway, cradling a contented Barclay in his arms. 'Jack!' smiled the sportsman, 'I found this little bundle scampering off down the stairs. Do you know anything about it?'

'Indeed I do,' said Varley. 'Skimpton: meet my aunt Lucinda, guardian of the bundle in question.' Skimpton, his face now ashen with fear, set down the dog and advanced stiffly towards her outstretched hand.

'How very pleasant to meet you Master Skimpton,' she offered warmly, 'I have heard much of your impressive sporting achievements. Tell me, what do you think of Barnchester's chances in the FA Cup?'

'Ugh, ugh...'

'Are you, like my nephew, keen on cricket?'

'W...w...w...'

'Skimpton loathes the game don't you old man?' put in Varley, helpfully. 'It's the only sport at which he doesn't excel.'

'What about chess? Do you play?'

But Skimpton was in no position to respond, for he was now gripped with a fierce paralysis, the inevitable consequence of finding himself in the company of a member of the opposite sex.

'Are you alright old man?' enquired Varley.

'Y...y...y...'

'Don't worry, Lucinda, he gets like this.'

'I hope it is nothing serious, Master Skimpton,' she said, 'I would hate to be the cause of any obstruction to your sporting efforts.'

Gradually though, an amazing transformation overcame the catatonic sportsman, for as she spoke, Skimpton felt his limbs spontaneously releasing themselves from their rigidity. Her voice was now somehow calming to him, even approachable, and he was astonished that, as he took her small hand in his, there was little evidence of stiffening in his body! By contrast he felt himself almost at ease – a condition which was entirely new to him when in the presence of a member of the female gender.

Barclay had pinned Varley down in a corner of the study, and Skimpton, without saying a word, floated easily into an armchair beside aunt Lucinda, who was now seated on the edge of the bed sipping tea. As she spoke, he found himself scrutinising her with all the wonder of a small boy presented with his first goldfish. There was something intoxicating in the musicality of her voice which banished all fear of muscular petrification, her words echoing soothingly in his head. Making no attempt whatsoever to respond to her questions, Skimpton contented himself by simply gazing into her face as one might an exquisite landscape by Poussin, comprehending little of its allegorical content, but revelling in its sensual beauty.

As she looked to her nephew for explication of his chum's extraordinary behaviour, Skimpton took Lucinda's hand once more and smiled beatifically, staring wondrously into her eyes.

'I...I was hockey captain when I was at school,' she stammered. But neither man nor beast in the room cared less. Varley was grappling with the dog as if his life depended on it, and Skimpton had quite clearly transported himself to a universe of his own construction, from where he fairly drank in her radiance, like a mother with a new-born child.

His eyes burned into hers as she went on to recount, with considerable humour, her recent adventures in foreign parts, and his hand gently squeezed encouragement during the more outlandish episodes. She was, he concluded, prettier than a shuttlecock in flight, more beautiful than a half volley into the net from thirty-five yards, more elegant than the curve of an archer's bow, and infinitely more streamlined than a well-seasoned javelin. Her eyes were deeper than the deepest dive, her lips fuller than the fullest toss, her cheeks smoother than a croquet lawn and her hands more dainty than a perfectly aimed grubber kick. More subtle was her voice than an exquisite back-hand drop shot, her wit quicker than a ten-speed Grecian Flyer travelling downhill, and her spirit tougher than a game of rounders against the upper fifth. In short, she was the most perfect example of anything Skimpton had ever seen.

*   *   *   *

Waking up some time later in his bed, after having passed out earlier in Jack Varley's study, Skimpton was surprised to find the dog's tail wagging in his face. Immediately, he looked about the room for Barclay's owner, but could see no sign of aunt Lucy.

Stumbling, somewhat befuddled, into his chum's room, Skimpton found Jack Varley enjoying the company of young Dick Parr, captain of the Junior Cricket Eleven. 'Now remember, Parr,' instructed Varley, 'never take your eye off the ball.'

'I say, Jack,' interrupted Skimpton, 'do you know anything about this dog which is at present resident in my room?'

'It belongs to my aunt Lucinda,' replied Varley tartly, 'and if my memory serves me correctly, you agreed – somewhat rashly in my opinion – to take charge of it for a period prior to her return from foreign parts.'

'When was this?'

'Some hours ago, before you fainted.'

'But it is against school rules to keep pets!'

'As indeed I attempted to point out to you.'

'When will she return?'

'I am afraid the woman left in rather a hurry without furnishing me with that information.'

'I say!'

'Now, if you don't mind, Skimpton, I have pressing business here with young Parr.'

As he was traversing the corridor in something of a daze, Skimpton encountered his young fag Piggot. The junior was decked out in brand new sporting togs, and brandished a grin the size of a banana. 'I have cleared the gymnasium, Skimpton,' he beamed, his prominent front teeth thrust forward at what seemed like an impossible angle, 'in preparation for our lusty session on the vaulting horse!'

'I beg your pardon Piggot?' came the dreamy reply.

'Do you not remember, Skimpton? You offered to assist me!'

'Did I?'

'Indeed so, sir!'

'Well…go and make a start, Piggot, and I shall be along shortly.'

'But I am unable to leap high enough without your help,' pleaded the junior. 'And the upper-fifth will be in there in half an hour doing their physical jerks!'

'Then I suppose we shall have to postpone activities until a later date.'

'Yes sir.' Piggot, utterly deflated, felt his lower lip quiver, and shifted his weight from one foot to the other, quite unsure where to place his heavy heart. Skimpton, completely oblivious to the youngster's disappointment, returned to his study.

*   *   *   *

Later that day, Cocky Peacock was arranging his few possessions in a characteristically spartan manner about his study. Apart from a few racy books and his clothes, the dandy had very little which might point to their owner's carefully cultivated and ostentatious persona. Indeed, in terms of home comforts, his quarters were more akin to the gaol cell he had briefly occupied subsequent to his misdemeanour in the billiard hall, than they were to anything else; a simple scattering of utilitarian belongings with which he appeared more than happy. Seated at his desk, he was perusing, with little enthusiasm, a copy of the school magazine, the mildly satirical *Fractured Lives*, and considering whether to offer his services as a columnist, when there occurred a knock at the door. His visitor was Marcus Dent, in sombre mood, his eyes fixed on the floor as he entered.

'Marcus!' hailed Cocky. 'I've just been reading this. It's quite appalling.'

'I know.'

'Listen…'

With all the skill of a seasoned orator, Cocky began reciting from the poetry section of the pamphlet.

Sing a song of rugger
Though your face be caked in mud
With the sticks in sight, the ball in flight
Awaits the mighty thud.

'Drivel' said Dent.

Sing a song of scrumming
When a vict'ry's in the air
For you'll 'wheel and take it with you'
Playing hard and strong yet fair.

'Cocky,' said Dent, seating himself on his chum's bed. 'I am in need of a wangle.'

'I hear you can procure one from behind the bicycle sheds for 1/6. Failing that, there's always the long-jump pit.'

'Listen,' said Dent, rising and pacing the room like a tragic actor, 'this may be my final term at Faysgarth, and it's imperative that I come up with a first-rate autumn jape to maintain my position. I know some of the fellows here think I'm already over the hill.'

'I say!'

'True. I have just been publicly ridiculed by two third-formers.'

'Really?'

'And fallen for a petty fourth-form prank involving a tin of paint and several school ties.'

'How distressing for you.'

'Don't worry, I'm having Spate ambush them later, armed with tar and feathers.'

Peacock shuddered at the prospect of Spate being given authority to perpetrate such an act, for though his tongue spewed forth invective with unbridled brutality, the sprightly misanthrope remained ideologically opposed to physical violence. 'So,' he pontificated presently, 'you have come to me for assistance?'

'I'm not thinking straight, Cocky,' stated Dent, agitatedly. 'This place is driving me potty. I must prove that I am still on the ball, otherwise the remainder of the term will be hell.'

Cocky Peacock poured himself a glass of tonic water, and Dent a tumbler of Scotch. Pulling a chord beside the fireplace, he then moved his chair to a position directly opposite his friend who was now seated on the bed. He handed Dent his drink and placed himself on the chair, crossing his legs. Some seconds later, a further knock on the door heralded the arrival of a third-former who entered without much ceremony, carrying a silver bucket containing ice. His duties were performed in silence with speed and efficiency, and it was only after he had departed that Dent registered that the youngster had been completely naked.

'Don't ask,' said Peacock. 'It was his choice.'

Peacock manoeuvred the ice cubes around in his glass and stared at Dent. Smiling confidently, he leant back in his seat, adopting the slightly disinterested pose of an illustrious barrister sizing up his client. Dent, by contrast, was sitting forward, head bowed, hands thrust between his thighs, feet tapping on the floorboards, like an anxious schoolboy waiting to be reprimanded by the head.

Presently, Peacock too leaned forward. His face now within an inch of Dent's lowered crown, he could just make out the specs of green paint still matted in his friend's hair. 'Why don't we blow the place up?' he said, calmly.

Pausing for a moment before responding, Dent raised his face to peruse his chum's expression, expecting to confirm that his suggestion was in jest. 'Blow the place up?' he said.

'Why not?'

'You mean put a bomb under Faysgarth?'

'Several, I would imagine. It is rather a large place.' Peacock grinned expansively, obviously delighted with his dramatic proposal. 'It would undoubtedly be a topping ruse,' he smiled.

'Cocky,' said Dent, 'you must be completely mad.'

*   *   *   *

On his way to dinner that evening, Dent's spirits rose immeasurably at the sight of Skimpton in receipt of a thorough ticking off from Colonel Coombes. Apparently, while showing a prospective new master around the grounds, the chemistry Colonel and his companion had been attacked by a dog, supposedly under the supervision of Faysgarth's most trustworthy pupil. At the height of the hullabaloo, the ever-helpful Dent had stepped in and offered to escort the visitor around the quad, leaving the Colonel free to beat Skimpton senseless for breaking school rules with respect to the keeping of pets.

The stranger turned out to be an amiable gentleman of German origin, by the name of Müller, who was considering taking up a position in the languages department, vacated by the recently departed slacker, Frobisher. Dent playfully discouraged the master as best he could, describing Faysgarth, picaresquely, as 'a putrefying potato full of worms' at one point, and suggesting that Herr Müller might better occupy his time trawling the bars and nightclubs of his native Berlin.

For his part, the extravagantly moustachioed Prussian, still shaking from his tempestuous encounter with Skimpton's four-legged fiend, seemed more concerned to ascertain whether the dog's presence in the school was permanent. Dent calmly assured him that the pooch was only a temporary menace, yet no less dangerous than many fourth-formers – an assertion prompted by his own recent, distressing experiences.

At the school gates, they were interrupted by the unmistakable resonance of Binns's voice spraying about the quad and eating into the brickwork like a powerful industrial acid.

'Marcus!' he now volleyed, from only a few feet away. 'Have you seen this?' He held out a copy of the *Barnchester Chronicle* and pointed to a report near the foot of the page. It read:

Local woman absconds from labratory
Important papers missing

'Well?' said Dent, mystified.

'Don't you notice anything remarkable?'

'There is an an "o" absent from the word "laboratory" but that is not particularly noteworthy, given the typographical inaccuracy for which that particular organ is somewhat famed.'

'I say, well spotted!' admired Binns.

'And a capital letter missing from the word 'Russian', of course, towards the end of the item.'

'Look at the picture!' exploded Binns, for the benefit of the entire county.

Before investigating the issue any further though, Dent, remembering his obligations to the German, turned to offer Herr Müller an apology for his reverberating friend's vocal eccentricity. But the master, who had until then been observing proceedings from a short distance, his fingers thrust deep into his ears, could now be seen shuffling off down the drive, with a view – Dent assumed – to preserving his eardrums for future use.

Presently, the Main Houseman returned to Binns's newspaper, his eyes skimming down the page and coming to rest on the photograph, attached to the article to which the mis-spelt headline belonged. 'Hmmm,' he mused, 'very interesting.' The information contained in the piece, he now devoured with considerable interest, as it referred quite unequivocally to the young woman he had only that day met for the first time. The accompanying photograph confirmed as much, for it was a rather fetching picture of Varley's aunt.

*   *   *   *

Skimpton, painfully prostrate on his bed in Second House, had good reason to bemoan the absence of his fag Piggot, for the severe lashing he had been awarded by Colonel Coombes had left such a network of deep and virulent gashes on his hind quarters, that only a particular combination of lotions and ointments, applied by an attentive assistant, would relieve the agony. Piggot, though, had long since been driven away by the threat of dismemberment at the paws of Barclay, man's supposed best friend. Now placed resolutely in the middle of the floor, the dog panted impatiently, wagging its tail and barking occasionally as an indication that it was in pretty urgent need of food.

'Are you hungry then, my little monster?' asked Skimpton wanly, sipping from a cup of beef tea he had painfully prepared earlier.

'As a matter of fact, I am,' replied the dog scornfully. 'Ravishing. What are you going to do about it?' Barclay then shot a cynical glare at Skimpton and gave out a series of threatening growls. Realizing that his present predicament precluded him from defending himself from any attack the quadruped might choose to launch, the debilitated Deputy Head Boy reached into his tuck box and flung two stale apple turnovers at the pooch.

Tossing the confectionery smartly into his body via the mouth, the dog then confronted Skimpton again, implying that he had need of further sustenance. This time, though, his guardian had nothing to offer, other than a friendly pat on the head.

It was then that Skimpton noticed for the first time the heart-shaped charm attached to the dog's collar. As he reached to grasp it, a sharp pain shot up his arm as Barclay's teeth sank into the flesh on the back of his hand. Withdrawing it immediately, and abandoning all intent with regard to the curio which the dog appeared to guard with such ferocity, Skimpton – for perhaps the first time – began to regret the presence of the canine at Faysgarth. Having quickly polished off his hors d'ouevres, Barclay had soon tired of waiting around for his main course, and was now prowling the room wearing a dangerous scowl. Skimpton, fearing for his furniture and clothing, shouted for assistance from Jack Varley, little realizing that, like Piggot and others before him, he too had deserted Second House, fearful that they might end up in the clutches of Skimpton's irascible canine companion.

*   *   *   *

At that moment, Varley was enjoying the more convivial atmosphere of the Senior Common Room, where he was engaged in an entertaining game of chess with, of all people, Horace 'Cocky' Peacock.

Consequent to the newspaper report, the quad had been reverberating with rumour on the subject of his absent aunt all afternoon. In between moves, Varley, assuming that his adversary was as absorbed with it all as was everyone else, was setting down his views at some length. 'If you ask me,' he said, 'she's gone totally bananas.'

'Who has?' sighed Peacock.

'Why, my aunt, of course!'

The game had been in progress for some minutes now, and Peacock was beginning to tire of his opponent's tedious obsession with his relative, and now attempted to steer the conversation elsewhere. 'I must say, Varley,' he commented, 'I do admire your cravat. Is it silk?'

'Actually, it's sarsenet. I had it fashioned by a man in Guernsey from the lining of one of my father's old blazers.'

'How ingenious.'

Peacock's flattery, though, only temporarily distracted Varley from his recital of displeasure, and he proceeded to plough on. This time though, the dandy gleaned a morsel of interest from the other's catalogue of grievances.

'Would that be Skimpton the runner?' canvassed Peacock, pausing over a queen.

'The same. She has roped him in on her tom-fool prank.'

'Really?'

'Between you and I, he's agreed to take care of her dog.'

'For mercy's sake, that's strictly against school rules! Until when?'

'Whenever she returns from wherever she's holed up, of course!'

'You don't think she's been abducted then?'

'Not in the least. If you ask me this fellow with whom she has been dallying is more than likely behind it.'

'You mean the Russian chap who has also gone missing?'

'Indeed. It's pretty serious actually. I was called to the Head's study this afternoon to answer questions from a Detective Inspector Collin C. Henessy from Scotland Yard. I didn't mention the dog, of course, for fear that Skimpton might come a cropper. Little did I realize that he would be foolish enough to take it for walkies whilst the Colonel was about.'

'Forgive my asking,' said Cocky, finally moving a knight to take a pawn, 'but what's he like, exactly, this Skimpton fellow?'

'A damn fool but a rattling good sportsman. This business will end in disaster for him, I am certain.'

'Why?'

Varley sighed, expansively. 'I suspect,' he said, 'that he has fallen in love with my aunt.'

'Fallen in love? The silly chump. Shouldn't he know better?'

'Of course! Besides, she's smitten with this fellow Tilkowski with whom they think she's done a bunk.'

'The Russian?'

'That's him.'

'Does Skimpton know this?'

'Certainly he does, but he's like a runaway train once he gets something into his head. It's like when he decided to take up the organ. Three years we had to endure him thumping away at it under the dubious tutelage of old Meades in the chapel. He only gave up after some kind soul poured cement into the pipes.'

Peacock, his mind circling menacingly above the information being delivered with reckless enthusiasm by Varley, was also calculating how best to dictate the course of the chess game so that his opponent could enjoy a narrow victory. 'Do we know what the nature is of these papers with which she and her Russian cohort have absconded?' he enquired, earnestly.

'I have no idea. But between you and I,' responded Varley, replacing Cocky's queen with his own bishop, 'she's been engaged in some sort of scientific experimentation. Highly hush-hush.'

'And where do you think she has gone?'

'Who knows? Probably miles away by now. But I'd hazard anything she'll be back for the dog. She adores the little mutt.'

Peacock, exacting swift retribution for the loss of his queen, removed Varley's bishop and replaced it with one of his own. 'You know,' he said at length, 'I don't know about you but I simply can't make head nor tale of this love business.'

'I am glad to hear you say it,' agreed Varley, 'for it's all a complete mystery to me too. I should hope Skimpton's thrashing by Colonel Coombes will teach him to stay well clear as well.'

'Colonel Coombes?'

'Psychotic chemistry man, hopelessly short-sighted. Once he gets going with that birch of his it's every man for himself! You should see the marks on Skimpton's back! Like railway lines at a busy junction. And the bruises on his legs fairly glow like burning embers!'

'How very vividly put.'

'Do you think so? I so enjoy words. I had a mildly satirical piece published in the school magazine last term. *Sing A Song Of Rugger*, it was called. I wrote it at Skimpton's request, though I'm a cricket man myself.'

'Do you know, I think I read it!' enthused Cocky. 'Very good it was too!

Sing a song of rugger
Though your face be caked in mud...

'I say Peacock, jolly well remembered!' Varley, delighted that his work had apparently made such a favourable impression, began reciting the entire poem, before triumphantly excommunicating his new chum's bishop, and replacing it with his own queen. 'Skimpton, of course hated it,' he said, 'didn't get the joke.'

'I say, poor show!'

'You know something Peacock,' said Varley, grinning, 'I think you and I are destined to become firm friends!'

'I am sure of it!'

'Although you'll have to improve somewhat on the chess board if our alliance is to sustain.'

'Oh yes, why?'

'For that, old man,' declared Varley, claiming a remarkable victory, 'is checkmate!'

*   *   *   *

Erich Müller was a small, rotund character of about fifty, whose arrival at Faysgarth was greeted with some relief by those taking the German option. After the ineffectual solecisms of the dithering Frobisher, Herr Müller's obvious competence and affable manner were judged to be precisely what the Languages Department required to help it out of the doldrums.

Amongst the boys, the genial German was particularly popular, as they revelled in his extended anecdotes about his exploits as an Olympic athlete before the Great War. Quickly establishing a keen interest in school sports, Herr Müller made himself universally available to every aspiring athlete, especially those whose interests leaned in the direction of the forthcoming Cross-Country Championships, to whom he offered particular advice and encouragement.

The personable Prussian's wider sphere of knowledge was extensive, and covered many fields; he possessed a discerning musical ear, dabbled in painting, and had been seen deep in discussion with Colonel Coombes well into the small hours, about matters scientific.

He spoke with such a pronounced German accent that it often bordered on the caricature, and he took great delight in the boys' efforts to impersonate him, deeming that their attempts, rather than challenging his authority, might improve their pronunciation of the language!

Indeed, the only pupil who failed to strike a chord with Herr Müller was the new dandy of the Upper Sixth, Horace 'Cocky' Peacock, whose extravagant behaviour and appearance soon caught the eye of the German, and for which he issued unusually severe punishments. Herr Müller took particular exception to Peacock wearing a flower in his buttonhole during his lesson one day, and there began a dissonance between the two of them which usually resulted in Peacock being lumbered with countless lines extolling the virtue of masculine restraint.

Skimpton, on the other hand, was especially favoured by the German master. So much so, in fact, that at their first meeting late one night in the school grounds, as Skimpton was out walking Barclay, Herr Müller promised to say nothing to Colonel Coombes about the presence of the dog – so long as Skimpton undertook to do all he could to defeat Cocky Peacock in the forthcoming race. An arrangement with which the sportsman was only too happy to comply.

By this time, though, plans were already underway not just to thwart Skimpton's sporting aspirations, but to implicate him in a fiendish plot to destroy the school he loved.

It was now the beginning of October and Skimpton had been playing host to Lucinda Varley's mongrel Barclay for over two weeks, retaining the tyke in his study during the day and letting him out only very late at night. This routine, though by and large workable, was not without its inconveniences. For though he had begun to grow quite fond of the little mutt, the dog's presence in Second House had all but lost Skimpton his friends, as well as the services of his fag. But so brightly did the image of its owner shine in his memory, that these minor distractions meant little to the Deputy Head Boy, for so long as Barclay remained under his care, he knew that there was a strong probability that he would see Lucinda Varley again.

Then, quite out of the blue, a letter arrived for him with a West London postmark.

'My Dear Skimpton,' it read.

Forgive me for not writing to you earlier but, as you may know

I am in hiding and have feared to venture out, even to the post box! I write to enquire of your health and that of my darling dog Barclay. I am sure that you are keeping him from harm, for, even in the brief time I spent with you, I could tell you were a gentle soul, and indeed one to whom I now find myself deeply indebted.

One day, Skimpton, I am certain that we will meet again, in more leisurely circumstances, when I am sure we will get on famously, for I sense we have much in common. Our short discourse last month at Faysgarth I have to admit to finding quite moving – I do hope you felt the same.

I cannot give details about my present predicament for reasons of personal safety, nor can I reveal my precise whereabouts, but should you choose to write c/o the above address, your words would, I am sure, bring some welcome respite to my situation.

With fondest regards,
Lucinda Varley.

Skimpton was unable to attend to his school work that morning. He remained, for some hours, imprisoned in his armchair re-reading the letter from Varley's aunt. Nor did he venture forth to the running track that afternoon, where he had arranged to meet Herr Müller for a thorough training session, choosing rather to lock himself in his study and set his mind to composing a reply.

*   *   *   *

Meanwhile, over in Main House, a furious Marcus Dent, two broken teeth testimony to him having fallen for yet another juvenile prank perpetrated by rebellious fourth-formers, had called a meeting of his cronies. Subject: mischief. 'Now,' barked he, 'what have you found out about Varley's aunt, Binns? And speak quietly.'

'Well, Marcus,' whispered the dunce, 'apparently our beloved

Deputy Head Boy's in love with her.'

'Is he now? Leaving him open for manipulation. Cocky?'

'I have already set the wheels in motion, Marcus,' assured Peacock, 'If all goes well, after we've blown up Faysgarth all the accusing fingers will be pointing in one direction: Skimpton's.'

'Splendid. Now Spate, what about these explosives?'

'I have placed an order for them with my father's shady contacts in the East End of London, Marcus.'

'Topping.'

'When's the blast to take place, Marcus?' asked Binns.

'During the cross-country race,' put in Cocky, 'as everyone will be lining the route, we can avoid any bloodshed when the place goes up.'

Dent, whose present mood had inclined him considerably further in the direction of wholesale slaughter than had Peacock's, nodded his reluctant assent. 'You must consent to run, though, Cocky,' he insisted, 'for I intend to open a book on the outcome and make a bob or two. Once the bomb goes off, you'll most likely be the only one left running.'

'Very well,' said Cocky, 'but I insist something is done about that venomous Kraut Müller. He's making my life a misery.'

'Spate,' demanded Dent, 'see to it, would you?'

'I want no killing,' said Cocky.

'Very well. Binns, you do it then.'

'But I've always found Herr Müller such a pleasant chap!' protested the idiot.

'In that case,' hissed Cocky, 'you may undertake to supply him with the 30,000 lines he requires from me before to-morrow morning. "I must not wear perfume in class".'

'Me?'

'Yes, get on with it!'

Binns looked to Dent in a pathetic attempt to secure support, but his lord merely scoffed at him and pointed to the door. 'You too, Spate,' he instructed. 'Go and devour one of the fourth-form for me, someone must be made to pay for that pathetic jape with the ball bearings this morning.'

'Right away Marcus.'

After Spate's departure, Peacock stretched out on Dent's bed, as his pal prepared them drinks. 'Whatever do you see in those fellows?' he asked.

'They have their uses,' replied Dent.

'I loathe all this violence you go in for at Faysgarth.'

'Desperate times require desperate measures, my friend,' said Dent, pouring himself an enormous vodka.

'You are sure,' said Cocky, 'that you wish to go through with all of this?'

'Of course. The sooner we dispatch this godforsaken place the better. If I leave Faysgarth at the end of this term under anything other than a very dark cloud then I shall endure a torrid time at Cambridge. Anonymity, albeit temporary, Cocky, is something I simply will not countenance. Cheers.'

*　　*　　*　　*

On the drive, Herr Müller was straining to keep pace with Skimpton, as the latter, missive to his beloved in hand, trotted through the school gates destined for the village post office. 'How is zat dog of yours?' enquired the German.

'He is in good health, thank you, Herr Müller,' came the polite reply.

'You have, as yet, given me no explanation for your absence from zer runnink track zis mornink, Skimpton.'

'I am afraid, sir, I had school work to catch up with.'

'You remember our agreement,' gasped Herr Müller, coming to a breathless halt some yards behind Skimpton. 'You must verk hard to beat zis Peacock character. I hear he is a fine runner even zo he is, how shall we say, a perwert!'

Unsure of the precise meaning of this last phrase and anxious to catch the five o'clock post, Skimpton did not tarry to reply, merely hoisting a valedictory wave towards the master before darting off in the direction of the village. Herr Müller, feeling quite faint from the effort of pursuing his favourite pupil, coughed violently and spat fiercely onto the ground, expelling from his mouth the unpleasant taste of Cocky Peacock's name.

*   *   *   *

Meanwhile, events were moving apace around the dormitories and corridors of Faysgarth School. Word had spread that Marcus Dent had been caught out by another petty autumn jest, involving a quantity of caviar and some tiny ball bearings. As he had, as yet, offered no autumn skulduggery of his own, it was assumed – by the lower caste – that Faysgarth's Maharaja of Mischief had finally run out of poppadums.

Rumours were circulating that moves were afoot, from within the ranks of the Upper Fifth, to topple Dent and his fawning courtiers from their hitherto unassailable perch of tyranny. As the week wore on, whilst Dent himself remained personally untouched, it was his adherents who took the brunt of the punishment. The hapless Binns was diverted from his job of scaring off Cocky Peacock's Teutonic tormentor Herr Müller, when he was chased around the quad by a fearsome band of revolutionaries screaming for blood. He was later left hanging for several hours by his feet from a chemistry laboratory window, and thrashed pitilessly by Colonel Coombes for his pains.

Whilst attempting to exact Dent's retribution on the audacious youngster responsible for the ball bearing prank, Spate found himself at the mercy of a baying crowd of buccaneers armed with wet towels and a seemingly irrepressible desire to whip their quarry to within an inch of his life. This he escaped with only by the skin of his teeth, after promising every last one of his persecutors generous quantities of fireworks from his personal supply.

Several more of Dent's lesser satellites suffered even greater punishments. Alec 'Dodger' Downing, the fifth-form poisoner, suffered acute stomach pains after being forced to eat his own ear wax by a band of second-formers, eager to prove their worth in the revolt. Littleworth Senior, manufacturer of unusual instruments of torture, by special appointment to His Majesty Prince Marcus of Dent, was strapped to his own pummelling device for three days, emerging with a permanent shake and an impenetrable stammer.

Perhaps the worse victim of Faysgarth's insurrection, though, was young Freddie Cherrington, whose only crime was that he had the misfortune of being distantly related to Dent on his mother's side. He was given a complete blood transfusion by members of the third-form, who replaced his own supply with that of a rabid goat. Pleading with Colonel Coombes for assistance as he convulsed on the ground in the quad, the ill-fated Cherrington was told to 'straighten himself out and stop playing the silly billy' – an irony which was not lost on the perpetrators, who were observing from a distance. He was eventually taken to hospital, where – it turned out – he remained until well into his thirties.

*　　*　　*　　*

As is often the case in revolution, the temperature of the Faysgarth rebellion eventually subsided through lack of coherent leadership. Marcus Dent, though, remained shaken by the various audacious challenges mounted to his authority, and was convinced that his position as champion cheat was far from secure. It was essential, he felt, that the momentous prank being prepared by himself and Horace Peacock should not go off half cock, or worse still, be seen to fail.

Agitated, he now paced his friend's study, his nails bitten to the quick, his confidence all but shattered. 'How will people know that it is me behind the jape?' he worried, 'and if they do, what's to stop me going to gaol?'

'Trust me, Marcus,' reassured Cocky. 'We shall wait a suitable period before putting it about that you masterminded the whole thing. The police know they will never convict the likes of you purely on rumour and innuendo, for it is obvious from your accent that you will encounter no trouble securing the services of a top defence lawyer. Were you a member of the working classes, however, things might be very different.'

Peacock, since his ignominious expulsion from St. Hugh's the previous year, had rather taken to railing about the inequities of the class system, and had even poured scorn on the public schools, which he now saw as an anachronism in the modern world, favouring rather, the more meritocratic system being canvassed by various notables at the time. Aware that immediate imperatives often lead to political allegiances losing focus, Dent worried somewhat over his friend's motives for wanting to demolish Faysgarth. 'You realize Cocky,' he said, 'that this is only an autumn jape. We're not starting some appalling revolution, you know.'

'Today Faysgarth,' intoned Peacock, 'to-morrow the world! Remember, so long as these ghastly institutions stand, bolstering the pillars of privilege, we shall remain a backward nation, clinging vaingloriously to our dubious past as temporary respite from a grasping and envious present.'

'Well I hope you know what you are doing,' said Dent moodily.

'I am fully in control, thank you Marcus,' came the confident reply. 'Now if you don't mind, I have an article to write for the school magazine.' On Peacock's desk lay a satirical piece, as yet unfinished, entitled *Faysgarth Daze*, written under the pseudonym 'Wolfgang Plankton'. As he ushered Dent from the room, however, it was other, more pressing matters which occupied his mind, and after bolting the door, he reached into his pocket and produced an envelope which had been delivered that morning.

Bearing a West London postmark, the missive was addressed to him in the unmistakably florid hand of his brother Dickie. Inside it was another envelope, as yet unopened, bearing a Faverstock imprint and addressed, in a rather less ambitious script, to a Miss Lucinda Varley. The letter contained therein made fascinating reading for Horace 'Cocky' Peacock, for it had been written by one of his schoolfellows; a young worthy smitten with the painful joys of juvenile yearning.

'My Darling Lucinda,' it began.

'I cannot say how delighted I was to receive your letter, and to learn from its content that your feelings, even if in a small way, might reciprocate my own...'

* * * *

Peacock's unwitting correspondent was at that moment day-dreaming in his study, when his reverie was interrupted by a knock at the door. 'Skimpton,' hailed Herr Müller from the corridor, 'I must speak viz you!'

A full ninety seconds later, an exhausted House Captain emerged from his fantasy and greeted the German wearily. 'What is it Herr Müller?' he sighed.

'I vos vorried,' said Müller, 'zat again zis afternoon you missed training.'

'Ah yes. Won't you come in?' Herr Müller looked uneasy, glancing past Skimpton into the study, attempting to ascertain whether or not the dog was in residence. 'It's alright,' said Skimpton, 'Barclay is out gallivanting with some third-formers. I have already telephoned for an ambulance. Can I get you anything? Tea? Coffee? Perhaps a game of cards?'

'Schnapps?'

'I'm afraid I only play whist, but if you'd like to outline the rules...'

Herr Müller seated himself on Skimpton's bed and attempted to engage the abstracted Senior in conversation of a sporting nature. Skimpton's contributions, however, were desultory, and his guest was forced to keep things ticking along with a lengthy account of his various experiences as an Olympic runner. With colourful enthusiasm, he recounted tales of his many successes and took great care to stress the importance of a supple pair of running shoes together with a diligent attitude to training.

Skimpton, though, listened to not a word, for his mind had taken flight, and was hovering over very different territory; one with waterfalls and cherry trees, olive groves and fluffy clouds, very much like the landscape of love.

When eventually his exalted senses once more fluttered earthwards and graced reality with their presence, he discovered, with some relief, that Herr Müller had taken his leave. He was settling in his battered old armchair preparing to read, for the five hundredth time that day, Lucinda Varley's letter, when another knock at the door announced the arrival of Jack Varley. 'I say Skimpton,' said Varley tartly, 'might I have a word?'

'My dear fellow! Do come in.' Varley too hesitated, ascertaining before entering, that his limbs were safe from a further mauling by his aunt's dog. 'Walkies,' said Skimpton, smiling.

'I have been asked by Colonel Coombes,' stated Varley, 'to speak to you about your school work.'

'Oh yes?'

Skimpton bore a serene smile which Varley immediately recognised as being identical to the one customarily adopted by his friend when he had no intention of taking any heed of his chum's advice. Varley, nonetheless, persisted. 'You see, Skimpton,' he said, 'he is rather concerned that your concentration appears to be slipping. I realize that the forthcoming Cross-Country Championships demand considerable attention from you at this time of year, but an average mark of just seven and a half percent will very soon begin to test the patience of even the most lenient of masters. Quite what such a performance will provoke from Colonel Coombes I shudder to think.'

Skimpton sallied forth with a resigned sigh, as if the threat posed by the homicidal chemistry master amounted to nothing more than a mere trifle. Fixing his friend with a quizzical look, he said, 'Have you read Shakespeare, Jack?'

'I am conversant with the set texts, that is all' came the icy reply.

Skimpton threw back his head, appeared to gaze at the ceiling for some seconds, before he began reciting, seemingly from memory:

Some glory in their birth, some in their skill
Some in their wealth, some in their body's force
Some in their garments, though new-fangled ill
Some in their hawks and hounds, some in their horse...

And when he had finished a few minutes later, there ensued a lengthy silence, in which Skimpton seemed happy to wallow. Varley, by contrast, was far from comfortable with the dramatic pause, nor the means by which it had been achieved. 'I had no idea you revered poetry, Skimpton,' he said flatly. 'Do you know what it means?'

'I've a rough idea.'

'I doubt it,' came the immediate, terse response. Varley, suddenly mad as a hornet, then turned on Skimpton. 'Why don't you stop playing the fool,' he fumed, 'before you are ousted from Second House and brandished a half-wit?'

'Can I offer you some muffins Jack?'

'Do you not realize what an idiot you are making of yourself? Before long the whole school will be laughing at you!'

'Nonsense! They are far too busy laughing at Marcus Dent. I hear he bit into a batch of ball bearings...'

'That may be true, but it is only a matter of time until someone reports you for harbouring that wretched dog!'

'Then you had better contact your aunt and request that she return for it.'

'I don't know where she is. Do you?'

'Haven't the foggiest old chap. How about some hot buttered toast?'

'No thank you Skimpton. I have been offered a game of chess

in the Senior Common Room.'

'Oh yes? Anyone nice?'

'Horace Peacock, as a matter of fact.'

'Oh dear. Isn't he reputed to be a trifle suspect?'

'Not in the least. I really do not know where you get your information from these days, Skimpton. Cocky's a trifle eccentric but at the same time a thoroughly decent fellow, with a level head on his shoulders – which is a damn sight more than can be said of a few people round here.' At which Varley turned on his heel and departed, returning the door smartly to its frame as he went.

Half an hour later, Skimpton was gazing from his window at the leafless branches shivering in the moonlight, a book of romantic poetry to hand, when he came across a few lines by a Frenchman named Le Comte de Bussy-Rabutin, which he felt encapsulated his mood perfectly:

> *Absence is to love what wind is to fire;*
> *it extinguishes the small, it inflames the great.*

A further knock at the door heralded the appearance of Piggot. Skimpton greeted his fag warmly, though the apprehensive junior hovered nervously in the corridor as he sought assurance that his life would not be put in jeopardy were he to enter. 'Lucky for you, Piggot,' said Skimpton benignly, 'Barclay is absent.'

'I am sorry to have made myself scarce recently Skimpton,' said the youngster, offering a weak smile.

'Think nothing of it. Can I tempt you with a brandy ball before the pooch finishes them?'

'No thank you, sir,' said Piggot, looking about the room nervously, and hopping in his characteristic manner from one foot to the other.

'Are you in need of the lavatory young man?' asked Skimpton.

'No sir. I...I have come to speak with you about your dog... Barclay.'

'Oh yes?'

'Well, some of the younger chaps, who, for reasons best known to themselves, like to organize late night feasts in Dead Man's Wood, were wondering if it were possible...you see some of them have been bitten rather badly.'

'Listen to this, Piggot, tell me what you think:

Such is the love I feel in my heart
My soul yearns for succour when 'ere we're apart.

'What do you make of it?'

'Very...heartfelt, sir.'

'Do you think so? Juvenile stuff, I know, but I'm hoping to move on to a more mature style next week.'

'Skimpton, the dog...' At that moment, there was a scurrying outside the window, as the animal in question leaped onto an adjoining wall and scurried onto the sill. Through the casement and inside the room within seconds, he charged across the floor with some ferocity. Discarding the dead vole with which he had arrived, Barclay leaped for the door, colliding painfully with it as it was hastily slammed shut by the retreating Piggot.

'My little daaarling,' smooched Skimpton, scooping up the squawking whelp. 'Have you hurt yourself? Let daddy kiss it better...'

*   *   *   *

'Another game?' ventured Jack Varley, cheerfully clearing the chess board after another resounding victory over Cocky Peacock.

'I am afraid you are far too good for me,' lied the latter. 'Besides, I have more lines to write for the abominable Müller – "I must not paint my nails in class".'

'Rotten luck,' sympathised Varley. 'I tell you what, leave it to me. I shall get young Parr to do them for you.'

'I say, that's uncommonly decent of you. Are you sure he won't mind?'

'Of course not. He's a frightfully accommodating young jackanape. Give me a sample of your handwriting.'

Taking out his best fountain pen eagerly, Cocky Peacock shaped up to write out a few words for Varley, but at the last moment appeared to change his mind. 'On second thoughts,' he said, 'I'd better get Binns to do it. I used him last time and I don't wish to offend. By the bye, any news of your errant aunt?'

Varley eyed the room cautiously and beckoned the other closer. 'As a matter of fact,' he whispered, 'I have received a letter from her only today.'

Peacock, in the process of popping a mint humbug into his mouth, seemed suddenly in imminent danger of choking to death. Indeed, so violent was the fit of coughing, that Varley felt impelled to assist. Slapping his convulsing friend smartly on his back had the effect of propelling the offending confectionery straight from Peacock's mouth, sending it soaring across the room where it hit a boy named d'Arbly smack between his eyes, snapping in two his pince-nez.

'I say, Cocky,' gasped Varley, 'are you alright?'

'Yes, yes.' Now fortified with a glass of water, Peacock appeared to regain his composure. Until, that is, Varley imparted his next tranche of information.

'I am considering telling Skimpton,' he said.

Some moments later, Peacock was proffering Varley a towel by way of assisting his friend in the removal of the water which, subsequent to it being ejected from the former's mouth, was now irrigating the other's face. He seemed determined to dissuade Varley from his proposed course. 'Are you sure that's wise?' he urged, somewhat agitated. 'After all, it will only distract him further.'

'Perhaps you are right.'

'Did she say when she intends returning?'

'Early next month. The letter was posted in France. My guess is she's holed up in the family cottage in Brittany with this Russian fellow Leopold Tilkowski. I'm convinced she'll want to be back for my dad's birthday, which is on the sixth.'

'The day after the Cross-Country Championships. In that case it is imperative you keep the letter from Skimpton. We don't want him getting distracted and going to pieces on the day of the race.'

'Good thinking. Between you and I, Cocky, I believe he's already half way round the bend.'

'What makes you say that?'

'Spends half his time mooning about his room reciting poetry.'

'Crikey!' Cocky Peacock then gave out a momentous sigh as Varley gathered up the chess pieces. 'I must own, Jack,' he said, 'all this business is baffling to me!'

'It's pretty bizarre, I am sure. Never mind, just continue to play with a straight bat, Cocky, and you'll be alright. I must be off now.'

'I'll walk with you to the quad.'

'Topping. Do you fancy pausing at the long-jump pit on the way?'

'Certainly.'

As the chums exited into the unseasonably warm evening, Varley was compelled to admit to himself that he felt rather more at ease in the company of Peacock than he had for a long time with his particular pal Skimpton, for their banter had taken on a gaiety which had been sadly lacking of late in Second House. Sensing this, Peacock took up the baton of conviviality. 'I hope you won't consider this remark in any way inappropriate,' he smiled, 'but I have been eager for some time to pass comment on how glossy your hair has been looking recently. Surely you have been applying some miraculous potion to it to achieve such noteworthy results?'

'On the contrary,' corrected Varley, 'merely an inexpensive brand of tonic my mother sent to me. She discovered it on sale for 1/6 in an Oriental emporium in the Burlington Arcade!'

'Really? I should be more than delighted if you could procure some of that for me!'

'I'll see what I can do!'

*   *   *   *

Over in Main House, Marcus Dent was officiating in his study at a rather thinly attended meeting of the Speculative Finance Committee. Much to his dismay, only a handful of bets had been taken on the outcome of the County Cross Country Championships, all the clever money going on Algernon Grimshaw, the fancied scholarship boy from Rainingham. Cheered by his boorish parents, Grimshaw had won the Monktonshire Three 'A's in dense fog the previous year. However, it was felt that in normal conditions that he was no match for either Cocky Peacock or Skimpton.

Dent had put it about that Peacock, preoccupied with his feud with Herr Müller, would perform well below his best, and everyone knew that Skimpton was in love, so didn't stand a chance.

Wrapping things up on a disappointing evening's business, an irate Dent rounded on his clumsy aide-de-camp Binns, poking him spitefully in the eye by way of a prelude to a sustained verbal assault. 'Why have you not dealt with Müller as I instructed?' he screamed, as Binns crumpled to the floor.

'I have had no time Marcus,' wailed the shirker, 'what with copying out Peacock's lines for him.'

'Get a squirt to do that for you,' roared the monster, 'I will not have Cocky worried by the German. See to it, Binns, or I shall end your life for you!'

'Right away Marcus.'

Taking his cue from Dent's impatient incisiveness, Binns exited the building, and marched purposefully in the direction of the refectory. Gaining entrance in the darkness to the kitchens via a side window, and making much noise in the process, the partially deaf bungler flung open the nearest cupboard. Picking his way through the contents after they had emptied themselves onto the floor at his feet, he selected a very large frying pan of the cast-iron variety and tested its weight in his hand. From there it was a short distance across the quad to the master's quarters, where darkness indicated that the rooms' occupants had retired to bed. Progressing unchallenged through the front entrance, Binns bounded up to the first floor. Scanning the names on the doors with the aid of a lit match, he soon located Herr Müller's domicile. Once inside the room, Binns quickly ascertained the whereabouts of the German, who appeared to be recumbent in his bed in the darkness, and reaching for his spectacles.

'What? Who is zer?' demanded Herr Müller, now fumbling for the bedside lamp.

'Herr Müller?' enquired Binns calmly.

'Yes. Vot do you vant?' Binns made no reply. Instead he merely stepped forward and brought the frying pan crashing down on the German's skull. There was a brief silence before he raised his weapon once more and smashed it a further time onto his victim's head, a procedure he repeated five times in all, with varying degrees of success, as the flailing Müller attempted to defend himself from the blows. A noise in the corridor prevented Binns from continuing his violent routine to its deathly conclusion, and he made good his escape by climbing from a window and shimmying down a drain pipe.

Before disappearing into Main House, his mission accomplished, Binns launched the frying pan mirthlessly into the air, and was inside the building whistling to himself when it plummeted through the chapel's ancient stained-glass windows, coming to rest in the tenor section of the choir stalls.

*   *   *   *

Some time earlier, Cocky Peacock, armed with his scurrilous journalistic piece intended for publication in the school magazine, was interviewing a youngster on his way from a late-night feed in Dead Man's Wood. 'Behind the cricket pavilion, you say?' asked the dandy.

'Yes sir, there you will find a path which leads through the copse. Travel along it for 250 yards, and take the right-hand fork.

This will eventually lead you to a semi-derelict building, a former coaching inn, I believe. Enter through the front door and you will see a staircase immediately to your right. Descend this and you will discover yourself in the somewhat labyrinthine cellars, which are arranged roughly in the shape of an 'H'.'

'Would that be a capital 'H' young man, or lower case?' teased Peacock.

'Upper case sir. Sans Serif. You will be entering from the bottom left, so to speak. The area housing the printing press and editorial staff is at the top right. Beware of obstacles, it is very dark.'

'Thank you young man, and your name?'

'Ramsey sir.'

'Very thorough. Well done. Scholarship boy?'

'Temporary secondment, sir.'

'Something of a demon on the soccer pitch I gather?'

'I try my best sir.'

'Jolly good. Keep it up, Ramsey.'

'Thank you, sir, I intend to.'

Some minutes later, entering the dank, cheerless headquarters of the school magazine, Peacock was confronted by a strange voice exuding portentously from the darkness. 'Halt!' it said. 'Who goes there?'

'A friend.'

'Prove it.' The tone was deep and resonant, the elocution precise and measured, giving the impression that the speaker had been resident in the basement for some time, waiting to confront his visitor. The only visual indication of his presence was the eerie glow of a cigarette.

'I have something for you,' offered Peacock, 'a contribution to *Fractured Lives*.'

'Is it amusing?'

'I hope so.'

'Splendid. Is it...dangerous?'

'That is for you to decide.' Peacock stepped forward, the blinding beam from a flashlight now directed at his face. Try as he might, he could make out nothing of the mysterious figure to whom he now handed a copy of his article.

'Do you smoke?' asked the enigma, tossing his burning cigarette end at Peacock's feet, and immediately lighting another.

'No thanks.'

'You are very wise.' The inquisitor then turned his attention to Peacock's article, shining his flashlight onto the title page. 'Hmmm...' he mused, from within a swirling cloud of smoke, *Faysgarth Daze*. Under what name do you wish your piece to be published, assuming it is of the required standard?'

'Wolfgang Plankton.'

'An ingeniously constructed moniker. Leave it with me. Now go.'

Upon his return to Main House, Cocky Peacock found himself somewhat troubled by the preceding exchange with the strange individual in the murky bowels of the old coaching inn. Indeed, so perfunctory and unreal had been the experience that he began to believe that he might well have dreamed the whole thing. However, a quick glance at the small hole burned in his shoe by the mysterious fellow's cigarette proved beyond doubt that the singular encounter *had* actually taken place.

Just then though, all thoughts of the matter were banished, for, in common with everyone else in the school, Peacock jumped to his feet as the unmistakable sound of breaking glass from the direction of the chapel shattered the silence, and invaded the quadrangle like an army of infantrymen rattling sabres.

*   *   *   *

Although Binns's tumultuous disposal of his mighty weapon that night disturbed many a Faysgarthian's sleep, to say nothing of the numerous Monktonshire residents also roused from their slumbers, it was a good three days before Herr Erich Müller emerged from his repose. Nursing a momentous headache, and with a proclivity towards dizzy spells, the genial German staggered from his quarters in little doubt as to the identity of his assailant.

Vowing severe retribution for the culprit, he set about the task of finding evidence to prove his hypothesis with an energy that many saw as excessive, bearing in mind his impaired faculties. To this end he interviewed over fifty boys and detained Nancy, the kitchen assistant, in his study, questioning her for some three hours on the subject of an errant frying pan found in the chapel and stained with blood. After two days of fruitless investigation he collapsed into his bed suffering from exhaustion, cancelling all his lessons.

Meanwhile, the morning's gossip about Herr Müller's attack bypassed Skimpton, for The Royal Mail had delivered him with another mellifluous missive from his sweetheart:

My darling Skimpton,

L'absence est a l'amour ce qu'est au feu le vent;
Il eteint le petit, il allume le grand.

I hope you adore poetry as I do, my sweet, for I look forward to sharing many evenings by the fire reading verses together.

My temporary confinement has been made immeasurably easier by your letter. I do not know how long present circumstances will prevail, and still cannot reveal – even to you, my love – the reason for my self-imposed banishment. It sufficeth to say that I hope soon to be by your side and hear once again your gentle voice.

I hope that you are exercising thoroughly for your forthcoming race, and that a great personal victory will ensue. But if what you tell me of your masters' intransigence with respect to your academic responsibilities is true, I suspect that Faysgarth does not deserve any credit in such a triumph!

I look forward to your next letter, the thought of which raises my spirits instantly, as indeed does the memory of your beautiful smile and natural grace.

One of my regrets at present is being deprived of my organ – did you know that in the past I have been given access on a regular basis to the gigantic instrument in Barnchester Cathedral? I so love music. Perhaps if you have any proficiency at the keyboard, we could attempt some duets by Buxtehude in the chapel when next I am at Faysgarth?

Finally, I regret to say that I have no photograph of myself to send, as you requested. But be not too disappointed, my sweet, for very soon I hope to entrust you with the real thing!

My heart is yours,

Lucinda.

*   *   *   *

Two days later, in Main House, Cocky Peacock was putting the final touches to another article for the school magazine. Wolfgang Plankton's previous dispatch, the mischievous *Faysgarth Daze*, was a huge success, with its pedantic, mildly satirical tone and thinly disguised aspersions on the veracity of Colonel Coombes's claims with respect to his war record. The author had also subtly perpetrated the notion, partly to protect his own anonymity, that the column was actually the work of Marcus Dent, who had subsequently been happy to bask in its reflected glory. Indeed, the promise contained therein of 'major revelations' in the next issue, relating to an 'enormous conspiracy' had the combined effect of spreading an unease which suppressed further revolt, and promoting a gleeful atmosphere of anticipation in the quad, unknown at Faysgarth since the days of regular trips to public hangings.

Replacing the top on his pen, Cocky began reading aloud, with some relish, from his latest composition:

Faysgarth For Me by Wofgang Plankton.

Faysgarth, for me, is a place of contrasts. On the one hand, the searingly banal, on the other, the mind-numbingly dull. Encroaching events, however, invite wider comparisons this week, and with the County Cross Country Championships rapidly approaching, one's mind harks back to those heroic athletes of ancient Greece, striding out bare of foot across the rocky terrain. The unforgiving Mediterranean sun bearing down on them like an angry god, these early Olympians must surely have envisaged for themselves a place in Elysium as their tired legs propelled them to momentous victory.

A far cry, then, from our own sloppy ditherers, sloshing about this sorry, rain-soaked county, the reach of their ambitions limited to the dismal classrooms of the Monktonshire Clerical College, or the provincial university, wearily ploughing its furrow of scholarly mediocrity.

Not for them the glamour of academic innovation and prize-winning discovery, assumed to be their rightful destiny by the inhabitants of more auspicious institutions. Nor for them the drowsy, highly polished tradition of the judge's bench, or the dizzy heights of political office. For we Faysgarthians will leave those glittering prizes to others, as we resign ourselves to the scruffy inkwells of the Civil Service and the company of the petty thief and rancid vagrant in the lower law courts.

Before submitting entirely to this mawkish assessment, perhaps I should take a few seconds to investigate the possibility of a ray of hope to illuminate Faysgarth's dingy corridors. For, amidst this quagmire of complacency and undistinguished effort, is there any endeavour at which the school truly excels? Any seed of comfort in this slurried landscape of bourgeois vicissitude?

At the risk of sounding flippant, might I direct the reader's attention to the school's outstanding record in the field of the practical joke? The autumn jape for which Faysgarth is so rightly famed? The pointless, yet fiendish and ingeniously engineered wangle, so devastating for its victims, so hilariously diverting for its perpetrators... about which I shall reveal more next week...

Now, further to my assertions last time on the subject of our beloved chemistry master's less than scrupulous attention to detail with reference to his activities during the last war, I should like here to highlight various inconsistencies relating to the qualifications our resident scientist claims to possess...'

*   *   *   *

Prancing over the quad a little later, his article tucked neatly under his arm, Cocky Peacock encountered Herr Müller, apparently suffering one of the dizzy spells which had plagued him since the vicious attack upon his person earlier in the week.

'I was sorry to hear of your accident, Herr Müller,' intoned Peacock, stifling a grin. 'I hope you have not been unduly inconvenienced.'

'It vos no accident, Peacock,' scowled the German bitterly, 'as I suzpect you vell know. I vos attacked in my bed vis a cooking utensil.'

'I say, what rotten luck,' returned Cocky gaily, 'are you yet recovered? You don't look too well, is there anything I can do?'

'You can put a stop to zat atrocious row emanating from zer chapel!'

It was indeed true that the music which at that moment was flooding into the quad was of a kind only dreamed of in the most punishing recesses of a modern composer's atonal imaginings, and would not have seemed out of place in a particularly sonorous abattoir or horror picture. What was worse, its volume appeared to be increasing considerably, straining further Herr Müller's refined musical sensibilities. Grimacing determinedly, and somewhat unsteady on his feet, he presented a pitiful sight to Peacock, who – bearing in mind his previous fractious dealings with the German – knew that it would require the master to endure far greater discomfort than the incompetent thunderings of a tone-deaf organist for him to afford the tormented Prussian any degree of sympathy. 'I see what you mean, Herr Müller,' he volleyed over the din, 'but I am afraid I cannot be of any assistance in that respect as I have a deadline to meet.'

'In zat case you vill write out for me two souzand times "A Man Should Not Skip In Public".'

Peacock, though, was already on his way, mincing off provocatively in the direction of Dead Man's Wood. 'Unfortunately, Herr Müller,' he shouted, 'I am unable to hear you above the sound of the organ!'

'Come...come back here you...you...HUNDERTFUNFUN-SEIBZIG!'

*   *   *   *

The tuneless exertions of the Faysgarth kapellmeister did not escape the attention of Marcus Dent that morning either. Relaxing on his chaise longue with an early spritzer for company, and surrounded by several hundred pounds of explosives, recently delivered from Poplar, East London, he summoned his blundering cohort Binns to provide explication. 'It's Skimpton, Marcus,' shouted he, 'apparently he has decided to re-acquaint himself with the chapel organ.'

'Not again!' wailed the rotter. 'We had enough of that last time. Spate...'

'Yes Marcus?' replied the angular henchman, sensing violence with the eagerness of a dog being summoned to its din-dins.

'Disembowel him.'

'Right away Marcus.'

'I don't think that would be a good idea,' interrupted Cocky Peacock, floating in through the door.

'Oh yes?' sneered Dent. 'What would you suggest?'

'Leave him to me.'

'To tell you the truth, Cocky,' said Dent, 'I'm getting a trifle worried about this fellow Wolfgang Plankton. If I'm to take credit for his literary dispatches I think perhaps I should know what he's up to.'

'There is no need. All you have to do is to make sure the bomb goes off at the right time.'

'Don't worry,' reassured Dent, stroking a stick of dynamite suggestively, 'that is all in hand.'

'About the payment for the explosives, Marcus,' put in a worried Spate, 'some of these fellows from the East End can get mighty jumpy. Remember it was only through the good offices of my father that we were afforded credit facilities in the first place. We couldn't allow his reputation to be compromised in any way.'

'His reputation?' shrieked Dent. 'Why, the man's an embezzler and a pimp! A brigand and freebooter of the lowest order. Don't talk to me about his reputation. You are not having second thoughts are you Spate?'

'Not at all.'

'Binns?'

'No Marcus.'

'Then worry not. The Speculative Finance Committee will cough up the readies for the explosives once I have collected all bets on the outcome of the race, and placed them with an associate in Faverstock. The favourable odds he has offered me will ensure an adequate return, I promise you.'

'But what will happen if Cocky doesn't win?'

'Cocky *will* win, won't you Cocky?'

Peacock was seated at the desk perusing his nails and scoffing at the typographical errors in that morning's *Barnchester Chronicle*. 'Of course I shall win,' he boasted. 'It is practically a foregone conclusion.'

'Now,' said Dent, knocking back the remainder of his drink decisively, 'the question remains what to do with these lovely explosives, for I will not have them cluttering up my quarters for the next three weeks.'

'Listen to this,' cut in a laughing Peacock, '*Valuable fur oat stolen from Barnchester residence.*' Do they employ no proof-readers?'

'Can't we put them in the Senior Common Room?' suggested Binns, when the guffaws had subsided.

'Good idea,' said Dent sarcastically, 'perhaps you would like to design a large notice to attach to them, Binns – Please Do Not Touch. Explosives To Be Used To Blow Up Faysgarth On November Fifth.'

'I know where we can hide them,' said Peacock. 'Binns, Spate...meet me round the back of the cricket pavilion at eight o'clock tonight.'

*   *   *   *

The following day saw the eagerly awaited publication of the school magazine, and Faysgarth fairly buzzed with talk of Wolfgang Plankton's latest tantalisingly seditious submission. Skimpton, though, having read the piece, could not see what all the fuss was about, dismissing its cynical tone as affected and clumsy, and branding the content as merely mildly treacherous. He did, however, read the revelations about Colonel Coombes's dubious academic record with some interest.

Returning to Second House from a forty-five-mile run, he was greeted in the quad by both the friendly tones of the chapel bell and the unwelcome bonhomie of Herr Müller, with hand outstretched. 'I am glad to see zat you have decided to recommence your training, Skimpton,' beamed the German. 'You know zat zer championships are less zan a month away?'

'I am aware of the date of the event, Herr Müller,' came the laconic reply, 'as it has special importance in our country's history.'

'Ja, of course! Guy Fawkes und zer gunpowder plan!'

'Indeed.'

Herr Müller then began a lengthy appreciation of the customs of his adopted country, even fighting off one of his dizzy spells to extol the virtues of maypole dancing. The spirit with which he attempted a demonstration of the same was a measure both of his affection for tradition and his determination to retain Skimpton's wavering attention. 'You know, Skimpton,' he volunteered, 'zere are two sinks about your country zat I do not understand. One, zer pansies...'

'That, if you don't mind me saying so, sir, is as prosaic an observation as I have heard in a long time, for what is there to comprehend in a flower?'

'Zat is not quite what I meant. And two, zer belts.'

'I see. Any particular belts?'

'Zer church belts! Why are zey always so appallingly out of tune?'

'I suppose it's traditional, Herr Müller.'

'You see, Skimpton, we Germans are a musical people. Our country has given the world Bach, Beethoven und Brahms. Our ears are easily offended.'

'I understand,' came the tart riposte. 'We English feel the same about foreigners crucifying our language.'

'I wonder, do you know, Skimpton,' asked Müller, undaunted, 'who it is who has been punishing zer chapel organ of late?'

'Haven't the foggiest, Herr Müller.' replied Skimpton tetchily. 'Now if you will excuse me, I have work to do.' At which, the sports captain turned smartly and marched off in the direction of the chapel organ, with the intention of delivering its keyboard with a further thrashing.

*　　*　　*　　*

The zealous commitment with which Skimpton had resumed his training in the following weeks did not pass without comment amongst Faysgarth's amateur pundits. And as the days went by, all the clever money had been shifted from the shoulders of Rainingham's plucky scholarship boy Algy Grimshaw, and onto Skimpton's more muscular frame.

Knowing full well that his explosive interruption would ensure that his man would be the only competitor to finish the race, Marcus Dent transferred every penny of his takings from the Speculative Finance Committee to the premises of a local turf accountant, placing them squarely on Cocky Peacock at five-to-one.

Having calculated gleefully that his potential earnings could well exceed £17,000 and with over a week to go, the bounder was settling comfortably in his study smoking a small Cuban cigar. Much to his annoyance though, his pleasing monetary conjectures were interrupted for the third time that day by a further attempt by Skimpton to master the keyboard music of Dietrich Buxtehude. Several agonising minutes elapsed before the School Scoundrel rose angrily from his chaise longue and took an iron poker from the fire, fully intending to desecrate the sanctity of the chapel by beating its resident organist's brains out.

Outside in the quad he encountered seventy other boys, all similarly armed, and with precisely the same objective. With fearsome expressions, the army of musical malcontents braved the hail of dissonance which rained onto them from the House of God, and converged on the chapel's ornate eighteenth-century portico.

Then, as suddenly as it had started, the playing stopped. An agonising cry echoed from within, and the soldiers of silence stood perfectly still, praying that some sensitive soul had stepped in to do their work for them, an accommodating assassin who had finally put paid to the maniacal kapellmeister. Seconds later, Skimpton appeared, hobbling in the doorway, his face contorted with pain. 'I say chaps,' he gasped, 'would someone give me a hand? I think I've pulled a hamstring reaching for the crescendo pedal!'

Returning chuckling to his study, Marcus Dent reflected joyfully on Skimpton's injury, and the relative tranquillity which would now return. Then he stopped in his tracks as the smile slid from his face. Realizing that his financial plan would be in ruins if Skimpton did not start the race the following week, he hailed – through his study window – Cocky Peacock who was conversing with a third-former nearby. 'Cocky!' he rasped urgently. 'I must speak with you!'

'Can you not see,' returned the fop sharply, 'that I am chatting to this youngster here?'

'It is imperative that we talk. Skimpton has just injured himself on the organ and may be unfit for the race.'

'I see,' responded Peacock impatiently. 'Now run along Jeremy,' he said, resuming his conversation with the junior, 'and remember: disregard what you have heard. These feelings are very common in a person of your age. Just try to be yourself.' At which, the youngster trotted off.

'What are we going to do?' grated the cad in desperate tones, in his study a few moments later.

'I don't see the problem,' said Cocky, 'even if Skimpton doesn't run we'll still be able to implicate him in the blast.'

'You don't understand! I've taken bets on him winning! If he doesn't start I'll have to give the money back!'

'How unfortunate for you.'

'But I've already put it all on you, you fathead!'

Peacock ushered his quaking friend over to the chaise longue and sat him down carefully. 'Calm yourself Marcus,' he soothed. 'Leave it to me. I shall see that Skimpton takes part in the race, so long as you keep that filthy German off my back.'

'I shall have Spate kill him if you like.'

'That won't be necessary. I am quite happy with him debilitated through dizzy spells, though I fear they have all but subsided.'

'I shall see to it that he doesn't bother you, Cocky. Is there anything else?'

'A new pair of shoes wouldn't go amiss. My best pair suffered an accident at the hands of a careless chain smoker. Something buckled with a French heel would be nice...'

*   *   *   *

Later that day, Skimpton, alone in his room but for the company of Barclay, lay on his bed, composing in a sober hand, a poem intended for his beloved:

Orphans of fortune, we two are entwined

Our hearts bound together o'er space and through time...

'Skimpton!' came a familiar voice from the corridor.

'I am afraid that I am unable to open the door for fear of aggravating my injury, Herr Müller.'

'No matter. I heard viz considerable distress of your accident, Skimpton. I hope I did not offend you zer oser day.'

'That is quite alright.' As Herr Müller proceeded to offer suggestions for treatment of his young protégé's pulled muscle, Skimpton penned a dedication to his love, at the foot of the page:

For Lucinda, for ever.

He then placed the ode, together with a recently drafted and fragrant letter, into an envelope, and began writing out the address.

'If zer is anysink I can do to help,' offered the German, 'then you must let me know.'

'I fear there is nothing that can be done, Herr Müller,' said Skimpton, licking the stamp. 'I believe I may well be forced to withdraw from the race.'

'Wisdraw from zer race?'

'I am afraid so.' Herr Müller waited for a moment in silence behind the door, before his shoulders buckled under the weight of a heavy sigh. Choosing to spare Skimpton his disappointment, he said nothing more before walking disconsolately away.

As he approached the top of the stairs, he was surprised to hear Skimpton calling him, and turned to see the latter's head poking from behind the door. 'On second thoughts, Herr Müller,' he said, 'there is something you can do for me.'

'Anysink, Skimpton, anysink.'

'There's a letter I require posting, if you would be so kind.'

*   *   *   *

Having dispatched Herr Müller on behalf of his errand, Skimpton was not to see the German for some time, for the latter went missing the following day. The general assumption was that he had finally succumbed to his unsteady spells and taken himself off for proper treatment. Skimpton though, did not rule out the possibility that he had been stricken by some profound form of Teutonic melancholia after hearing of his withdrawal from the race, and half expected the master's stricken body to be found washed up on a beach somewhere.

The day after he sustained his injury in the throat of the chapel organ, Skimpton was astonished to find himself in the company of Horace 'Cocky' Peacock in his study. His ostentatious cross-country rival had called unannounced, wearing a peach silk blouson beneath his school blazer and a particularly powerful brand of *eau de cologne* which prompted Skimpton to open the window some seconds after his visitor's arrival. After the usual pleasantries were negotiated with some stiffness, Peacock declared immediately the reason for his presence; astonishingly, he had come to offer his assistance to Skimpton in an almighty push for fitness in the final days before the race!

Taken somewhat aback by this uncommonly sporting gesture, Skimpton at first suspected it might be a ruse to tempt him into some uncomfortable pederasty in the gym. Tentative intimations by him in that direction however, proved fruitless. Could it be that Peacock's proposal was genuine?

Skimpton hesitated before composing his response, and struggled to the kettle by way of buying time to think. It was certainly true that, after a good night's rest, the strained muscle was not nearly as painful as before, and he even found that he could put some weight on his left leg without too much pain. Was it not about time, thought the game sportsman, that he stopped moping around and made every possible effort to recover? Did he not owe it to his fellow Faysgarthians, Peacock included, to fight for his fitness as if his life depended on it? Indeed, should not the latter's presence, as a representative of the school, already have prompted him into a more positive attitude? After all, surely the injury had now fulfilled its primary purpose, that of providing the inspiration for a rattling good poem in honour of his girl! And there were six full days before the race! More than enough time for one so young as he to recover from such a setback. As for Cocky Peacock, the boy who now sat in his study radiating both bonhomie and a rather pleasant bouquet in equal measure, had not he heard Jack Varley extolling the fellow's virtues with almost unseemly dedication for weeks?

So, with rekindled enthusiasm and a hearty handshake, Skimpton and his fellow Faysgarthian set about concocting a plan of action, for the young stickler of Second House loved nothing better than a monumental battle against the odds. Light training in the gym to start, followed by a leisurely swim in the River Monkwash, and a thorough and vigorous rub down. Then, later in the week, out onto the track for a steady trot, with Cocky pushing the pace as the days went by.

By the first Friday of November, with the County Cross Country Championships beckoning the next day, Skimpton had more than satisfied his young trainer's requirements, as his leg seemed to gain strength almost by the hour. Then came the final test; a ten-mile run through open countryside.

Over fields they pressed as far as Faverstock Common, neck and neck, and then home via the river and Dead Man's Wood. A successful circuit of the quad left Cocky gasping for air and Skimpton eager for more, for he now felt fitter and more robust than ever, all thanks to his team-mate's hard work over the previous days.

As they dried themselves after a bracing shower, Skimpton felt the moment right to express his heartfelt gratitude to Peacock. Proffering his hand, he said, 'I don't know if I'd've been able to do it without your help, Cocky, so thanks a lot.'

'Think nothing of it,' returned the other, 'you have worked hard and deserve success.'

After they had finished dressing, Peacock gathered up his kit bag and made to leave. Pausing in the doorway, he turned to Skimpton, the slightly troubled expression on his face implying that he might be about to impart some information of sizeable import. Instead, though, he remained pensively silent, rooted to the spot. 'Was there something Cocky?' prompted Skimpton.

'Nothing,' replied the other, still somehow preoccupied. 'You are a fine fellow, Skimpton,' he said flatly, staring thoughtfully at nothing in particular. 'An admirably determined individual with great stamina and good legs. I wish you every reward for your endeavours.'

'Thank you, Cocky.'

*   *   *   *

As they walked from the changing rooms, the surprisingly troubled mood which accompanied them descended into the kind of silence reserved for particularly melancholy funerals. Just as a perplexed Skimpton was about to enquire after his new friend's puzzlingly introspective demeanour, a familiar voice beckoned from the quad.

'Skimpton!' it said, 'I am happy to see zat you are runnink again!' It was the rounded figure of Herr Müller, his face illuminated by an enormous smile.

'Herr Müller!' greeted Skimpton warmly, 'I am glad to see you alive!'

'Steady on! It takes more zan a bash on zer snout to kill off a Prussian! And you – vot of your injured leg?'

'Cured! All thanks to Cocky here. I mean Peacock.'

'I hope you are feeling better Herr Müller,' put in Peacock graciously.

'Yes,' came the mirthless reply, 'I am sure you do.'

'What can we do for you Herr Müller?' asked Skimpton.

'I should like to speak vis Peacock, in private if you don't mind.'

'Of course, sir, I'll run along.'

'Skimpton!' called Herr Müller. 'I have somesink for you, and will, if I may, wisit you in your study later.'

'Very well sir. Good to have you back on board, Herr Müller!'

The master, now apparently less shaky than he had been before his temporary departure, watched Skimpton disappear into Second House before turning his attention to Cocky Peacock. 'So,' he said firmly, 'you have been helping Skimpton vis his training?'

'He is a very conscientious athlete, Herr Müller. I now fear that I will be hard-pressed to beat him in the race to-morrow.'

'Good. Zat is as it should be. I do not pretend to understand why you are doink zis, Peacock, especially since you appear to have taken such pains to make a fool of zer fellow.'

'I'm sure I have no idea what you mean, Herr Müller,' came the rather apprehensive reply.

'You may have been wondering where I have been these last few days, Peacock, ja?'

'I had no idea you had departed the school, if I am to be scrupulously honest.'

'I shall enlighten you. I vos asked by Skimpton to deliver a letter earlier zis week addressed to a Miss Lucinda Varley in West London, zer relation of a pupil at zis school, I gaser.'

'Varley's aunt, I believe, yes.'

'However, when I attempted to hand over zer missive personally at zer Hammersmith residence, I was confronted by your brother, a decidedly noxious personality who introduced himself as 'Dickie Peacock'. A quick scout around the flat revealed no evidence of Miss Varley's presence...'

'Herr Müller, I can explain...'

'You have been involved in a dezpicable prank, Peacock, involving zer duping of a fine and upstanding member of zer school. Zis conclusion I have reached after reading zer letter written to Miss Varley by Skimpton, in zer firm belief zat he has been engaged in a romantic correspondence vis zer woman for some time.'

Peacock turned a drastic shade of green, and a bead of sweat appeared on his forehead, travelled the length of his nose and dropped solemnly to the ground.

'You are a miserable young man, Peacock,' resumed Herr Müller. 'A degenerate of zer lowest rank, possessink, as far as I can tell, no redeemink features. I intend, in zer fullness of time, to voice to zer police my suzpicions regarding zer identity of zer cowardly maniac who attacked me viz a frying pan in my study. I tell you now zat you are zer chief suzpect, Peacock. As for zer race to-morrow, I strictly forbid you from taking part. Further to that...'

'Let me stop you right there Herr Müller,' interrupted Peacock forcefully, and manhandling the German into a nearby doorway. 'No one, least of all you,' he continued, 'shall prevent me taking part in the race to-morrow, and I shall tell you precisely why. I had cause, the other night, during the course of my journalistic researches, to check up on some records in a library book – sporting entries relating to the Olympic Games. Imagine my surprise, then, as I scanned the details relating to the Marathon of 1912 to find no record whatsoever of an Erich Müller taking part, let alone receiving the bronze medal as you have led us, with such wearisome regularity, to believe.

'Indeed, I had to scour my memory for some minutes before I recalled where I had heard the name of the German competitor who is credited in those same records as coming third that year.'

Herr Müller's face, already by this time a pale shade of grey, now turned completely white, and soon it was his turn to irrigate the pathway with perspiration.

'Yes, I know who you really are,' resumed Peacock, decisively 'and have a pretty shrewd idea why you are here. So, if you wish me to keep your identity a secret long enough for you to pack your bags and get out of Faysgarth, then you will kindly desist from interfering in any way with my preparations for the race to-morrow. Now, if you don't mind, I have to manicure my nails.'

*　　*　　*　　*

'This bit's even better!' roared an ecstatic Marcus Dent, reading to his chums from an advance copy of *Fractured Lives*. 'Listen: "One of my regrets at present is being deprived of my organ... bla bla...I do so love music"!'

Spate was choking on the floor with laughter, and was soon joined by Binns, after the latter's slower brain had caught up with Wolfgang Plankton's revelations. Dent, beside himself with excitement, roared onwards. 'Why, Cocky's published the entire correspondence! Listen: "Perhaps if you have any proficiency at the keyboard, we could attempt some duets by Buxtehude when next I am at Faysgarth"!'

Spate stuffed a handkerchief into his mouth to stifle the screams, while Binns rolled about the floor vibrating with mirth. Dent, crimson with glee, composed himself and continued. ' "My Darling Lucinda, I am considering having my hair cut, please let me know of any particular style you favour"!'

By this time, Binns was turning blue, the blood vessels pulsating dangerously at his temples, for the sensational content of Wolfgang Plankton's latest dispatch in the school magazine outshone any amusing jape he had yet encountered.

' "I am pleased to announce, my love, that I am making steady progress on the organ, encouraged by the hearty support of my schoolfellows, and, having exhausted the works of Buxtehude, I am now acquainting myself with Johann Sebastian Bach's famous *Toccata and Fugue* in D minor, BWV 565"!'

At this, Spate started pounding his head violently against a wall, Binns having apparently passed out under the bed. Dent, his face contorted with hilarity, could hardly form the words with his mouth. ' "If I am fortunate enough to win the forthcoming race, my darling, it will be for you, my sweet, for you are dearer to me than even my favourite rugger boots. Your love means more than any medal or trophy, except, perhaps, the Monktonshire Hockey Cup, which – due to the fact that it has thus far eluded me – is a trophy I particularly cherish..."!'

Here, Spate relinquished all control, flinging himself over Dent's desk, convulsed in agonising laughter. Indeed, the very room itself now appeared to be joining in, vibrating like an empty waiting room when the Flying Scotsman thunders through. Books had started hurling themselves in gay abandon from the shelves when an irate Cocky Peacock appeared and brought matters abruptly back to earth. 'Where did you get that?' he demanded wrathfully.

'It's an advance copy,' said Dent, 'Spate was given it by your friend in the dungeon.'

'Has anyone else seen it, Spate?'

'Not as far as I know, Cocky.'

'I left strict instructions for all copies to be held back until after the start of to-morrow's race. Timing is imperative. No-one must breathe a word of its content. Do you hear me? Binns?'

'Yes Cocky. I'm not deaf.'

'Yes you are,' corrected Dent.

'Spate?' continued Peacock.

'Of course, Cocky.'

'You're not getting cold feet are you, either of you?'

'Not at all.'

What his co-conspirators didn't know was that, before his latest spat with Herr Müller, Peacock himself had been on the verge of abandoning the whole project. The sheer force of Skimpton's irrepressible personality and courage in the previous days had convinced him that the plan was no more than a petty prank utterly unworthy of civilized fellows. Müller's invective, though, stiffened his resolve. He now hated Faysgarth and everything it stood for more than ever, and was desperate to see it – and, for that matter, all other institutions like it – wiped from the face of the earth.

'I love this last letter,' said Dent, in placatory tones. 'Tell me, Cocky, has Skimpton received it yet?'

'It will arrive to-morrow.'

'Excellent. That should really drop him in it. It's very, very clever, Cocky.'

'Thank you. Now: the race starts at three, and the magazine will be distributed soon after. School, of course, will be empty as everyone is under orders to cheer our fellows on. That is the time to set up the explosives, Spate.'

'What time shall we actually light the touch paper Cocky?' asked Binns.

'Three-thirty on the dot. It is imperative that the school is completely destroyed, every rotten brick of it. Do you understand?'

'Absolutely.'

'Good. I shall now retire to my room for what I am certain will be a fitful night's sleep.'

'What shall you be wearing for to-morrow's shindig, Cocky, as a matter of interest?' enquired Dent, apprehensively.

'Rest assured that I have devised a sufficiently eye-catching ensemble, Marcus, to more than satisfy the aesthetic requirements of my adoring fans.'

After his friend had departed, Marcus Dent gave out one more chuckle and turned to his trusted cohorts. 'You have everything you need, Spate?' he asked.

'It is all in my room, Marcus. There is still the matter of the payment for the explosives, however...'

'Yes, yes, yes. Now, Binns, I have one further favour to ask.' He then took out a small sachet from his breast pocket, upon which was printed a caricatured illustration of a mischievous youngster, grinning. The garish colours gave Binns the unmistakable impression that the item had been purchased from one of Dent's favourite joke shops. 'Find some way of getting the contents of this packet into Skimpton's running shoes before to-morrow, would you?' said Dent.

'What is it, Marcus?'

'Look on it as a sort of insurance policy.'

*   *   *   *

Skimpton, meanwhile, was pouring himself a mug of cocoa in preparation for an early night. Barclay, upon hearing revels in Dead Man's Wood, had taken himself off with the intention of assaulting a few third-formers and stealing their food. Consequently, when Herr Müller knocked on his door, Skimpton was able to invite the German into his study without fear of unnecessary bloodshed.

After the preliminary greetings, the master presented Skimpton with a small parcel. The schoolboy discarded the wrapping fervently, revealing a cardboard box, inside which was a brand-new pair of running shoes. 'I say, Herr Müller,' he exclaimed, 'these are absolutely spiffing! How did you know my size?'

'Your feg, Piggot, seems to know most sinks about you!'

For a moment, as he gazed, enraptured, at the gleaming white boots, Skimpton was so blissfully happy that he could almost have kissed Herr Müller, but remembering that to do so would almost certainly lumber him with a hefty punishment of lines, he decided it would be wiser merely to proffer his hand in the traditional manner. 'Thanks awfully, Herr Müller,' he said earnestly. 'These shoes are a corking gift. And what with my others holed, you've done me a topping favour!'

'Put zem on!'

'Why of course!' Skimpton threaded the leather laces eagerly, caressing the shoes proudly as he did so. They were obviously very expensive, made of white, stained calfskin and as supple as a pair of carpet slippers. 'There!' he cried, jumping to his feet and hitching his pyjama trousers to afford Herr Müller a sporting view of the footwear. 'If these don't win me the championship then nothing will!'

Herr Müller smiled to himself, stretching his limbs wearily as they overflowed Skimpton's battered armchair. Relaxing, his arms now hanging loosely, he seemed to fumble about beneath his seat for a second, and then produced a partially eaten dog biscuit.

'I try everything to keep him amused,' explained Skimpton, 'but he escapes!'

'And what of zer owner, Skimpton, when will she return?'

'I have no idea. You'll have to ask Jack Varley – it's his aunt, you see.'

'Yes, of course.'

After Herr Müller had departed, Skimpton carefully removed his new running shoes and placed them on a chair by his bed, so that when he awoke they would be the first thing he'd see. After hanging up his dressing gown he clambered into bed wondering whether he would have time to get a haircut to-morrow before the race. Varley's aunt, in her latest missive, had made no mention of any particular fashion she preferred, so he would probably leave it to the discretion of his usual man in Faverstock, an entertaining fellow who charged sixpence and spoke authoritatively on most subjects.

*   *   *   *

The next day brought a bitterly cold November wind; the morning air was as sharp as a butcher's knife and the ground as hard as differential calculus. At six-thirty, Skimpton emerged from a freezing shower, his limbs refreshed and relishing the prospect of a gruelling day's sport. Piggot had already laid out his togs in the dressing room, and now all that remained was for him to prepare mentally for the main event of the day.

As was his custom, he followed a strict itinerary; breakfast in his room of dry toast, porridge and lemon juice, a thorough cleansing of the teeth and gums using a proprietary brand of soot, followed by an hour or so in the music room enjoying repeated playings of his one gramophone record, *Has Anybody Seen My Tiddler*, by the talented music hall artiste of yesteryear, Fred Harrison Winner.

However, upon returning to his study after his shower, having only just embarked on his trusted routine, Skimpton was waylaid by the arrival of a letter. The handwriting on the envelope he recognized immediately, for he was certain it was that of Varley's aunt. Anxious to hear news of his love, Skimpton tore at the seal, fumbled open the contents and devoured the words contained therein.

My Darling Skimpton,
    Since I have heard very little from you of late, I must assume that your sporting preparations have taken preference over our correspondence. I understand, my love, for I should hate your performance to suffer on my account.

Skimpton felt an immediate pang of guilt at having somewhat relegated Lucinda in his thoughts recently. Though, he puzzled, had he not sent – via Herr Müller – a letter only a few days previously? Certainly, the poetic efforts contained therein elicited no mention here. Perhaps, thought he, the German had suffered a dizzy spell and omitted to post it?

Apart from a humorous suggestion relating to his masters pestering him about school work, and a brief, playful discussion on the subject of hair styles, the most arresting piece of information in the letter concerned Lucinda's intention to visit Faysgarth that afternoon to see him run in the cross-country race. She would catch the train, she said, and hopefully be there by three o'clock, although her situation dictated that she might have to adopt a disguise. However, she teased, it would be worth it to see her Skimpton, and confirm their affection for one another. The missive then returned to its melancholic key by way of a coda, and Skimpton, though delighted at the prospect of her visit, could not dispel the guilt he felt at evidently being the cause of Lucinda's dolefulness. What could he do to prove to her his love?

Pacing the room in roughly the manner of a romantic artist, he glimpsed his face in the mirror and was immediately stricken with a profound loathing for himself. Then it occurred to him, as he stared accusingly into his own eyes; there *was* something he could do that would prove beyond any doubt his love for Varley's aunt. A course of action that would show everyone that in the romance department this particular fellow meant business. To this end, he put on his cap and departed for Faverstock, and the tonsorial emporium of a wise gentleman who he knew would not disappoint.

*   *   *   *

As the morning wore on, preparations were made at Faysgarth for the arrival of the many visitors expected later in the day. Colonel Coombes supervised the installation of a rope barrier which would line the majority of the route, and a refreshment tent serving alcoholic beverages was erected, primarily for the benefit of Lord and Lady Edgerton, who had promised – as usual – to turn out.

Jack Varley, casting a benign eye over proceedings, reprimanded Binns after discovering the waster hanging around the changing rooms suspiciously. Later, he bumped into Cocky Peacock stretching himself near the long-jump pit, and was happy to wish his erstwhile chess challenger the best of luck.

Marcus Dent was taking final bets on the outcome of the race, behind locked doors in Main House, everyone's pocket money going on Skimpton. His dangerous sidekick Spate, meanwhile, lurked with characteristic menace about the quad.

After lunch, the crowds began to arrive. Unlikely-looking competitors from Rainingham and St. Hugh's jostled for a share of the crowd's attention, as supporters cheered their arrival. As an activity, long-distance running can occasionally lend fleeting celebrity to the least sporting of fellows; the stringy buffoon on the rugger pitch can frequently impress with his stamina over field and gate, and a surprisingly strong finish after ten miles of dogged perseverance can often be delivered by the most minuscule of duffers in the boxing ring. Unaccustomed as many of them were that day to their temporary fame, a sizeable number of these fellows exhausted themselves well before the trigger on the starting pistol was pulled, as a result of them showing off to the crowd too vigorously.

In the category of miniscule duffers, though hardly lacking in discipline and stamina, resided young Algernon Grimshaw. Though stunted of growth in his early years as a result of poor nutrition, this five-foot fifth-former was known to perform particularly well on heavy ground. A tenacious little battler, Algy was accompanied to most competitions by his voluble parents, purveyors of meat and its various bi-products from their butcher's shop in Flatley, Northern England. His father, George Grimshaw, a former miner, had been the lucky recipient of a sizeable sum by way of compensation for an accident at the coalface which left him susceptible to nerves. This modest windfall had enabled him to leave his job at the colliery, open his butchery business, procure a pair of ill-fitting false teeth for his wife and – with the aid of a small scholarship – send his only son to a relatively inexpensive minor public school. His boy, if not the most popular pupil at Rainingham, was certainly the fastest over long distances, and – if rumour was to be believed – was also streets ahead of the others academically. A source of considerable pride, as well as frustration, to his parents, Grimshaw could often be seen being both spoiled and at the same time berated by his father, who, it was widely held, had rather misplaced his sense of proportion after he had come into money.

As three o'clock approached, the good-natured crowd began buzzing with excitement, lining the fifteen-mile route in places some four or five thick. Previous years' races at other schools had been marred somewhat by jostling here and there amongst the onlookers, and there had even been a few fainting incidents. This time, though, the thoroughness of Colonel Coombes's organization of the event meant that Constable Stubbs, the local bobby, was managing to maintain public order without much effort. He did this merely by parading his mighty frame conspicuously and belching loudly at regular intervals.

The St. Hugh's contingent was the first out of the dressing rooms. By and large a pretty indifferent-looking bunch, they appeared to be lacking the inspiration provided in previous years by their erstwhile star performer, the controversial Cocky Peacock.

Then came the Rainingham lads in dazzling blue togs, led by the diminutive Algernon Grimshaw, who, noticing his parents nearby, immediately ran in the opposite direction. 'Come on Algy!' encouraged his father loudly. 'Tha can 'ammer this lot!'

'That's right!' added his mother, removing her false teeth for added volubility. 'There's 'alf a crown for yer at 'ome if yer win!' Grimshaw, stricken with embarrassment, pretended to do press-ups, as many present sniggered behind cupped hands.

Still being picked out for ridicule some minutes later, and conspicuous because of the initials embroidered onto his vest in bright red letters by his mother, Grimshaw was thankful for the eventual arrival of the Faysgarthians. In particular Cocky Peacock, who rather stole the limelight in a white pleated singlet with an embroidered flower motif and matching tutu. In his lacquered hair was placed an ivory rose, on his lips a ruby smile.

'By bloody 'ell!' declared a dismayed Mr. Grimshaw vehemently. 'Look at the state on that!'

His wife, though, was searching in the mud for her dentures, and it was some seconds before she noticed the object of her husband's derision. As Peacock stretched his muscles on the grass nearby, Grimshaw let rip with further disapproval. 'Sling 'im darn't'cells,' he offered, 'he's nobbut a bloody queer!'

'Leave 'im be, George,' urged his wife. 'It teks all sorts.'

Everyone collapsed in paroxysms of laughter as Grimshaw trawled through his steamy catalogue of northern invective, much to everyone's amusement and education. Rather than displaying any sign of offence though, Cocky Peacock laughed loudest, affording all present scintillating views of his salmon pink drawers.

The reaction to Peacock's appearance was no more dramatic than that which greeted the next arrival from the dressing rooms. For, apart from sporting a dazzling new pair of running shoes, which in themselves would have attracted considerable comment, Skimpton trotted out into the fray with his head completely shorn of any vestige of hair! 'By Christ!' exclaimed a bewildered George Grimshaw, 'this'n looks like a billiard ball!'

'If yer ask me,' added his wife with a laugh, 'he's been feightin' wi' a lawn mower – and lost!'

This comment was greeted with rather less enthusiasm than had been the previous remarks, for Mrs. Grimshaw had been attempting to insert her false teeth as she spoke. This, combined with a marked thickening of her accent as a result of them still being caked in mud, meant that none of the schoolboys present had much of an idea what she had said.

'Come 'ere lad!' beckoned Mr. Grimshaw, covering his wife's embarrassment, 'a bit o' spit on me 'anky an' that bonce o' yours'll come up a treat!' Since it was more clearly articulated and contained no difficult vocabulary which might confuse the schoolfellows, this utterance was greeted with renewed enthusiasm from behind the ropes.

Skimpton though, appeared far from happy. His eyes scanned the crowd for any sign of Varley's aunt. But she was, alas, nowhere to be seen. In addition, his head, the subject of much hurtful mockery, was beginning to feel very, very naked indeed. Also conspicuous by his absence was Herr Müller, whom Skimpton hoped to question about the stray letter. He was also anxious, given the German's enthusiastic assistance in recent weeks, that he be present to see him perform in the big race, and it seemed ludicrous to think of the amiable Prussian missing the event. As if these disappointments weren't enough, his new running shoes were also proving far from comfortable, and he now almost wished he was wearing his old ones.

Thankfully, the confusion was brought to a halt when Colonel Coombes, in the middle of one of his deathly public addresses, accidently fired the starting pistol, and a deafening roar from the crowd propelled the runners down the hill and off in the direction of Dead Man's Wood.

As the competitors disappeared into the trees and the crowd dispersed, hoping to catch up with them at later stages of the race, the empty school buildings stood guard proudly atop the hill. But like a decrepit old soldier standing to attention, Faysgarth, that November afternoon, though impressive of countenance, must itself have been lost in dreams of bygone glories as it gazed out over the Downs. For when a young woman stole through its gates, crept stealthily up its drive, traversed silently the quad and penetrated Second House, she did so entirely un-noticed.

Having mounted the stairs, she progressed down the corridor and arrived at the door to Skimpton's study. Finding it unlocked, she stepped inside, where, to her amazement, she discovered Herr Erich Müller pinned against a wall by a growling Barclay.

'Lucinda!' he cried.

'Leopold! What on *earth* are you doing here?'

*   *   *   *

Ten minutes into the race, and copies of *Fractured Lives* were circulating amongst the crowd like the flames of a forest fire. A list of runners was included across the centre pages, but this item held little interest for the Faysgarthians present, every one of whom had turned directly to Wolfgang Plankton's latest dispatch, *Faysgarth Mon Amour*.

On the farthest edge of Dead Man's Wood, Skimpton and Cocky Peacock lay just behind the leaders, striding pace-for-pace. Ignoring the ridicule still being hurled at him from behind the ropes about his bald pate, the young worthy attracted his team-mate's attention. 'Cocky,' he gasped, 'these new running shoes are killing me. I can't go on.'

'Nonsense,' came the reply. 'They are calfskin. Why, you can't buy any better!'

'But my feet are burning inside them!'

'Well, if the worse comes to the worse you can have mine!'

'I won't hear of it.'

'Nonsense. These conditions suit you far better than me. You are much more likely to beat Grimshaw. Do you think you'd fit into these?'

'I don't think so,' said Skimpton, glancing at the other boy's feet, 'they're far too big.' Now prancing about like a clown, Skimpton was obviously in a state of some discomfort, for both his feet seemed like they were on fire, so grievously did they itch. 'I am going to have to stop, Cocky,' he rasped.

'Do you have another pair?'

'In my study. I am sure I can get them and re-join the race.'

Cocky looked at his wristwatch, a worried look on his face. 'Whatever you do,' he instructed, 'make sure you are out of the school buildings by three-thirty. Don't ask why.'

'I should hope to be back up here with the leaders by then,' laughed Skimpton, 'otherwise it won't be worth doing! Cheerio!' 'Good day to you.'

*   *   *   *

Meanwhile, Lucinda Varley was fighting off Barclay's affectionate greeting as Herr Müller recovered in Skimpton's armchair. 'I vos sure you would return for zer dog,' he said, still shaking.

'But how long have you been at Faysgarth, Leopold?' she asked.

'I took a temporary position in zer Languages Department under an assumed name after ascertaining zat you had visited your nephew here and deposited zer dog.'

'You were hoping to retrieve the results of the Z52H Project, I presume, to give to your friends in Germany?'

'I have, zese days, very few friends in my home country, Lucinda. However, your first assumption is correct. My intention remains, though, to eradicate all evidence of our work for zer good of mankind. Zat is why I have been, for some time, destroying all documents relating to zer project.'

'I see,' said Varley's aunt, her curiosity pricked. 'Then you are not a spy?'

'Not at all. I am, as you are well aware, a physicist. But first and foremost a human being, and can no longer allow zis vile and potentially catastrophic work in which we have been engaged, to continue.'

'But you know as well as I that if we do not undertake this research someone else will.'

'Zat is a matter between zem and zeir consciences. I presume you have secreted zer formulae in zer locket around zer dog's neck?'

'How did you know?'

'Just a hunch. I gave you zat locket as a birthday present, I knew you would not leave it behind wizout good reason.'

'When the files first started to go missing, I resolved to copy all subsequent results onto microfilm, and hid it in the locket.'

'And since I have now destroyed zer originals they are the only record left of our work, is zat right?'

'That is correct.'

'Zen I must request zat you hand over zer locket.'

'How do I know you are telling the truth, that you will not pass on the information elsewhere?'

'You have only my word.'

'Then you are attempting to take advantage of the vulnerable position in which I find myself with respect to you.'

'What do you mean?'

'You know how I feel about you, Leo.'

The German appeared uncomfortable with the direction in which the conversation had turned, and cleared his throat before continuing. 'It is true zat I have suzpected for some time zat you have been harbouring thoughts of an affectionate nature towards me. But I have to tell you zat, fond as I am of you, Lucinda, I cannot for various reasons concern myself wiz any kind of romantic affiliation. I vill say no more.'

Lucinda Varley seemed puzzled at the German's reluctance to elucidate, and an awkward silence descended between them. Finally, having apparently reached some sort of conclusion as to why her inclinations towards the man she knew as 'Leopold' could not be reciprocated, she gave out a lengthy and crushingly disappointed sigh. 'I see,' she said.

'It gives me no pleasure to find myself in zis situation viz you, I can assure you.' Now standing by the window, the German produced a revolver from his jacket pocket, and – somewhat unsteadily – aimed it at Barclay. 'Time is runnink out, Lucinda,' he said, 'and unlike zer Englishman I do not intend to put zer velfare of zer dumb animal before all oser considerations. Now please, take zer locket from zer dog's collar and hand it to me.'

At that moment, the door burst open and Skimpton, his running shoes in his hands, strode manfully into the room. 'That's enough Herr Müller!' he declared. 'Now give me the gun!'

'Skimpton!' exclaimed the Prussian, 'what has happened to your hair?'

'I should have thought that was obvious,' replied the House Captain, winking conspiratorially at Lucinda Varley, 'I have had it shaved off!'

'But why?'

'Never you mind, just hand over the weapon.'

'But what are you doink here? Surely zer race is not finished!'

'I have returned for my old running shoes, Herr Müller. As you are probably aware, the pair you so kindly gave me had been impregnated with a very unsportsmanlike substance.'

'Vot are you talking about? I know nosink of any "unsportsmanlike" substance! Skimpton, viz all due respect, you do not understand vot is going on here.'

'On the contrary, I understand only too well. You are a German spy, Müller, and have been deceiving us all along!'

'Skimpton,' interposed Varley's aunt, 'I think perhaps...'

'Leave this to me darling, for I have heard everything from outside the door.'

'What do you mean "darling"?'

'Skimpton,' said the German, 'all zis has nosink to do viz you.'

'In so far as it is taking place in my study, Herr Müller, it has everything to do with me!'

'Perhaps you are right,' returned the Prussian, 'but before I explain, I sink you should know zat zis is not zer young woman viz whom you believe yourself to have been corresponding over zer last few weeks. You have been zer subject of a cruel hoax.'

'You should know, you filthy coward,' retorted Skimpton, 'for is it not you who have perpetrated the cruellest deception of all? Leading us all to believe you to be a decent fellow and former Olympic athlete? Do you not realize what effect it might have on the younger members of the school, who have idolized you this term, when they discover you to be no more than a cranky fifth columnist?' At which the furious sportsman closed in on his prey, his hand outstretched, his eyes teeming with hatred, and his socks fully charged with Marcus Dent's itching powder. 'Now don't be a fool,' he insisted, 'and give me the gun.'

'But Skimpton,' faltered the German, 'zer race!'

'Zer race can vait!' hissed Skimpton, his shadow now looming over the older man like a sentence of death. The Prussian, forced backwards into Skimpton's leather armchair, his hand shaking visibly, directed the barrel of the revolver straight at the chest of his favourite pupil.

'Skimpton! Be careful!' urged Lucinda Varley, backing into the doorway with Barclay.

'Don't worry, my sweetheart,' assured he, now towering over the cowering German. 'Everything is under control.'

*   *   *   *

The thunderous roar of the explosions could be heard as far away as the outskirts of Barnchester, where farmers reported it to have been louder, even, than the noise of their tractors. The race leaders had just reached Faverstock Common, to be greeted by a large crowd, when the series of blasts from Faysgarth fairly shook the ground. Colourful plumes were sent high into the murky November sky, after a number of initial detonations produced an enormous plume of black smoke. This was quickly followed by an horrific display of coloured arcs – presumed to be the contents of Colonel Coombes's chemistry laboratory – shooting through the low cloud like dazzling streamers.

Screams were heard from all directions and several boys almost fainted with shock. The runners were startled into motionlessness, like petrified citizens of Pompeii, the lights from the explosions reflecting in their thunderstruck, rain-washed faces. 'I say!' gasped a shocked Faysgarthian, 'Skimpton's only blown up the school!'

He was instantly collared by an irate and anguish-filled Jack Varley. 'What do you mean, you silly ass?' he demanded. 'What has Skimpton got to do with this?'

'But it's here,' replied the fourth-former, 'in the school magazine. This character Wofgang Plankton's been pretending to be your aunt and getting Skimpton to do all sorts of dotty things like shaving his head and learning the organ. Now he's *really* done it!'

Varley snatched the copy of *Fractured Lives* from the boy and, as the crowd – many of them openly weeping – pushed past him, scanned the pages. Racing through the account of the correspondence between his best pal and the boy who had posed as his aunt, he paused to concentrate on one section of a letter, supposedly from his aunt:

As for my tonsorial preferences, my darling, I declare that I should even love you with no hair at all – perhaps even more so – for you would be such a novelty, so shorn, that every girl in

Monktonshire would surely be out in her Sunday best seeking your favours!

Quickly reading on, his attention finally settled in disbelief on the most devastating paragraph of all:

I am certain, my love, that these masters and boys who appear to be pestering you so callously about your scholarly performance and other matters, are not fully appreciative of how lucky they are to have one such as you in their midst. If I were you, I would be tempted to put a bomb under the place and have done with them all!

Varley, taking into account the foolhardy nature of Skimpton's behaviour of late, occasioned by what he had taken to be the promptings of his aunt, paused to consider the import of that final sentence:

If I were you, I would be tempted to put a bomb under the place and have done with them all!

Just then, though, the diminutive Piggot arrived, his porcine features fraught with worry. 'Varley!' he gasped. 'Skimpton's disappeared from the race! They're saying he's destroyed the school! Is it true?'

'You'd better read this,' replied Varley flatly, 'and make up your own mind.'

As the final volleys echoed across the hills, Varley, like a blind man lost in a maze, foraged about his brain in search of another explanation, any escape route from what now seemed an unavoidable conclusion. Surely his old friend would not perpetrate such an act of apocalyptic vandalism, for he loved Faysgarth even more than dear life! There must surely have been a mistake, he thought, either that or he was certainly in the throes of some appalling nightmare! Stunned, and almost unable to summon up the breath required to do so, Varley ran over and joined the crowd, and, like one irresistibly drawn into a vacuum, moved towards the school, still shrouded in smoke, hoping, even now, that it might still be there.

*   *   *   *

Mr. and Mrs. Grimshaw in the meantime, had chosen to set aside the apparent demolition of one of Monktonshire's foremost minor public schools, and were enjoying a picnic tea on the farthest edge of Faverstock Common whilst awaiting the appearance of their son, Algernon.

Assuming that the tumultuous commotion beyond the woods would have dampened many a competitors' vigour that afternoon, they were confident that their well-drilled and determined son's appearance was imminent, as the top card in a very depleted pack. However, so profound was their disappointment when, rather than Algy, Cocky Peacock was

first to emerge from the distant brouhaha, that a distracted
Mr. Grimshaw, believing he was devouring a pork pie, bit into
a boiled egg, still in its shell.

There was no mistaking Peacock though. And a very sorry
sight the formerly decorous Faysgarthian made too; his outfit was
spattered with mud, his previously coiffured hair now flattened
to his pate and dripping wet, and his makeup dancing a sprightly
tarantella all over his face. With his arms hanging loosely at
his side, and his feet dragging in the mud, the dandy looked
desperately out of sorts and drained of spirit. As he eventually
passed them, the Grimshaws slurped anxiously on their brawn
sandwiches, washed down with thick, black tea – apart from
Marcus Dent, the only spectators left.

A few seconds later, their son popped up, strolling over the
common with apparently not a care in the world, his hands
thrust into his pockets like an Ascot beau. 'What's tha playin' at?'
screamed his father, expelling egg shell from his mouth as he did
so, and racing up to Algy to box his ears. 'It's not ovver yet, tha
knows! Tha's got that jessy to beat yet!'

'But I surmised it had been called off!' protested the boy.

'Well dunt surmise nuthin',' walloped his father. 'There's
another five mile to do! Now get on wi'it!' At which, his son
dutifully picked up speed.

'Try not to be too 'ard on t' lad, George,' pleaded Algy's
mother. 'You know 'ow you get.'

'Do you want me a laughin' stock in Flatley or what?' snapped
Grimshaw. 'Because that's what I'll be if 'e dunt win today!'

Elsewhere, Marcus Dent had caught up with an exhausted
Cocky Peacock on the road from Faverstock to Faysgarth village.
Upon finding the weary competitor hunched over a fence gasping
for air, Dent was furious. 'What on earth are you doing, Cocky?'
he rasped. 'Do you have any idea how much money I have riding
on you this afternoon?'

'I can't go on,' admitted Peacock.

'What do you mean? You must!'

'Just so that you can make a fast buck? This whole wretched business was ill-advised from the outset.'

'Well you devised it, you poncy little twerp! What has happened to all your revolutionary fervour?'

'I draw the line at needless loss of life.'

'There's no making an omelette without cracking eggs, Cocky. I should have thought you would have realized that.'

'Look: Skimpton may be a complete buffoon, Marcus, but he doesn't deserve to die like a dog.'

'Oh, don't talk nonsense.'

'He returned to his study twenty minutes ago and is certain to have been caught up in the blast.'

'You are being ridiculous.'

'I blame you for this, Marcus. You knew I wouldn't countenance casualties.'

'There have been no casualties.'

'And it may seem ludicrous to you, but I've actually grown to respect Skimpton over the last few days. He's shown a courage and resolve that one simply can't help but admire.'

'Good grief! One might almost believe that you had grown in love with the dear fellow!'

'Don't be absurd. I just don't relish the thought of being implicated in his death, that's all.'

'There haven't been any deaths.'

'If you think I'm just going to stand by and…what do you mean there haven't been any deaths? Anyone within five hundred yards of that blast would have been hard-pressed to hold onto his limbs! Now, I know how much delight you Faysgarthians seem to take in injuring one another, but I tell you this…'

'There have been no injuries either, for there has been no bomb.'

Here Cocky paused and looked Dent quizzically in the eye. 'What do you mean,' he said, 'there has been no bomb?'

*   *   *   *

As the jumble of spectators picked their way through Dead Man's Wood, the tearful youngsters of Faysgarth leading the way, a small dog appeared before them, dodging this way and that, in an attempt to locate a route through their ranks. Then, the sound of gunshots nearby added to the confusion, for now the crowd knew not which way to turn. Lady Edgerton began screaming and was wrestled to the ground with rather unseemly relish by her husband, and encouraged by him with considerable urgency to keep quiet.

As another shot rang out, Herr Müller appeared from behind a tree, flourishing a revolver and apologising for any inconvenience he might be judged to have caused. Enquiring from the crowd as to which direction the dog had run, the panting Prussian appeared confused and somewhat unstable as he waved his weapon about him crazily. Taking his unpredictable manner into account, the three hundred and fifty stunned spectators' understandable response was to remain utterly still and point, every one of them, in the direction of Faverstock Common.

The smell of burning now penetrated the nostrils, as smoke wafted through the trees. Some distance behind, Skimpton appeared with Varley's aunt. As Lucinda ran on ahead, in pursuit of the German, Skimpton found himself cornered by a dangerous-looking Jack Varley. 'What have you done to Faysgarth, you filthy rotter?' demanded the cricketer with as much threat as he could muster.

'I'm afraid I can't talk now Jack,' came the reply, 'as I must help Lucinda retrieve her dog.'

Varley, steaming with rage, grasped Skimpton by the throat. 'You cad!' he scowled. 'I knew you were barmy, but I never suspected you capable of this!'

'I am sure I don't know what you are talking about Jack,' responded Skimpton, 'now kindly unhand me, as I must capture Barclay before Müller gets his hands on him.'

'The world is crashing about our ears, Skimpton! And all you can think of is a damnable dog!'

'Look, Jack. I don't have time to explain now, so let me go or I shall punch your face for you.'

'Then do your worst, you bald-headed bounder! Kill me, if you like, for where you are going one more act of treachery will make no difference.'

A further shot echoed in the distance as Skimpton sighed and looked about him. There was nothing more for it, concluded he, and after withdrawing his arm very deliberately, he delivered his best pal a powerful blow to the right eye, sending Varley crashing, semi-conscious, into the bracken.

* * * *

Meanwhile, in the quad, Binns and Spate were clearing away the spent remains of the fireworks with which, at Dent's behest, they had so convincingly fooled everyone into believing the worst. 'I hope Marcus approves of our little display,' said Binns, 'though I suspect my hearing might well have suffered something of a further setback as a result of it.'

'I don't doubt that it has,' said Spate, entirely unheard.

Just then, the first band of bewildered spectators arrived, in the form of a battalion of lachrymose third-formers, led by an irate Piggot. After reassuring themselves with momentous relief that their beloved school was still standing, the emotionally volatile band of juniors turned resentfully on Dent's henchmen. It was a fuming yet erudite Piggot who immediately grasped the situation and spoke for them all. 'What do you mean pretending to blow up the school, you dirty pair of beggars?' he shouted angrily. 'Why, you are no better than slaves to Marcus Dent's twisted whimsy!'

'What's the matter with you?' retorted Binns. 'Everyone's seen a rattling good show, haven't they?'

'That is beside the point,' put in another youngster. 'You chaps have humiliated Skimpton with your potty pranks!'

'That's right,' enjoined Piggot. 'Come on fellows, let's scrag them!'

And as they chased the cowardly miscreants in the direction of Main House, so set were they upon revenge, that not one of them noticed that, over at the school gates, another pair of n'er do wells were arriving at Faysgarth; two young gentlemen whose record of violence and skulduggery in the East End of London was the cause of as much consternation in the local constabulary as had been the exploits of Binns and Spate at Faysgarth over the last few years. For, strolling down the drive at that moment were none other than Neville 'Knuckle' Knowles and Eddie Stiletto, purveyors of thuggery, stolen goods and, for a price, large quantities of explosives.

Stationing themselves near the entrance to the chapel, the unsavoury pair, sporting vulgar gangster suits and flashy, two-toned shoes, adjusted the brims of their trilbies as they surveyed the school grounds. 'This is the place alright,' sneered Knowles, winking shiftily at his partner.

'It's full of snobs!' added his mate.

'Course it is. Ripe kidnapping pickings.'

'Maybe next time.'

Just then, Piggot and his friends passed close by. Having given up on their attempts to punish Spate and Binns, their mission now was to inform everyone of what the sneaky blackguards had been up to with the fireworks.

'Oy you! Toff boy!' bellowed Knowles after Piggot. 'Where's 'Enry Spate's young sprog? He owes us money!'

Piggot, sizing up the fellows in an instant, took a few seconds to compose his response. When it came, it was of such incisiveness and condescension of tone that any sixth-form public schoolboy would have been proud to have the riposte accredited to himself, had they themselves been confronted with two specimens of such evidently suspect quality. 'If you are addressing me,' conjectured the junior firmly, 'then you will kindly endeavour to display at least a modicum of courtesy. I fully appreciate that where you come from such customs are probably about as rare as would be a ballerina in a bone yard, but until you undertake to learn at least the fundamentals of good manners then I am afraid I can be of no assistance to you. Good day.'

'Lumme!'

Furthermore, and before either of the ruffians had recovered from this verbal assault, they were both sent sprawling onto the gravel by a small dog which appeared from nowhere and sprang up at them viciously, before it disappeared into the chapel. Additional indignities followed immediately after, as a hail of bullets whizzed passed them, fired from a gun toted by an elderly gentleman who staggered up to them with his smoking weapon, and apologized profusely in a foreign accent before himself proceeding into the chapel in pursuit of the mutt.

Hearing the sound of a police whistle nearby, the East End ragamuffins were on the verge of cutting their losses and scarpering when they were further detained by yet another grievous attack upon their persons, in the form of a hail of debris which landed on them as a result of an enormous explosion in nearby Dead Man's Wood. More profound, even, than Binns and Spate's previous detonations, this present blast had the unmistakable timbre of genuine catastrophe, in that it appeared to rumble for some seconds before a deafening roar sent out a seething mass of undergrowth, masonry and glass in all directions. Knuckle Knowles was hit by a twisted section of what appeared to be a printing press, and his colleague just managed to avoid being decapitated by a sign with the word 'Stout' painted on it which flew past his head, missing it by a whisker.

How most of the Faysgarthians in Dead Man's Wood that afternoon managed to avoid injury from the massive explosion was a mystery to all. Though Cocky Peacock, putting two and two together half a mile away, was moved to conclude that the volatile combination of several tons of dynamite, previously hidden in a dingy cellar by Binns and Spate, under his own supervision, and a carelessly discarded cigarette end, likely disposed of in the same location, now meant that the school magazine would most probably be in urgent need not only of a new printing press but of alternative premises. In addition, it would seem safe to hazard that the same publication would also be looking to fill the vacant position of editor-in-chief in the not-too-distant future.

'WHAT IN GOD'S NAME IS GOIN' ON!!?' boomed Constable Stubbs as he bounded over the quad with Detective Inspector Collin C. Henessy of Scotland Yard, who had just arrived by motor-car.

'It's the old coaching inn,' said a voice, 'in Dead Man's Wood. It's just been blown to smithereens!'

'And Herr Müller's inside the chapel,' added another, 'after the dog with a gun!'

'Let me get this clear,' said the portly constable, anchoring himself and his rudimentary intellect securely to the gravel. 'The dog 'as a gun?'

'I think you should know, Constable' said Skimpton, arriving from the direction of Dead Man's Wood, 'that he is a German spy.'

All present fairly choked with amazement, as the policeman struggled to comprehend Skimpton's astonishing revelation. 'How can a dog be a German spy?' he demanded.

At that moment, another shot rang out, this time from the belfry, where Herr Müller could be seen balancing precariously, intent on capturing Barclay, who was perched on a parapet close by. 'It's imperative he doesn't get the dog,' urged Skimpton, 'for in a locket around its neck is information vital to national security!'

Constable Stubbs's narrow, reptilian eyes surveyed the Deputy Head Boy with obvious suspicion from their vantage point near the top of his vast body. 'Are you 'avin' me on?' he queried.

'No, Constable,' put in Varley's aunt, who had just arrived. 'It is essential that the scientific formulae contained in microfilm hidden in the locket don't fall into the wrong hands as, not to put too fine a point on it, the very future of civilisation may be at stake. It is vitally important, therefore, that we rescue the dog.'

'I see,' pronounced the policeman. 'In that case I shall 'ave to go after the little blighter myself!'

'Hang on Constable,' interposed Marcus Dent, who, with his cohort Binns, had also edged his way into contention. 'I have a better idea.'

'And who might you be?'

'Dent, sir. My father commands a high-ranking position in the government.'

'Does 'e now? Well let's 'ear your suggestiond, Master Dent.'

'Binns,' barked the School Scoundrel, 'get up in that Belfry!'

'Why me?'

'Because I say so!'

'But he's got a gun!'

At this juncture, Mr. Grimshaw intervened. Having left his wife at the running track awaiting the arrival of their son, the ex-collier had joined the kerfuffle with a view to lending his support in the persecution of the German. 'Go on, young 'un,' he urged Binns, 'do as this lad tells yer. There's thirty bob in me pocket for yer if yer stop that Hun gettin' 'old o' t'dog!'

'Go on, Binns!' urged a junior.

'Go it, Binns!' impelled another. 'Atta boy!'

A spontaneous round of applause broke out as Binns, groaning all the while, was unceremoniously propelled into the chapel by Marcus Dent. 'Right,' said Dent, addressing the crowd decisively, 'I need one more volunteer.'

Amidst the clamour of willing applicants was Constable Stubbs, who stepped forward from the scrum, dispatching several juniors to the ground as he did so. 'I'm your man Master Dent,' he declared, his whistle at the ready.

'Top hole,' said Dent. 'Come with me, Constable.'

*   *   *   *

In a soggy meadow on the edge of Dead Man's Wood, meanwhile, two doughty runners were taking a well-earned breather before the final stretch of the County Cross Country race.

'Ah dunt know abaht thee, Cocky,' gasped Algy Grimshaw, 'but ah'm knackered.'

'Likewise.'

'I 'ope me mam and dad dunt see us slackin' off.'

'I dare say they'll be waiting at the finishing tape with a few tongue sandwiches for you, eh?'

'Thing is, I hate tongue,' complained the working-class fellow. 'And brawn. And beef drippin'. And potted meat. To be 'onest wi' yer, these days I lean more towards a vegetarian diet.'

Peacock smiled and surveyed his opponent empathetically. 'They push you pretty hard don't they?' he said.

'Me dad goes in a mood if I get less then ninety-five percent in every subject.'

'Bad luck.'

'And if I'm issued wi' a detention or owt like that he starts chuckin' stuff abaht.'

'Really?'

'I got given t'cane for insubordination last term an' 'e stopped eatin' for a week! Me mam 'ad ter get me uncle Stan to force feed 'im in t'end.'

Sympathetic though he was to Algy's domestic tribulations, Peacock's attention was now diverted elsewhere. 'Wait a minute,' he said, 'what's going on over there?' Pointing to the garden of a large house about a quarter of a mile down the hill, he jumped onto a nearby fence to gain a better view of the two suspicious-looking characters attempting to gain entrance through a conservatory window.

'I dunt know,' said Grimshaw, 'but 'app'n we'd better investigate!'

*   *   *   *

At about the same time as Binns reached the top of the belfry steps, Herr Müller sent another bullet singing off the walls in the direction of Barclay, who let out a yelp and leapt onto a ledge. 'I say, Herr Müller,' implored Binns anxiously, 'do come down, there's a good fellow.'

'It is you!' exploded the German. 'You who hit me vis zer frying pan! I recognise your voice!'

Then, the small tower was awash with noise as Marcus Dent and Constable Stubbs, at its foot, swung with all their might on the bell ropes. On the drive, the crowd gasped as a terrified Barclay appeared to look down and crept gingerly along his ledge, literally shaking with terror.

'Aaargh!' screamed the German. 'Zer Belts! Zer Belts!'

Skimpton, peering upwards, Lucinda Varley hovering apprehensively nearby, found himself standing beside Jack Varley, who was sporting a rather persuasive black eye. 'Fancy old Müller turning out to be a German spy, eh, Jack?' commented Skimpton. 'I always suspected there was something unsavoury about him.'

'Listen,' said Varley quietly, 'about earlier...'

'Forget it old man. We all get the wrong end of the stick sometimes.'

'Indeed,' agreed Varley. 'I take it, then, that you have not yet read this week's edition of *Fractured Lives?*'

'Haven't had the chance old stick. Anything good in it?'

Varley produced a slightly singed copy of the school magazine and handed it to Skimpton. 'Page four,' he said, '*Faysgarth Mon Amour* by Wolfgang Plankton. I should sit down before perusing it if I were you.'

*   *   *   *

Confronting 'Knuckle' Knowles and Eddie Stiletto as the two trespassers tried to force their way with a crowbar into the large house at the foot of the meadow, Cocky Peacock and Algy Grimshaw found themselves facing a barrage of abuse for which neither of them was prepared. 'Look at this one!' railed Eddie. ' 'E looks like one o' the old tarts darn Brick Lane!'

'Yeah,' agreed his partner, 'after a night on the tiles!'

'Tha'd better watch what tha's sayin',' put in Grimshaw, 'or else tha might get us angry.'

'And who do you fink you are,' sneered Knowles, 'George Formby?'

'Tha can't get away wi' brekkin' inter private property, tha knows.'

'An' who's gonna stop us, you?'

Cocky Peacock, straining to glean some sense from these seemingly impenetrable colloquial exchanges, began to suspect that a sensible course might be to depart with a view to telephoning the police, and suggested as much to Algy. Grimshaw, though, had other plans, for the continuing taunts on the subjects of his diminutive stature and provincial accent had produced in him such a fury that he suddenly flew at the hoodlums, fists flailing.

So surprised were they at this frantic onslaught that the gangsters barely had time to defend themselves before Grimshaw had socked them both on the bean and launched a couple of vicious kicks to their shins, sending them sprawling onto the lawn. As they crawled off, howling with pain, in his direction, Peacock picked up a nearby spade, and as the ruffians reached him, the effeminate Faysgarthian bashed them both once with the tool, propelling them head first into a nearby ditch!

As the injured pair lay in their crater, covered in mud and moaning feebly, both Peacock and Grimshaw exchanged astonished glances, amazed at what they had achieved. 'That seems to have cracked it,' said Peacock, smiling. But the other, fists clenched tightly, face crimson with rage and body pulsating visibly, could only let out a series of disquietingly deep breaths by way of response.

Returning to the garden some time later, after having telephoned the police from a nearby house, Peacock was astonished to find his Northern friend apparently close to finishing off the cockney criminals. The spade in his hand, Grimshaw was feverishly shovelling earth onto them like a man possessed, burying the pair in the very hole into which they had earlier been forcefully dispatched. 'What in God's name are you doing Algy?' demanded a shocked Horace Peacock.

'I couldn't find any rope to tie 'em up wi',' explained Grimshaw, 'so I thought I'd weigh 'em darn wi' a ton of earth instead! They've got breathin' pipes.'

'I'm glad to hear it. Now come on, put that spade down. We've got a race to run!'

*   *   *   *

Outside the chapel, the crowd held its collective breath as it watched Barclay escape the clutches of Herr Müller by leaping like a terrified cat onto a suspect strip of guttering. What with the dissonant bells still clamouring in his ears and Binns's booming voice only feet away, the German looked to the heavens for respite, his hands clasped firmly about his bandaged head.

Lucinda Varley, beside herself with fear for Barclay, clung to Skimpton, as Lady Edgerton, obviously on the verge of another fervid outburst, bit deeply into her husband's hand with the excitement. Jack Varley, his injured eye throbbing with pain, stood beside Detective Inspector Collin C. Henessy, the policeman from Scotland Yard who had interviewed him several weeks before, at the start of this sorry episode. 'A dirty business, Detective Inspector,' he commented.

'What? Oh, indeed,' agreed a preoccupied Henessy.

Skimpton, however, his red face still buried in Wolfgang Plankton's purple prose, paid no attention whatsoever to the desperate struggles atop the chapel belfry. For such was the shame and embarrassment he felt at having fallen so spectacularly for the anonymous satirist's jape at his expense, his only inclination now was to slope off quietly to his study, lock the door, close the curtains, and remain there uninterrupted for the next fifty years.

That was until the unmistakable, and indeed unavoidable, bugle call to duty sounded, in the form of an anguished scream from Varley's aunt. 'SKIMPTON!' she cried, as her beloved dog lost its footing and plummeted earthwards. Looking up in an instant, the young fly-half sprinted over the drive and launched himself like a torpedo a good thirty feet, before snatching the dog literally inches from the gravelly jaws of certain death.

If Skimpton hoped that his amazing feat might have gone some way towards restoring his standing at Faysgarth, he was instantly disappointed. For, rather than the customary cheers which usually rang out after such a triumphant display of athleticism, he was greeted – as he handed over a quivering Barclay to its grateful owner – with a rather perfunctory and sarcastic round of applause from the crowd. Indeed, so severely had many of them suffered the dog's vicious attacks in previous weeks, that the overwhelming majority of Faysgarthians present, rather than rejoicing in its good fortune, were sorely disappointed not to see the pugnacious little pup's malevolent limbs splattered inexorably onto the drive.

'Is he down?' asked Marcus Dent, returning from his campanological exertions.

'We've got t'dog,' said Mr. Grimshaw, 'but t'German's still up there!'

'In that case there's only one thing for it,' insisted the school bounder. 'Skimpton...'

A few minutes later, with Dent and Constable Stubbs bouncing around for all they were worth on the bell ropes, and Skimpton's polyrhythmic pummelling of the chapel organ battering the eardrums of anyone within five miles of Faysgarth, Herr Müller, swaying dangerously, re-appeared atop the chapel belfry. His equally sonorous persecutor Binns, also present, was now obviously so profoundly deaf that he seemed totally oblivious to the appalling noise.

'Leopold!' wailed Varley's aunt. 'Please be careful! I love you!'

'What do you mean, Lucinda?' queried her nephew. 'That's Erich Müller up there!'

'No, Jack,' stated his aunt, 'that is Leopold Tilkowski, one of my colleagues in the laboratory.'

'The one with whom you are reputed to be in love?'

'Yes, if you must know.'

'But I was led to believe that the character to whom you were secretly attached was a Russian!'

'Where did you hear that?'

'Why, it was in The *Barnchester Chronicle*.'

'He is a Prussian, Jack.'

'Oh. But the newspaper said...'

'Perhaps you could get a part-time job there as a proof-reader. Sounds like they need one.'

'I'll take the locket, Miss,' came an authoritative voice nearby. At first, it wasn't clear from whom the order came, and it was only after a group of third-formers removed themselves that Detective Inspector Collin C. Henessy was revealed, his small frame having been lost in their midst.

'And who are you?' asked Lucinda Varley.

'This is Detective Inspector Collin C. Henessy of Scotland Yard, Lucinda,' interposed Jack Varley. 'He has been investigating the case for some time.'

'I see. Then I suppose you'll be wanting to arrest me for absconding with government property?'

'That won't be necessary Miss,' said the detective warmly. 'From what I have heard you have done the country some service by keeping the information out of the hands of undesirable aliens.'

As she handed over the microfilm to Henessy, Lucinda Varley glanced upwards, prompted by a further angry exchange between the German and his voluble oppressor Binns. 'Come on, Herr Müller!' screeched the latter. 'Take my hand!' The Prussian, though, appeared to be on the verge of reprising one of his dizzy spells, his eyes rolling, arms flailing as he staggered about the parapet, the increasingly deafening noise now bombarding his senses cataclysmically.

'Leo! Please be careful!' shouted Varley's despairing aunt. Finally, as the monstrous tumult reached its peak, evidently unable to take any more, the terrified Teutonic let out a blood-curdling cry, pleaded to the heavens and leapt into oblivion, plunging earthwards head first and landing on the gravel with a sickening crunch.

A few seconds' stunned silence ensued, broken only by the sound of Detective Inspector Henessy's car skidding off, and then by the jubilant cheers of the exultant Faysgarthians. 'Hooray!' they roared. 'Three cheers for Marcus Dent!'

Varley's aunt threw herself weeping onto her colleague's broken body. 'Leopold!' she cried. 'Speak to me! I never intended for this to happen!'

Presently, as everyone drifted away, shaking their heads in disbelief at what they had just witnessed, Skimpton emerged from the chapel, his ears ringing, his numb hands reddened from their pounding of the organ's keyboard. 'Is he dead?' he asked.

'I am afraid so,' came the tearful reply.

'Where is Detective Inspector Henessy?'

'He left a few seconds ago,' interjected Jack Varley.

'Without waiting to see what happened?'

'He didn't seem much interested in anything else once he'd got his hands on the microfilm.'

'I see.'

'If there is anything I can do, Lucinda,' added Varley, 'I will be in my study.'

After his friend had departed, Skimpton, caught in a whirlwind of conflicting emotions, felt anger rising in his blood. 'You had the locket all along didn't you, Lucinda?' he demanded.

'How did you know?'

'When I handed you the dog just now I realized it was missing.'

'I took it from Barclay's collar earlier when you were confronting Leopold in your study.'

'Then all this wretchedness...the death of a man...has been for the sake of a ...of a miserable dog?'

'Have you never done anything foolish, Skimpton?' asked Lucinda tersely. 'I didn't want to see him killed! I loved Leopold,

for he was a fine man and a brilliant physicist. I had no idea that
he was in such turmoil! What on earth have you people done to
him here over the last few weeks?'

'Then you no longer believe him to be a spy?'

'How on earth could he have been? Where would he have
taken the microfilm had he retrieved it from the belfry today?
There was no possibility for escape. I now believe that his sole
intention was to destroy the formulae, for that is what he believed
was the honourable thing to do.'

Beside the German's twisted, lifeless body, Skimpton noticed
a folded piece of paper which had fallen from his pocket. On it,
he recognized, in his own hand, the poem he had only recently
composed in honour of the young woman who, as yet, remained
unaware of the affection she had inspired in him.

> *Orphans of fortune*
> *We two are entwined...*

'And did he love you?' he asked.

'Not in the way that a man customarily loves a woman,' she
said, 'of that he was not apparently capable. I believe, though,
that he loved me in his own way.'

'I do not doubt it,' said Skimpton. Picking up the sheet of
perfumed notepaper and placing it in his pocket. 'Now if you will
excuse me, I have a telephone call to make.'

*   *   *   *

'Hello? Is that Scotland Yard? My name is Skimpton and
I'm calling from Faysgarth School near Barnchester. What?
Yes, *that* Skimpton. A former pupil? Well, my giddy aunt!
Congratulations! Thank you very much officer. What? No, I
have been forced to withdraw due to exceptional circumstances.
What I wanted to enquire about was...did you really? That was
a very close game indeed. Well, you know how these things are,

you're fifty yards out and just slam the puck goalwards and hope
for the best. Now, I believe that a Detective Inspector Henessy
was sent to Faysgarth today to investigate reports of a German
spy in connection with some official secrets. What? Yes Henessy.
He what? Really? Are you sure? I think that would be a very
good idea...'

*   *   *   *

'If they're not 'ere in t'next five minutes,' barked Mr. George
Grimshaw from his position beside the running track, 'I shall tek
meself off in one o' me moods.'

'Na dunt get into a dither,' soothed his wife, 'tha's dribblin'
piccalilli darn thi chin!'

'What's happening?' asked a tetchy Marcus Dent arriving at
their side. 'They should have been here ages ago.'

'And who are you?' enquired Mrs Grimshaw.

'This is t'young lad who I were tellin' yer abaht, mother,'
explained her husband. '"Is father's high up in t'government, and
'e's just saved t'world!'

'Marcus Dent's the name, Madam. Speculative Financier,
Faysgarth School.'

'In that case young man,' beamed an impressed Mrs Grimshaw,
'can I offer yer a mug o' tea and a brawn sandwich?'

'Not for me thanks.'

'I say! Might I try some?' It was Binns, ravenous after his
exploits in the chapel belfry, and brushing aside all in his way to
get to the food.

'After what you did up there lad,' laughed Mr. Grimshaw,
'you deserve a thumpin' great treat. Tek as many as yer like!'

'Mmmm...delicious!'

'Finest quality brawn that is, from Grimshaw's of Flatley.
Butchers of Distinction. Tek a couple more!'

'Thanks. Any chance of some of that tea?'

'Of course, lad!' offered Mrs. Grimshaw. 'But why does tha

'ave ter shout?'

'I am afraid,' explained Dent, 'my young friend here has developed a problem with his hearing of late, and is quite unaware of the distress caused by his booming delivery.'

'Oooh,' sympathised Mrs. Grimshaw, 'is there nothing that can be done?'

'I am afraid he is beyond hope, Mrs. Grimshaw.'

'I say!' screamed Binns, 'these brawn sandwiches are grimscious Mr. Scrumshore!'

'Eh?'

'It's Grimshaw,' said Dent.

'Pardon?' quizzed Binns.

'Grim.'

'What is?'

'Mr. Grimshaw!'

'Is he?'

'The gentleman's name is Grimshaw, Binns!'

'I say, what an extraordinary coincidence! Tell me Mr Grimshaw Binns, do you utilise a hyphen in your name?'

'Could you enlighten me,' interrupted Dent, trying to salvage some sense of intelligibility from the pitiful exchanges presently masquerading as conversation, 'what *is* brawn, exactly, Mr. Scrimshaw...GRIMSHAW!!?'

'Boiled pig's 'ead,' proudly stated the butcher.

'Jellied!' added his wife, smacking her lips together with relish, her false teeth making an unpleasant clacking sound as she did so.

As Binns immediately emptied from his mouth, with considerable alacrity, the masticated remains of the northern delicacy with which he had recently been so generously plied by the Grimshaws, Marcus Dent turned to his sorry cohort, a look of disdainful resignation on his face. 'How about sampling some pig's trotters next, Binns?' he suggested.

*   *   *   *

'Piggot!' hailed Skimpton as he crossed the quad and approached his young fag with some urgency. 'Where is everyone?'

'They are all at the running track Skimpton, awaiting the dramatic climax to the race,' replied the junior. 'You appear somewhat agitated, sir,' he added, 'I hope you are not unduly worried about what has appeared in the school magazine this week. For if that is indeed the case, I should like to reassure you that we younger Faysgarthians are still behind you one hundred percent, and will give you our total support in whatever course you wish to pursue in that respect.'

'Thank you Piggot. I am most grateful for this display of loyalty. But your assumption that a certain Herr Plankton's scurrilous tricks are responsible for my present preoccupation is in error, for I fear far more dangerous chicanery may be abroad. Do you recall a Detective Inspector Henessy being on school premises earlier today, Piggot?'

'I certainly do, Skimpton, and a mightily suspicious character he was too.'

'Very observant of you to have come to that conclusion, Piggot, for I have recently ascertained that your impression was absolutely correct. A high-ranking officer from Scotland Yard, a former Faysgarthian as a matter of fact, has just confirmed that this fellow Henessy left the metropolitan force under something of a cloud several months ago, and has been wanted in connection with offences relating to various breaches of national security for some time!'

'Don't worry,' said Piggot confidently, 'he won't get very far.'

'How do you know that?'

'I took the liberty of ensuring as much after I had noticed a ticket for the channel ferry on the passenger seat of his car.'

'Had it not occurred to you that the fellow was merely intending to go away on holiday or had business on the continent?'

'That was my immediate assumption, Skimpton, until I investigated the document more closely.'

'And what did you discover?'

'That the name on the ticket was Chesney Nicolls!'

'So, perhaps Henessy was picking it up for a friend?'

'Unlikely, Skimpton. Why, don't you see?'

'See what?'

'That "Chesney Nicolls" is an anagram of "Collin C. Henessy!" Now, I ask you, why would anyone want to conduct their affairs using two completely different names, the letters of which are entirely interchangeable?'

'Unless, of course, they were up to no good.'

'Excellently deduced, Skimpton, and precisely the same conclusion at which I quickly arrived. Further rooting around in the glove compartment produced even more incriminating evidence of Henessy's skulduggery; namely a passport bearing Henessy's photograph but inscribed with the name Chesney Nicolls! It was this discovery which led me to take steps to prevent the fellow from escaping too far.'

'What did you do, pierce his petrol tank?'

'That old trick did occur to me, Skimpton, but in the end, I chose another avenue of sabotage, removing, instead, a hose attached to the breaking system of the car, in the hope that the rascally driver would come a cropper in a ditch somewhere and knock himself out in the process!'

'Why, Piggot! You are an absolute beauty! Remind me to notch up an extra ten house points on your behalf when next I am in the junior common room!'

'Are you serious Skimpton? Ten house points? Why, that would put me on level pegging with Fothergill Minor, and he is reputedly a genius! Ten house points?'

'Why, of course, you deserve them! I don't suppose you got his registration number, did you?'

'U892L.'

'Well done. Now, all I require from you is that you wait here for the appearance of the Barnchester police, who will have been alerted that something is afoot by Scotland Yard. Explain all to them when they arrive.'

'Righto!'

'My guess is, this Henessy character's made off towards the coast on the south-bound B4357. Hopefully he has run into a hedge by now, and I will be able to catch up with him on my bicycle. Tally ho, Piggot!'

'Tally ho, Skipper!'

*   *   *   *

'So, let me get this straight, Mr Grimshaw,' said Marcus Dent, 'you race whippets for money? Is that correct?'

'Aye, we do that.'

'And you make a few bob out of it, do you?'

'Can do, dependin' on t'purse.'

'Intriguing.'

Ever on the lookout for new business opportunities, Marcus Dent had been grilling George Grimshaw for some time on the subject of his dogs, and was weighing up the possibility of importing the sport to Faysgarth. It would certainly be worth a try, he thought, and even if such an enterprise failed to catch on, he could always sell off the canine competitors to his schoolfellows as food. Just then, though, more immediate concerns thrust themselves forward, as all eyes turned to the farthest edge of the field, where the only two remaining contestants in the County Cross Country race were battling neck-and-neck. As they approached the sports field from Dead Man's Wood a mighty cheer went up. 'Come on Algy!' shouted the Rainingham lad's mother. 'Just a lap an' 'alf to go!'

Even from that distance, though, it was obvious that both Algernon Grimshaw and his plucky opponent were utterly exhausted, as they skidded clumsily in the mud alongside the rugby pitch, and struggled to stay upright.

With Peacock marginally ahead, as the two runners stepped from the slippery grass onto the shale running track at the far side of the arena, the plucky northerner began closing on his rival, and Marcus Dent started to look worried. 'Come on Cocky!' he bellowed anxiously, 'You can do it!' And as they neared, it was a toss-up for who looked the worse for wear, the two bone-weary athletes or the prostrate and burnt-out Constable Stubbs, who had been brought on a stretcher to see the climax of the race by a brace of burly sixth-formers, for the portly policeman had suffered a mild stroke as a result of his gruelling session at the end of a bell rope with Dent earlier in the day.

*   *   *   *

Meanwhile Skimpton, in search of the formulae relating to the Z52H Project, on the B4537 coast road, approached with some caution, a vehicle, registration number U892L, which had careered into a ditch, as it had presumably been travelling south. Its wheels still spinning and with steam shooting forth from under the bonnet it could only, he thought, have crashed minutes earlier.

Dismounting his bicycle, the brave schoolboy opened the passenger door and looked inside. Apart from an unconscious Chesney Nicolls, alias Detective Inspector Collin C. Henessy, his bloodied face wedged against the steering wheel, were two other fellows, both uncommonly filthy. One was out cold and the other was twitching on the back seat like a half-wit, and jabbering on senselessly. 'We only wanted a lift!' he stammered in a broad cockney accent. 'We ain't done nufink wrong!'

'Shut up, you fool,' said Skimpton, 'and help me manoeuvre this fellow, for there is something in his pocket of vital importance, and of which I intend to take immediate custody.'

*   *   *   *

The race, meanwhile, was shaping up for a thrilling finish, with Algy Grimshaw looking easily the stronger as the two runners rounded the bend near the long-jump pit. 'Go on Algy!' shrieked his mother, jumping on her husband.

As the bell sounded for the final lap, the two shattered combatants staggered past, Grimshaw pulling away slightly from Peacock. 'For Christ's sake, Cocky,' shouted Marcus Dent. 'Get a grip, you slack arse!'

'Come on Algy!'

With half a lap to go, and Peacock summoning every last ounce of effort to close the gap, disaster struck. Looking up the hill at Faysgarth, Peacock seemed almost instantly thunderstruck and suddenly confused. In truth, his exhaustion had provoked an hallucinatory vision which distracted him profoundly, for as he surveyed the school buildings, they appeared to be laughing at him derisively, from their haughty position of privilege and power.

Suddenly, he was no longer certain that he even wanted to continue, let alone win the race, and he slowed almost to a complete halt. Why, thought he, should he conspire with such an anachronistic institution as Faysgarth, and pursue goals which could only bring greater glory to the broken, grubby, corrupt system it represented? Why, indeed, should he attempt to win a race merely for the sake of satisfying the greed of his chum who, after all, had hardly carried out his side of the bargain?

Now dragging his aching limbs with very little enthusiasm, Peacock summoned no resistance when his legs buckled beneath him and he collapsed in a pathetic heap on the ground.

'Get up Cocky!' cried Dent, his eyes filling with tears at the thought of the enormous sum with which he would have to part in the event of Peacock losing the race. 'Pleeease! Pleeease, Cocky, I beg of you!'

'He's gonna win, mother!' bawled an emotional Mr. Grimshaw. 'Our Algy's gonna win!'

Their son, though, looked hardly certain to finish himself. Now staggering like a Saturday night drunk, the northerner seemed unsure quite which way he should propel his drooping body. His parents were beside themselves and would certainly have picked up their son and carried him to the tape had it been within the rules. The Faysgarthians looked on in horror as their man Peacock lay motionless on the ground, for surely all that was needed now to secure victory for their bitter rivals Rainingham was that their representative Algy Grimshaw hobble to the winning post only two hundred yards away!

Then Peacock heard a voice urging him on from the crowd, and it echoed in his head like a mantra. 'Come on Cocky,' it said, 'do it for me.' It was as if every esteemed sportsman in history were speaking to him, and that they were somehow reliant upon his victory to maintain their exalted positions in the great scheme of things.

'Come on Cocky, do it for me!' urged Skimpton, having just arrived on his bicycle to taste the last drop of the race. And to everyone's absolute amazement, Cocky Peacock did just that. Pulling together his shattered limbs and wringing from somewhere a last thimbleful of energy, the determined Faysgarthian picked himself up and began running again, slowly at first, then faster and faster until he fairly whizzed round the final bend. Algy Grimshaw was only inches from the tape, though, his parents urging him on, and it seemed certain he would lurch to an unlikely victory, when Peacock thrust past him at the very last moment to secure a sensational and momentous first place for Faysgarth! Yet another sporting triumph for the record books!

'Hurrah for Cocky!' was the cry. 'Hurrah for Faysgarth!'

'Hurrah for Skimpton,' muttered Marcus Dent under his breath, in a combination of relief and utter jubilation. For not only had he just avoided ruin by the skin of his teeth, but a combination of Cocky's victory and his own multifarious financial speculations had just won him nearly £19,000 – enough lolly to keep him at Faysgarth well into middle age.

'Well run, Cocky,' said Skimpton, helping the victor to his feet. 'That was a simply ripping finish.'

'How do I look?' asked the desperate dandy.

'Ghastly. But nothing that a freezing shower and a change of clothes won't put right.'

'Well done Cocky,' said Dent, joining the pair. 'Come to my room later, I have a fine pair of buckled shoes for you with a dainty French heel by way of reward.'

'Keep them,' rasped Peacock. 'I want nothing more to do with you.'

'As you wish.' Dent then turned his attention to Algy Grimshaw, who was being consoled by his mother with a large, fluffy towel and a pint of hot, black tea. 'Hard lines Grimshaw,' he smiled, 'you put up a rattling good show. If it's any consolation, my money's on you for next year. Where is Mr. Grimshaw, by the bye? I should like to speak with him on the subject of his whippets.'

'He's took 'imself off, Master Dent, distraught' explained Algy's mother. 'We won't expect to see 'im for a couple of weeks.'

'I say, poor show.'

'Doctor says it's 'is nerves,' said Mrs. Grimshaw.

'He's a bloody maniac,' dismissed Algy. 'He wants stringin' up.'

*　　*　　*　　*

Later, in his room, Skimpton was studying, with a magnifying glass, the strip of microfilm he had retrieved from Chesney Nicolls, the cryptographically disguised erstwhile Detective Inspector from Scotland Yard.

'How are you feeling, Skimpton?' asked Jack Varley, poking his head round the door.

'Jack!' greeted the valiant House Captain. 'A tad confused, to say the least. I can't make head nor tale of these formulae.'

'Give them here. I shall pass them on to my aunt. I am sure she will put them to devastatingly good use.'

Skimpton then dropped into his armchair, and took up, once again, that week's copy of *Fractured Lives*. 'What a business, eh, Jack?' he sighed.

'Indeed.'

'Any notion as to who this "Wolfgang Plankton" character is who's been stringing me along?'

'Haven't the faintest. I assumed it to be Marcus Dent, but he denies it categorically.'

'I dare say a visit to the address to which I have been writing would give me a pretty shrewd idea.'

'Shouldn't bother if I were you. Best put the whole sordid business behind you.'

'I've made an awful ass of myself, haven't I, Jack?'

'Afraid so, old bean. Don't worry too much, though. School-boys have very short memories. Another couple of trophies hoisted, a winning goal scored, a bull's eye here, a knockout there, and all this nonsense will soon be forgotten.'

'But what about Herr Müller...Tilkowski...whatever he's called?'

'That was not your doing, Skimpton. If anything, the blame lies with my wretched aunt and her unfathomable affection for that heinous dog.'

'But if I hadn't chased him like that, or hammered away at the organ...'

'He should have just come down from the belfry like a civilized fellow! Instead of which, he simply gave in to all that Teutonic hysteria.'

'I expect you are right, Jack, as usual. I just wish there was something I could do.'

'There is.'

'What is that?'

'Why, your best, of course!' Varley reached into his pocket and produced a paper bag. 'I've just seen Cocky Peacock, by the bye,' he said. 'He sent you this.' Varley then took from the bag a pink woollen bob cap with fur trim studded with imitation pearls, and tossed it to his pal. 'To keep your shiny pate warm!' he added affectionately.

'Good old Cocky!' grinned Skimpton, inspecting the dubious item with a sardonic grin. Placing it on his head, he reached into his top drawer and pulled out a bag of sweets. 'Now, Jack,' he said, 'what would you say to a fruit bonbon?'

*   *   *   *

In the basement of the kitchens beneath the refectory at Faysgarth can usually be found a small cat which answers to the name of Molly. Although the little beast is tolerated by the cook, there is an understanding between herself and her young assistant Nancy, who had taken rather a shine to the animal, that the kitten should be kept under strict control at all times. Indeed, so stringent are the rules regarding pets at Faysgarth that the cook herself could find her position in jeopardy should anyone discover the animal's existence.

Little wonder, then, that young Nancy had worked herself into something of a flap when Molly went missing that night. Searching the kitchens for some thirty minutes to no avail, the girl had all but given up hope when she opened a cupboard and discovered the errant pet in the arms of a member of the Lower Sixth-form, cowering in the gloom. 'Why Master Spate!' she cried. 'What on earth are you doing in there?'

'Ah,' said Spate, blinking his eyes repeatedly in an attempt to accustom them to the light. 'Hiding from a couple of fellows, as a matter of fact. Associates of my father's from London, to whom I owe rather a lot of money.'

'I see. And you thought you'd hold on to my cat for a bit of company, did you?'

'We sort of fell in together. I hope you don't mind.' Spate stumbled from the cupboard, handed the cat over to her owner, and stretched himself into his familiar, angular shape.

'I saw your firework display earlier,' said Nancy, cuddling her purring pet, 'it was most impressive.'

'Thank you.'

'The way you and your friends got everyone thinking that Master Skimpton had blown up the school. I had to laugh. And him with that bald head and all.'

'Bald head? Oh, yes...yes. It was all my idea, of course.'

'Now let me ask you something: it *was* Horace Peacock writing all that stuff in the school magazine, wasn't it? Only cook and I had a little bet on it. She reckoned it was Master Dent behind it, but I recognized the style, you see. I used to work at St. Hugh's when he got into all that trouble with the Lord Chamberlain's office. He's a very clever young man, isn't he?'

'I suppose he is. For a deviant.'

'He's certainly the only one with the nerve to pull off that kind of stunt. Not that you weren't the mastermind behind the whole thing, of course.'

'No! No, you are right. Peacock is a very fine wordsmith. You have made a very astute observation.'

Nancy then looked at her wristwatch and an expression of pure panic swept over her attractive, freckled face. 'Good Lord!' she said. 'Is that the time? I'm way behind. I've got a train to catch in half an hour and the stew to put on, and the cat to drop off before then!'

'I could do that for you! Make the stew, I mean!' suggested Spate, eagerly.

'Nonsense, Master Spate. I won't hear of it. There's all these chickens to chop up.'

'Can't be that complicated. Just pop them in boiling water with a spot of seasoning.'

'That's true. Cook'll be along later to add the vegetables. You sure you wouldn't mind?'

'Not in the least.'

'Only I've got to visit a friend of mine in London. A female friend, you understand, and if I don't get the eight-thirty train there isn't another one until nearly eleven.'

'Leave it to me. I could look after the cat for you if you'd like.'

Nancy paused, a look of anticipatory glee brightened even more her sunny features. 'Would you really?' she said. 'I usually drop her off with a lady in Faverstock, but I don't think I've got time tonight.'

'I am sure Molly and I will get on famously. You won't be away for long will you?'

'Only a couple of days. My friend's got two free tickets for the railway, you see, being a guard and that, and we're planning a trip to the seaside.'

'Your friend is a railway guard?'

'A lady railway guard!' she stuttered. 'There's only a few, you see, and she's…erm…she's one of 'em.'

'I understand. Well, I am sure you both will have a wonderful time!'

'I hope so.' Nancy smiled and looked slightly apprehensive at leaving Spate in charge of both her pet and to-morrow's lunch. In the end, she decided to take a chance on the young man's initiative and reliability, and with an air of cautious resolve said, 'I'll make tracks then!'

'That's a good one,' chortled Spate genially, 'make tracks… railway guard!'

'Oh yes!' laughed Nancy, handing the kitten back to Spate. 'She doesn't take much looking after doesn't Molly,' she said. 'Feed her a few scraps now and again and keep her out of the way of the old dragon.' The assistant cook then put on her coat, picked up her overnight bag, walked up to Spate and, standing on her tiptoes, planted a single kiss on his forehead.

'I say, steady on!' protested the embarrassed Main Houseman, wiping his brow with a handkerchief. 'Is there a telephone number I can call in case of…' But before he could say any more, she was gone.

And so it was that Spate's short-lived career as a master chef began. Having chopped the hundred or so chickens into quarters and transferred them into several large pots of boiling water, the culinary novice now warmed to his theme. Rooting through the cupboards with considerable enthusiasm, he found a veritable cornucopia of herbs and spices, all of which he added to the brew, together with tinned prunes, lettuce leaves and molasses all the way from the Nile Delta. Oat flakes, he used to thicken the broth, and several jars of dried anchovies mixed with liquorice root added just the right piquancy. By way of a finale, the gallivanting gastronome tossed into his bubbling creation several whole watermelons and the contents of an enormous jar of mulberry jam.

'That lot should tickle the fellows' fancy!' quipped he,

trotting out into the cold evening in pursuit of the cat. And as he traversed the quad, a whiff of gunpowder tickling his nostrils, he felt somehow light headed, as though for the first time in his short life, the cloak of undisguised menace had been lifted from his shoulders, and he entered Main House wearing a rather untypical smile, and with a definite spring in his step.

SIX

LA JIRAFA

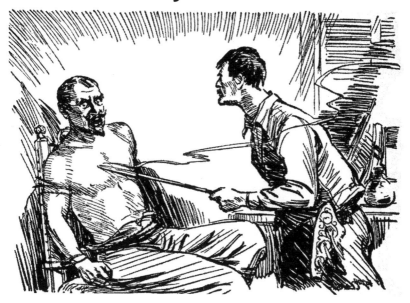

The toothache began some minutes into the Channel crossing. More precisely, within seconds of the disappearance from view of Dover's famous white cliffs. Skimpton had found himself a quiet spot on the aft section of the vessel which was now proceeding with some determination towards the coast of France, when, inhaling deeply from the salty air, he felt an unmistakable jolt of pain emanating from an upper right molar. Not yet severe enough to warrant the attention of a dentist, the problem – he concluded – was sufficiently painful to rank alongside his other numerous irritations regarding the trip.

It was Colonel Coombes whose idea it was to assemble a scratch team to compete in the International Schools' Hockey Tournament in faraway Barcelona. Since Faysgarth's First Eleven were required for important matches at home, a second team was assembled from various willing juniors and members of the Arts Option, all of whom were well-known duffers when it came to sports. Skimpton had been roped in despite his protests, in the hope that his captaincy might add a degree of mettle to the outfit, though quite how, given the irredeemably poor standard of his team-mates, was a mystery to the Deputy Head Boy.

Unfortunately, his participation on the tour meant him missing several vital rugger games, a state of affairs which the talented fly-half found frankly infuriating. Neither had his present mood been improved by the irritatingly esoteric nature of his schoolfellows' conversation during the arduous train journey from Barnchester. Rodney Carstairs, the puny fourth-form surrealist had answered questions for two hours on the subject of Dadaism and its influences, whilst his effete cohort, the lanky 'cellist Riley, had scraped away incessantly on his instrument, torturing the ears with the tuneless works of various Austrian composers, the names of whom Skimpton could not now remember.

And as if all this wasn't enough, Colonel Coombes, the myopic menace of the chemistry lab, who was ostensibly leading the party, had brought along a female companion, in whom he had been engrossed since the moment they left the school gates. This large, stout lady – the inspiration, Skimpton was convinced, for many a seaside postcard – had been introduced by the Colonel as his sister, though she, in turn, had expressed a heartfelt wish that the boys would know her simply as their 'aunty Betty'.

Skimpton was contemplating joylessly his immediate prospects, a finger thrust speculatively into the region of his upper gums, when he noticed Colonel Coombes on the upper deck nearby, his sister at his side. 'You see, Skimpton,' carolled the master, somewhat stiffly, 'my sister and I...'

'Colonel Coombes,' interrupted Skimpton wearily, 'you appear to be addressing yourself to a life jacket. Should you wish to speak with me I am located four paces to the front of you and two to the left.'

'Ah, yes!' said the Colonel, approaching Skimpton jauntily, a definite air of geniality in his gait. He was wearing an outfit Skimpton had never seen before; a nautical blazer, slacks and open-toed sandals, and were it not for the fact that his bowtie was half way round his neck, his hair in a state of some disarray and his spectacles perched at a crazy angle on his face, one might easily have confused him with a normal person going on holiday. 'You have been introduced to my...sister?' he asked gaily.

'Aunty Betty and I are already firm friends,' replied Skimpton disinterestedly, for such was his indifference to the entire venture that even his muscles couldn't bring themselves to seize up, as was their custom when in the presence of a member of the opposite sex.

'Jolly good,' resumed Coombes. 'Now, when we finally reach Barcelona, at twenty-three hundred hours, Continental time, my...your aunty Betty...and I will be departing immediately for a few days on the coast as we have business to attend to there. I am sure, therefore, that we can rely upon you to take temporary charge of the party.'

Skimpton did not respond, maintaining instead a hostile silence.

'We'll make it worth your while!' offered aunty Betty, in the jokey tones of a cockney street seller.

'Of course!' added the Colonel, 'there might be as many as fifteen house points in it for you! How does that sound?'

Skimpton stared at him blankly, and receded further into his sombre mood.

'What about five bob then?' said aunty Betty, rummaging around in her purse.

Skimpton could now just make out the coast of France in the distance behind his tormentors, his first ever sighting of a continent supposedly ravaged by civil strife and political uncertainty. His immediate concern though, was to escape the oppressive regime which had now cornered him near the life jackets. 'Two pound ten,' urged aunty Betty, 'and that's my final offer!'

Rather than dignify the conversation with a response, he turned gruffly, placed his arms on the rail and looked down at the foaming waves, parted by the enormous vessel's gleaming bulk. Perhaps, conjectured he, a meeting at the bottom of the ocean with the mighty Neptune would be preferable to enduring the further miseries that surely lay in store?

*   *   *   *

The train journey, subsequent to the party arriving at Boulogne, afforded no relief from the discomfort. After passing through the Spanish border, a tumultuous influx of humanity meant that what little available space became monstrously over-subscribed, and any lingering pretence at civilized behaviour was quickly discarded once livestock was introduced.

Skimpton was seated on a crate staring uncomprehendingly at a book about rugby tactics when he heard a voice apparently addressing him from close by. 'You wanna olive?' it said.

'No thanks.'

Skimpton's travelling companion was a greasy-faced young-ster of about twelve with long black hair and atrocious teeth. Grinning all the while, he proceeded to eat a whole jar of green olives whilst smoking the most evil-smelling cigarettes. 'My name,' he beamed, 'he is Sancho!'

'I am very glad to make your acquaintance, Sancho, I am sure.'

'You wanna smoke? Byooodiful cigarillos...?'

'No thank you.'

'You are...school?'

'Yes, I am school.'

'Me, I am soldier!' At which the boy stood up and saluted ostentatiously, knocking a cage full of birds from a luggage rack onto an elderly couple below.

'Very good,' said Skimpton. 'At ease.'

As the train made its slow progress through the warm Spanish night, Skimpton managed to escape his toothache and

the eager company of Sancho only by the occasional bout of
fitful sleep. Travelling at what could only have been about twenty
miles an hour meant that the journey was not only interminable
but hideously uncomfortable. The train's snail's pace allowed
hordes of people to throw themselves and their luggage onto it
at every station, whether it had stopped or not. Those who did
not find seats then proceeded to perch on each other's shoulders
and hang from the luggage racks like monkeys. The smell was
excruciating, the heat unbearable. And when, with apparently
only a few miles left, the train lurched to a standstill, Skimpton
was not astonished to find that the small pig, which had been
asleep on his lap since Figueres, had emptied the contents of its
bowels onto his flannels.

More surprising was the sound of horses' hooves outside,
accompanied by much whooping and barking of instructions
in Spanish. Then one of the doors was flung open and several
masked men entered brandishing rifles. 'Papers! Papers!'
demanded their leader impatiently, as his men ploughed through
the bodies. An urgent silence descended the carriage, as even
the sheep and goats seemed to sense danger and ceased their
noise. As identity cards were inspected, fearful whispers began
circulating like illegal contraband. 'Fascista! Fascista!' they said.
'Don Esteban! Fascista!' A young Spaniard, after protesting when
his papers were retained, was rewarded with a rifle butt to the
mouth which brought gasps from the passengers.

Finally, Colonel Coombes considered that he had seen
enough. 'Now look here you fellows,' he protested, clambering
to his feet, 'just what precisely do you think you are doing?'

'Who are you?' quizzed their leader, a malodorous fellow of
around forty, with an atrocious moustache.

'Sit down Archie,' hissed auntie Betty, smiling sweetly.

'I,' pronounced the master, 'am Colonel Archibald Coombes,
of Faysgarth School, Barnchester. One of Monktonshire County's
finest educational establishments, dedicated to the instruction of
boys between the ages of...!'

The bandit laughed scornfully and then sucked his teeth before turning his attention to the Colonel's angelic companion. 'And who is she?' he asked, smiling lasciviously.

'She,' responded the Colonel firmly, 'is my sister Betty!'

This revelation elicited even more hilarity from the Spaniard, and soon not only were his confederates joining in, but so, too were the rest of the carriage. 'Betty!' they cried. 'Betty! Betty! My seester Betty!'

By this time, three of the desperado's men had been dispatched to the farthest end of the carriage, where they had plucked Colonel Coombes from his seat before delivering him to their leader. 'You Col...o...nel Coom...bes, yes?' confirmed he, in a guttural English which the master found highly distasteful. 'Good soldier, si?'

'I was indeed privileged to serve my country during the Great War,' declared the Colonel proudly.

'Then you come with us, yes?'

'No!'

'YES!' roared the renegade, nodding to his men, who pounced on the hapless chemistry master and propelled him forcefully towards the open door.

'You can't do that!' protested Betty. 'He's...he's got qualifications!'

'Close up your mouth Betty,' snapped the leader. 'Your brother, he come to no harm. You...me...we make little agreement, yes? I gi' you my word, you gi' me a leetle kiss, si?'

'Not on your life!' retorted Betty. 'Someone call the police!'

More uproarious laughter greeted this latest demand, until the bandit, with a flourish of his hand, brought the hilarity to an abrupt halt. Descending onto one knee, he took up Betty's hand to kiss it. 'Señora,' he mooned, 'we *are* ze police!' He then gave out an almighty roar and disappeared through the nearest exit, his men following close behind, dragging a terrified Colonel Coombes with them.

'Archie!' cried a tearful Betty.

'Archie! Archie!' parroted her travelling companions sardoni-
cally, 'my brother Archie!'

Skimpton, who had been observing events with some concern
from the corridor, exchanged worried looks with his schoolfellows
as their aunty Betty began to sob quietly.

After the sound of horses' hooves had disappeared into
the night, the train recommenced its clackety journey and the
passengers began chatting gaily, almost as if nothing untoward
had happened. In desperation, Skimpton turned to young Sancho
for explanation. The youngster shrugged. 'The work of Don
Esteban!' he said, lighting another of his putrid cigarillos.

'What do you mean?' said Skimpton. 'What in Heaven's
name is going on?'

'Civil War, amigo!'

'Civil War?'

'Fascista, Communista, Anarquista!'

Skimpton, as was his custom when exceptional circumstances
demanded, placed his head firmly in his hands. And this time no
hint of adolescent melodrama accompanied the gesture.

'Do not worry,' said Sancho, 'I will take you to my *teniente*.
He will find your Colonel Archie.'

'Teniente?'

'He is a great man and a very brave soldier.'

'I see. And what is this fellow's name?'

'*La Jirafa.*'

*   *   *   *

Presently, after he had dragged his sleepy charges from the train
and marched them in single file along the platform, Skimpton
gathered together his fellow Faysgarthians and called a meeting
of the Second Hockey Eleven on the concourse of the Estación
Central in Barcelona.

'Now listen up you chaps,' said the Deputy Head Boy, 'I am
going to leave you in the capable hands of young Carstairs here,

who will see to it that you are all safely billeted at our hotel, the Falcon, which I gather is not too far.' He then beckoned Sancho into the fold and resumed his address. 'I,' he continued, 'shall be disappearing with this fellow here in search of Colonel Coombes, and may not be back for a while. Should any major problems arise, I am sure that aunty Betty will be on hand to offer advice.'

Skimpton had cause immediately to doubt this last assertion, as a quick glance in the direction of the street revealed that the Colonel's companion was already climbing into a taxi, with a view, he presumed, to securing a superior room at the Hotel Falcon. 'So,' resumed Skimpton with a brave face, 'all that remains is for me to wish you the best of luck, and to hope that you enjoy a good night's sleep.'

As the last of his weary schoolmates departed, Skimpton could not help but feel uneasy about leaving them under the dubious authority of Carstairs, the budding surrealist. He also knew, however, that circumstances had left him very little alternative, and that he owed it to them all to try and secure the release of Colonel Coombes.

Setting aside the last of his misgivings, Skimpton plucked from his bag a crisp, red apple and bit into it. The pain in his upper right molar was immediate and unbearable, and he briefly considered questioning Sancho on the subject of a dentist. A momentary perusal of the Spanish boy's gruesome arrangement of teeth, as he flashed another of his unsightly grins, indicated that – in all probability – the youngster would have not the slightest idea what he was talking about.

'We go?' enquired the young Spaniard.

'Yes, Sancho,' assented Skimpton, 'we go.'

*   *   *   *

The following morning, after a brief bus ride and an arduous trek on foot over rocky, inhospitable terrain, the unseasonally fierce morning sun beating down on them, an exhausted Skimpton

and his young Spanish guide arrived at the fortifications which
apparently – in that region – constituted the front line. These
scruffy trenches were populated by a rather shabby band of
individuals, most of whom were not much older than Sancho.
They were attired in little more than rags, some brandishing an
assortment of weapons which looked like they'd been salvaged
from the conflicts of previous centuries. Skimpton identified
an old Gatling gun, prostrate like a stricken animal, its inner
workings spilling out from its side, and several ancient muskets,
looking very much the worse for wear, in the custody of what
could only be described as snivelling urchins.

Sancho was greeted with enthusiasm at first by his pals, but
soon discarded once they had ascertained that he had brought
them no food. Presently, a man of muscular bearing jumped
from a nearby parapet and approached. He carried with him a
preoccupied air and wore dusty fatigues and a substantial sneer.
'Skeempton!' said Sancho. 'This is Comrade Bob Sidebottom
from Lancashire!'

Skimpton's face fell into an expression of utter dismay,
so amazed was he at finding another Englishman in such a
wretched hole. 'I am pleased to meet you, Mr. Sidebottom,' he
said, cupping his face as another jolt of pain shot through his
jaw. Sidebottom said nothing, and an awkward silence ensued. 'I
am afraid I have rather a severe toothache, sir,' added Skimpton,
smiling weakly. 'As a result, you may find the quality of my
speech somewhat indistinct.'

Again, the Lancastrian offered no response.

'He is here to see *La Jirafa*!' put in Sancho helpfully.

Bob Sidebottom laid down his musket, removed the spent
remains of a cigarette which appeared to have been nestling
inside his mouth, and, scoffing, scrutinized with exaggerated
suspicion the young fellow to whom he had just been introduced.
''Ave you ever been down a mine, lad?' he asked, at length.

'No sir,' came the lusty reply.

'What about a slum, 'ave yer ever lived in one?'

'Not as yet sir!'

'Thought not.' Bob Sidebottom then unclipped a flask from his belt and poured a murky liquid from it into a tin cup. 'You'll be thirsty after yer journey,' he suggested, proffering the semi-opaque substance provocatively. He spoke in a thick provincial accent which Skimpton found even more impenetrable than Sancho's primitive English. Sidebottom's vowels, in particular, were most bizarre, for they sounded like the noise a sheep might make if, for some reason, it were chewing on a piece of wood.

Skimpton eyed the drink uneasily. 'Get it down yer,' said Sidebottom. 'It's all there is.' At which Skimpton quaffed the turbid liquid in one. It tasted like a cocktail of paraffin, tobacco and mud. 'What about the rozzers?' resumed Sidebottom presently. ''Ave y'ever been beaten black and blue by a bobby?'

'Not really, sir, no, but at Faysgarth we have masters who can on occasion be more than a touch unscrupulous with the cane.'

'Fair enough. Come wi' me.'

They then traversed the length of the trench in silence, past unspeakable squalor, taking care to avoid the dead vermin, human faeces and the odd sniper's bullet which whizzed overhead. Though the ground was thankfully quite hard as it was springtime, the warm weather had brought its disadvantages, namely the tiny creatures with whom Skimpton now suspected he shared his clothes.

At the farthest end of the dugout was a small hut sheltering behind a mound of earth. Bob Sidebottom went inside and a brief exchange ensued, of which Skimpton heard but one word: 'toff'. After a few seconds, the Lancastrian re-appeared. ''E'll see yer now,' he said bleakly.

Inside the hut, and once his eyes had accustomed themselves to the gloom, Skimpton found himself confronted with a most curious sight. In the middle of the floor was a small writing desk underneath which a rat nibbled at a crust of stale bread. On top of the desk, in an obvious state of discomfort, crouched an extraordinarily gangly man in corduroy breeches, khaki puttees and a yellow pigskin jerkin. Around his head was a brown balaclava, and a knitted scarf covered both ears. As appeared to be the custom, a cigarette dangled from his mouth.

'Mr Jirafa?' enquired Skimpton.

'Indeed,' came the reply, in an unmistakably educated English accent. 'Do come in. What can I do for you?'

'I am in need of urgent assistance, sir. An esteemed member of staff from Faysgarth School has been cruelly abducted by a character known as Don Esteban. A fascist, I believe.'

'What rotten luck. Faysgarth, you say?'

'That is correct, sir. A party from the school is presently billeted in Barcelona, preparing to take part in a hockey tournament'

'I see. Faysgarth. Haven't heard of it. I'm an Eton man myself.'

Skimpton whistled, admiringly.

'Don Esteban, you say?' said La Jirafa.

'I was led to understand that you might know the whereabouts of the blackguard's hideout.'

'Of course. But first, be a fellow and get rid of the beastly vermin for me, would you? Can't stand the little buggers!'

On a nearby chair Skimpton noticed a leather holster in which resided a grubby-looking revolver. Needing no further prompting, he marched over to it, pulled it out, took aim and blasted the little creature into oblivion. 'I say! Jolly good shot!' cried La Jirafa, jumping from his perch and offering Skimpton his hand.

Alerted by the gunshot, Bob Sidebottom popped his head round the door, a look of bewildered alarm on his face. 'It's alright, Bob,' assured La Jirafa, 'everything is under control.' And then, returning to Skimpton, he introduced himself, formally. 'The name's Blair,' he said, 'Eric Blair.'

'I am pleased to meet you Mr. Blair.' It was only then, as he shook the other's hand, that Skimpton realized how unfathomably tall the fellow was.

'I am afraid there is very little food on offer,' said Blair.

'However, I do have two rather splendid cigars which my wife sent me. Would you care for one?'

Skimpton had never before smoked, but on this occasion a desperate desire to distract himself from the hunger which had been gnawing away at him for hours, prevailed, and he accepted the Englishman's offer. Taking the cigar from Blair, he put one end in his mouth and held the other carefully over the match's flame. 'I say,' he remarked, puffing away in precisely the same manner as he had seen characters do in films, 'this is delicious!'

*   *   *   *

Meanwhile, at the Hotel Falcon, a huge banquet was taking place in honour of the Faysgarth Second Eleven Hockey team, the only foreign outfit to have turned up for the forthcoming tournament. Requiring about the same amount of encouragement as had Skimpton before he dispatched heavenward the furry mammal, Carstairs had embarked – whilst standing on his head in the ballroom – on a rousing rendition of *Rule Britannia*, using a comb and a piece of tracing paper. At the conclusion of the performance, Señor Suarez, the Minister of Culture, rose to his feet and led the applause.

A dapper fellow at five foot one, with a distinguished shock of coiffured grey hair, and wearing an expensive suit with a remarkable bowtie, Suarez was undoubtedly the brains behind the whole tournament, and he immediately recommended himself favourably to the Faysgarthians by announcing that they would be awarded an honorary bye to the final, an event he hoped would be attended by a contingent of visiting statesmen from Russia.

A subsequent improvised recital, based around an atonal theme of his own composition by Riley on his 'cello, emptied the hall in seconds, by which time Carstairs had noticed that something had been written on his napkin. It read: 'If you value the life of your Colonel you will lose the hockey game.'

Unsure quite what to do with this worrying piece of information, the young surrealist took the note directly to his aunty Betty, who was recumbent in her room, appearing to have found solace in a bottle of Scotch. 'Wassa problem?' she slurred, after reading the note. 'You just lose the game!'

'We'll probably do that anyway,' replied the Dadaist, 'especially now Skimpton's gone. But as for throwing it away! We may be artists, aunty Betty, but we are also Faysgarthians. Besides, how do we know that we can trust these fellows to keep their word?'

'Can you think of a better idea?'

'It depends from which angle I choose to approach the issue,' mused the fourth-former loftily, 'as a surrealist or as a Faysgarthian. For, you see, a firm adherent to the former would, I am sure, attempt to devise some strange and provocative performance, inspired by the dilemma. But a loyal servant of the latter would, I know, feel it his duty to instigate an immediate and thorough investigation.'

'I beg your pardon?' replied a dumbfounded aunty Betty.

'Your mouth is open, madam,' observed Carstairs, 'I suggest you close it before a mosquito flies inside and bites you on the tongue.'

*   *   *   *

'Now let me get this straight,' said Skimpton, puffing on his cigar like a Wall Street tycoon. 'You are fighting here on behalf of the republican regime against the fascists, led by this fellow Francisco Franco and his cronies, of whom Don Esteban is reputed to be one.'

'That is correct,' replied Blair.

'However, the government, in your opinion, is now nothing better than a handful of puppets controlled by the Russians, and dismisses you chaps as hopeless Trotskyists and pesky anarchists.'

'More or less. Anarcho-syndicalists to be precise.'

'Be that as it may. But what precisely do you consider yourself to be, Mr. Blair?'

'I,' pronounced he triumphantly, 'am La Jirafa!' At which point he stood up and struck his head painfully on a wooden beam.

Skimpton pondered for a moment the complex political picture which Blair had just painted for him, and at length, spoke again. 'I don't suppose you have anything for toothache, do you?' he asked.

'I believe there to be a small quantity of oil of cloves in my knapsack,' said Blair, 'you are quite welcome to search for it.'

Skimpton had the stuff out and was applying it to his gums even before the other had finished speaking, and a few moments later was in a position to continue the discussion. 'You say there are many Englishmen out here fighting for socialism and democracy,' he queried, after the soothing substance had begun to take its effect. 'But on which side?'

'There are so many different factions, Skimpton,' said Blair resignedly, 'it is sometimes difficult to keep track of them. You see, the Spaniards are, by and large, a decent, jolly bunch. Perhaps that is why they possess so little expertise in the organisation of wholesale conflict; their hearts don't appear to be in it! In short, these chaps couldn't organize a piss up in a brewery, if you receive my meaning.'

'So what do you think will happen?'

'Who knows? I suppose eventually the war will end. At this moment, I just hope it will be sooner rather than later.'

'The quickest way of ending a war,' declared Skimpton sagely, 'is to lose it.'

'Very well put,' said Blair, obviously impressed. 'I shall write that down in my notebook.' After having done so, the battle-weary Englishman stubbed out his cigar and immediately began rolling a cigarette. 'Can you handle a rifle, Skimpton?' he asked.

'Indeed, sir. We have an excellent Officer Training Corps at Faysgarth.'

'Jolly good. Tonight, we will sneak behind enemy lines. Don Esteban's headquarters are situated not half a mile from here. If your Colonel Coombes is being held prisoner there, we should have little trouble releasing him whilst his captors are asleep.' Blair then blew the dust from an ancient Mauser and handed it to Skimpton. 'I keep this for special occasions,' he said. 'You are welcome to it, though I cannot vouch for its efficacy.'

'Thank you, sir,' said Skimpton, taking reluctant possession of the decrepit old weapon. 'Why do you think they have abducted him?' he asked at length, 'Colonel Coombes, I mean.'

'Perhaps they thought that he was a member of the International Brigades like myself. Men such as he with a military bearing are invaluable to our side, Don Esteban knows that.'

'I see,' said Skimpton, somewhat unconvinced, for he could not for the life of him comprehend how anyone as deranged, unpredictable and visually impaired as Colonel Coombes could possibly be considered invaluable to anyone, ever.

'By the bye,' said Blair, 'I shouldn't bother with all that "sir" business around here if I were you. You are in the midst of what we call a "People's Army" here, Skimpton. We tend to refer to one another as "Comrade".'

'Very good, Comrade Blair. There is one other thing which puzzles me, though. Why would anyone wish to concern themselves with urination arrangements in a beer manufactory?'

*   *   *   *

Before the reception in the ballroom of the Hotel Falcon had ended, Rodney Carstairs had instructed one of his fellow Faysgarthians to procure written directions to the school at which the following day's hockey final was due to take place. These were drawn up by the Minister of Culture himself, the resplendent Señor Suarez, and delivered to Carstairs in the lobby.

Having left his aunty Betty in something of a drunken stupor in her room, the troubled fourth-former was casting a cursory glance over Suarez's hieroglyphics when he was struck dumb with an immediate realization. The handwriting on the map matched exactly that of the message referring to Colonel Coombes that had been scribbled onto his napkin! There could be only one explanation: The Minister of Culture himself was implicated in the plot to abduct the Colonel!

An immediate enquiry was called for, and to this end, Carstairs proceeded to the hotel's reception to seek information about the location of the Ministry of Culture. He then stepped out onto the busy Ramblas, destined for the government building, which he had ascertained was housed in a large, ornate building only a short distance away.

Some minutes later, hesitating outside the main entrance, Carstairs spied a formidable-looking guard stationed in the marbled lobby of the Ministry building, and, rather than risk a confrontation with the fellow, decided to attempt to gain entry through the rear. Quickly locating an alleyway, the young surrealist escaped the busy thoroughfare and soon discovered himself in a sunny courtyard immediately behind the building. Directly, a flight of stairs presented themselves, leading to what he assumed was the basement, where a partly-opened door invited his penetration. Upon reaching the bottom step, though, he was startled by a piercing scream issuing forth from an upstairs window, the sound of which sent a flurry of birds high into the air from a nearby almond tree. The cries were unmistakably those of a woman in a state of some considerable distress. The wailing continued for some seconds until a man's voice interrupted them in harsh, strident tones. There then followed a series of violent crashes, accompanied by further hideous screams. When they eventually ceased, it was with a horrible and spine-chilling finality.

Needing no further evidence to support them, Carstairs's suspicions were now confirmed; clearly the building was being used for purposes of imprisonment, torture and death – a fate which, if it had not already caught up with him, surely awaited Colonel Coombes. That was unless something could be done, and quickly.

Gaining swift entrance to the basement, the determined young Dadaist silently scaled the stone stairs, stopping at the fifth floor when he heard further worrying ejaculations nearby. Passing through a large polished wooden doorway, he found himself in a carpeted hallway with doors leading off to what he took to be offices. Behind one, men's voices boomed in Spanish. Gingerly, he crept closer and listened for a few seconds. As he was about to move away though, he heard clear mention of Colonel Coombes's name, followed by raucous laughter.

'Can I help you, Master Carstairs?' said a voice from behind him. Startled, the Faysgarthian turned to face his questioner. It was Señor Suarez, the shady Minister of Culture himself!

'I...er...was hoping to have a word with you sir,' blurted the youngster, swallowing hard.

'Certainly, please come into my office.'

Suarez led the way into a large, opulently decorated chamber, his pungent *eau-de-cologne* swirling menacingly around like a dangerous swarm of bees. The room had the unmistakable feel of quality about it, from the stained wood and heavy curtains to the polished leather chairs. Settling himself behind his enormous desk, Suarez leaned back in his chair, lit a cigar and ran his hand through his thick, carefully manicured hair. 'Now, my friend,' he said, 'what can I do for you?'

'I mentioned to you earlier,' said Carstairs nervously, 'that the leader of our group, Colonel Archibald Coombes, had been abducted by bandits...'

The Minister of Culture put up his hand, indicating that he wished to hear no more. 'As I have already told you,' he said with more than a hint of irritation, 'we are doing all we can, save actually over-running the fascist lines.'

'I realize that, sir, but...'

'I assure you there is nothing more that can be done.'

'Yes, sir, but...'

By this time, though, Suarez had all but disappeared behind the cloud of smoke, having slunk lower and lower into his decorously leathered throne. 'Would you care for a cigar?' he asked, now little more than a disembodied voice behind the desk.

'No thank you,' said Carstairs, tersely.

A lengthy silence then followed, and the schoolboy began to fidget apprehensively in his chair, for such was the thickness and impenetrability of the smoke, that Carstairs was now unsure of the precise location of Suarez, if indeed the fellow were still in the room.

Then, suddenly, the Spaniard's face thrust out at him from the fog, an expression of pure delirium on his face. 'Now,' he exclaimed purposefully, 'let's talk surrealismo!'

*　　*　　*　　*

Twenty minutes later, the wily Carstairs emerged from the Ministry of Culture, having secured from its debonair Commissioner permission to stage an open-air performance along Dadaist lines the following day on the Ramblas.

After the schoolboy had disappeared into the crowd, *en route* to the Hotel Falcon and his companions, the pitiful screams and ruthless, goading voices issued forth once more from a window on the fifth floor of the Ministry, as students from the Barcelona School of Speech and Drama, temporarily relocated there after earlier street fighting, tackled once more the violent interrogation scene from Thomas Kyd's play *The Spanish Tragedy*.

*　　*　　*　　*

It was early evening in the trenches, and the flaming sun sank finally out of sight behind the fascist lines. Skimpton awoke to find his skin crawling with fleas and his shoe being nibbled by a rat. These discomforts, together with an aching hunger and a grinding toothache had combined to prevent the hockey captain from enjoying anything more than sporadic repose that day, and he now felt miserably tired and was missing his chums at Faysgarth terribly. What would Jack Varley be doing now, he wondered? Most probably enjoying the company of some young cricketing colt in the long-jump pit, if he knew his pal! And what of his trusty fag Piggot? Pestering one of the masters, in all likelihood, with his seemingly unquenchable thirst for knowledge!

Just then, a sniper's bullet screeching overhead punctuated the arrival of Eric Blair, as the eccentric Englishman launched his lengthy frame through a wall of sandbags, coming to rest with an almighty thump on the unyielding floor of the trench. Immediately, a group of hungry desperados gathered around him, including Bob Sidebottom and young Sancho, each hoping for one of the potatoes he had bravely picked from no-man's-land, and which he now emptied from his knapsack.

At that moment, Skimpton could not help but feel admiration for the tall, stringy fellow who sloped around like the long-necked quadruped after whom he had been affectionately named. For although undeniably reckless – his head invariably protruded dangerously above the parapet – and unquestionably dotty, *La Jirafa* was undoubtedly a decent sort of fellow; a courageous man many miles from home fighting for principles the young sportsman found it practically impossible to comprehend.

As the hungry crowd dispersed, clutching their feeble culinary swag, Blair settled himself next to Skimpton in a small foxhole and offered to share with him a rather grubby-looking spud. 'When exactly does the fighting take place?' queried the Faysgarthian.

'Oh, never,' came the jaunty reply. 'We've been stuck in these positions for months. With no orders to move we can do nothing.'

'But what about the snipers?'

'They just loose off a couple of rounds when the mood takes them. I suppose there's a sort of gentleman's agreement that no-one will actually get hurt.'

As Skimpton munched away on what was essentially his dinner, a sudden look of alarm gripped Blair's face. 'I hope,' he said, 'you are going to leave some of that tettie for me!'

Skimpton handed over the remainder of the root vegetable with a smile, and wiped his mouth with a handkerchief. 'Tell me, Mr. Blair,' he said, 'this fellow Sidebottom – what does he do in England?'

'He is an ironmonger in Bolton.'

Skimpton nodded and stroked his chin thoughtfully. 'And where is that?' he asked, for geography was not his strongest subject.

'It is in the north, near Wigan – a place I have recently had cause to visit.'

'Really? And how did you find the people up there?'

'Living in great squalor, my friend. Which is why so many of their menfolk are out here.'

'How do you make that out?'

'Because they are fighting for a revolution similar to the one they hope will one day take hold in Britain.'

'Well, let's hope when it happens, it's a little better organized than this shambles, what?'

'Hear hear, Comrade Skimpton,' laughed Blair, for he knew full well that the young man had hardly considered the wider social consequences should his enthusiastic wish for successful proletarian rebellion ever become a reality. 'And what of you, amigo,' resumed Blair as he lit yet another cigarette, 'what do you propose doing with yourself after leaving Faysgarth?'

'I intend becoming an explorer, sir, and a loyal servant of the British Empire!'

'Forget it,' dismissed Blair, 'the Empire is finished.'

'Do you think so?'

'Believe me. I was in Burma for five years.'

'The Far East! Wizard!'

'It was the worst mistake of my life. The colonies, my friend, are little more than a racket designed to cause upheaval in faraway lands so as to make as much money as possible out of their unfortunate inhabitants.'

Blair drew urgently on his cigarette and turned to Skimpton in the hope that he had provoked the schoolboy into an impassioned riposte. But his companion was already beating a path through the jungles of Borneo whilst snoring loudly.

*   *   *   *

Skimpton did not wake until nearly eleven-thirty that night, when Blair presented him with two rounds of ammunition for his Mauser. 'The time has come,' declared *La Jirafa* with mock gravity, 'to release the Colonel from his confinement!'

'I come too, si?' It was Sancho, panting like a dog and eager to see some action.

'I am afraid not, Comrade Sancho,' said Blair firmly, 'you must stay here and provide cover.'

'But I have no weapon!' protested the young Spaniard. 'There is only one rifle between ten and he is broken!'

'Then you must shout if you see any movement in the fascist lines, comprende?'

Sancho scoffed and spat a mouthful of tobacco onto the ground.

'Comprende?' repeated Blair.

'Si Señor,' said the boy, crestfallen.

Some moments later, Skimpton found himself crawling on all fours in the pitch darkness of no-man's-land. The ground was hard and unforgiving, and pretty soon holes had appeared in his trousers, as the sharp stones cut his knees like razors.

Presently, having negotiated the perfunctory arrangement of barbed wire, he and Eric Blair found themselves within an ace of the fascist trenches, and were soon able to observe the enemy at close hand. A small group of men were huddled around a candle, some six feet away, engaged in an animated game of dice, a desultory pile of coins and a few grubby notes before them on the ground. If these sorry fellows constituted the enemy, thought Skimpton, then the republicans had little to fear, for they were a pitiful bunch. Their khaki uniforms were all but threadbare, and the wretchedness of their conditions more than compared with the primitive facilities he had just left behind. There were no visible supplies and the fellows looked tired, underfed and lousy.

After a few minutes, Skimpton, concealed behind a nearby mound of sandbags, found himself following the contest avidly, and he eventually noticed that Blair had also become quite transfixed by the game. The rules appeared to be quite simple; each player threw six die, of which only the ones and fives scored, each producing one hundred and fifty points respectively. The winner was the first to reach five thousand. The obvious clown of the group, whom they called Gonzalez, needed but fifty to win, with the rest lagging far behind. Gonzalez was already in a state of some agitation, and when he threw and no five appeared, seemed to be on the verge of exploding with frustration. A few seconds later, and again he threw, but still no five showed, much to the amusement of his friends, whose scores were now creeping up. Eventually, Gonzalez took up the die again. He kissed each one individually, crossed himself whilst looking up to the heavens, and tossed them onto the ground with a flourish. Still the number five failed to appear!

The next round saw his adversaries' scores threatening to overtake Gonzalez at the last hurdle, and there was much good-natured ragging and more than a little dubious gamesmanship. Finally, with all scores standing at four thousand nine hundred and fifty, the joker gathered up his die once more. Skimpton fairly willed him to throw a winning five, and had to restrain himself from encouraging the jocular Spaniard from the sidelines, so fixated had he become with the game. An eerie silence fell upon the competitors as a grinning Gonzalez rattled the wooden cubes in his hands in the rhythm of a fleeting samba, before confidently releasing them to the ground. Three, two, six, four, two...five! A moment's silence was followed by a huge cheer as all present hailed Gonzalez's magnificent victory!

Bullets hummed overhead from the opposing trenches as Gonzalez was scragged playfully by his fellow fascists. 'Gonzalez!

You have won again!' came a distant cry from the republican side.

'Si!' whooped the excited victor 'Five pesetas!'

'Good old Gonzalez!' breathed Skimpton, rather too loudly, for he felt a hand grasp him by the collar and propel him some yards out of the way, as Eric Blair considered that it was now about time they made themselves scarce.

A few seconds later, the intrepid pair pressed on silently, and were soon atop a nearby hill, some fifty yards behind enemy lines. From there the lights of Don Esteban's impressive hacienda beckoned. Quickly covering the remaining ground, they found themselves peering in through a window, the flames from a blazing fire illuminating their grubby faces. Inside was a portly man in uniform who stood before the fire feeding raw meat to a large, dangerous-looking dog.

'That is nothing like the man who abducted Colonel Coombes from the train,' stated Skimpton, flatly.

'Madre de Dios!' came a voice from behind, 'you are right amigo!' It was Sancho, flagrantly disobeying orders and squeezing in between them.

'What are you doing here?' fumed Blair under his breath. 'I told you to stay put. Do you people have no respect for your superiors?'

'We are republicans, Señor Blair,' retorted Sancho haughtily, 'we have no superiors!'

'Then get out of my sight before I give you a comradely cuffing about the ears!'

'Triste, Señor Blair,' murmured a deeply repentant Sancho, 'I want to kill fascista!'

'Then try somewhere else. I hear they have plenty to choose from in Germany at present.'

Sancho then began weeping loudly. Don Esteban looked up and Skimpton clasped his hand firmly over the young Spaniard's mouth and pulled him to one side. The corpulent fascist approached the window and peered out into the gloom for several uncomfortable seconds before smiling drearily to himself and returning to the dog.

A quick check around the rear of the building revealed no evidence of Colonel Coombes's presence, and the three set out disconsolately on the journey back.

It was four in the morning when a weary Skimpton dragged himself over the sandbags and flopped down into the familiar home trench. Blair followed some moments later and immediately began rummaging through his pockets in what quickly turned out to be a fruitless search for his tobacco.

'I picked up a potato,' said Skimpton plaintively, 'would you like it?'

'You haven't got a fag, have you?' said Blair.

'Indeed I have, sir.'

'Splendid!'

'His name's Piggot and he's in the third-form.'

Blair smiled and lay down on his side, his head resting on his knapsack, his teeth grinding for want of nicotine. Skimpton sighed. His eyes were smarting through lack of sleep and he could hardly muster sufficient energy to talk, let alone eat. 'Where's Sancho?' he said.

'He can perish for all I care,' replied Blair, yawning.

*　　*　　*　　*

They awoke a couple of hours later to the sound of gunshots. It was now light and there were definite signs of activity in no-man's-land. Sancho, having mistaken a ditch some five hundred yards out for his own lines, had fallen asleep and been disturbed by a stray fascist out searching for food. Witnessing the confrontation, Bob Sidebottom had fired off a few rounds from his rifle before it jammed and all but exploded in his face.

When Skimpton popped his head above the parapet to see what was happening, the fascist soldier was chasing Sancho, his revolver spewing bullets in all directions. Skimpton instantly took up his weapon, as did Blair, whose rifle practically snapped in half with the first shot.

Sancho was now running for all he was worth towards them, fearing for his life, though the enemy soldier now appeared content merely to stand his ground and fire gleefully at the boy's feet. Skimpton cleared his eyes of sleep and prepared to take aim.

'For pity's sake, man,' roared Blair, 'what are you waiting for?'

And as the bullets continued to pepper the ground around the fleeing Sancho, the Deputy Head Boy from Faysgarth lined up his quarry in the sights, trying to remember all he had been taught in the OTC. His finger crept towards the trigger, his left hand steadying the barrel, and his eye focused on the distant uniformed figure who was now hooting uproariously at the whole affair. It was at that moment, when he heard the laugh, that he realized that the character at whom he was peering through his sights was none other than the fascist japer Gonzalez.

'Fire, you fool!' screamed Blair. 'Fire!'

But Skimpton hesitated. His mind flashed to the dice game the night before, and he remembered the fleeting joy he had felt at Gonzalez's pathetic victory. He could now hear Sancho screaming only yards away. Perhaps the danger was passed, he thought, and looked to Blair for confirmation of as much. The Englishman, though, seemed intent on seeing blood being shed. 'Shoot!' he urged.

Skimpton once more took aim, this time several yards to the right of Gonzalez, and squeezed the trigger resolutely. The kick-back from the ancient weapon sent the sportsman hurtling backwards, and he crashed painfully against the opposite wall of the trench.

'Good shot, sir!' cried Blair. 'You've hit him!'

Skimpton sank to his knees, for this was the last thing he wanted to hear. He had not bargained on the appalling inaccuracy of the old rifle over long distances, and now rued the day he'd ever picked up the wretched thing. As Sancho hurled himself into the dugout, Gonzalez's agonising groans could be heard faintly in the distance.

'There'll be all 'ell to pay now,' commented a gloomy Bob Sidebottom. 'Them fascists'll not be too 'appy about that.'

* * * *

Presently, a lorry arrived with supplies of bread and tobacco, and *La Jirafa* arranged for Skimpton to return with it to the city. After a light meal of dry bread and goat's milk, he said his goodbyes to Blair, Sancho and the obdurate Bob Sidebottom, and climbed into the back of the dilapidated vehicle.

The journey was some two hours in duration, over unforgiving, pitted roads, and though the truck's primitive suspension afforded Skimpton little by way of comfort, he did manage a few minutes' sleep here and there. He dreamt of Gonzalez and the dice game, and of Colonel Coombes on horseback, surrounded by whooping Spaniards.

On the outskirts of Barcelona, the roads became more even, and the busy sounds of the traffic filled Skimpton with anticipatory glee at seeing his fellow Faysgarthians again. His tooth, though, was again throbbing as he had – some time before – used up the last drop of the miraculous potion given to him by *La Jirafa*.

He was dropped off on the busy Ramblas, a thoroughfare so vibrant and colourful that it seemed unthinkable that a state of civil war existed in the region immediately surrounding the city. At the far end, near the Hotel Falcon, there appeared to be taking place some sort of street carnival with dancing and music, and, not wishing to get caught up in the crowd, Skimpton took a back route to the hotel.

Once inside, he discovered that his schoolfellows had already departed to the Joseph Stalin Grammar School, where the hockey final was due to take place shortly. He quickly managed to locate his luggage and was shown to his room.

After a brisk shower, which thankfully seemed to expel from his person the parasites which had been tormenting him for the last day or so, he climbed into a change of clothes and ordered a well-earned glass of lemonade from room service. Having seen the refreshing drink off in one mighty gulp, the young rouser collected together his hockey togs and set off in search of his team.

However, once out onto the Ramblas, he encountered great difficulty fighting his way through the street revellers, many of whom seemed to be engaged in the most curious of activities. One fellow was leaping around in a diving suit, another appeared to be attempting to set fire to a tuba! A young woman was brandishing an umbrella made of mud and a group of youngsters were singing madrigals with loaves of bread tied to their heads! There were even people prancing about naked! It was quite the most bizarre spectacle Skimpton had ever witnessed. Some distance away, a large metallic structure with what looked like an elephant's trunk attached to its front was being wheeled noisily down the street, and in the middle of it all a seemingly ordinary-looking fellow in a dark suit and bowler hat was wandering around with a serene expression on his face, and occasionally kicking people up the backside! Swaying above the crowd was an enormous banner depicting Leonardo da Vinci's *Mona Lisa*, onto whom some mischievous fellow had painted a moustache, and nearby, on top of a grand piano stood a mightily bemused-looking horse!

As Skimpton pushed his way to the front of the crowd, all became gradually clear, for, on a podium above the throng stood the energetic young surrealist Rodney Carstairs, spouting on about Dada into a megaphone, accompanied by his chum Riley, screeching away in a demented fashion on the 'cello. Next to them on the stage was aunty Betty, obviously the worse for drink, dancing the foxtrot in her swimsuit, with a bicycle wheel bolted to a wooden stool.

'Is Dada dead?' screamed Carstairs passionately, to the delight of the crowd. 'Is Dadalive? Dada is! Dadaism!'

'What on earth is going on?' demanded an uncomprehending Skimpton.

'I have organized a spontaneous celebration of surrealism,' responded Carstairs, 'so as to create a massive diversion. You see, I intend storming the Ministry of Culture building, where I believe Colonel Coombes is being held prisoner!'

'I say!'

Carstairs then took up his megaphone again, quickly whipping up the crowd into a further frenzy. 'Dada! Dada! Dada!' he boomed. 'Viva Tristan Tsara for he is the father of Dada!'

'But how do you know all this?' asked Skimpton.

'Why, I have studied surrealism since I was very young, and am considered in many circles to be something of an authority.'

'I mean about Colonel Coombes, you fathead!'

'Oh, I see. I received a ransom note from the Minister himself, Suarez, saying that the Colonel would come a cropper if we didn't lose the hockey final. Upon further investigation I found evidence of detentions and torture in the Ministry building.'

'Good Lord!'

'Dali! Dali! Eau de toilette!' cried Carstairs, to the obvious delight of the crowd. Riley was now plucking away at his 'cello strings violently, an improvised *pizzicato* theme.

'Is there anything I can do?' asked Skimpton.

'Get yourself quickly to the Joseph Stalin Grammar School, and play a blinder for Faysgarth. I shall slip away shortly, when the violence starts, as, surely it must, given these Latin temperaments. I will endeavour to release the Colonel. Riley and I will do our best to make the second half.'

'Good show!'

'Yes, it is rather, isn't it?' put in Riley, wryly.

*   *   *   *

Meanwhile, back at the front, Eric Blair and his comrades were coming under heavy fire from the fascists, furious at the shooting of their colleague Gonzalez. Reinforcements arrived in the form of a renegade anarchist contingent known as 'Los Dementes' – their nickname an unequivocal reference to their apparently unrivalled lack of intelligence. They had brought with them an Englishman whom they had captured, they said, as he was on his way to fight for the fascists. Having decided that his military expertise would be of much greater benefit to the republican side they had decided to transport him on horseback directly to the front lines. Unfortunately, though, the group's map-reading skills had not been of the highest standard and, had their disgruntled prisoner had a mind to do so, he might have renamed his captors 'Lost Dementes', so far from the correct route had they wandered the previous day.

'Can you cope with an old Mauser do you think, Colonel Coombes?' enquired Blair, as the bullets hummed about his head.

'Certainly,' came the confident reply. 'Why, in the Great War...'

'Jolly good,' interrupted Blair, handing the chemistry master the same rifle which, only shortly before, had been used to such devastating effect by Skimpton. 'The barrel may be a little shaky,' he said,' but it won't let you down if you hold on tight!'

*　　*　　*　　*

Upon his arrival at the Centro Segunda Enseñanza Joseph Stalin, Skimpton found the hockey final already under way. With barely seven minutes gone and playing with just eight men, the Faysgarth team were already five goals down.

The grandstand was packed with excited Spanish boys, in the middle of whom was a row of dark-suited men, including the smarmy Minister of Culture, Señor Suarez. His Russian guests were particularly conspicuous, with their sombre expressions, and – even though it was a warm spring day – overcoats, gloves and fur hats. Behind each goal was a gigantic portrait of Joseph Stalin, a stern-looking fellow with dark hair, guilty eyes and a preposterous moustache.

Quickly changing into his togs, the skipper took up his stick, ran onto the field and re-organized his team. A five-goal deficit was a handicap he could well have done without, especially since he had not slept for two nights and his toothache had returned with a vengeance. He decided that the best policy would be to play in goal in the hope of containing the Spanish boys until the arrival of Carstairs and Riley, for though neither of them could be relied upon to perform adequately, at least the numbers would then be equal, and there was a chance that no further concessions would occur.

Skimpton performed his duties as goalkeeper with characteristic grit and passion, turning away shot after shot, as his team-mates flailed hopelessly with their sticks. On the stroke of half-time and with the score standing at seven-nil in favour of the opposition, Carstairs and Riley arrived with bad news. It appeared that Colonel Coombes was not, after all, being held at the Ministry of Culture as they had assumed, for a quick scout around the building on the Ramblas had revealed that the screams Carstairs had taken to be those of prisoners suffering hideous torture were merely the voices of drama students rehearsing a gruesome Jacobean tragedy.

From the stand, Suarez beamed mirthlessly at Carstairs as if to indicate that he knew precisely what the boy had been up to all along. His Russian visitors had by this time relaxed somewhat, and were busy lighting cigars and chatting gaily.

After a brief discussion it was decided that, whatever the fate of Colonel Coombes, the Faysgarth team owed it to themselves and their school to go all out for victory, and to that end it was decided that the goal should be left unguarded in an almighty effort to score.

From the whistle, Skimpton, in agonizing pain from his upper right molar, took possession of the ball like a kestrel onto a sparrow, steering it skilfully through the opposing defenders as if they didn't exist. A petulant thrust sent it to Riley, and the lanky 'cellist did well to push it inside to Carstairs, who gathered it up tenderly. Unfortunately, being something of an artist, he required too much time to complete the move, and a clumsy Spanish tackle sent the rubber spinning into space down the right.

Racing over, Skimpton thrust his stick sideways at a crazy angle and just managed to keep possession. With the goal in sight, he raced forward, sidestepping neatly a desperate challenge, and WHANG! He sent the ball spinning and humming into the back of the Spanish net! Seven-one!

'Hoorah!' cried his team.

'Viva Stalin!' shouted Señor Suarez, entirely for the benefit of his Russian guests.

For some minutes, the game seemed evenly poised, with the Faysgarth boys' renewed enthusiasm and superiority in out-field numbers more than making up for their obvious lack of skill. Both sides sensed that control at this stage might be imperative if ultimate victory were to be secured.

Finding himself in something of a pickle down the left, Carstairs hooked a bad pass to Skimpton, who was placed under immediate pressure by a burly Spanish forward. A momentary lapse in concentration led the skipper to opt, disastrously, for a loping back-pass to his non-existent goalkeeper! Immediately realizing, after executing the move, that the Faysgarth net was unguarded, the County hop-skip and jump champion fairly flew half the length of the field as the ball raced along the ground for a certain own goal. At the very last second, with humiliation staring him in the face, Skimpton launched himself like a gazelle into the air, leaping a good thirty feet to turn the ball round the post.

The crowd was amazed, and soon many were openly cheering the Faysgarth boys, much to the disgust of Señor Suarez who sat with his arms folded, an expression of pure hatred on his face. 'By Jove!' whistled Carstairs. 'That was frightfully well played by Skimpton. His athletic powers border on the unreal.'

Ten minutes later, after Faysgarth had pulled back two more strikes from corner penalties, the scoreboard showed seven-three in favour of the Spanish side. Riley, gaining in confidence, rounded a cumbersome defender and flicked the ball cheekily to Skimpton, who trapped it for the oncoming Carstairs to wallop into the net. Seven-four, and encouraging play by the stringy 'cellist who, only the day before could not tell a hockey stick from a jelly baby!

The Faysgarth team was now playing as if jet-propelled, and Skimpton had quite forgotten his toothache when another chance presented itself. Running onto yet another defence-splitting pass from Riley, the captain flicked the ball into the crook of his stick, checked himself and looked up, with only the goalkeeper to beat. Taking careful aim for the second time that day, he again froze on the spot.

'Shoot!' cried a nearby Faysgarthian.

'Shoot!' screamed Riley.

'Blancmange!' bellowed Carstairs, for whom the entire match had become an extension of his earlier performance on the Ramblas.

But it was no good. Skimpton felt as if he were drugged or in some sort of dream, for there, behind the goal, standing at the foot of the glaring portrait, looking decidedly dishevelled and more than a little sheepish, was Faysgarth's famous chemistry clot Colonel Archibald Coombes CBE, his swaying sister by his side.

'Shoot man! Shoot!'

Skimpton's concentration though, had completely evaporated, and he had only a vague awareness of the approaching goalkeeper, and heard little more than a rush of air as the Spanish boy's stick made contact first with the puck, and then, crunchingly, with his palpitating jaw.

*   *   *   *

Regaining consciousness some time later in hospital, his head all but encased in plaster, Skimpton discovered to his amazement that the adjacent bed was occupied by his old comrade from the republican trenches Eric Blair, or *La Jirafa*, as he was known. A brief and difficult initial discussion revealed that the two of them now shared an acquaintance, an individual who appeared to have been responsible, in Blair's case directly, for the horizontal nature of their present predicaments.

After Colonel Coombes had turned up at the front during heavy fighting, Blair had presented him with a rifle with which to defend himself, assuming that he might make better use of the weapon than would any of the Spanish juveniles. He was rewarded for his confidence in the master with a bullet through the throat, an accident the myopic chemistry man blamed on his faulty Mauser.

With possibly irreparable damage to his vocal cords, Blair, who had escaped death only by a fraction of an inch, had been left with somewhat limited powers of verbal expression; namely the odd grunt and squeak. His main frustration, however, was his apparent inability to inhale cigarette smoke, the stuff having a tendency to escape through the hole in his throat before carrying out its acrid business in his lungs.

Skimpton, too, found himself rather restricted in the conversational arts, his jaws having been wired together as a result of a hairline fracture. Still, thought he, his injury had its positive side; he no longer suffered the toothache which had blighted so much of the trip for him, since his tussle with the Spanish goalkeeper had left him with the loss of a tooth in the upper right region of his mouth.

At first, time passed slowly for the two invalids, both finding the enforced silence extremely frustrating. A visit by Carstairs, however, livened things up enormously. His colourful account of the remainder of the trip caused much painful hilarity as the two let out strangulated screams of delight which brought hospital staff running from all directions.

After Skimpton's departure from the hockey game, according to Carstairs, Colonel Coombes's sister, the redoubtable aunty Betty, had taken it upon herself to play as substitute, much to the fury of the Spanish dignitaries. She and Riley had combined in the final minutes to form a formidable duo and the dispirited Spaniards were finally routed thirteen-seven!

Buoyed by his team's triumph, Carstairs had collared the appalling Suarez and delivered him with a severe roasting over the latter's dirty trick with the napkin. The fourth-former even reported that he had been applauded for his efforts by the Russians, who seemed to find the entire business hilarious!

Furthermore, that night, during the victory celebrations at the Hotel Falcon, Colonel Coombes flying in the face of convention, had proposed marriage to his sister, and after she had agreed, declared that he intended to make certain enquiries of the ship's captain on the journey home!

If Skimpton's remaining time in hospital was relatively serene and uneventful, the days spent there by Eric Blair were punctuated by a series of bitter arguments with the hospital staff, who put his irascibility down to a deprivation of nicotine.

Capable doctors and livestock were his primary sources of irritation, in that – according to Blair – the place suffered both from a criminal scarcity of the former and an unhealthy abundance of the latter. When an old woman arrived to visit her ailing husband bringing with her his favourite sheep, in the hope that it might raise his spirits, Blair complained vehemently to a passing surgeon. He was threatened with an instant, un-anaesthetized appendectomy for his pains, and told, in no uncertain terms, that he was a nuisance and that if he valued his life he should keep his mouth – and throat – shut.

Eventually though, the indefatigable Englishman did put his strengthening vocal cords to some good use. Skimpton was relieved to learn from Blair the fate of Gonzalez, the fascist joker. The bullet the Faysgarthian had released in his direction had only grazed the Spaniard's arm, apparently, his cries of agony being produced merely for the purpose of fooling his chums.

One evening, Blair, uncommonly cheerful – for his throat had now healed sufficiently for him to successfully partake of several dozen cigarettes a day – made an announcement. 'I intend,' he intoned squeakily, 'to write a best-selling book about my recent experiences. I shall set it in an hospital where the patients conspire against the doctors and overrun the place. They then replace the previous authoritarian regime with an egalitarian system with all private provision cancelled for the foreseeable future. In time, however, the patients' leaders betray them and they soon suffer worse treatment than before. The doctors return and are offered massive sums by the treacherous turncoats to perform expensive treatments on them.'

Skimpton was impressed by Blair's idea but suggested that, given present conditions, the story might more appropriately be set in a farmyard, adding that it might even be jolly if the animals could speak. Blair laughed heartily, was momentarily intrigued by the idea but in the end, dismissed the narrative as utterly preposterous.

SEVEN

SKIMPTON SHOWS HIS CLASS

'So, this is the johnnie is it?' said Skimpton, holding up the silver coin to the light.

'No,' corrected his fag Piggot, 'that's his mad brother Rodolpho. He was deposed a year ago.' Rummaging through his collection, the third-former then produced another, shinier example of Boravian coinage. 'That's Maximilian there,' he said, pointing to the profile contained thereon.

'Oh yes,' said Skimpton, 'I can see the family resemblance. They both have similar noses.'

'My family and I all have brown eyes,' offered Piggot, flashing his protruding teeth at Skimpton in an ugly grin.

Skimpton, for a moment, regarded his fag with an air of dismissive bafflement before turning away. Flicking the coin casually, the Senior gazed out of the window of his study.

'Just think,' he said, 'King Maximilian of Boravia at Faysgarth! What a lark!'

'It's not the first time there's been a Monarch present at King's Day, apparently,' said Piggot, with a titter.

'Oh yes?'

'According to Hurlingham Minor, who's been rooting through the records, some fourteen years ago the festivities were graced by the presence of one Wilfred K. Monarch, the county's Chief Sanitary Engineer!'

'Very amusing. You should consider a career in the music halls.'

'It wasn't, by all accounts.'

'What do you mean?'

'Amusing. He closed the place for six months condemning the lavatories as a disgrace.'

'As indeed they still are.' Skimpton tossed the Boravian coin to his fag and ruminated on the subject of water closets for a few moments. 'Piggot,' he announced presently, 'I hereby entrust you with the task of ensuring that, on King's Day this year, washroom facilities at Faysgarth are fit for use by a crowned head.'

'Really Skimpton?' enthused a delighted Piggot.

'The job is yours if you want it.'

'Why, thank you sir!'

'We don't want this fellow returning home to Boravia with ghastly stories of the lavatorial kind, do we? There may be an international incident, and before we know it our two countries could be at war!'

'That is hardly likely, Skimpton.'

'And what would you know about it?'

'My feeling is,' stated Piggot authoritatively, 'that, even if their head of state were insulted in such a way, violent hostilities with respect to Great Britain would not figure very prominently in the minds of the Boravian people.'

'And why not?'

'Because, Skimpton, there are only 315 of them. They would be outnumbered 126,984 to one, based on figures from the last census.'

Skimpton smiled at his fag feebly. It crossed his mind to reprimand Piggot for his cockiness, but in the end, he merely pointed to the door and ordered him from the room.

King's Day had, for many years, been an annual event at Faysgarth. Commemorating the return to England in May 1660 of Charles II after twelve years in exile, the school's celebration had been the brainchild of a desperate headmaster in the 1850s who hoped that a fabricated link between Faysgarth and the House of Stuart might improve dwindling rolls by attracting pupils from north of the border. However dubious its origins and merits though, the idea seemed to work, and numbers increased considerably, though for some years rules relating to the school uniform had to be temporarily relaxed in order to accommodate the wearing of kilts.

Apart from the jollity and feasting, the main event of the day was the annual archery competition in which Senior Faysgarthians competed for the title of King's Bowman. Skimpton though, having easily triumphed in the competition for the previous three years, was beginning to tire of the whole business, with its dreary succession of civic dignitaries and inebriated parents. The announcement in Full School Assembly that morning, however, of the arrival of one of Europe's esteemed sovereigns, had rejuvenated him no end, and he now looked forward to the event with considerable enthusiasm. For, even if Boravia did amount to little more than a few scrubby fields on the borders of Czecho-Slovakia, a victory in the presence of its king would certainly be a feather in his cap, to say nothing of the pride it would bring to his father, should the old man choose to favour the event with his presence.

With three months to go, Skimpton calculated that, given his other sporting commitments, he might just be able to put aside Tuesday and Thursday evenings for target practice, leaving the rest of his free time to devote to the remainder of the soccer and rugby fixtures.

Reaching into his sports cupboard with a feeling of joyful expectation, Skimpton carefully liberated his four-foot, finely sprung bow from its hibernation. Twanging the string playfully, he began whistling his favourite tune, *Has Anybody Seen My Tiddler,* by way of an accompaniment. The result, he thought, was musically very pleasing, the taught cat-gut providing a rather effective *pizzicato* counter-melody to the main theme. The bow had been presented to him as a birthday present some years before by his father, who had himself achieved some success with it as a schoolboy, and Skimpton looked upon it as a trusted old friend, and one in whose company he now felt very relaxed, as he luxuriated in its re-acquaintance.

'That is a very pretty tune, Skimpton,' came a voice from under the bed. 'My parents and I sing that one round the piano when we are at home.' It was Piggot, finally locating the last coin in his collection.

'I thought I told you to get out!' snorted an irritated House Captain.

'Has anybody seen my tiddler?' sang Piggot chirpily. 'Tiddle iddle iddle iddle iddler.' My parents and I are thinking of starting a singing group. Do you think I have the requisite talent, Skimpton?'

'Look, Piggot,' said Skimpton, fitting a feather to his bow and preparing to aim it straight at his fag, 'I have studying to do for my history.'

'Of course,' said the fag, moving nervously to the door. 'I hear you're bottom, Skimpton.'

His fag-master looked momentarily puzzled. 'My bottom is of no concern to you, young man,' he said sternly. 'Now be off before I fire one of these arrows into you!'

'Tiddle iddle iddle iddle iddler...'

*   *   *   *

Skimpton's indifferent results in recent examinations had become the source of much amusement to his fellow Faysgarthians, and had even elicited an irate letter from his father, furious that his son should be letting the family down by coming bottom in any subject.

Invariably managing just above average marks, Skimpton had suffered last term, as his heavy fixture list had interfered with his usual timetable of last-minute cramming. The distressing consequence of this could be viewed by all on the Senior Common Room notice board, where the embarrassing results had been posted.

A downward fluctuation of a few percentage points here and there, he could easily countenance. But when a score plummeted to a measly eleven percent, as was the case with his history, even Skimpton was forced to admit that punishment might be in order. Fully expecting the dreaded call from Colonel Coombes, he had, each morning, fortified his trousers with exercise books. But when, as the days went by, no such summons appeared, he breathed a momentous sigh of relief and resolved to do better next time.

Then the letter from his father arrived, and such was the magnitude of the dunce's subsequent guilt, that he almost felt like taking himself off to the Colonel's office, selecting one of the chemistry man's more dangerous weapons, and delivering himself with a thorough caning.

History was a subject for which Skimpton possessed much enthusiasm, but of its detail, his deficient memory retained precious little. He loved reading about the intrigues of kings and queens, the exploits of generals and the wheedling of politicians, but unhappily, when faced with an examination question about them, he could rarely remember any of their names.

Neither had his tutor, the elderly Mr. Larkins been of much assistance, his droning monotone having sent the sports champion into a deep sleep on many an occasion in class. Skimpton's chum Jack Varley on the other hand, invariably sailed through the examinations without very much effort, and usually came top – a position from which he frequently teased his less academically able pal.

As he crossed the quad later that day, *en route* to his next encounter with his least successful subject, Skimpton passed a group of fifth-formers chatting idly. 'Have you seen the history results?' asked one, turning to his friend and sniggering.

'Yes,' replied the other loudly. 'I see Skimpton's bottom!'

'What's it like?'

'Pink and very pimply!'

On his arrival at the classroom, Skimpton suffered further ragging. On the blackboard, one of his artistically gifted classmates had sketched a series of illustrations depicting the posteriors of famous historical characters. Between George VI's voluminous backside and a rather scruffy appendage, labelled as belonging to the Russian mystic Rasputin, was a detailed depiction of a public schoolboy's hind quarters, his trousers round his ankles. The caption, written below, read:

SKIMPTON'S BOTTOM IN HISTORY

'Alright you fellows,' said the failure, 'I'll wager anybody five pounds I don't come bottom this term!'

'You're on,' pledged Marcus Dent, recognizing a safe bet if ever he saw one.

What Skimpton did not know, and what Marcus Dent had kept securely under his hat, was that, some minutes before, whilst delivering to the third-form a typically prosaic lecture on the Peloponnesian Wars, old Larkins had finally and quite literally bored himself to death. In an attempt to avoid further distress to the boys, the master's corpse had been removed to the chapel by a platoon of burly sixth-formers, where it stayed until an ambulance arrived and promptly took it away.

The result, much to Skimpton's dismay when he was informed of the death, was that Faysgarth was now bereft of a senior history master. A flustered Colonel Coombes arrived towards the end of the lesson and announced that the boys should fend for themselves with regard to the forthcoming external examinations, at least until a suitable replacement could be found.

Bearing in mind Faysgarth's less than sparkling reputation for its treatment of staff, the boys knew that this process could easily take years to complete.

*   *   *   *

For the next two weeks, whilst Skimpton attempted to make sense of the Hundred Years' War, his classmates, liberated of Larkins's tenuous supervision, amused themselves in a variety of ways. Marcus Dent read *The Racing Chronicle,* Jack Varley played chess, Binns and Spate lit small fires in their desks, and various other individuals slipped away quietly to enjoy each other's company in the long-jump pit.

One sunny Thursday evening on the sports field, as Skimpton was preparing to release another feather from his finely-tuned four-footer, he was distracted by a dull, droning sound in the distance. This continued for several minutes until its source was revealed to be a small biplane which appeared over the treetops above Dead Man's Wood. Circling the skies for a good fifteen minutes, the crate eventually made off in the direction of Faverstock Common.

A few minutes later, Skimpton had taken up his bow once again with a view to loosing off another arrow, when the plane reappeared. Flying low over the sports field, the bright-red biplane banked suddenly and proceeded to attempt a seemingly suicidal loop. Screaming earthwards over the cricket pavilion, the shuddering crate appeared destined for destruction as the pilot visibly struggled with the joystick in an attempt to complete the foolhardy stunt. Apparently out of control, the plane hurtled towards a group of boys practising in the cricket nets, scattering them in all directions.

Finally, after its undercarriage had practically parted a third-former's hair, the bus righted itself in the nick of time and its pilot forced down the stick, bringing the plane to earth with a grievous thud and swinging it to a halt in the middle of the cricket pitch.

The pilot was immediately mobbed by a squadron of cheering boys as he climbed from the cockpit, his flying boots churning the wicket as he strode from the machine.

'That was a mighty dangerous manoeuvre, if you don't mind me saying so,' castigated Skimpton, in something of a fume.

The pilot removed his goggles, underneath which he wore a monocle. 'I agree!' he giggled, in a childish voice which elicited more fervent cheers from his juvenile admirers. He was a youngish man with a discernible air of frivolous irresponsibility about him, and Skimpton felt certain that he had seen the fellow before, perhaps in one of those aggressively unfunny films they showed at the Majestycke in Barnchester.

'She's a mighty fine crate, sir!' squawked a junior. 'Do you mind telling me what sort of a 'plane she is?'

'She's a Sopwith Scout, sonny,' said the stranger, proudly. 'But I call her *The Scarlet Lady.*'

'I say, that's a super name!' enthused the youngster.

'And jolly apt, too,' added the airman, 'for she's red hot and purrs like a she-cat!'

'I wonder if you would mind,' said Skimpton, with a hint of outrage, 'informing me of your identity?'

'Who wants to know?'

'I am Skimpton. Captain of Second House and Deputy Head Boy.'

'Congratulations.' The individual removed his flying gloves and helmet in a pretentiously ornate fashion, producing gasps of wonder from his worshippers.

'You realize that you can't leave your machine there,' said a steadfast Skimpton.

'Who says?'

'The cricket pitch is due to be rolled to-morrow.'

'Rolled? Where to? Ha ha!' The man's infantile laugh irritated Skimpton immediately, for it sounded like the noise a poodle might make if its head were caught in a revolving door. 'The name's Bamber,' the man said. 'Philly Bamber. I'm the new history master at Faysgarth.'

Further cries of excitement greeted this doubtful revelation, though Skimpton felt it best to keep his suspicions to himself. 'I see,' he said, dutifully, 'in that case we are all very pleased to meet you, I am sure.'

Bamber donated the boxing champion the limpest of hand-shakes before turning once again to his audience of young sycophants. 'I say you fellows,' he hailed, 'what do you call a fly with no legs?'

'I don't know sir!' replied one of them merrily. 'What do you call a fly with no legs?'

'A currant! Ha ha ha!'

Skimpton waited patiently for the resulting hysteria to abate before speaking again. 'Perhaps you would like me to take you to see Colonel Coombes, Mr Bamber,' he ventured. 'He tends to take charge of things around here.'

'Plenty of time for all that,' came the jokey response. 'Now, who's for a turn in the crate?'

'Me sir!'

'Me sir!'

Ignoring the pleading Juniors, Bamber smiled to himself and turned to the Deputy Head Boy. 'Skimpy?' he said.

At this greeting from the stranger, the smile which Skimpton had so assiduously maintained for the purpose of gleaning information, took immediate leave of his face, dropping to the grass, then burrowing deep into the ground and finally dissipating very close to the earth's core. For there were a few things in life which irritated the rugger captain more than being called 'Skimpy'.

'Well, Skimpy?'

'I shall decline your invitation on this occasion, sir,' replied Skimpton flatly, 'for I value my life far too dearly.'

'Trifle scared, eh? Oh well, we'll have to give one of these little turks a treat instead!' At which point Bamber scooped up a terrified Piggot, who had merely wandered over to see what all the fuss was about.

'B...b...but sir!' spluttered the youngster, sparks flying from his protruding teeth, 'I d...d...don't want to go!'

But Bamber would have nothing of his protestations, and with a hearty giggle, dumped the squirming third-former brutishly into the passenger seat. He then climbed into the cockpit himself and commenced starting up the engine, as half a dozen of his new acolytes did their best to rotate the propeller. Within seconds, the pistons spluttered to life and, laughing uproariously, the chortling pilot let out the throttle. 'Tally ho!' he cried, confident that he was about to award Piggot the thrill of a lifetime. 'Toodle pip! Ha ha ha ha!'

*   *   *   *

In the event, Piggot returned that evening from his aerial excursion over the Monktonshire Downs so rattled with terror that the resulting silence gripped him for the remainder of the term. No amount of effort from Skimpton over the coming weeks could coax from the junior any sort of a voice, neither could his masters fathom the problem. Finally, after a week or so, the stricken third-former was left alone in his silence to conduct his affairs on his own, his spirits low and his nerves shattered.

During this period, Skimpton, too, was not feeling his usual self, going about his business in a seemingly permanent state of ill-humour. Not only had he lost the services of a trusted and loyal fag, but his preparations both for the forthcoming history examination and the King's Day archery tournament were progressing far from satisfactorily. The blame for these deepening difficulties, as he asserted frequently, lay undeniably at the door of Faysgarth's new history master, Philly Bamber.

Whilst the newcomer's increasingly eccentric aerobatic displays suggested that as a pilot he might make a good history teacher, his equally inept performances in the classroom suggested quite the opposite. From the outset, it was obvious to all that his knowledge of the subject for which he had been engaged to teach was minimal. Rather than trying to pretend some sort of proficiency, Bamber made no attempt to conceal his ignorance, and even made frequent jokes on the subject, humorously dubbing himself 'History's Happiest Ignoramus'! As a result of his dereliction, classroom activities continued much as before; newspapers were read, chess was played, fires were started and company was most certainly enjoyed in the long-jump pit.

*　　*　　*　　*

One afternoon in class, as Skimpton was grappling with a mighty volume entitled *The Thirty Years' War (1618-48)*, he was interrupted by his light-minded tutor, who for – some reason – had decided to feign interest. 'Oh yes, I know that lot,' said Philly Bamber, glancing at the forbidding text as though it were an invitation to a society dinner. 'Gustavus Adolphus and all that!' Skimpton pressed on with his studies, trying to ignore the pest. 'I'm thinking of giving flying lessons on Tuesdays and Thursday evenings, Skimpy,' warbled the twit, 'would you be interested?'

'Those nights I have set aside for archery practice, Mr Bamber,' replied Skimpton curtly. 'I hope once more to secure victory in this year's King's Day tournament.'

'Jousting?'

'Archery.'

Bamber looked unimpressed. 'Oh well,' he said, 'have it your own way.'

Skimpton looked up from his book and viewed the master coldly, as the latter hovered nearby, eager for approval and desperately trying to think of something amusing to say. His weak chin and pathetic monocle seemed to embody all that was lax about those educated at great expense at the inferior public schools dotted around the nation. Even the fellow's name invited derision – Bamber, Bamber, Philly, Philly, Bamber. It sounded to Skimpton like a character from a child's book.

Although he had succeeded in gaining a degree of popularity, even amongst certain vacuous factions in the Seniors, Bamber's determined brand of asinine garrulity and frequent recourse to childish voices held little sway with Skimpton, for the sportsman's preoccupations at that time lay in more sober directions.

'Have you heard this one, Skimpy?' trilled the master defiantly. 'What do you get if you cross a tube of glue with the King of Mesopotamia?'

Skimpton sighed vehemently, and would certainly have hurled his tormentor through a window had he not noticed Colonel Coombes passing at that moment. Instead, he resigned himself to the subject about which he was attempting to learn, and, hoping to stump the master into a tactical withdrawal, said, 'Mr Bamber, I am soon to embark on an essay about the war at sea, 1915-16. Do you know anything about battleships?'

'Well I've played it if that's what you mean,' returned Bamber. 'Why, do you fancy a game?'

*   *   *   *

Later that day, a depressed Skimpton was keeping guard over a pair of kippers, boiling in a frying pan in his study, Philly Bamber wrestling with his *Scarlet Lady* in the skies above, when he spied the solitary figure of young Piggot wandering aimlessly in the quad below. There was something unsettling about this Bamber business, thought the season's leading goalscorer, but try as he might, he was unable to put his finger on precisely what it was.

A knock at the door then preceded the entrance of Jack Varley. 'I say!' said he, 'them kippers smell topping! Any going spare?'

'Of course, old man,' smiled Skimpton, 'pull up a side plate!'

Varley picked his way through the mountain of worthy texts that now littered the floor of his pal's study, removing exercise books by the dozen before finally settling in Skimpton's battered old armchair. 'I must say, Skimpy,' he breezed, 'you do seem to be taking this history lark rather seriously!'

'You forget, Jack,' responded the other, 'I have an inferior memory to train, an angry father to placate, and five pounds resting on my performance in the coming examinations. Now, would you prefer your kipper on your plate or on top of your head?'

'Whatever do you mean?'

'If, as I suspect, your preference is for the former, then I suggest you refrain from using that hateful moniker, for you know full well that it is a name I positively loathe.'

'You mean "Skimpy"?'

At this, Skimpton, with a flourish, placed the boiled fish onto the top of his friend's head, garnishing it with a knob of butter and sprig of fresh parsley. 'I say! Watch out, why don't you!' protested Varley, removing the kipper from his crown and hurling it back into the pan.

A lengthy, doom-laden pause ensued as the fishes boiled furiously on the old primus. 'It's just that,' resumed Varley presently, 'I've heard Philly Bamber call you it recently and thought it rather quaint.'

'To tell you the truth, Jack,' stated Skimpton, 'I've had about enough of this silly fellow Bamber, and his idiotic nicknames, to last me a lifetime. For, apart from being appallingly unfunny and a perfect menace in the skies, the man is a mental blizzard! A chimpanzee would be more use as a teacher of history.'

'I agree,' said Varley with a chuckle, 'but I still find him rather invigorating.'

'You can afford to, Jack, chances are you'll walk your history exam, Philly Bamber or no Philly Bamber.'

'I hope in all this hard work you are not losing your sense of humour, Skimpton,' offered Varley. 'The man's doing his best!'

'The man is an imbecile, Jack!' retorted Skimpton, smartly walloping another kipper onto Varley's plate.

'Look, Skimpton, with regard to your exam, if you think it would help, I'd be more than willing to offer some extra tuition. How's that sound?'

Skimpton was genuinely impressed by this kind offer, and his mood softened considerably. 'I say, Jack,' he said, 'would you really?

That's awfully charitable of you. What about Thursday evening?'

'I thought you practised archery on that day?'

'That's deferred, I am afraid. I've given up trying to compete with *The Scarlet Lady*'s groans of delight as she deposits boys from five hundred feet.'

'I see.' Varley, having polished off his kipper, then retired into another uneasy silence.

'Well?' said Skimpton.

'Well what?'

'What about Thursday?'

'That might be a bit difficult, Skimpton. You see, I have a flying lesson with Philly that evening.'

Skimpton sent his fork flying across the room, and as it collided noisily with his boxing trophies, he rounded on his housemate. 'Look here, Jack,' he fumed, 'if you wish to waste your time with that maniac, hurtling through the air strapped into his deadly assemblage of wires and canvas, then that is your concern. But do not bellyache to me in the coming months on the state of the wicket. For, in case you hadn't noticed, your beloved Bamber's blasted biplane is churning deeper furrows into the popping crease than would a thousand clumsy batsmen. And that is to say nothing of the effect on our previously tranquil surroundings of *The Scarlet Lady*'s thunderous two-stroke engine!

'In addition, I do not suppose that it has occurred to you that there might be anything slightly suspicious about our senior history master's rather dainty monocle, which appears to contain no glass whatsoever! Or is this perhaps just another one of his zany eccentricities, the comical side of which appears, yet again, to have eluded me?'

Skimpton now took up the frying pan in which the last kipper was boiling, and thrust it resolutely at his chum. 'I tell you now, Jack,' he said, 'there is something decidedly fishy in the follies of Philly Bamber. And I intend to find out what it is!'

*   *   *   *

The House Captain's subsequent investigations in that respect, however, revealed precisely nothing. Even a midnight foray into the files in the school office, relating to teachers' appointments, proved fruitless, the only information relating to Bamber's employment being the statutory terms of contract. Even the new senior history master's apparent lack of both references and qualifications caused Skimpton only temporary puzzlement, in that a quick glance through other masters' credentials revealed that neither appeared to be required to secure a position at the school. Indeed, records showed that Mr. Perivale, the recently appointed art master had, only six months before, completed a prison sentence for forging banknotes, and the new Head of English, Mr Gareth Wyn-Jones, had evidently been hired in the full knowledge that, as a native Welsh speaker from a remote community in Cardiganshire, he possessed only elementary knowledge of the language he was being employed to teach!

Towards the end of term an incident occurred which merits description. During a history lesson, an increasingly distracted Skimpton was attempting doggedly to catalogue the main events of the French Revolution, the usual classroom shenanigans assaulting him from all sides. Finally, his irritation on the point of boiling over, the unhappy scholar attempted to attract the attention of Mr Bamber, who was playing noughts and crosses with Binns on the blackboard. 'Yes! What is it?' spat the master impatiently, eager to continue with his game.

Unsure quite how to put into words his keen sense of frustration, Skimpton merely fumed for a moment before resorting to an academic platform from which to challenge the monocled wastrel. 'I wonder, Mr Bamber,' he hissed, 'if you would be so kind as to recommend a suitable title on the subject of The Reign of Terror?'

Bamber paused for a moment and laid down his chalk on his desk, as his audience quietened themselves for a witty riposte. 'There's a fascinating chronicle on that subject entitled *My Life At Faysgarth*,' he quipped, 'by Colonel Archibald Coombes!'

The class duly erupted into gales of laughter, as Bamber returned to his game on the blackboard, leaving Skimpton literally shaking with fury. 'Mr Bamber,' he said, 'do you know nothing of the subject you are supposed to teach?'

'Indeed I do, Skimpy,' he said. 'History, in my view, is nothing more than a glorified roll call of the deceased, most of whom met their death through either exploitation, execution, or gonorrhoea.'

'Hear hear!' agreed Binns.

'Study of the subject, in my opinion,' continued Bamber, 'amounts to little more than a turgid test of memory, requiring neither imagination nor insight.'

'Hooray! cried the class.

'I'll second that!' laughed Jack Varley, throwing his chess board gleefully into the air as all present whooped their approval of Philly Bamber's pungent wit. Other boys then joined the celebration, jumping onto their desks and chanting their hero's name loudly. 'Bamber! Bamber!' they cried, 'Philly Philly Bamber!'

Just then though, when the uproar was at its height, the door opened with a terrifying suddenness, and from behind it emerged a wrathful Colonel Coombes, fairly steaming with vexation. 'Quiet!' exploded the apoplectic chemistry Colonel. 'What in God's name is going on? You boy, sit down!' Jack Varley moved swifter than Skimpton had ever seen him, even between the stumps for the First Eleven, as he swerved deftly to avoid the Colonel's perilously swiping palm. 'Mr Bamber,' hissed the frenziedly myopic master, turning to address Marcus Dent, the only person possessing a modicum of authority in the room. 'I should be grateful if you would spare me a few moments in my office at lunchtime!'

'Of course, Colonel Coombes,' said Dent, calmly folding his newspaper and smiling at Bamber portentously, 'I should be glad to. Shall we say one o'clock?'

After the Colonel's departure, a silence enveloped the classroom, matching in its intensity the one which you might imagine was afforded Robespierre as he crouched at the feet of *Madame La Guillotine*, awaiting her final act of correction. 'I say chaps,' joked Bamber airily, as he unbuckled his belt, 'might anyone lend me a few exercise books?'

*   *   *   *

The same silence which greeted Bamber's last sombre quip was carried over into lunch, as the sound of his agonising cries at the hands of Colonel Coombes's fury put paid to all attempts at cheerful conversation in the refectory. During the afternoon, the news emerged that not only had the revered master received some thirty strokes of the chemistry man's birch, but that his flying lessons, so popular with the boys, were to be curtailed forthwith. The lacerated Bamber was also informed that if he failed once more to maintain civilised order in his class then he would suffer immediate dismissal without pay.

Blame for this dismal state of affairs was laid squarely on Skimpton. Many felt that he had been responsible for the cancellation of Bamber's flying lessons, as someone had put it about that he had reported the reckless aviator over his ploughing up of the cricket pitch. This scurrilous assertion Skimpton denied vigorously. His protestations though, fell on deaf ears, and there remained much talk in the corridors of him having turned abnormal, as it was deemed that only a particularly twisted and sadistic individual would report anyone to the Colonel in his present mood, no matter what his crime.

Skimpton's critics also included Jack Varley, who had taken to sounding off against his erstwhile pal in the quad. And despite his continued protestations of innocence, pretty soon, the most popular boy in the school found himself reduced to the position of least favoured pupil at Faysgarth. Indeed, the only individual prepared to associate with him at this time was his melancholy fag Piggot, though as the third-former was still stricken dumb as a consequence of his distressing experience with Philly Bamber in the skies above Faverstock Common, communication – mutually supportive or otherwise – was somewhat restricted.

One evening, after many days' exclusion from his school-fellows' discourse, a distressed Skimpton, his profound sense of isolation threatening to overwhelm him, knocked on Varley's door in search of conversation. Inside he found his chum entertaining young Dick Parr, captain of the Junior Eleven at cricket. 'Hello, Jack!' volunteered the House Captain bravely.

'Skimpton,' replied Varley, flatly, without looking up.

'How do you fancy a turn in the nets? I'll do my best with the bowling.'

'No thanks. I have pressing business here with young Parr.'

'What about a game of tiddlywinks then?'

'I think not.'

'Perhaps another time then?'

'As you wish.'

At this, Skimpton returned to his room, picked up a book on the crusades, and looked at its pages without taking from them one jot of meaning. After about half an hour he took himself off to the school office, hoping to sneak a quick telephone call before anyone noticed. This exercise, too, proved fruitless, as no-one answered at the number he had been given for use in an emergency. For it was testimony to the depth of Skimpton's despair that he had taken the unprecedented step of attempting to contact his father, as a measure of last resort.

*   *   *   *

The next night, Skimpton's soccer team failed to turn up for training, and the following Saturday the First Fifteen declined to take part in the final rugger game of the season if he were included in the team. His decision to stand down did nothing to reduce the contempt in which he was now held by his schoolfellows, and even some of the masters now refused to teach him. A quasi-humorous address he had hastily composed on the subject of songs from the music halls, which he delivered in Full School Assembly, was received in total silence.

History lessons proceeded much the same as before, in that no attempt whatsoever was made to study the subject. The quiet manner in which his classmates now went about their various activities though, relieved Skimpton greatly, as he continued to prepare himself as best he could for the forthcoming examinations.

The only distractions came, predictably, from Philly Bamber at the head of the class, as he chuckled at the funny papers and passed the occasional snide remark about Skimpton's studiousness. When, one afternoon, he learned of his least favourite pupil's disastrous marks the previous term, the capricious Bamber laughed so loudly that his young acolytes feared another calamitous intervention by Colonel Coombes, and threatened their precious master with lines if he did not shut up.

Bamber seemed particularly amused with reports of the jokes about Skimpton's lowly position in class, and made much smutty reference to the Deputy Head Boy's posterior in the weeks to come. Skimpton, for his part, took his punishment with a stoicism bordering on the heroic, and sought refuge in his solitary timetable of swotting and archery practice.

*   *   *   *

On the morning of the external examinations, a sombre Bamber stood before his class immediately prior to them tackling the paper, and delivered a salutary speech. Still in some pain from the thrashing he had received from Colonel Coombes, he spoke in measured, stately tones. 'I should just like to say a few words,' he began earnestly, 'to thank you for the hard work you have undoubtedly declined to put in this term. You have most certainly, the vast majority of you at least, made my job considerably easier as a result.

'I know, for I have observed you all closely over the last few weeks, that there has been stiff competition for the title of laziest boy in history, and I must admit to a certain admiration for your almost universal lack of effort in this respect.

'Almost all of you, in his own way, has contributed impressively to this fine record of scholarly under-achievement, a surely-unequalled display of communal indifference to the subject supposedly under scrutiny, and one worthy of recognition.

'I am pleased to say that, after only a short time under my humble tutelage, your term work has been uniformly poor, if not for the most part entirely invisible. And for that consistent lack of effort I offer my thanks to you all.

'All, that is, except one.'

Here, Bamber paused for dramatic effect before continuing, as all heads turned to Skimpton.

'For there is always one individual who lets the side down, is there not? The one who, as the rest knuckle under to some diligent time-wasting, can invariably be found at the front of the class, his head sullenly sandwiched between the pages of a pertinent text. The one who, when others are assiduously engaged in throwing their futures down the drain, can always be seen out of the corner of one's eye revising sedulously, his papers stacked neatly on his desk. He is the boy who persists with his 'relevant' questions, whose inkwell never runs dry, and yes, is the studious fellow who is always last out when the bell goes.

'And yet, this individual is not a dull boy. Far from it, for he is a sportsman of quite startling ability. And in common with many of his ilk, possesses a natural and, I suspect, hereditary impercipience in matters academic which might, even now, bring him the prize you all seek. Taking this into account then, only a fool would underestimate his potential for failure in the approaching examination.

'I therefore warn all idle hopefuls, in their quest today for the coveted dunce's cap, not to rely on the fickleness of the gods for victory, for in many cases, triumph will not be achieved through any mystical talent for incompetence. No! It will be won only through good old-fashioned indolence – a vital concept I invite you to consider in the coming hours, in the hope that you will not be distracted from its pursuit.

'For, if this crucial element is at any time absent from your endeavours today, then do not complain to me if, after the results are posted and your eyes have descended to the foot of that ladder of merit, you find...Skimpton's bottom!'

Bamber then departed the classroom, leaving his pupils to complete the examination entirely unsupervised.

* * * *

In the week leading up to the King's Day celebrations, Skimpton intensified his training for the archery tournament, and, in the absence of any other positive aspects to his life, began looking forward to the prospect of retaining his title in the esteemed presence of King Maximilian III of Boravia.

Marcus Dent's loyal battery of misfits and deviants, meanwhile, put it about that their leader intended to assassinate the Boravian Head of State with a view to stealing his country and ruling it with an iron fist. This rumour, though completely fictitious and entirely unsolicited by Dent, was afforded much credence when, on the morning of the festivities, an unusually observant Colonel Coombes discovered a large bomb placed beneath the podium upon which the King was to be accommodated. The device was removed to the farthest end of the rugby field by an explosives enthusiast from the fifth-form named Grayson. His decommissioning of the incendiary at great personal risk earned him ten team-points from a grateful Colonel Coombes. Dent, meanwhile, was promptly locked in the games hut under the eagle eye of Wilf, the groundsman, and Constable Stubbs, who had been drafted in to oversee security matters.

After a morning's target practice and an hour and a half in the music room re-acquainting himself with his favourite gramophone record, *Has Anybody Seen My Tiddler* sung by Fred Harrison Winner, Skimpton installed himself in his study and awaited the possible arrival of his father. Word had reached him that the old man, pending business commitments, intended to put in an appearance that afternoon. Skimpton, though remained dubious, having been let down by the fellow too many times before.

From his position overlooking the quad, he took great pleasure in the sight of his beloved Faysgarth decked out in its holiday clothes. The gay bunting fluttered excitedly about the place whilst the colourful tents on the sports field fairly shimmered in the early summer sunshine.

Atop the chapel steeple, radiant and alert in the stiff breeze, was the Union Jack, beside the yellow and green flag of Boravia. The cricket pitch, thankfully relieved of the presence of Bamber's wretched biplane, though still bearing the deep scars left by the

Scarlet Lady's tyres, looked luscious in its anticipation of the coming season, for around its boundary the dewdrops had gathered as if waiting for the first ball to be bowled.

Skimpton delighted, too, in the jaunty aspect of the many fascinating side-shows whose pleasures awaited temptingly; the coconut shy, the skittles game, the goldfish frolicking jovially in their glass bowls. And then there was the Faverstock Old Soldiers' Brass Band, assembling their instruments and tuning them conscientiously whilst the archery targets were rolled into place at the very centre of proceedings.

This was the Faysgarth Skimpton loved – a place of pageantry, history and, above all, sport.

Strolling outside in a crisp pair of flannels and a freshly laundered shirt, the amiable House Captain, forgetting that he remained the subject of much hostility at the school, was surprised when he was jeered by a group of fifth-formers as he tried to engage them in good-natured banter. 'Hallo, you fellows,' he hailed, 'what about making yourselves useful and tying a few guy ropes?'

'Shut up, Skimpton,' came the witless response from their leader, 'go and tie them yourself.'

Undeterred, Skimpton hailed his pal Jack Varley, who had recently arrived with his parents from the railway station. His hearty greeting though, was returned with little more than a formal salutation, and a slightly embarrassed silence ensued between the two. His friend's father, the formidable Major Charles Varley, on the other hand, seemed pleased to see Skimpton, for the two had always got on. His timid, minuscule wife, aware of Skimpton's customary discomfiture in the presence of ladies, offered a considerate, modest greeting, and, smiling, withdrew slightly. The friendly exchanges, however, were curtailed abruptly when Varley dragged his parents off to meet another, more favoured, schoolfellow.

As time wore on, various modes of transport deposited more parents and guests. Lord and Lady Edgerton, the wealthy art connoisseurs, arrived by motor car with Barney Binns, greasy theatrical entrepreneur and begetter of Faysgarth's famous loud-mouthed lout. The volatile aristocrats appeared to be in the throes of one of their legendary squabbles as they stepped from the Bentley, the oily theatrical attempting vainly to referee the contest. 'Might I suggest...' offered Binns.

'If you'd wanted the Sisley, Rupert,' hissed Lady Celia, 'then you should have put in a bid for it!'

'You forget,' returned her husband acidly, 'that you had already spent a sizeable proportion of our wealth on those ghastly Piranesi engravings.'

'But I liked them!'

'Why, they are little more than architectural diagrams!'

'Do you think,' interjected Barney Binns, 'that we might postpone hostilities until...'

'And you can shut up, you slimy little twit!' thundered the Edgertons, in perfect synchrony.

'Dad!' boomed a stentorian voice from the far end of the cricket pitch, for it belonged to Barney Binns's fulminatory progeny. 'Can I have some money!!?'

Glancing about him, Skimpton became aware of the sinister presence of Marcus Dent's dangerous henchman Spate, who was prowling the quad with his mother. A surprisingly statuesque woman of remarkable beauty, she appeared to be chatting amiably to herself whilst her son kept his distance and sneered at everyone in sight.

And then came Piggot and his somewhat distressing parents, both of whom wore rather scruffy clothes and carried about them an air of unkempt academia. Piggot's father was a youthful university lecturer and both he and his wife seemed to be handicapped by front teeth which protruded so dangerously that Skimpton feared he might be impaled upon them should he wander too close. 'What do you think we should do with our son, Master Skimpton?' pleaded a concerned Mr. Piggot. 'He seems to have lost the will to live, let alone the power of speech.'

'Give him time, sir,' advised the Deputy Head Boy, as he dodged his questioner's dangerous dental protrusions. 'I am sure he will recover very soon.'

'I hope so,' volunteered Piggot's mother, 'for we are hoping to form an amateur singing group soon, of which our son – as the treble – will form an integral part.'

'We intend calling ourselves "The Singing Chestnuts",' put in the father, 'for as you can see, we all have brown eyes! It is a family trait!' At which, all three of them smiled hazardously.

'By jingo!' declared Skimpton, stepping backwards a yard. 'You are absolutely right! I am sure the venture will be a great success!' He then turned his attention to his fag. 'In the meantime, Piggot,' he said...

'Yes sir?' interrupted the boy's father.

'I was addressing your son, Mr. Piggot,' said Skimpton.

'Very good sir.'

'I hope, young man,' resumed Skimpton, 'that you have not forsaken your duties with regard to the lavatorial facilities, as we agreed. For the King of Boravia is expected very soon, and will doubtless wish to avail himself of them.'

Piggot then turned very red and looked extremely guilty. 'We'll sort that out immediately,' stammered his father hastily. 'Come on you two!' At which, *The Singing Chestnuts* departed to scrub clean the latrines.

Next to arrive were the ladies from the Faverstock Towns-women's Guild, who toppled from their charabanc and stationed themselves on the quadrangle lawn with their picnics. There was much gaiety amongst their ranks as the indefatigable Lady Farkham-Trillyon waltzed serenely with herself, a cup and saucer in hand. Many of the older boys openly lined up for views of the stunning debutante Fay Manners-Henderson, but soon dispersed as the fearsome Baroness Edwardes-Hawke advanced towards them brandishing her parasol.

By now, Faysgarth was fairly teeming with visitors, and yet there was still no sign of Skimpton's father. The Deputy Head

Boy was not too concerned though, for precedent indicated that, if his pater turned up at all, he would most probably be late. It was therefore a sanguine Skimpton who sauntered over for a quick word with Constable Stubbs outside the games hut. 'Still keeping an eye on our dastardly usurper, Constable?' he greeted.

'Young Dent is securely bound and gagged, Master Skimpton,' replied the policeman, 'he should present no further threat. I 'ave just dispatched 'is parents with instructions to secure the services of a barrister.'

'Dent certainly appears to have scuppered himself this time,' observed Skimpton. 'It seems hard to believe that he would be behind such an heinous plot.'

'The workin's of the criminald mind, young man, are complicated and hexceedin'ly dirty. A short spell in custody should soon sort 'im out.'

'That seems uncharacteristically benevolent of you, Constable Stubbs, if I might say so!' teased Skimpton.

'Don't get me wrong, if it were up to me, I'd lock the blighter up and throw away the key. But I am afraid we live in flimsy times, Master Skimpton, and one such as I must go with the flow.'

Just then, a tumultuous fanfare from the Old Soldiers' Brass Band heralded the arrival of Maximilian III, King of Boravia, whose impressive Packard was drawing up at the red carpet on the drive. There to receive his Magisterial Eminence was Colonel Coombes, who proceeded to open the wrong door of the car and bow ostentatiously for the benefit of the chauffeur.

Presently, the King emerged, to a clamour of cheering from the crowd, many of whom waved Boravian flags in his honour. He was a youngish man of about thirty, wearing a pale-yellow uniform decorated with various medals, and he smiled generously whilst waving to everyone around.

'Looks a bit young for a King if you ask me,' asserted Constable Stubbs, assuming erroneously that anyone was listening or cared what he thought.

Immediately, Colonel Coombes delivered a typically long-winded and lacklustre speech of welcome, to be followed by a much more rousing oration by the King himself, whose remarkable facility with the English language impressed everyone.

'And furthermore,' he concluded, 'as a keen sports fan I look forward particularly to this year's archery tournament, and the tussle for the title of King's Bowman. In addition, I should like to offer the eventual winner the opportunity to visit my country and do battle with our own supreme archer, a highly talented individual with whom I am very well acquainted, since that person happens to be none other than myself!'

The King's humorous, sardonic tone was well received by the assembled crowd and he was afforded a lengthy and genuinely appreciative round of applause.

The likely winner of King Maximilian's generous addition to the prize money, however, was absent at that moment, and it was not until nearly three o'clock when he finally appeared, during the playing of the Boravian national anthem. 'If you see Philly Bamber,' said Skimpton quietly to his fag Piggot, 'inform me immediately. Do you understand?'

Piggot nodded.

At length, Colonel Coombes called together the competitors and, at considerable length, outlined the rules of the contest. The King of Boravia observed with keen interest from the nearby platform, which only that morning had hidden Marcus Dent's explosive surprise. But as the Colonel droned on, almost losing himself in the regulations, Maximilian's attention began to wander and he now looked regally about him, acknowledging the crowd.

'Now,' pronounced the Colonel, 'there are sixteen of you, separated into groups of four, is that correct?'

'That is indeed the case, Colonel Coombes.'

'Each group is to shoot at one of the four targets, every boy firing a dozen arrows at eighty yards and six at sixty yards. Is that clear?'

'As crystal, Colonel.'

'The first and second highest in each group will go forward to the next round and the lowest two will drop out.'

'...will drop out. As in previous tournaments.'

'As you all know, we are honoured this year to have in our midst King Ferdinand of Bavaria...'

'Maximilian of Boravia.'

'...who has generously offered a free, all-expenses paid, luxury holiday in his country to the eventual winner. This, I am happy to say, will be in addition to the usual prize of five shillings and sixpence which is traditionally accorded the successful participant.'

'Thank the Lord for that.'

'Now! Let the contest begin!'

Archery was a sport which Skimpton held in the highest of esteem. For, just as the running of a tortuous marathon somehow made him feel at one with those ancient Greek Olympians, so did the firing of an arrow from a rattling bow convince him of his spiritual connection with those valiant English archers of bygone times.

His present instrument, he felt, would more than compare with those of his forebears, for it was both highly responsive and impressively long, and he loved nothing more than to take it in his hands and perform miracles with it in front of the public. If only his father could be here now to see how much affinity there existed between his son and the supreme weapon of toxophily with which he had been bequeathed. However, as time wore on, Skimpton became less hopeful that he would see his dad that day.

In the first round, Skimpton was drawn against a fine archer who luxuriated in the unusual name of Seth Spottiswode, and the tall, thin sixth-former built up a considerable score of sixty-three, with three golds (or centres), after he had loosed a dozen arrows.

The other two boys in his group were clearly too nervous to bother about, and it was an apparently confident Skimpton who took up his bow and fired off his first arrow. Dismay! He had missed the target! This pitiful start prompted much hilarity in the crowd, and one audacious fourth-former even ran up to Skimpton as a joke and offered the reigning champion the use of his spectacles!

His next arrow eventually found its way into the black, scoring but one point, and it was only because the other two boys in his group had been so useless, all their arrows failing even to reach the target, that the highly regarded sportsman was able to progress to the next round. Even then he did so having only accrued a measly ten points.

'Piggot,' said Jack Varley, surveying the scoreboard ruefully, 'there's something wrong here.'

'I agree,' enjoined the fag's father, for his son's mind was elsewhere.

'Either Skimpton's come down with an acute attack of nerves or someone's been tampering with his arrows. Run along to the gym and fetch some replacements, would you?'

'Right away.' At which, the senior member of *The Singing Chestnuts*, having previously been dispatched by Skimpton to clean out the filth from the Faysgarth lavatories, departed in some haste to do the urgent bidding of the House Captain's best friend.

In the next round, Skimpton found himself in even greater trouble, languishing in last position and in danger of suffering an ignominiously premature departure from the tournament. Perhaps it was as well, thought he, that his father was not present to witness the heavy defeat which now seemed inevitable.

But what had gone wrong? He had been shooting marvellously in recent days, and these were his new tournament arrows, previously unused and in immaculate condition!

These concerns, though important to Skimpton, were nothing compared to his unease over the apparent disappearance of Philly Bamber, who had still not shown his face that day. And, as he worried himself into something of a lather, his next, possibly final, turn approaching, the sportsman was taken aside by a solemn-looking Jack Varley.

'I don't know what the trouble is, Jack,' he despaired, 'I can't seem to shoot straight!'

'Let me see those arrows,' urged his chum.

Skimpton removed one of his choice feathers from his quiver and Varley held it up for close inspection. 'Just as I thought,' he said. 'The shafts are bent. Someone's probably soaked them in water and eased them round.'

'By George! Who would do such a thing?'

'Probably the same person who has been intent all along on spoiling the day; the dirty rotter who planted the bomb – Marcus Dent, of course!'

'I can agree with only part of that thesis, Jack, but don't have time to say why.'

'Very well. Here are some replacement arrows for you, courtesy of Piggot Senior.'

'Excellent. Tip him for me would you, Jack?'

'Of course.' And as Varley wandered over and thrust sixpence into the grateful hand of Piggot's father, Skimpton took his new quiver of arrows and prepared to do battle with renewed vigour.

'Good luck, Skimpton!' shouted Jack Varley, his face sparkling into a grin.

'Thanks, Jack,' returned his pal.

With his next dozen arrows, Skimpton astonished the crowd by shooting three straight golds, together with three blues, totalling forty-two, securing him second position in his group and a place in the last four.

Lady Edgerton seemed particularly impressed. 'I say Barney,' she breathed, 'this fellow Skimpton's rather tasty.'

'Yes, he is,' agreed the impresario, 'in a characterful sort of way.'

'He'd be perfect for your musical production of *The Dream*.'

'Perhaps I'll audition him.'

'He'd make a perfect *Lysander*.'

'Do you think so? I was thinking more in terms of his *Bottom*.'

'Were you indeed?'

In the next round, Skimpton, now shooting excellent arrows, built up a formidable lead with a score of 119, his nearest rival, a fifth-former by the name of Templeton, managing a worthy 112 before bowing out.

So, the stage was set for a nail-biting final round, in which Skimpton was matched against his old rival from the preliminaries, the stringy sixth-former Seth Spottiswode. Skimpton's remarkable comeback was acknowledged by the young King of Boravia, who nodded his encouragement as the sports supremo fitted his first arrow.

With it, he scored a gold, and his second and third struck red – twenty-three points. Steadily, his score from eighty yards mounted, and soon it was an apprehensive Seth Spottiswode who took up his bow, facing a mammoth total of eighty-one points to beat. Immediately, he loosed seven splendid arrows, scoring five golds and two reds. The next three, though, were disappointing, two blacks and a white, but his finish was exemplary, two more emphatic golds. Eighty-four points!

Sportingly, Skimpton granted Spottiswode his request to continue with his last half dozen arrows, and in complete silence, the sixth-former strode up to the sixty-yard mark. The tension in the hushed crowd was tangible, and King Maximilian of Boravia was literally on the edge of his temporary throne as Spottiswode loosed the first of his arrows. Gold - nine points! Followed by another of the same – nine more points! Then a red – seven points, a blue – five points, and to finish, a final gold for a mighty total of 123 points, the highest score by far that day!

The crowd cheered wildly as the plucky contender took his seat and awaited Skimpton's response. Rarely had the champion been called upon to defend a title in such dramatic circumstances, for he now needed no less than forty-three points for victory. Before drawing, Skimpton sought out Jack Varley's face in the crowd, and his housemate grinned encouragingly.

His first three arrows could not have been better, all of them straight golds – twenty-seven points, and all thoughts of Philly Bamber banished from his mind. As he prepared to take aim with his next arrow, however, the sound of a distant aeroplane scythed through his concentration, and his next two attempts reflected the unease which was obvious to all; a red and an amazingly disappointing white, adding only eight further points, eight left to win.

'Come on Skimpton,' urged the King of Boravia, 'go for gold!'

Steeling himself for the final effort, the appalling noise of Philly Bamber's biplane drifting down through the clouds, the champion knew that only maximum points from his final arrow would ensure him the title; anything less would bring victory to his opponent and a smile to Seth Spottiswode's spotty face.

As he carefully placed his feet behind the line, the crowd, as one, held its breath, and, as Skimpton slowly raised his bow, several ladies from the Faverstock Townswomen's Guild developed breathing difficulties, collapsed and were taken away on stretchers. The noise from *The Scarlet Lady*'s engine was now much louder, as she dodged beneath the cloud and approached at around 400 feet. Placing his last arrow in position, Skimpton withdrew his arm and took meticulous aim at the target. The plane was now coming in low over the pavilion, its stuttering engine backfiring wildly as the crate screamed towards them.

'Is it a flying display?' asked Lady Farkham-Trillyon, as screams rang out from the crowd.

Skimpton took a deep breath, his muscles straining with the tension, before astonishingly he turned about, lifted his bow to the heavens and sent his final feathered messenger shooting skywards, towards an entirely new target, the one painted on the underside of Bamber's wretched biplane, and situated directly beneath *The Scarlet Lady*'s frenzied pilot! Upwards it flew, smooth as anything, as the crowd gasped in terror, for they could clearly see that Bamber was brandishing a weapon! 'Why! It's a stick grenade!' exclaimed Spottiswode, at which everyone dived for cover. At that moment, though, Skimpton's final arrow reached its destination, travelling straight through the very centre of the painted target, it ripped through the *Scarlet Lady's* canvas-clad underside, continued its determined path through her flimsy girdle, up into the seat, and lodged itself firmly in the pilot's rectum! 'Aaaaaargh' screamed Philly Bamber, at a volume which echoed out over the Monktonshire hills, and drowned out momentarily the noise of the Sopwith Scout's fearsome two-stroke engine. 'AAAAARGH!'

As the machine lurched sideways and Bamber struggled to release himself from his painful orificular intrusion, the grenade tumbled from his grasp and exploded some thirty yards away near the long-jump pit, frightening two third-formers who were wearing only bathing trunks.

The crowd winced audibly as the horribly impaled history master fought a desperate battle with his machine, and many averted their eyes as he eventually thrust it down for an agonisingly bumpy landing on the deeply furrowed cricket pitch.

As the plane lurched to a halt, all eyes turned to Piggot, who had put up his hand and jumped to his feet. 'H...h...h...' he stuttered, as everyone looked on in amazement. 'H...h...h...'

'Go on, Piggot,' impelled Skimpton.

'Ha...ha...ha...'

'What's the joke, Rupert?' asked a baffled Lady Edgerton. 'Have I missed something?'

'Ha...ha...ha...'

'Come on, son,' urged Piggot's father, 'spit it out!'

'Ha...ha...ha...has anybody seen my tiddler? Tiddle iddle iddle iddle iddler!'

And as Piggot sang, amidst much cheering and jubilation, his parents embraced, for although their son's silence had deprived *The Singing Chestnuts* of a talented descant to carry the tunes, he had emerged from his quiescence with an even more impressive *basso profundo* to underscore their cherry-lipped harmonies!

I caught that little fish with some cotton and a pin

Oh how I laughed when I dragged him in
But coming home, Oh dear oh
That rude boy Dicky Diddler
He poked his fingers in my galipot
And pinched my tiddler.

Many in the crowd then moved to the cricket pitch to revel in Philly Bamber's discomfort in the cockpit of *The Scarlet Lady*, some of them even mercilessly imitating his cries of pain.

Skimpton found himself alone, but for the company of a somewhat shaken King Maximilian III of Boravia. 'I suppose,' said the marksman, firing a last arrow nonchalantly into the gold, 'you thought you'd seen the last of your brother?'

'Indeed,' replied the monarch, 'for we exiled Rodolpho immediately after his deposition. My subjects would no longer tolerate his lunacy.'

'They have my sympathy. I suspected he might be mad to seek employment on the staff at Faysgarth.'

'I assume he thought that his position here would give him a chance to have another pot-shot at me. He's always trying to bump me off, for he hates me, purely because I don't share his sense of humour.'

'I think he felt the same about me for precisely that reason, Your Excellency.'

'He'd also, I think, like to get his hands on the crown again, for his ambition is to turn our country into a massive joke shop. Just as a matter of interest, which name did he use this time?'

'Philly Bamber.'

'Oh, yes. He invented that one at Harrow.'

Just then, a searing cry was heard from the cricket field, an ejaculation so strangulated and blood-curdling that everyone within hearing grimaced fearfully. For they all knew that the pitiful howl meant that the Old Harrovian from Boravia had finally been uncoupled from his beloved biplane, and would very soon be in need of stitches in a very sensitive area of his body.

Maximilian III stood up, indicating that Skimpton's audience with him was drawing to a close. 'My offer of a trip to Boravia still stands,' he said. 'Your marksmanship has indeed done me a great service today. Although I am unsure whether, bearing in mind the last arrow's final murky destination, so prestigious an accolade as that of King's Bowman is quite appropriate!'

'I am certain that it isn't, sir!' said Skimpton, affably.

'Now, if you will kindly direct me to your 'kupitalom' facilities, I will make brief use of them and then be on my way.'

'With great pleasure Your Majesty. Please follow me.'

*   *   *   *

As Skimpton was making his way to his study a little later, he was hailed by one of Marcus Dent's auxiliaries near the entrance to Second House. 'Binns!' he laughed. 'What brings you to this end of the quad? Not mischief, I hope.'

'I am under instructions to congratulate you, Skimpton,' replied the loud boy, with uncharacteristic formality.

'Hang on a minute! I'm not sure whether that last arrow counted!'

'That is not the accomplishment for which I am here to pay you tribute.'

'Then it must be for the dramatic saving of King Maximilian's life this afternoon, which I affected by skilfully incapacitating his treacherous brother, thus changing the course of European history. Believe me, it was nothing.'

'Neither is it to that equally laudable achievement that my message of felicitation pertains,' said Binns, 'although the subject of history is not one to which my mission is entirely unrelated.'

'Good Lord, Binns! Have you perchance swallowed a dictionary?'

Binns reached into his blazer pocket and produced a crumpled five-pound note, and handed it to Skimpton. 'This is from

Dent,' he said. 'The history results have just been posted.'

'And..?'

'You're top.'

'What!!?'

'With eleven percent. The rest of us have failed to make double figures, I am afraid.'

'Bless my soul!' declared a flabbergasted Skimpton. 'Well, if I'm top, who's...'

'Varley, with nought.'

'My giddy aunt! Varley's bottom, eh? I never thought I'd live to see that!'

At that moment, there was a flurry of activity in the drive as King Maximilian leapt into his Packard before the motor skidded off at considerable speed.

'The Boravians must have just found out the bad news,' said Binns.

'And what's that?'

'According to the radio, the Germans have just overrun their country.'

'I say, poor show.'

'They're threatening to do the same to nearby Czecho-Slovakia, apparently.'

'Really? Well, I dare say it will all blow over. Is there anything else, Binns?'

'No, I'd better go and see my father off, as he's promised me rather a lot of money when he dies.'

'Very well. Good day to you.'

Upon entering his study, Skimpton was pleasantly surprised to find a magnum of Champagne awaiting him, courtesy of 'an admirer' (this later turned out to be Lady Celia Edgerton, but that is another story).

As he stood by the window observing his schoolfellows bidding tearful farewells to their parents, he reflected on the extraordinary events which seemed to punctuate his life at Faysgarth, and wondered if his future in the adult world would be nearly as exciting. He had heard it said that a fellow's schooldays were invariably the best of his life, and he worried somewhat that the road ahead might not be so full of adventure, and the bracing challenges afforded by one of the county's foremost minor public schools.

Just then, a knock at the door heralded the arrival of Jack Varley, who marched into the room purposefully. 'Skimpton!' he saluted.

'Jack!' said the other.

'Hallo? Champagne! Who's this from?'

'Never mind that. What a lark, eh? Old Bamber turning out to be a deposed royal!'

'Incredible,' said Varley crisply.

'Imagine it, King Bamber of Boravia!'

'Indeed.'

'I should have realized earlier,' said Skimpton, 'I'd seen him, you see, on one of Piggot's foreign coins. I knew who he was the moment I set eyes on the King when he arrived. They both have similar noses, don't you think?'

Varley remained silent, seating himself at Skimpton's desk like a doctor preparing to impart grave news to his patient.

'My guess is,' continued Skimpton, 'that it was he who tampered with my arrows out of pure spite. The bounder probably sneaked in here when we were sweating away at that bally exam. Soon sorted him out with the old arrow up the jacksy, what?'

'You have every right to feel pleased with yourself, Skimpton,' said Varley.

'Especially since I've just heard the history results and discovered you're bottom!'

'How unfortunate.'

'Not in the least! I won five pounds from Marcus Dent, look!' Skimpton placed the money proudly onto the desk but Varley ignored it, choosing instead to clear his throat and adjust his cuffs ceremonially.

'Sit down, would you, Skimpton,' instructed he, solemnly.

'What on earth's the matter, Jack?'

'I have some very important news to impart to you.'

'If it's about Philly Bamber forget it. As far as I'm concerned that's all water under the bridge.'

'It has nothing to do with Philly Bamber, or King Maximilian, or any of that stuff.'

'Well, what is it, for Heaven's sake?'

'I recommend again that you seat yourself, Skimpton,' repeated Varley, 'as you may find what I have to say very shocking.'

'Why? Whatever is it?' quizzed Skimpton, feeling his legs starting to shake as he lowered himself onto the arm of his favourite leather armchair.

'I have just received news of your father, Skimpton.'

'Really?' the sports champion was now slightly concerned that something untoward might have happened to the old man. Unwilling, almost, to admit that possibility to himself, he frowned and gazed disinterestedly out of the window. 'I'm dashed peeved he wasn't here to see my triumph,' he complained, edgily.

'I am sure you are. I have to tell you that he wasn't here, Skimpton, because he was held up on business.'

'Typical,' scoffed the other, allowing himself a small sigh of relief. 'Is that your news?'

'Part of it.' Varley then looked his pal squarely in the eye, and his face gradually lit up in an enormous grin. 'The other part,' he added, 'is that he's just arrived and is waiting for you outside!'

At that moment, the door swung upon, and in the corridor stood Skimpton's beaming father, proffering a large bag of fruit bonbons.

'Dad!' exclaimed Skimpton.

'I'm very late, I'm afraid,' said the other.

'Of course you are! You've missed everything! We've had a ripping time of it of late, haven't we Jack?'

'We have indeed, Skimpton. We have indeed.'

Acknowledgements

Has Anybody Seen My Tiddler
by AJ Mills and Frank W Carter, 1913

The Black Footballer by R.A. Moss
– Mammoth Book for Boys, 1934

Original cover illustration by CP Shilton

Thanks to the following, all of whom at various stages
have helped in the writing of this book:
Simon Armstrong, Simon Banham, Deborah Benady,
Maxwell Hutcheon, Rob Jarvis,
Ciaran McIntyre (1947-2019) and Caryl Phillips.

Printed in Great Britain
by Amazon